A CHARMING SEDUCTION

Rose took a sip from the canteen Dillon offered her; the wine warmed her. "Have you ever been in love, Dillon?" she ventured.

"That's one sticky wicket I've managed to avoid. The sea . . ."

"Is your mistress," Rose completed for him. "If I were allowed to have a mistress, I'd be the same way."

"If you could accept that you are a woman," Dillon said, offering her more wine, "and a remarkable one at that, you'd be astonished at the resulting satisfaction."

"Then would you kiss me like you did this morning?"

"I kissed you to prove a point, Rosie. To show you that you are a woman."

"Then let's do it again." Rose planted her lips upon Dillon's, drawing his head closer, running her fingers through his hair. At first it was like kissing a rock, but it wasn't long before his mouth softened against hers.

He pulled her to him tightly. "If we keep on like this," he murmured, "there'll be no stopping."

"Do you want to stop Dillon . . . *really?*"

His silence was as loud as any answer he might have made.

"Make me glad I'm a woman, Dillon!" Rose pleaded in a voice as velvet and stirring as her touch. "You're the only man who can."

Dillon felt like he was being consumed by the fires of hell, while heaven beckoned within his grasp. "Ah, Rosie!" he whispered. Heaven was not to be denied. There was no alternative but sweet capitulation.

Border
Rose

Linda Windsor

Zebra Books
Kensington Publishing Corp.
http://www.zebrabooks.com

ZEBRA BOOKS are published by

Kensington Publishing Corp.
850 Third Avenue
New York, NY 10022

Zebra and the Z logo Reg. U.S. Pat. & TM Off.

First Printing: July, 1998
10 9 8 7 6 5 4 3 2 1

Printed in the United States of America

One

The shroud of fog finally lifted from the choppy green waters of the Atlantic. By midmorning occasional glimpses of land could be seen to the west as the *Border Rose* cut smoothly through the foaming crests of the waves. Her figurehead, a blue-eyed maiden with up-swept ebony hair and cheeks as flushed with color as the exquisitely carved rose she held to her ripe young bosom, bore a striking resemblance to the young lady at the ship's rail. They not only shared the same coloring, but the same name.

The lady, however, was as much alive as the wood replica was inanimate. Her hair was more than black, boasting the shimmering array of colors on a raven's wing exposed to the sun. As for her eyes, blue was inadequate to describe the range of hues that could change quick as the weather from a deep violet to a pale sky, reflecting her mood. Most of the time they were what the family called Beaujeu blue, aglow with the same qualities as the sapphire itself.

That was their hue now as Rose Marie Beaujeu, daughter of merchant and shipbuilder John Beaujeu of Castine, somberly appraised a tiny white speck of sail in the distance. Was it friend or foe? Her heart struck a double beat as the latter crossed her mind. The *Border Rose* was riding low in the water, shouting the fact that she was loaded with cargo. She was a fit prize for any bluenose, as the seamen and privateers from the maritime provinces to the north of her Maine home were referred to.

Damnable war, she thought, turning to eye the quarterdeck where Captain Nathan Malone was also watching the strange ship in the distance. Time was, seeing a ship from Scotia or Brunswick was welcome, a chance to exchange amenities, news, and sometimes supplies. Even after President Madison and his Warhawks declared war against Great Britain, New England had no quarrel with their Canadian neighbors and wanted to continue its neutrality. True, it had lost some sons to England's naval impressment, but surely the peaceful settlement of the issue, which had been in the process when hostilities were formally announced, should have been given time to come to fruition, rather than coming to this.

Nate's face was a mirror of the danger of the situation, but her first cousin did well to hide the other emotions Rose suspected he endured with each sighting of sail since his escape from Halifax the year before. Like most of his fellow New Englanders, he'd been against the war with England . . . until he and his brother Edward were taken from their own ship and impressed into the British navy.

"What do you think, Captain?" Rose called out.

"Too soon to tell, Rosie. Come take a look!"

Rose carefully lifted lilac skirts, beautifully adorned with looping soutache the same darker hue as the sash about her high-waisted dress, and took Nate's proffered hand. How much easier things had been when she was younger and scampered about her father's ship with small trousers made to wear beneath her dress for just such occasions. Now that she'd attained womanhood, there were so many restraints put upon her.

"I can't see her colors," Nate remarked as he handed her the glass. "But she's Baltimore built."

Rose breathed a sigh of relief. The ship had a raking stern and bow, with little freeboard showing at her waist, unlike the *Rose*, which, while sharing the same degree of rake for speed, boasted higher sides at the middle to weather the rougher seas of the north.

"No doubt about it. They don't build them anywhere else like that. She's going thirteen knots, if she's moving a bit!"

"The *Rose*'ll do that much, when she's not loaded to the hilt."

Rose returned her cousin's grin. The same thought had crossed her mind. What a race that would be, her ship against a Baltimore schooner. Her ship, Rose reflected, beaming as she handed the glass back over to her cousin. She still could not believe it was finally true.

Her brother Jack Beaujeu had received his own vessel from the family shipyard ten years before, after managing to graduate from college, despite numerous threats of dismissal and fines over matters ranging from attending a theater in Boston to drinking at a local grog house. When their father, John Beaujeu, insisted she attend a young ladies' academy in New York, he dangled the same sort of prize before Rose. She, too, would own her own vessel and profit from it.

Her mother had grown up on a merchant vessel and continued to make the sea her home when she married Captain John Beaujeu, a noted privateer during the War for Independence. Rose intended to follow in her mother's footsteps, but upon Kate Beaujeu's death, John, recognizing the need for a strong feminine hand on his wild and impulsive daughter, sent Rose to live with his family in Albany and attend the small, but fashionable ladies' academy there.

What a time she'd had at first, adjusting to the dull,

disciplined atmosphere of the academy. Shipboard life required discipline as well, but it was never as boring as that which Rose endured for the last few years. If not for her land-loving family, she'd have never survived. Her grandmother Tamson and her aunt Arissa proved to her that she could become a lady and still enjoy life.

What adventures they told her about! Rose wouldn't have believed them if Grandpère Alain and Uncle Phillip hadn't confirmed them. It ran in the Beaujeu blood to take the scripture about loving thine enemy to heart. Her grandfather and grandmother had been enemies during the French and Indian War. His French Canadian sisters all married colonials, and his Montreal-born daughter Arissa fell in love with American army intelligence officer Phillip Monroe of New York during the Revolution.

"Cap'n, she's hauled her wind and headed straight for us now!" one of the men shouted from the rail.

"Keep her away from our stern!"

Although she was not well versed in combat at sea, Rose knew enough to realize Nate wanted to avoid the aggressor's favorite raking maneuver of cutting across the victim's back and shooting stern to stem with her guns.

"Do you think the captain wishes to exchange salutations?" Rose turned to her cousin, who once again had lifted the glass to examine the approaching vessel.

Nate was lost in his observation, his fair sun-bleached hair whipping about his face in the warm breeze. Then, suddenly, he exclaimed, "I think I've seen that figurehead before! Henry, take a look and see if that isn't the *Lucinda* out of Philadelphia."

The first mate took over the glass. "Aye, that be who it is all right! I'd know that redheaded siren anywheres."

Judging from the smirking, silent exchange between the two men, Rose would bet a good sum that a buxom redhead named Lucinda was at the center of the intrigue.

"Cap'n's name's Figgs, 'Zekial Figgs, as I recall."

"No, it's the *Hawthorne!*" Nate remembered. "Lucinda was the captain's . . . er . . ." He glanced at Rose, somewhat embarrassed.

"Figgerhead," Henry provided helpfully. Then, just as quick to change the subject, he asked, "Think we should change our colors?"

"Not until they're closer. No sense in taking any chances."

The *Border Rose* currently flew the Dutch flag, proclaiming neutrality for safety's sake. Once their company's friendliness was established, the Stars and Stripes would be hoisted. If the stranger tried to take them, they'd do battle beneath their country's flag.

"Should I pass out the guns?"

Rose shifted her gaze sharply from the approaching vessel to see Nate answer with a nod. Upon seeing the alarm on her face, he smiled reassuringly. "I don't think it's a bluenose privateer. I know the ship."

"Well, there's no harm in being prepared."

She returned her cousin's smile, yielding completely to his authority. Nate was a capable captain. Like Rose, although nine years her senior, her maternal cousin had been born on the water. She couldn't have picked anyone better to captain the *Border Rose,* aside from her father who'd retired from the sea at her mother's death. Unless, of course, it was herself.

Before it could gain ground with her thoughts, she dismissed the latter idea. Young women did not captain ships, and the precious few older ones who did were usually widows taking over their husbands' affairs. Besides, even if Rose had held a glimmer of hope of continuing her life on the sea, the war had snuffed it. Her father had even wanted her to take the overland route home, rather than the much easier sea one, because of the dangerous bluenose privateers and English warships attempting to plunder and blockade the eastern coast.

Rose, however, was able to cajole Nate into taking her. When her New York family objected, she'd flung back at them, "How can this Beaujeu 'love her enemy,' if she never gets to meet him?"

It had been a lighthearted jest, of course, for she had no desire to meet the enemy, much less fall in love with him, but her point had been made. She had obeyed her father's wishes to attend school and then take over the position he'd created for her by building a new schoolhouse in the town, but she was not going to be denied the single pleasure of sailing home on her own ship.

"If your father says one word of reprimand to you, you must remind him of the day that he left his home to go to sea. That, too, was in the midst of a war," Grand-père Alain had informed her when they'd said their good-byes on the Dutchman's wharf.

"Sound the men to quarters!"

Nate's booming voice gave Rose a start. Even without the benefit of the glass, she could see the approaching ship had tacked and was flying Dutch colors from the quarterdeck. The men on deck sprang into action. Up from the lower deck spilled the small assembly of sharp-shooters Nate had hand-picked to take to the mast tops or scaffolding high amidst the sails, their rifles and kits in hand. Below, she could hear the scraping of the furniture being cleared out of the way of the gun crews and the loud hiss of the galley fires being put out.

A sudden burst of gunfire gave Rose a start. The shot went far beyond the bow of her ship, landing harmlessly in the water. Heavens, but the Baltimore-built vessel had practically sailed up on them in minutes! Now she could see the men working in the riggings and a fair size crew moving at the rail.

"Ahoy there! What ship are you?"

A man stood at the other ship's rail, one foot perched on a ratline. In his hand was a speaking trumpet which emphasized the robust baritone of his voice. His dark hair was gathered in a queue and a red neckerchief was tied about his forehead. Casual as he appeared, he had the look of a bird of prey eyeing a potential victim. Although she couldn't see them, she knew his eyes were dark, dark as his ship was black.

"Cap'n, look at her side real close. I'd bet me mother's own heart there's gun'nels with crews ready to fire behind that painted canvas."

"Ahoy! I said what ship are you?" the man at the rail shouted again.

"Then we're outgunned!" Nate swore under his breath.

Rose saw it, too. The sun was now glancing off the painted canvas covering the gun ports on the side of the ship, meant to give her a harmless appearance. Their worst suspicions were true, she thought, raising her gaze to the stranger's masts where figures more numerous than the few sharpshooters the *Rose* carried were no doubt measuring Nate and Henry in their sights at that very moment.

As Nate raised the speaking trumpet to his lips, Rose snatched it from him. "Follow my lead, Cousin, and pray the captain is a gentleman."

"We're the *Border Rose* of . . ." Rose purposely let her voice trail off, as if it had been swept away by the breeze. "Go to my cabin and get the pink petticoat hanging on the back of the door. Strike the Dutchman and raise the petticoat instead. Hurry!"

"Bring her round his bow! Hard about!" Nate shouted to the shocked crew after nodding for Henry to carry out her order. He could see her idea was already working, for the stranger on the rail had been struck dumb by the answer of a female voice.

"Swing wide and give us space, lads. Idlers, keep down," he cautioned the armed men who'd stripped the masts of the cutlasses hung conveniently there for just such an occasion. "Tell the gunners to keep the gun ports empty. Make them think we're harmless, lads."

Although Nate's sharp eyes swept the deck assessing their readiness, he spoke aside to Rose. "The first shot fired, you get below and stay there! One hair of your head gets ruffled and I'd sooner swing from a yardarm in Halifax than face your father."

In a flash, Henry Malloy rushed past them and handed the pink silk petticoat to a crewman, who hoisted it to the very top. Meanwhile, taken aback, the privateer worked the great sheets of sail that had brought her so quickly upon them, sheering off course, no doubt to regroup. Even as she did so, the deceptive canvas was shed, as if to intimidate the ship flying the pink banner from the top of the mainmast.

"Davy's bones, she's hoisted the Red Jack!"

True enough, the privateer's flag had now replaced the Dutch. No longer was there any semblance of a doubt as to the ship's intentions. As she sailed past, Rose caught a glimpse of the gilt-painted nameplate on her stern: the *Thorne,* hailing from Halifax, Nova Scotia.

"Blast it, the bluenose bastard must have claimed the *Hawthorne* as prize and refitted her for privateering!" Nate cursed vehemently. "No doubt Figgs is wasting away in a prison ship by now."

"We gonna try to beat her to the coast?"

Nate shook his head at the mate's question. "The wind's in their favor, not ours, but, thanks to Rosie's quick thinking, we've bought some time to plan."

"Maybe we could come about again and I could try

to reason with the captain. Perhaps if he thought I was master of the ship, he would let us pass."

Rose's heart beat fast as her words rolled out. She looked at Nate expectantly, delighted at his compliment about quick thinking.

"He'll try to take us, whether we offer a fight or not. The question is, whether to fight."

Amazed that surrender even crossed Nate's mind, Rose stared at the young man. Nathan Malone detested the British. No amount of preaching could offset the scars on his back, or the empty grave in the family cemetery with his brother Edward's marker on it.

Wrapped in a canvas sack with eighteen pounds of shot for weight, he'd been left to a watery grave somewhere off Prince Edward Island. Nate managed to escape overboard in Halifax Harbor and make his way home overland. The fact of the matter was, Nate would face a noose in Halifax as a British deserter, not an American prisoner of war.

"They may simply take the cargo and specie and let us be," the mate suggested.

"I'm not about to let that sneaking bastard take my ship!" Rose averred.

"I was wondering how long it would take for that fancy schooling to wear off." The humor in Nate's eye, however, was short-lived. "But I'll not risk you getting hurt. I shouldn't have let you talk me into bringing you along in the first place."

"This is my ship, is it not?"

"Aye, but . . ."

"And you are my captain, aren't you?"

"I am the captain, Rosie. I'm responsible . . ."

"For these men and my ship. Well, why not ask them what they want to do. Lie down and let the bluenose take us, or give him his trouble's worth?"

"Rosie . . ."

"By damn, Nate, I'm not going to be responsible for the capture of this ship and her men, at least not without a fight."

"They might let us go on parole."

"And they might not!" Rose argued. "And you know very well you'll swing if they find out who you are!"

A huzzah from the deck gave evidence that their voices had risen sufficiently to involve the crew. Encouraged, Rose went on. "And I have a plan!"

Nate's look was dark. "And what is that, madame? Shall we stroke them into submission with silk and lace?"

"Use me as an asset, not a liability!" Rose shot back, holding her ground. "I'll call the ship close as I can on the pretense of negotiating. That we've not raised enemy colors or tried to run may keep them off balance enough for me to succeed. After all, how threatening is a ship captained by a woman and flying a petticoat banner?"

"If we could git close enough to take down her masts and shred her canvas with chain and grape . . ."

"And take a broadside," Nate pointed out.

"Maybe, but the gun deck can give good as it gets, especially if we fire before they do."

"I could give a signal, a certain phrase meaning fire at will. I could tell the captain I've no choice but to strike my petticoat for him."

The corner of Nate's mouth twitched, despite his effort to remain in control. "That figurehead doesn't do you justice, Cousin. It looks too innocent." Turning to the main deck, he called out to his crew. "What say you, lads. Shall we serve our mistress by fighting or surrender?"

The belligerent answer was unanimous. Rose could hardly hear Nate as he raised a warning finger at her, but she could well read his lips. "At the first shot . . ."

"Why, I'll go below, of course," she finished primly. "I don't want to get in the way or cause any distraction among our men."

It seemed an eternity before the two ships squared off again for another pass. Nate was careful to keep to the wind's advantage, but the privateer skillfully managed to keep her pace. Again she was headed alongside, surely with the intention of cutting across the *Border Rose*'s stern, if the sweeps had to be manned to do so. With Nate close by at the helm to prompt her or take over if need be, Rose stood at the smooth gilded rail, inhaling the salt air as though it sustained her courage and calm.

Thankfully the unshaven rake poised at the rail of the other ship could not see that she needed two hands to hold the speaking trumpet, lest it tremble enough to bloody her lips. It wasn't that she feared so much for herself, as she did for the others. She was bound to take the same risks and determined to suffer the same fate as her men, whatever the outcome. Be it a wild celebration of escape, or, better yet, taking the *Thorne* as a prize, or sharing the brig in the hold of the dastardly black ship approaching the starboard bow, she was ready for it.

"*Border Rose,* you've a gift for covering your stern!"

"As any lady of breeding should possess, sir," Rose quipped. She heard Nate make a gagging sound, surely swallowing his reprimand for her risqué reply.

A rich peal of laughter wafted across the space between the two ships before the captain spoke again. "I like a woman with a quick wit. Perhaps, milady, you'll be good enough to put over a boat and bring your papers and avoid a distasteful confrontation."

Rose was distracted by a series of loud whispers passed along until they reached the quarterdeck. The speaker for the other ship, as well as the helmsman, was in the sights of the *Rose*'s sharpshooters in the topmast. Time was of the essence, but if violence could be avoided . . .

"I thought as a gentleman, you would allow a lady to pass unhampered, sir. This is my ship and I've heard the Crown frowns on its men assaulting a lady and confiscating her property."

"The Crown means properties of a more personal nature, like that fetching piece flying at the top mast, milady."

"Any time, Rosie," Nate muttered under his breath.

She'd had to try. The resignation in her answer rang true. "Very well, sir, you leave me no choice. I suppose I must *strike my petticoat* . . ."

Before she could finish the command, rifle fire cracked from the tops of the forward, main, and aft riggings of the enemy ship. Across the water, the captain leapt to cover, as though the unprovoked attack had startled him as well. Even as two of the *Border Rose*'s marines pitched forward against the netting in the mast top, Nate shoved Rose toward the aft gangway. "Fire at will!" he shouted, his voice fading in the responding thunder of the guns beneath them.

At the same time, the railing on the top deck exploded with the impact of the enemy's return broadside. Rose grabbed the rope rail to keep from pitching headlong down the narrow steps to the main deck. The ship felt as if it had been struck twice, but one of the recoils was from their own gunners, who were now reloading furiously on the main. In the midst of the din of shouts and smoke, the firefighters tossed seawater on a section of the deck littered with burning tatters of canvas which had fallen through the main hatch from above. Others were spreading sand and dodging the boys running powder as needed to each of the gun crews.

Black choking smoke pervaded the low-beamed

space. It stung Rose's eyes to the point of blurring. From the forward main the first of their four starboard guns roared again, followed by the second and so forth until the one next to her bellowed.

Prepared this time, she grasped the rope rail of the hatchway to maintain her footing and blinked to clear her vision. How could Nate expect her to go to her cabin, when he and her men were fighting to save her ship? Rose started down to the berth deck, where Doc Ames was in charge of setting up a makeshift hospital. After living with her aunt Arissa, who was still sought out by her neighbors for her medical know-how, Rose was no stranger to the sight of a bloody injury. She'd helped her aunt from time to time, but never had she dreamed she'd have to put the experience to use.

The ship reeled again, this time from the enemy fire, and the deck heaved precariously to the larboard. The answering report of cannon shook the very timbers beneath them as the *Border Rose* gamely righted herself. Spurred on by the increasing ferocity of the encounter, Rose stumbled down the narrow hatch to the berth deck, half blind and nearly deaf from the roar of the guns, but not deaf enough to ignore the anguished screams of the first men victimized by the deadly enemy bombardment.

Two

The fighting was more savage than Captain Dillon Mackay had anticipated. Their victim had taken down the *Thorne*'s forward mast and riddled her canvas with the first shots, too damned lucky a strike for the harmless merchantman it first appeared to be. Only seasoned gunners were that good. Nor were the men of the *Border Rose* simply sailors. He'd lost a helmsman and suffered a bullet's graze himself because of the keen-eyed riflemen in her mast tops. They were either dead now or had abandoned their lofty perches in the hail of grapeshot he used to return the favor of the tattered sails dealt him.

The decks of both ships were bloodied and splintered, their freeboard pierced with shot. Dillon climbed aboard the *Border Rose* to receive her papers and specie from her first officer, the captain having been wounded and taken below just before the surrender.

Now the fires had been put out on both ships and already the carpenters were plugging the holes in their sides. Canvas was being taken down, mended, and replaced. They could hobble back to Halifax after the *Thorne*'s other prizes without replacing the foremast. In the meantime, they'd refit both ships as best they could and then get underway with a prize crew aboard their newest acquisition.

Miraculously, the damage was mostly superficial, a tribute to the builders of both ships. Yet, it was only a cursory glance the captain of the *Thorne* gave the *Border Rose* itself. He was more concerned with the prisoners, and, in particular, a certain lady who had unforgivably lowered his guard by taking advantage of his innate respect for the gentler sex. Yet, nowhere among those men held at gunpoint by his marines was the lithe figure in lilac he'd seen on the quarterdeck.

"Where is your lady captain?" Dillon addressed the man in a battle-tattered shirt who stepped up to meet him. "I hope she was not injured in the fray."

At first the man looked blank. Then suddenly he chuckled, his uneven teeth white against his powder-blackened face. "Miss Beaujeu is below, but the lady's not hurt, sir."

"Beaujeu?" Dillon repeated in disbelief. Immediately a small cherubic face came to mind, rosy lips parted to expose two perfect rows of tiny pearllike teeth. "Higher, Dillon, higher!" the miniature dark-haired princess in crinolines and trousers had goaded him as he carried her piggyback up to the mast top.

That was some twelve years ago, when he was but a cabin boy on Captain John Beaujeu's *Katie Marie,* named after the man's wife and the child's mother. Dillon had gone to sea in the summers between schooling and learned the ropes under Captain John so that he might take over his father's merchant fleet someday. His father and the Beaujeu family had been fast friends and, on occasion, partners.

Wishing he'd listened to that inner voice which told him to let the lady and her ship pass, Dillon glanced toward the aft hatchway. Nearby, men were working to remove a section of the mast that had been cut clean by chain shot and hung only by the ropes.

"The captain, now," the seaman went on, "he went

below to the hospital after orderin' our colors struck. The lady's tendin' 'im, her bein' his cousin. Cap'n Nate Malone is his name."

"Then he knows the whereabouts of the ship's papers?" There was some solace in the fact that Dillon wouldn't have to take them from the lady, whether she was truly little Rosie Beaujeu or not. These matters were best settled among men.

"Well, I sure as Davy's bones don't have 'em."

Dillon turned to his own first officer. "Mr. Green, use the able-bodied prisoners to transfer the wounded to the *Thorne*. Then select a prize crew for this ship."

"There's only one problem, sir."

"Only one?" Dillon couldn't help his sarcasm. The day had been hellish and promised to be even more so.

"Sir, this is our fifth prize. Considering the number of lads wounded, we don't have enough now to outfit her."

Dillon nodded grimly. Damnation, it was bad enough to have had to do such damage to their prize in order to subdue her, but to have to sink her after such a fight because he lacked enough able crew to man her was unthinkable. There had to be a way.

"I'll speak to the captain and see if we might make some sort of arrangement. There are times we have to bend the articles," he sighed, fully aware of the set of rules laid down for all privateer captains and crew. He'd paid a handsome bond guaranteeing to keep them, but short of sinking the *Border Rose*, he would have to improvise.

His first officer stopped him again. "Captain, I thought you might like this."

Hesitating, one foot on the rung of the step leading below deck, Dillon turned to see a grinning James Green holding out a silk and lace-bedecked petticoat, the one

that had flown as a banner on the mainmast and confounded him and his crew.

"You have to admit, it was pretty effective."

Dillon took the flimsy garment. "Thank you, sir." His
answer was strained through taut lips. Ignoring the soft
feel of the surrendered banner as he wadded it under
his arm, he started below again. It was strange to find
such finery in the midst of shattered timbers and shred-
ded canvas. Like its owner, it had no place in battle.

Dillon should have been somewhat gratified to see that
the berth deck was as full of patients with as varying degrees of wounds as his own, but he wasn't. He had no
thirst for blood, only for victory and fortune.

Aware of the wary eyes upon him, Dillon made his
way through the makeshift pallets on the floor, searching for one who might be the downed captain of the
vessel. The bloody bandages and groans from those
past preserving their dignity in the face of the enemy
were enough to make a man mad with frustration at
the futility of it all. Brave as these fellows had fought,
they'd been foolish to do so. They were outgunned,
outmanned, and, with their heavy cargo, outrun.

Dillon couldn't imagine a cargo so valuable as to be
worth the shattered ship and mangled bodies, when
they might have surrendered and been treated with the
utmost regard. He'd had bigger vessels surrender without objection upon realizing that his ship's speed and
his men's training more than offset their ability to fight
it out.

If it was the hangman's noose or a prison they feared,
he'd have been willing to parole the blokes and put
them off on one of the neutral islands to the north
sooner than be bothered with taking them into Halifax.
The courts and prison ships were inundated with
American prisoners as it was. If only they'd been willing

to negotiate. No doubt the lady in lilac had something to do with the fickle decision.

Dillon called out above the din of the infirmary. "I would speak to your captain!"

A short, stocky man in a blood-soaked coat rose from working on the shattered leg of a pale and trembling seaman. "Cap'n Nate ain't up to speakin' to no one right now." He nodded to a fair-haired man, who'd been set apart from the others. "Took some of the aft rail in the shoulder."

Not exceedingly tall, but broad-shouldered and sturdily built, the captain of the *Border Rose* had the look of the Malone clan into which Captain John Beaujeu had married. They all had blond hair and blue eyes from what Dillon recalled, and, except for the bloodstained bandages swathing his naked shoulder and his uncommon pallor, this one was as robust as the lot of them. Nonetheless, the man was clearly unconscious. One of the cabin boys continued to wipe the dried blood from his arms and chest with a damp rag without getting the slightest rise.

Dillon saw no sign of the lilac-clad female who'd precipitated all this. "Then I'll speak to your owner. I understood she was here."

"Miss Beaujeu is in the captain's cabin, sir. He sent her there soon as our colors were struck. No disrespect intended, sir, but I've got more men bleedin' than I got hands to help 'em."

"By all means," Dillon replied instantly, motioning for the ship's physician to return to his work. "Your mates will be down presently to help transport them to my ship, where you'll have the assistance of our own physician."

He left the infirmary and nimbly climbed back up the hatch aft of the littered gun deck to access the officers' mess, which was lined with their cabins on both sides. At the stern quarters, he came upon two of his

marines standing guard outside a polished door leading
to one of two aft cabins. The top panel of rich red mahogany was adorned with a carving of a single rose
growing wild around a ship's anchor.

The lady on the other side had to be Rosie Beaujeu,
the little jack tar who'd had the run of her father's ship,
despite her mother's watchful eye. No doubt this ship
had been built and named for her, and the artisan who
did the carving was as enamored with the cherub as
Dillon had once been.

"Stand aside, gentlemen. I'd have a word with the
mistress."

Instead of the instant obedience Dillon expected of
his men, one of the marines put his hand out in warning. "I wouldn't go in there just yet, sir. The lady says
she has a blunderbuss and will blow the first man what
attempts to open that door to bits."

"We could'a forced it, sir," the other chimed in,
"but ye said the lady wasn't to be harmed. She's got
the wind full in her sail and been bustin' up things
inside with gale force. Short of takin' her down with
pistols, we didn't know what to do but keep her
penned up till ye came aboard."

Look at it, Dillon! Isn't God wonderful? Again Dillon recalled a small wonderstruck face framed in short dark
curls and turned upward toward a thunderstruck sky.
The child's chubby finger pointed to the bolts of lightning hurling downward to stir the waves tossing the ship
into further turmoil. Rosie had wanted to go up to the
mast top to watch the storm, but her parents had forbidden it, of course. She hadn't been the least frightened by the thunder and lightning, but thrilled by it.

Had their battle thrilled her or frightened her? he
wondered, idly measuring the rose on the door as if it
were the lady on the other side. Had she taken up the

blunderbuss in fear of injury or was she still riding high on the adrenaline of the fierce conflict?

"Rosie Beaujeu, is that you in there?"

"Who calls me so familiarly?" a feminine voice demanded in return.

If she was frightened, it didn't tell. Her reply was as saucy as it had been when enticing him close enough to give her snipers a good shot at him and to present her gunners with an unobscured sweep of his sail and masts.

"An old friend, milady, one who would not have fired a single shot, had he known it was you who sailed the *Border Rose.*"

That wasn't exactly true, Dillon realized, for a prize was a prize, and they were political enemies. However, he'd have certainly tried harder to take the ship without heavy casualties and damage.

"If you are a friend, sir, I should hate to face you as an enemy."

"Milady, you cannot remained holed up in the captain's cabin indefinitely. Your ship is taken and already your men are being transferred to the *Thorne.* Since Captain Malone is unconscious, it seems, we need to discuss the terms of surrender with you, your being the ship's owner."

"I'd know to whom I am surrendering, sir" came a somewhat breathless reply.

Something scraped across the floor and there was the hurried patter of slippered feet on the planking. What the devil was she doing, Dillon wondered. A picture of her trying to roll a cannon ball through the door came to his mind, but he dismissed it as absurd.

"Rosie, Captain Dillon Mackay of the *Thorne* has taken your ship as a prize of war. Now that I know who you are, I wish no further . . ."

"Dillon?" Disbelief resounded from the other side of the door. "Dillon!"

The latter echo was one of recognition and relief. Suddenly the door was unbolted and in its place, a living rendition of the *Border Rose*'s figurehead stood smiling at him brilliantly. For a moment, Dillon was stunned. He'd thought the girl fetching enough, what he'd seen of her across the distance between their ships, but only a step away from him, she was positively stunning.

The smudges of soot on her face could not detract from the china-perfect features he remembered, nor were the bloodstains on her dress able to deter him from appreciating her now-ripened figure caressed by the smooth-textured garment worn without its full scheme of petticoats. Her gemlike gaze held him speechless with the sudden rush of warmth and gratitude that filled it. No sky had ever been a more vibrant blue than her lovely eyes.

"Thank God it was all a mistake!" she whispered, her voice breaking for the first time. The glaze in her eyes, which he judged to be from shock, made them appear deeper than any sea on which he'd sailed. "I . . . I'd prayed so hard that something or someone would save us and here you are!"

She leaned the lethal blunderbuss against the wall and reached for Dillon's arm, pulling him in. "And it is you, except that you're full grown! Look at you, half naked and hairy as a heathen!"

"My men don't wear shirts as a means of . . . of identifying each other in battle, milady." Dillon stammered, momentarily thrown by the lady's bold observation.

As though she did not trust her eyesight, she ran her fingers over the rough shadow of a beard on Dillon's chin and then dropped them to the lightly furred plane of his bare chest.

"Too many to pluck, I'll wager," she murmured.

Her seemingly bizarre comment was not lost on Dillon, who, when his body was starting to sprout the manly crop, had suffered such curious abuse tolerantly from his petite shipboard shadow. A fiendish thought of reciprocation darkened his mind for a moment, and the effect on him drove home the fact that he'd been too long without female companionship. The two men watching them with interest and the responsibility of securing two ships, however, proved as sufficient as a dousing of icewater in maintaining his battle-hewn senses.

"I believe this is yours, milady," he said.

Her bewildered attention shifted from his chest to his face, and then to the pink petticoat that had flown over the valiant battle.

"So it is," she acknowledged flatly, looking at the garment with the same hypnotic fascination she'd shown with him.

Rose wanted to shake her head, to clear away the insipid daze that had sufficiently numbed her to fear and the loud anguish of the wounded in order to bandage and stitch according to Doc Ames's instruction. The good man had done his best, as had she, but not even her aunt Arissa's training had been enough. There were some men who'd needed more. After the third blanket-covered face, she'd stopped counting. Not even her childhood knight in armor could change that.

"What a horrible, horrible mistake we've made!" she choked out, turning away to try to master the tears that suddenly spilled over her cheeks. Dillon always told her real sailors didn't cry. "I don't know how many men we've lost, and the ship . . ."

Dillon put his hands on her shoulders, swearing silently. The sea in wartime was no place for a woman. John Beaujeu must have been out of his mind to let his daughter sail a merchantman in these waters, but then,

Rosie was used to getting her way. This time, however, was going to be different. Shares were due his crew for a prize hard won, whether the captain was sympathetic to the ship's owner or nay.

"Rosie, I need the ship's papers."

"What for?" The girl turned and wiped her eyes on the sleeve of her spencer jacket, pulling it open in the process to reveal the matching bodice beneath where her bosom rose and fell with the distracted rhythm of her breath.

Here was no feminine trickery, Dillon knew. She truly didn't understand the situation at hand.

"It's the custom for the captain or master of a prize to hand over her papers and specie to the capturing captain."

"But you just said if you'd known it was me . . ."

A shock even greater than that to which she'd succumbed cut Rose off, abruptly clearing her mind. Dillon Mackay had not made a mistake in taking the *Border Rose*. He had every intention of claiming the ship as a prize, even though he now knew it belonged to her. Well, damn his handsome bristled hide to hell!

"I thought you'd have acted the gentleman and turned away from us if you'd known it was my ship." Her reply was more accusation than observation. Gone was that wild, lost look and in its place a frosty one cold enough to chill the warm air in the close quarters. The bitterness in her mouth invaded her tone as she went on. "Imagine my naiveté to think you might still do the same."

"We're at war, Rosie."

"You owe my father!" the girl argued back. "He taught you everything you know."

"And I intend to treat you with the best of care until you are safely delivered to your home, but . . ."

"So this is what you've come to," she derided, gath-

ering fire all the while. "I can't believe I wanted to
marry you when I grew up . . . a man who would turn
on his own friends! A man who covers his guns with
painted canvas and sneaks up on an innocent ship under a false flag! God may forgive you for this, Dillon
Mackay, but I never will!"

"We're at war, Rosie," Dillon repeated, wiping his
hands on the long length of his thigh to keep from
drawing frustrated fists before the hysterical girl.

"You bluenose bastard, I'll see shrimps fly before I
hand over our papers!"

"Have it your way then, blast it!" Uncertain as to
which was worse, bewildered tears or this maddening
defiance, Dillon turned to his men. Either way, he had
time for neither. "Search the cabin. I'll take the young
lady with me."

Rose snatched away from Dillon's grasp and stumbled
backward beneath a gaping hole which had been torn
out of the quarterdeck above the captain's desk. "I'm
remaining with my ship."

His patience wearing thin, Dillon moved toward her.
He was tired and there was much to be done so that
they could get underway, rather than sit in the water
and wait for an American warship or privateer to slip
up and take both disabled ships.

"Damn it, Rosie . . ."

Above deck a horrendous snap followed by a clamor
of warnings froze Dillon in midstep. With the lashing
hiss of a thousand cats cutting through the air and the
thunder of a magazine explosion, the ceiling overhead
suddenly started down, or at least part of it did. It was
only Rose's terrified scream that managed to thaw Dillon sufficiently to leap for her, but he was too late. A
large, jagged piece of the destroyed aft mast, which had
apparently broken loose from the riggings that held it

suspended above deck, plunged into the captain's cabin, driving a wedge between Dillon and his prisoner.

As he called out Rose's name, he was suddenly smothered in the heavy canvas which toppled in behind the mast. In a tangle of broken lines and torn sail, Dillon cut his way free with the combined help of his own men and three of the captured crew who had lowered themselves by rope through the opening the moment the girl's scream registered above deck. Fiercely, they tore through the litter of sail, shrouds, braces, and lines. Dillon felt a cold blade of apprehension where the girl had earlier placed a warm, tentative hand against his chest. By all that was holy, she had to be in there somewhere!

"Look there, sir!"

He saw it the moment his man spoke. It was a weakly flailing arm covered in torn lilac sarcenet. The rest of the girl's figure was smothered in the sail that had fallen about the jagged mast, which lay across her. Despite the sick fear that clenched his stomach, Dillon began to cut and tear away a section of the heavy shroud which had secured the aft mast to the side of the ship before it was blown loose during the battle.

"Hang on, Rosie, we'll have you out of there in a flash," he consoled the struggling figure, praying all the while that it was only the weight of cloth and line pinning her down.

With the help of his men, he managed to haul the heavy shroud aside and shove his arms beneath the oppressive fire-singed sail to secure a better hold. No more had he buried his hand in the wreckage than he withdrew it with a startled yelp.

"Keep your bloody hands to yourself, you blithering traitor! I'd sooner suffocate!"

A quick glance at the perfect row of teeth marks on his wrist reassured Dillon that blood had not been drawn. Tempted as he was to leave the damsel to fight her own way out of the tangle that had miraculously spared them both, he motioned toward the moving pile of sail.

"Dig her out . . . and watch yourself! And there's still five pounds to the man who finds the ship's papers. I've two ships to make ready for sail," he added, a reminder aimed more or less at himself.

Dillon climbed topside three rungs at a time. The fresh blast of salt air acted as a balm to his riled state. Inhaling deeply, he scanned the chaos on the deck, which seemed mild compared to that below.

"The lass is all right, isn't she, boy?"

The *boy* that followed the question brought Dillon about face-to-face with the first mate of the *Border Rose* again. This time, however, he studied the man's weathered angular face with its oversize and slightly off-center nose more closely. The years had salted the older man's hair and claimed some of it about his forehead, but there was no mistaking his patronizing tone. Henry Malloy, the bosun of Beaujeu's *Katie Marie*, wasn't capable of speaking to his apprentices any other way.

"I'm a captain now, Mr. Malloy. I didn't recognize you at first, sir."

"So I see, but the lass . . ."

"Is fine. A bloody miracle, but fine . . . and stubborn as ever."

"Didn't get the papers, eh? I'm not surprised," his prisoner snorted, not the least intimidated by Dillon's authority. Yet, when he spoke again, there was respect for it, as much as the man was capable of mustering. "Might I see for myself, sir?"

Henry Malloy was an old salt, tried and tested in the ways of the sea. Furious as he used to make his young apprentice, he and Captain Beaujeu were among the best a young man could learn under.

"Aye, but I'd have a word with you first, sir, since the captain isn't able to speak for his men at the moment. We've a delicate situation at best."

"Humph! *De-lee-cate* is a mighty fancy way o' sayin' we've blown ourselves into a pickle. Must be all that high and mighty schoolin' yer mama insisted on." Again there was no disrespect in the twinkling gray gaze peering out from beneath brows thick as a thunder-cloud. It gave the man a fearsome look, even when he was having fun, which he was at the moment.

Dillon grinned in return, grateful to have a reason-able individual to deal with for a change. "I see you've assessed the situation already." He clapped Malloy on the back. "Now, I'm not asking you to turn traitor to your country, but it would be a shame to have to sink the young lady's ship for lack of manpower, much less to have to put up with your company all the way to Halifax. I would have my crew continue to respect me."

Again Malloy snorted as he walked beside Dillon to the stern rail, around the gaping hole where the fallen mast protruded. "There's no chance they'd do other-wise from what I've seen, sir."

"I said get away from me! I can walk on my own!"

At the sound of the feminine outrage echoing below deck, the first officer drew his lips into a wry purse. "O' course, I'd be speakin' of the men only. A strong-willed woman, why, that's a horse's market ye'll have to cross on your own."

"You've no idea where the ship's papers might be?"

"Oh, I knew where they were . . . sealed in a small keg in the captain's locker."

If that were so, his men would turn them up in short order. Something, however, about the crash before he entered the captain's quarters and the young woman's breathlessness on the other side of the locked door gave Dillon cause for doubt. Rosie Beaujeu had hidden them for spite, and his smarting hand was testimony that she was not about to disclose their location to anyone, especially to him.

Dillon grimaced in exasperation. War was a man's affair and had no place for a woman, especially one with the temperament of a bloody hurricane.

Three

By nightfall the forward mast of the *Thorne* had joined the aft one of the *Border Rose* in a watery grave, along with the rest of the worthless debris from the two ships. Lanterns were hung stem to stern while the men of both crews struggled to repair the rigging and replace canvas. The holes in the freeboard were plugged and sealed with tarred hemp. Had the battle lasted one round longer, one or both ships would have gone down, Dillon mused as he climbed across the rails of the ships, which had been lashed together in the becalmed sea so that the combined crews might repair both as needed.

Now he had a prize, worse for battle, and no papers for her, which meant no inventory of the hold, no idea of the amount of liquid specie or spendable moneys aboard, and no proof that she indeed belonged to the crew of the *Thorne*. Possession of the papers was almost as important as that of the ship.

When his crew had not turned them up, further questioning revealed that Rose Beaujeu had destroyed them. She'd flung the deed at him with that irrepressible tilt of her chin he recalled from another time. It was hardly an honorable or responsible act, but what could one expect of a hysterical woman? Ship's owner or nay, he'd have never let her know where the papers were kept had *he* been her captain.

He looked to the new wood braces in the riggings, bleached compared to their weathered counterparts, where some of the prisoners worked with his own men to reef the patched sail. At least he had been able to work out an equitable arrangement with the *Rose*'s first officer. His remaining able crew had agreed to work with Dillon's scant prize crew in order to get the ships to a friendly port. In return, he'd release the Americans on parole. There were harbors along the northern New England post where British ships continued to trade for American supplies as usual.

It was not a matter of politics, but of economics, what with the increasing effectiveness of the English navy's blockade. The captain of the Castine ship and his crew could find their way home from there, where, despite their parole, Dillon knew they'd be at sea again as soon as they could find a ship. It was in their blood, just as it was in his. That made them brothers, war or not.

"Glad to have you back aboard, sir," his first officer greeted him as he started across a main deck amidst the men sweeping up the fresh wood shavings left by the ship's carpenters. "We've a bit of a problem with the lady."

"She's ill?"

Even as he asked, Dillon knew better. She'd tossed her bonneted curls in aloof defiance, refusing the sling he'd had rigged to decently transport her over the rail. Then, with the train of her rent skirts pulled between her legs and tucked into the front of her waist, trouser fashion, she'd climbed over the rail as gamely as a Turkish corsair. If the girl had just come from a ladies' school in New York, her father had wasted his coin.

"No, just in an uncooperative humor, sir. I've been

as polite as I know how to be. I admit, I'm at a loss as to what to do!"

Dillon had no doubt of that. If the problem lay with anyone, it was with their fair prisoner, not James Green. His first officer was the epitome of gentility and breeding, as well as a first-class seaman.

"There we go, lads. She's fit to sail, if she ever was!"

The bosun's pleased announcement reminded Dillon of what he'd been about to tell his first officer, when the subject of Rosie Beaujeu had interrupted his thoughts. Besides, the young man looked as though he needed bolstering.

"You've done well with the ship, Mr. Green, and in time, too, by the look of the sky. The moon'll hold water."

"Aye, rain's in the making, sir, but the lady . . ."

"I'll speak to her."

"Thank you, sir."

Dillon only hoped young Green learned to keep a better poker face before he became a captain. Despite his penchant for formality, the man wore his heart on his sleeve for all to see.

"Your sympathy for Miss Beaujeu is understandable, Mr. Green, but evidently your undoing." Forcing a wry smile, Dillon started for the aft hatchway.

"Sir, she's not in your cabin!"

Halting so abruptly that the younger man stepped on the back of his heels, Dillon pivoted and steadied the flustered officer.

"S-orry, sir! She's in the brig . . . with the wounded."

"In the brig with the wounded?"

Green nodded at Dillon's terse echo.

Dillon shoved past him and stalked across the main deck toward the forward hatch, this time far outstepping his junior officer with his long, purposeful gait. Fate had damned him to capture a female in the war at sea. He was double damned that she was Rosie Beaujeu. But he would not be triple damned by having her in the brig with the male prisoners.

The third set of steps led down to a dimly lit corridor where heavy grating separated the prisoners from the guards' apartment. Because of the scarcity of crew, two armed seamen stood watch, rather than the *Thorne*'s marines. Having to duck because of the low beams, Dillon seized a lantern and held it up so that he might peer through the iron-and-wood bulkhead.

The group was unusually silent, a miserable lot, from the look of their bloodied bandages.

"Rosie, what the devil are you about now?" he demanded, searching the figures for the irksome girl.

"The name is Miss Beaujeu to you, sir."

The cool answer came from the front corner of the cell. Dillon dropped to his haunches. She was kneeling next to the *Border Rose*'s captain, who was obviously ill at ease.

"Captain, do you hold by this—a woman in a ship's hold?"

"Indeed not, Captain Mackay. Unfortunately, no reasoning of mine has been able to change her mind and I am not able to physically remedy the situation." There was genuine disappointment in the man's voice.

"If I'm a prisoner, I belong here."

Dillon cocked a curious brow at the girl who crossed her arms as if the matter were settled. "Milady, you are aware that, while Mr. Green's quarters open into my own, you will be afforded the utmost privacy. Few ships can offer someone in your circumstances better."

"Her original owner built the room for his wife so she could get away from the business of the ship," First Officer Green put in. "And one of your trunks is already in there."

He at least was afforded her attention. "Where's the other?"

"On your ship, milady."

Dillon flashed a dark look at James Green before turning back to the iron grille separating him from the prisoners. The female didn't need to be reminded of an indeed sore subject. *Her* ship!

"As a guest, Miss Beaujeu, will you accept Mr. Green's quarters?"

"If I were your guest, Captain, you wouldn't take the *Border Rose* from me."

Dillon's head ached abominably. He rubbed his temple as if to ease the pressure about to explode there.

"Rosie," Nate Malone intervened wearily, "I speak for the men. We don't want you here."

"I committed to fight with you and I'll face the same fate."

"I'm the captain and I say accept the gentleman's hospitality."

"Well, I'm the one who'd have to suffer the company of a man who would take my ship from me like a common thief."

"And *I'm* retiring to my quarters!" Dillon announced, pushing up to his feet as though ending the argument. "Guard, if the lady changes her mind, Mr. Green's quarters will be ready. Otherwise, see that she has everything she needs."

"But, Captain!" James Green protested. "You can't leave her in there!"

Dillon smiled, despite the fact that he wanted to pull the stubborn female through the grate with his bare hands. "Indeed I can, sir. This is a ship, not a nursery, and I am a captain, not a nanny. Gentlemen," he addressed the imprisoned crew of the *Border Rose,* "you have my sympathies, but far be it for me to force a lady to take the offered quarters against her will. Mr. Green!"

"Sir!"

"You may join me presently for a well-deserved pitcher of rum and double rations to both crews tonight, as well as those men in here that want it . . . and the lady, of course," Dillon conceded with a grace he was far from feeling.

"Aye, aye, sir."

"That's mighty generous of you, Mackay."

"Decent behavior deserves decent treatment, Captain Malone. Perhaps tomorrow, if you are up to it, you will join me for supper and we can ignore this damnable war for a pleasant hour or so."

"I look forward to it, sir."

"And Miss Beaujeu is invited, I'm sure," First Officer Green reminded Dillon timidly.

Dillon glanced at the young lady, who refused to acknowledge his presence, much less his hospitality. "If she can tear herself away from the comforts and pleasure of our brig, of course." He afforded his prisoners a cordial but costly nod of his aching head. "Good night, sirs . . . milady."

The man had no shame or conscience, Rose mused, watching as the tall lean captain of the *Thorne* retreated up the hatch, his upper torso, still naked and more magnificent than such a rogue deserved. It had glistened like his varnished boots in the lanternlight. Muscle had evidently replaced the good nature of the young lanky seaman she used to idolize on her father's ship.

Dillon must have at least turned thirty by now. No, thirty-one, she calculated. She recalled the men teasing him about his slow progress with puberty, calling him Peachfuzz. Naive, she'd thought that by plucking out his few sprouts of chest hair, it might somehow keep him from aging until she caught up with him. Now that manhood had darkened his soul as much as it had shadowed his chin, she realized she was even a greater fool to think she might shame him into releasing her crew and the *Border Rose*.

Instead, it was she who was forced to capitulate. Even after she'd tied up a blanket to separate her visually from the others, she wasn't out of earshot. Quiet as they tried to be, she could still hear the men grumbling about her obstinacy. Between that, the snoring, and other poorly disguised bodily sounds that made her burn with horrified humiliation, she was on the verge of tears when the night watch left and the midwatch came on. Worse, she needed to use the necessary and would not be reduced to the communal chamber pot, regardless of her blanket bulkhead—not with twelve men a whisper away.

"Rosie, for the love of God, leave us! 'Tis a miserable situation that has the men bilging under their breath and they'll not stop complaining until you go!" Nate whispered through the flimsy boundary. "Captain Mackay has offered a gentleman's hospitality. Women are not designed for the damned brig of a ship!"

Unable to argue that point or put off her decision any longer, Rose grudgingly asked one of the guards to deliver her to First Officer Green's abandoned quarters. Aside from the moonlight shining through the glass in the stern counter, the captain's cabin was dark when she was shown inside. That he'd answered the guard's knock with a growling "Show her to Green's berth and be done with it!" told her the rum he'd consumed in celebration of his victory had not improved his humor. It also rubbed in the fact that he'd been expecting her to give in all along.

She rushed into the first officer's cabin and closed the door behind her with a slam. Instantly she recognized the porcelain commode which had come from her own quarters on the *Border Rose*, as well as the matching washbowl and filled pitcher that were nested in a copper shaving basin built into the bulkhead. The trunk Mr. Green had mentioned was jammed beneath the stern window at the foot of a narrow berth, a masculine modification of what had been the former lady occupant's settee, for Rose could see where the back had been removed from the wall behind it.

Once Mother Nature was appeased, she lost no time in taking advantage of the niceties provided by the considerate Mr. Green, for she would not credit Dillon Mackay with the slightest kindness. Her knight of long ago had tarnished with age and greed. And, she realized to her dismay, after performing a much needed toilette and changing into a clean muslin shift, he snored fierce enough to swell the ship's sides like a blowfish!

With the break of day, activity once again ensued on the decks, stirring Rose from the restless sleep that the increasing roll of the sea had finally brought on. Outside the cabin, she could hear the voices of the ship's company over the clinking of cups and dishes and could only guess that, either forgotten or ignored, she'd been allowed to sleep through breakfast. Her stomach growling to remind her of the small portion she'd consumed of the fish stew served the prisoners the night before, she slid off the berth and hurriedly threw open her trunk.

Mr. Green had said there was to be a burial service for those from both ships who had not survived the bitter fighting and she needed something suitably dark, since she'd never suffered mourning clothes to be part of her wardrobe. Rummaging through her things, Rose noticed for the first time that they were not as neatly arranged and folded as they had been when Aunt Arissa's servant packed the trunk. Some items, particularly those of an intimate nature, had been wadded and shoved around the edge of her dresses and petticoats.

Her lips thinned and indignation flushed her face. How dare the man search her trunks, for there was little doubt in Rose's mind that Dillon had overlooked the one still aboard her ship. His brand of hospitality was indeed as questionable as she'd suspected. It was one thing to be robbed of her ship, but this was a violation of a personal nature. The very idea that Dillon Mackay's hands had touched those things she wore against her naked flesh was . . . well, it was as indecent as touching her outright!

By the time she'd donned an indigo frock made somber enough by a black inset on the bodice and sleeves, Rose had worked up a piping steam. Without taking time to find a bonnet to cover her tumble of dark curls, she threw open the cabin door, ready to confront the rogue on whom she wished the most disagreeable aftereffects of his rum-soaked evening. Instead of finding him still wallowing in his berth, however, she found the bed neatly made and the cabin, which he kept better tended than his person, abandoned.

Also deserted was the officers' ward through which she'd been escorted the night before, although their breakfast dishes had not yet been cleared by the steward. Losing momentum temporarily, Rose negotiated the steps to the quarterdeck, where she could hear her captor's ringing voice above the strain of the lines and the creaking of the ships being coaxed apart by the contrary current.

Dillon was back to her, his broad shoulder span testing the fit of the russet broadcloth jacket tailored to it when she emerged topside.

"Captain Mackay, I'd have a word with you this very moment!"

The bane of her existence turned a clean shaven face

toward her. But for the sardonic lift of his brow, he'd the astounding appearance of a gentleman ready for a church social with his clean muslin shirt and fawn breeches trimmed to black polished boots.

"I hardly think now is the time to shove in your oar, milady."

He even held a Bible, the recognition of which knocked the last of the wind from Rose's blustery sail. Subdued by the reverence of her surroundings, Rose turned toward the main deck where both ships' companies, including the wounded, had been assembled topside. At the rail of each ship were the canvas-wrapped bodies of those who had not survived yesterday's battle. How could the man even think to send her dead to their watery grave without her presence? Was there no end to his insensitivity?

Rose bowed her head and found what was left of her voice.

"By all means, proceed, sir."

"Yea, though I walk through the valley of the shadow of death . . ."

Dillon went on to finish the Twenty-Third Psalm, reciting rather than actually reading from the open leather-bound book before him. As his rich baritone rose above the sounds of the ships straining to be parted by the restless sea, Rose made the mistake of permitting her gaze to wander to the deck of the *Border Rose* where eight bodies lay at the side. Although she could not see the faces, she knew their names. She'd been with Nate when Henry Malloy reported the names of those whose families would have to be contacted. She'd written them in the log for her cousin before he handed it over to Mr. Green.

Old Huck Wilson, the man who'd painted the figure-head his brother had carved, was among them. A master gunner who'd cut his teeth on John Beaujeu's privateer during the War of Independence, he'd been crushed when one of his carronades was blown off its cradle by enemy fire. Rose had held his hand as he slipped his dying wind, all the while swearing over the fact that his crew's last shot had gone high because of a sudden swell.

"They must'a been shootin' at gulls!" he'd sworn with a horrid, unforgettable rasp that had awakened her more than once during the night, leaving her damp with perspiration.

Eyes blinded with raw emotion, Rose tried to shake the haunting image. When they cleared, the present bore down in its place. It was Jam Wilson she now saw standing stoic and ready to consign his brother's body to the sea they so loved.

"May the one God of heaven and earth and land and sea take these valiant men to His bosom."

An early-morning breeze wailed through the lines above them as the bodies from both sides were committed to their watery grave. Above the mournful windsong, their ensuing splash echoed in eerie cadence. Rose tried to swallow the painful blade fixed in her throat, but it would neither go up nor down.

War had sounded so exciting when she'd reveled in the tales of her relatives. In her naiveté she'd envied them. The last twenty-four hours, however, had robbed her not only of her ship but her innocence. Just as she'd seen Dillon for what he was, she'd also witnessed the glory of battle blackened by death and gore.

"Pipe the men to quarters! Strike a light now! Guard, see the prisoners below and secure," she heard Dillon command, his sanctimony now replaced with unquestionable authority. The service was over and life was going on. Once again the captain of a privateer, he extended his hand to his first officer.

"God's speed, Mr. Green. Keep your course for Grand

Manan in sails' sight, that red sky willing. If not, we'll meet you there."

"Aye, sir! Thank you, sir!"

Rose noticed for the first time since emerging on deck the rosy pall of the morning horizon. The northwest breeze was starting to frost the tops of the ocean crests, its chill marking a decided change from the balmier clime of the previous day. Rose crossed her arms with a shudder. Mother Nature had not lost all her wintry breath with the coming of spring and, like the tide of grief building within Rose's chest, she seemed fit to burst with it.

Eight men from the *Border Rose* and . . . She hadn't counted those on the *Thorne's* deck. Somehow she couldn't bring herself to wish it were as much or more, even if Dillon's crew was the enemy.

"Milady, I have a ship to get underway, so please say what you will and get below before you catch your death and blame me for the weather as well as the war."

Accompanied by a unified shout at the rails, the lines binding the protesting ships together were cast, providing a distraction so that Rose might sort her beleaguered thoughts.

"I . . ." Never feeling more lost or inadequate, Rose drew a steadying breath and turned to face Dillon. "I don't appreciate your commencing the burial without me," she blurted out. "They were my men, too!" This wasn't at all what she'd intended to say. Worse, she could hardly speak, not without the risk of sobbing like the baby Dillon had accused her of being.

"We thought you needed your rest more than further distress, milady."

"And don't call me milady!" she rallied in desperation. "I'm an American woman, not one of your aristocratic hens!"

"*Madame* then."

The anguish in her throat was literally strangling her, yet she could not allow it to escape. But there was no shame in retreat, she thought wildly. Many a brave warrior did so, to come back another day, when he was stronger and better able to battle the overwhelming odds. She knew what she had to do and hastily.

"Thank . . . thank you, sir!"

Just then the bosun's voice boomed from the main deck. "Stand firm, lads, here we go!"

On the heel of his warning, the ship plunged into a trough between the green swells of the ocean and rolled heavily to starboard. All that had been battened down held its place. Above them, the men in the lee of the furling canvas nimbly balanced in the riggings like acrobats on a high wire, but Rose, caught off balance physically and emotionally, teetered backward into their captain's outstretched grasp.

"Whoa, Rosie!"

As she fell against him, she was astonished to find that, even through his jacket and shirt, he was as warm as the air was chilling and as unbending as the raking masts now snapping with renewed canvas hungry for the wind. She found herself holding desperately to the proverbial any port in a storm, the port of her vowed enemy's embrace in the storm of her despair.

"Mr. Hanson, take over and keep to Mr. Green's stern!"

Dillon's voice thundered from his chest, even as he cradled her head against it. Then there was no longer any need to support her own weight, for he'd somehow slipped his arm beneath her knees and scooped her off the deck as easily as he'd done when she was small. How desperately she needed *that* Dillon now!

Except there was more to her distress than a skinned knee or wounded pride. Her very soul had been rent in two. Half had sunk beneath the green swells gradually growing in size about them and the other pulled ahead of them with sails tall and majestic as a North Atlantic iceberg.

"I wish *I* was in a sack!" she sniffed miserably, drawing up her feet so that Dillon could maneuver unhindered down the hatchway.

The ship rolled as it struggled to assume its course and another man might have stumbled on the steps, but not Dillon. He descended them as if he knew them by heart, no matter which way the sea toyed with them. That much about him had not changed.

"N-Nate was going to surrender and I stopped him," she blurted out. "They'd all be alive now but for me!"

Dillon never answered until they were inside the stern cabin and he'd carried her into the small quarters adjoining his own. Gently depositing her on her unmade berth, he cupped her trembling chin in his hand and leveled a dark and somber gaze at her.

"They were a sad loss, but that's the way of war, Rosie. It doesn't allow for our wants or best of intentions. Things would be a lot better between us if you'd think hard on that."

"But I had my reasons, Dillon!" Now that she'd started to unload her burden of guilt, Rose stopped reluctantly. She dared not tell him, for fear he might renege on his promise to parole Nate, sooner than take him to Halifax where his life might well be endangered.

"So do I, Rosebud."

Dillon had no more intention of calling the distracted girl on the berth by the pet name he'd dubbed her with years ago any more than he'd contemplated carrying her below. It just happened. The fact was, he'd take musket balls over a woman's tears any day, which was another reason females had no place in war. They were like delicate flowers, even if this particular one was as prickly as her namesake.

Despite more than one healthy portion of rum, he'd not been able to sleep for thinking about the abuse of her confinement with twelve seamen in such a dark and hellish place as the brig. After all, she was clearly not herself. On the other hand, she'd been so damned maddening!

"And I thought if I could lure you close enough, we stood a fighting chance. The snipers had you in their sights and then your men started shooting."

His quandary of whether to stroke or strangle the comely creature was instantly settled by the accusation. She hadn't listened to a word he'd said.

"By God, woman, I will not apologize for surviving! I, frankly, am glad not to be keeping company with Davy Jones in a canvas sack!"

"I wasn't asking for an apology. I only meant . . ." Rose backed against the bulkhead as her suddenly incensed companion leaned over, his clenched fists driving into the mattress on either side of her.

"But if it makes you feel better," he raved on, "I've had the man who fired the first shot dealt two lashes at daybreak."

Her startled expression grew even wider. "Why in heaven's name would you punish someone who saved your life?"

"Because he disobeyed my orders! Although why I expect a woman to understand the importance of discipline, I can't imagine."

"I seem to recall a time when you had trouble with it," Rose shot back with matching cynicism. "The brig was your home when you first came on with my father."

"And I seem to recall a time when you were sweet and lovable. It's a bloody shame the playful kitten became a vicious cat!"

"Why . . ." Rose struck out at the handsome face not inches from her own, but before she made contact, her wrist was caught in a viselike grip. "Get your hands off me, you bluenose bastard! 'Tis bad enough you've had them all over my intimate things!"

"Your what?"

"My clothes, you dullard! You had no right to search my belongings! What were you looking for, gold thread? Or perhaps you intended to steal my jewelry as well as my ship!"

"Madame . . ." Damning daggers flew at her from glittering ebony. "I was searching for the ship's papers!"

"I told you I broke open the cask and tossed the paper through the stern portal. Now will you kindly unhand me?"

Despite her false bravado, she winced when Dillon threw up his arms and backed away in stammering outrage. "I—I cannot believe that you would be so stupid as to toss over a fortune in specie!"

As though he feared the devil rising within him would drive him over the brink of restraint, he started to turn toward the open door and stopped. Again he raised his hands, but instead of making another threatening gesture, he dug them into his hair, grasping his temples.

"No, belay that!" he ground out.

His face had turned a mottled shade and he spoke as if invisible fingers were choking him and plucking on the cords standing out on his neck. A number of words were chewed and swallowed, all surely unfit for female ears, before he finally settled on an edited version.

"By the saints, I believe you just might be so foolish as that!"

Even though she saw it coming, Rose flinched at the slam of the cabin door. Her wide gaze still fixed where the dark tempest had stood but a moment before, she tried to sort through the scene which had just unraveled like a taut, frayed line to figure out what exactly had transpired. One moment she was basking in Dillon Mackay's comforting nearness, pouring out her very soul, and the next they were going at each other like two bull whales with sore noses.

Doubling her pillow behind her, she propped it under her neck and closed her eyes in weary resignation. She wasn't accustomed to losing control and crying.

She must have lost her mind to think Dillon Mackay's brief show of concern for her was genuine. All he cared about was the blasted papers she'd hidden along with her jewelry in the captain's cabin of the *Border Rose*. He hadn't listened to her at all, not like he used to.

Well, damn his boots, he could keelhaul her and she'd still not tell him the truth. Not as long as there was a remote chance of taking her ship back.

Four

"Even if we were fit, I'd not have my men party to it!"

Despite his earlier declaration that he was much improved, Nate Malone looked horrible in the dim swinging light of the brig. Rose wasn't used to seeing her cousin so unkempt. Not that he was a vain man, he was simply fastidious. Still, he was no more able to lead his men into taking over the ship in the midst of a storm than his men were. The able crew was riding it out with Mr. Green on the *Border Rose,* bound by their word and the added weight that Dillon Mackay held their captain hostage.

If only Nate could lead a rebellion and take the undermanned *Thorne* while its crew was conveniently occupied by Mother Nature's fury . . .

"I gave my word, Rosie."

"But this is war and I thought . . ." The single guard who'd climbed to the deck to see how his shipmates fared stepped down a few rungs and settled there, watching her, so Rose brightened her voice. "So you've been well fed?"

"The same fare as the ship's crew," Nate replied.

"And the doctor?"

"Is a cut above Doc Ames. His infirmary's well supplied with opiates, what with the *Thorne*'s being a pri-

vateer expecting to need them. I don't know how Peaky
would have managed without them."

Rose glanced over at the young top man whose name
had been shortened by his fellow seamen from Harrison Edward Peacock. He was as oblivious to the reckless
toss of the sea as the rain beating down upon them as
if the ocean had been upended. The men had wedged
blankets about the sleeping man to keep him from moving and aggravating the stump where his crushed leg
had been amputated by the *Thorne's* surgeon.

"And you, Cousin? How are you, Rosie?"

"I don't think I shall ever forgive myself, Nate,
but . . ." She took a bracing breath. "I shan't forgive
Dillon Mackay either. I never dreamed he'd keep her,
once he realized it was my ship."

"He couldn't let her go if he wanted to, Cousin."

"He's the captain. He could do anything he chose to
do!"

"We signed contracts, Rosie . . . articles, guaranteeing to follow a prescribed behavior."

"*We?*"

"There was a letter of marque in those papers you
destroyed," Nate reminded her. "Which was a hellova
thing to do. You should have turned them over."

"I'd sooner die!"

Nate fell back against the bulkhead and shifted to
ease his shoulder. "Well, it's done," he said. "But
Mackay'd have mutiny on his hands if he let you have
your ship after the fight his men put up to take it.
They're due their shares according to the articles. It's
the law, Rosie," he said in a raised voice to silence the
protest building behind the obstinate purse of her lips.
"As for you, I'd suggest you act the lady your father
spent good coin to make you. Believe me, Cousin,
Mackay could be considerably less gracious a host. He's
going to parole us, Cousin."

There was no need for Nate to elaborate. By not having to go to Halifax as a prisoner, he was not risking the certain noose awaiting him there. Rose glanced up at the guard sitting at the top of the hatchway and was reassured he was preoccupied with the storm.

"You gave your word to help him to a neutral port for refitting, but, beyond that, are you bound to let him sail off with my ship?"

"Well, no, but . . ."

"And you've every authority to take his ship under your letter of marque, do you not?"

"Cap'n John's mite has a point," someone put in from the darkness of the cell beyond them.

" 'Twould be fair turnabout if we could do it, sir," another added thoughtfully. "Just to take the ships, mind ye. We could parole Mackay an' his men."

"Aye, just to square the rigs with 'em, Cap'n, no more."

"Naturally we would reciprocate with the same hospitality we've been afforded." Rose fairly beamed at the unexpected rise of support. "And we'd move only if the risk was minimal, no more bloodshed than necessary."

"I think we're all agreed on that," Nate relented warily.

Rose accepted the little ground she'd gained. There was a long way between here and Halifax before total surrender became a necessity. The damage that forced them to put in at a neutral port at least evened the odds against them. "Just think on it, men, and be ready should the opportunity present itself. That's all I'm suggesting."

Although the deck was pitching, Rose climbed to her feet and walked to the hatchway. Her cloak and skirt daintily gathered in one hand, she started up the rungs, accepting the guard's assistance with a smile.

Nathan Malone stared after her with a mixture of annoyance and admiration. She'd suggested nothing that had not already crossed his own mind as he'd discussed their terms of surrender with Captain Mackay. He had given his promise of support so far as to get them to a port where the ships might be refitted and he and his men could be released. God knew he didn't want to give up his ship. He'd manned her with a crew that had previously known battle to avoid just that.

Game as Rosie was, however, he'd been reluctant to go any further and risk possible harm to her. Her father would never forgive him, nor would he forgive himself if something should happen to her.

"That's Cap'n John in a skirt, if he ever existed at all. I wasn't at all s'rprised when she come trippin' down here, them Beaujeu blue eyes all a sparkle, that she was up to somethin'."

"Wasn't there a story about her daddy doin' the same to some British jack durin' the independent war?"

"Aye, took back his own ship and the Red Jack's, too."

The round of comments was enough for Nate. If she hadn't had it before, Rose's ploy with the petticoat and willingness to face the same fate as her men to the letter had won her their undying devotion, even if they hadn't wanted to share the brig with her. His cousin's visit had sparked more life among the beleaguered seamen than any of his words of encouragement. Had she pressed a bit harder, there'd have been a mutiny right there in the brig.

"Most females'd be pukin' their guts out in their cabin in this gale, but not our Rosie."

Nate caught himself in the midst of testing his injured shoulder and grimaced, partly from the pain and partly from the spontaneous chuckle that shook him. "No, not our Rosie."

"And that cap'n thinks he's smellin' hell right now!"

Nate laughed outright. "Like as not, instead of worrying she'll have sand in her ears by morning, she's dancing on the deck right now."

That they might be washed up on a beach by morning had crossed Rose's mind. Rain was pouring through the aft hatchway like a waterfall. It was ice cold and made the planking dangerously slippery as it rushed to the drains on the side. Keeping one hand on the bulkhead, she carefully made her way across the deck, which bucked wild as any horse she'd ever seen. Above the hammering of the waves against the freeboard, Rose could barely hear the shouts of the men topside, fighting the elements with their wit and bare hands.

It was a magnificent storm, she had to admit, and they were riding it out in admirable fashion. Like herself, they loved the sea and were given to take her moods, both good and bad, with a thrill no other mistress could give them. Without regard for the pelting sheets of water, Rose braved her way to the quarterdeck, where she might catch a glimpse of the violent match.

Most of the canvas had been reefed, and that which was modestly furled hurled the ship across the pitching ocean into the gray unknown ahead of them. The falling curtains of rain blocked the afternoon sun, reducing visibility to zero. She could barely make out the dangerous game in the mast tops, where a single misstep meant the loss of life. Dillon Mackay's seamen appeared to be holding their own, at home like monkeys in a tree.

The ship's wheel on the quarterdeck was lashed to hold a steady course against the raking claws of the elements. Even so, three men, including the captain, manned it, their clothing plastered to their skin by the wind-driven downpour that stung Rose's cheeks and pushed back her hood. As she tried to pull it up, the ship suddenly swooped down off a giant swell and her stomach seemed to drop out from under her along with the deck on which she huddled.

Her hold returned judiciously to the rail, the hood abandoned, a smile of delight spontaneously claiming her lips. Her aunt Arissa and grandmother had often dubbed her mad when she reveled in the fierce majesty of a storm, warning her to have more respect for nature. The truth was, Rose had great respect for it. She believed in taking every precaution, but saw no call to fret when there was nothing she could do to stop it and yet so much to appreciate.

Naturally, she wouldn't think of venturing topside unnecessarily, although, if she had a rope to tie about her waist . . .

The music of the thrashing sea invaded her thoughts. There was something in its midst which did not belong, a roar, but not like the wind whipping through the lines and braces and sweeping into the open hatch around her. Crashing rather than hissing, it bore more resemblance to the sound of a battered surf or of the storm-tossed waves breaking over shallows.

But not in the open sea! Her alarm struck Dillon Mackay at the same time. "Hard a starboard!" he shouted hoarsely above the din. "Quick, lads! We're headed ashore!"

No shore was visible to the human eye, but his men sped to unleash the wheel to change the deadly course. The rope, swollen and wet, resisted their efforts. The young captain pulled a knife from his boot and hacked away at the rope.

As though she held the blade in her own hand, Rose tightened her grip on the rail with each frantic saw of the line, for she knew Dillon had heard the same thing as she. They must have been blown off course and were approaching shoals of the mainland or of the many islands dotting the coast.

A storm on the open sea was a wild but relatively safe ride for a well-built vessel, but the same in shallow water promised a journey straight to Davy Jones's locker. Rose came to her feet on the rungs, clinging to the swaying rail, and prayed for the rope to give way while there was still time to steer the vessel clear of the submerged rock and sand awaiting them.

With an answering snap, the line whipped around the spinning wheel. The men leapt to it; captain and crew fought to master the willful wheel.

"Pull!"

Two seamen appeared from below and raced topside, as though summoned by some unseen telegraphic signal. Drawn from where she'd pressed against the rail to get out of their way, Rose followed them and grabbed at the loose line Dillon had cut earlier. Acting only with inborn instinct, she wrapped it about her arm for a firmer grip and lent her strength to the united effort.

The wind played havoc with her skirts and cloak. It was blowing strong enough to unhair a dog and the materials were not tarred for protection like foul weather gear, so Rose was soon soaked to the bone. Yet she was not cold, not any longer. Like her fellow shipmates, she was enveloped in the dead heat to save the ship against the lethal rock-studded coast that lay in wait for them.

It seemed to take an eternity before the buxom figurehead of the *Thorne* finally turned her nose up and started out for sea again. Once the wheel jerked viciously out of their grasp, snatching away the line and Rose's sleeve with it. A terrible grinding sound followed, one that tore the breath from her chest. Even as she sprawled backward upon the slippery planking, where the backwash of the deck swept her into the scuppers, she prayed desperately that the rock scraping the

Thorne's underside would skim no more than barnacles off.

Although blinded by the slapping rain, Rose managed to grab hold of a cleat next to the drain and there she lay, wedged against the bulkhead until the ship made its shuddering turn into the waves and the blade of rock beneath them had retreated. The five men still struggled to keep the wheel under control, three holding the new course, while two sought to lash fresh line to it. It had been close, very close, she thought shakily.

But for Dillon Mackay's finely hewn senses, she might be clinging to a piece of wreckage. A good captain needed no daylight, but could navigate by the sound of the sea, her father had said many times. She remembered his tying her to the aft mast and sharing over the roar of a storm what he heard and what it meant. He'd done the same with Dillon, insisting, above the young man's protest, that a rope be used sooner than lose the green son of fellow captain and friend overboard.

"Cap'n, we're takin' on water in the aft hold!" a sailor shouted from the hatchway.

Dillon's curse surely stoked the fires of hell. "Turn the prisoners out of the brig and put every one that's able to the pumps."

"Captain!"

"What the devil is it, Hanson?" Dillon swore as his junior officer held up a soaked rag in his face.

"Lace, sir! It was caught in the line tied to the wheel!"

With an oath, Dillon snatched the material from the man, examining it himself. It was lace and there was only one source of such a frill on his ship. The coppery taste of dread rose in the back of his mouth as he scanned the water-swept deck around them but saw no sign of movement, aside from that of his men above through the driving sheets of water.

"Take over, sir. Keep her steady!"

The soaked cloth wrapped about his hand, Dillon started for the hatch. She wouldn't have. She couldn't have, he argued against the nightmarish notion that Rose had been tossed over the side while he'd struggled to save the ship. Surely the girl had more sense than to leave her cabin!

Look, Dillon, isn't God wonderful? The recollection of rain-splattered cheeks, rounded even more by the delight on the little Rosie Beaujeu's face spurned Dillon down to the berth deck without touching the steps. His muscles and joints stung with the hard landing on the lower deck, but he forced his legs into action, racing through the empty officers' mess to his cabin.

Everything was in its place, from the books on the railed shelving crowning the perimeter of the room, to his shaving basin nested in the washstand. He could hear his navigation instruments rattling safe inside his desk, exactly where he'd put them. Rose Beaujeu, however, was not where she belonged. The open door to her small cabin banged against the wall with each roll of the ship and the floor itself was flooded with water.

Rushing into the cubicle, Dillon saw the problem immediately. The window in the stern counter had worked its way loose during the rough-and-tumble passage and seawater had rushed in and swamped the cabin, washing the bedding off the berth and spilling over into his own quarters. Even her trunk, which had taken four men to bring aboard, had overturned and feminine garments were strewn about like the hooked rugs always tripping him at the family home his stepmother had refurbished.

Reluctant to step on the delicates, much less be found tangled in them, Dillon leapt across the water-soaked mattress to secure the battered casement. Just as he landed, another swell flooded into the room, knocking him backward over the edge of the bedding. Although he scrambled to brace himself, the paneling was wet, offering no rescue whatsoever from the blunt edge of the berth awaiting his head.

"Dillon!"

God deliver him, he was hearing the missing girl, but the blinding pain in his head refused to let him see her. He blinked furiously to clear his eyesight until he was able to focus in the storm-dimmed light on the drenched urchin frantically gathering his head into her lap.

"Are you all right?"

But for the pain and common sense, he'd swear he was drunk as a Portuguese fisherman. "Aye, that is . . . I think so."

"Wait here!"

The lap which had pillowed his head suddenly disappeared, leaving Dillon to catch himself on his elbow as the girl sprang to her feet and lunged at the swinging window. Waiting for the ship's motion to work with her rather than against her, Rose pushed the casement to and, with the click of the bolt, secured it against the angry saltwater clamoring against the glass to gain entrance.

"Where the ballyhoo of blazes have you been?"

"Visiting the brig!" she answered breathlessly. "The men are fine, but we're taking on water! I heard the scrape."

Dillon eyed the hand extended to him and pushed himself upright. If he didn't know better, he'd have sworn someone had split the back of his head open with a cleaver. Swaying with the roll of the ship, he grasped the edge of the berth for support.

"That's not the only place—" He broke off as the girl in the shamelessly clinging dress shed her water-laden cloak, exposing a bare arm—white, smooth, and blurring like the rest of his sentence. The words swimming evasively in his head, he held up the hand wrapped in the missing sleeve of her garment. "My God, Rosie, not the . . . the wheel . . ."

"Dillon?"

There were two of her now and both grabbed at him when he started forward. Yet, neither of their arms were sufficient to keep him from plunging into the bottomless darkness. It opened before him, swallowing him and most of his senses. A few remained behind, clinging stubbornly to the dangling threads of consciousness.

He heard the anxious pitch of Rose's "Oh, God, Dillon, you're bleeding!" The more she shook him, the faster his brain seemed to spin inside his skull. "Oh, damn, Dillon, look what you've done!"

As if he'd intentionally knocked himself senseless! Despite his lightheadedness, Dillon felt like the deadweight he was as his smaller companion struggled to lift him. Only a miracle saved her from dropping his head on the floor after she'd managed to drag him into the other room. As it was, it was her slippers that softened the blow when she lost her grip.

"I don't think I can get you up there!" she panted.

Up there? Realizing her intention to put him in his bunk, Dillon groaned in protest, but Rose slipped her arms beneath him and lifted him with a labored grunt. What he'd intended as an emphatic "No!" resounded only in his mind. Then even that was stomped out by the slam of his upper body on the floor, as, once again, he slipped from the girl's tentative hold. The resulting agony filled his senses with a blinding white light, which blessedly went out in total almost as soon as it had appeared.

A lantern hung uncommonly still on its sling across the room when Dillon's consciousness returned with a hellacious throbbing at the back of his neck. From what he could gather, the gauze bandages enveloping his head and nearly covering his eyes were all that kept his skull from splitting in two. The only pounding he heard was not that of the ocean hammering at his ship, but of his erratic pulse. And there was humming somewhere close by, soft though it was in comparison.

Venturing to open his eyes beneath the lip of the bandage covering his brow, he came to focus on a slender feminine form bent over his sea chest, her short shift revealing a riveting share of shapely leg. As she straightened and shook out a pair of neatly folded breeches, Dillon realized it was no shift at all, but one of his shirts. It was also evident, with the light of the ship's lantern behind her, that a shirt was all the young lady wore.

Now there was a vision to distract a man from his aches and pains! Dillon would have thought he was dreaming, but, aside from the pleasure his eyesight dealt, every other sense was playing hell with him. His head felt like a football after a hard game. Nonetheless, he held back the protest aching to escape his lips lest he alert the lady to his observation and end this heavenly display of allure.

An abrupt knock on his cabin door, followed by his junior officer's voice, fouled his plan. "Miss Beaujeu, may I come in?"

"Just a moment, sir!" Idle humming turned to frenzy as the young lady rushed to make herself presentable. Hopping on one foot, she shoved her other into his trousers and then repeated the little dance with the reverse before tugging them up and tucking his shirt in the oversize waist. Even as Dillon drew his gaze from the firm thrust of her bosom beneath his shirt to speculate as to how she would keep the canvas pants up, she fished a length of cord about them and fetchingly pulled them in. His bell bottoms swung about her ankles as she ran barefoot to open the cabin door.

"He's not stirred a bit, sir," she said as Mr. Hanson entered the room. "But the doctor and I were able to pull off his wet togs and get him into his bed."

Dillon touched the side of his hip with his hand in disbelief and found that he was naked as the day he'd been born. This had to be a dream!

"I'd have a report on my ship, Mr. Hanson, and be quick about it!" he rallied, determined to separate fantasy from reality once and for all.

Rose fairly jumped out of her skin at the sound of Dillon Mackay's voice and pivoted to see the very much awake man rising on his elbow. "What . . . How long have you been there?" she stammered. "I mean . . ."

"Long enough, madame."

A scarlet flush spread from the top of her head to the very tips of her toes in the wake of the thorough sweep of her patient's knowing gaze.

"The ship's still afloat, sir, but we took a terrible beating," Hanson said.

"And the men?"

It was a shame he'd lost that innocent look she'd admired while he slept. It was the first time since they'd met again that she'd not felt intimidated by him. He hadn't taken long to recoup that swaggering authority, she mused grudgingly.

"All well, sir. They're at the repairs, but we've a tear in the larboard side, just at the waterline. Never once heard *She sucks!* from the pumps all night long. We're heading for an island in the distance, sir, so the carpenters can get to it at low tide."

"Ground her?" Dillon queried. It was difficult to sort out the information amidst the painful beat of his pulse, but he had to. A captain had no business in his quarters at a time like this, especially when the pumps had yet to suck air, indicating considerable water still lay in the bilges.

"No, sir, tie her over like the lads did in France."

"Aye, of course. What island is it?"

"As near as Captain Malone and I can figure, sir, it's an unnamed one south of Fundy." Upon seeing Dillon's scowl, Mr. Hanson added quickly, "Don't you worry about a thing, Captain. I've got the situation well under hand. I believe Captain Malone is a man of his word. He's been helpful as can be."

His prisoner was running his ship, while he was laid up with double vision and a bursting head and Mr. Hanson saw no reason for him to worry. Dillon forced himself upright, but refrained from continuing to his feet at Rose's disconcerted gasp.

"The doctor said you should rest! I put three stitches on that hard head of yours."

"You?"

"Doctor Gibbons fell during the storm and sprained his right hand. It's swelled big as a shank of ham," Hanson explained.

"Well, well, it seems you've finally found a niche for yourself, although I'm just as glad I did not awaken to find you coming at me with a suturing needle."

He hadn't meant to be funny, but Rose smiled. She had become a beautiful if troublesome young woman. Quite lovely, even in his clothes.

Dillon drew his gaze away from her. "That's all, Mr. Hanson. I'll be topside shortly to assess the situation for myself. Oh, any sign of Mr. Green?" he added as thought of *Border Rose* came to his gradually clearing mind.

"Not yet, sir. The weather's still lifting but I'll let you know the minute we sight sail. Anything else?"

"Not at the present, Mr. Hanson. Dismissed."

Waiting until the door was closed behind his junior

officer, Dillon slid off the bed, pulling the sheet with him. His prize could be anywhere and as damaged as the *Thorne* after riding out the storm. However, he had confidence in Mr. Green's command. As he considered the possible consequences, he nearly forgot Rose's presence.

"Umm . . . I'll wait for you to dress in my cabin!"

The fetching blush which had touched the girl's face earlier bloomed again, a hot pink against the loose curls of her unbound hair. The raven tresses fell just short of her shoulders, long enough to pull up in that pert pile of ringlets which tumbled in natural disorder from her ribbons and combs.

"But why, madame? As I understand it, I've nothing beneath this blanket you've not already seen."

Much as his head ached, Dillon found himself unable to resist the temptation to keep the young lady off balance. He had the edge and was not one to let it pass.

"Stripped me of my wet togs, I believe you said. And it must have been by your own tender hand, what with the doctor's handicap. Did they teach you such things at your ladies' school?"

Rose wavered only a moment before seizing the offensive. "I peeled you like a banana, you herring choker! But since I saw little enough to merit a second look, I feel my time better spent restoring my quarters to order. Good day, sir."

Dillon laughed despite the heat racing up the cords of his neck and inflaming his face and scalp. The girl, however, had not noticed, for she spun on the balls of her feet and stomped toward the small adjoining cabin.

"I'm afraid I can't say the same," he called after her, halting her as though he'd caught her by the scruff of the neck. "I don't think I've ever seen you more charming, Rosie, either in or out of my clothes."

"The storm swamped my trunk. I shall return these as soon as my own dry, Captain."

The blanket still wrapped about his waist, Dillon closed the distance between them and leaned over to whisper in her ear, "I'll look forward to it, madame."

Brushing his lips away as though a worrisome gnat, the girl afforded him a cutting glance over her shoulder. "I may have grown up, Dillon Mackay, but I've not lost my mind. And I'd suggest you get dressed before you get yourself another black eye to match the one I accidentally gave you while you were out."

Before he could answer, the door to the cubicle slammed in his face. The small shaving mirror anchored to it swung back and forth where the blue-black swelling she'd claimed credit for looked back at him, robbing him of reply.

Five

By nightfall the *Thorne* was safely moored in a small quay sheltered by a natural breakwater of rock. While the wooded island's natural cove seemed the perfect place to repair the ship, it was also the worst for a privateer to be caught. They would be literally high and dry by daybreak, although Dillon *thought* he was in friendly waters.

In the full wrath of the blow, those of the *Border Rose*'s crew who were able had pulled together with his own men at the pumps to save the ship. Tonight, they would celebrate as one crew in thanksgiving for the safe reward of their combined efforts with extra rations of rum.

The tempting scents drifting through the ship from the galley made Dillon's stomach growl as he nodded to the night watch before going below to his cabin. He himself was to dine with Captain Malone. Dillon looked forward to an evening of relaxation, dry clothes, and the subsequent good night's rest promised by them. With first light, he would be back to the business of repairing his ship, replenishing what supplies they could from the island, and getting to a port where he could arrange transportation for his parolees.

The sooner the better, he thought, disliking the idea of being stranded, helpless like a turtle on its back during low tide. He halted at the door to his quarters. After a short debate with his conscience as to a captain's right versus propriety, he knocked.

Rose Beaujeu hadn't left the quarters since the storm had abated, but then, strange as her behavior was, that didn't surprise him. Why would she venture topside when it was perfectly safe to do so? That made entirely too much sense. Although, her medical prowess had impressed him.

He touched the back of his head, which was still tender, but had ceased to give him thunder. The ship's physician commended her most highly when Dillon had gone below to check on the invalids. Of course, the physician wasn't the one with the cut over a blackened eye and a gash on his head resulting from her lack of good judgment.

"Rosie— Miss Beaujeu?"

"You may enter, sir!"

Dillon tripped the latch. However, he stopped short just inside the door, for the entire room was draped in feminine apparel of every description. He couldn't even see the windows in the stern counter, or the perpetrator of the outrage, for that matter.

"What the—"

A defensive voice from the adjoining quarters cut him off in explanation. "My things were soaked, Captain Mackay. It's either this or the deck."

Dillon held his tongue. One blasted petticoat on a top mast had nearly sunk his ship. He poured some Madeira from the decanter with matching goblets of purple Spanish glass he kept on his desk, a ridiculous gift from his fickle stepsister, as inappropriate as her choice in husbands.

"Has the *Border Rose* been sighted?"

Women had become the bane of his existence. Men

he could have flogged. "Not yet, madame. Perhaps tomorrow. Will you join me with a glass of Madeira?"

"Do you think you should indulge in spirits with your head wound? I would think you'd be dizzy enough."

"Thanks to your needlework, my head is well enough to indulge my needs. Will you join me?"

"You've nothing lighter, like a sherry?"

"Not on a man's ship. Where the devil are you? I feel the bloody fool speaking to a row of empty frocks."

"Mending your dress shirt! Just pour the drink and I'll join you shortly. I need this light."

Dillon scowled. "I wasn't aware my shirt needed mending."

"It didn't" came the unabashed reply. "It hung on the hinge of your chest when I was looking for something to wear. I thought it was the least I could do to repair it."

"The least." He downed the glass and poured himself another, although he doubted there was enough Madeira in his private store to offset the effect of his present company.

When that had been finished at his leisure, he dodged a batiste shift, a camisole, and a corset, devoid, he noticed, of the padding often needed to round out the female figure, before finding his washstand at the edge of the feminine menagerie. Next to the basin lay his razor, soap, and talc. Pleased that at least some things were still normal, Dillon stripped to the waist and performed a quick bath before lathering his stubbled chin and moving in front of the mirror.

No more had he put the blade to his jaw when the door upon which the mirror was mounted flew open, knocking it askew and nicking his earlobe in the process.

"Dillon! What have you done to yourself!"

Dillon's beribboned companion hurriedly grabbed a towel and dabbed at his bleeding ear.

"Why didn't you say you were behind the door? Would you like me to shave you? I used to help Aunt Arissa with her patients . . ."

"Good Lord, no!" The girl had to be crazed to think he'd let her near his neck with a razor. What she missed by design, she'd make up for by accident.

Rose bit her tongue at the outburst. She'd made up her mind to let Dillon Mackay go on thinking she was a harmless, helpless female, anything to lower his guard so he'd not suspect a thing when she and her crew made their move to retake the *Border Rose*.

"Well, I'm sorry!" she enunciated, adding dourly, "I should have knocked before exiting."

She couldn't let her imagination run wild toward the worst, just because the *Rose* hadn't been sighted since the storm. She *couldn't!* A good captain kept a becalmed manner.

"I don't enjoy being like this!" she blurted out. "It's just that . . ." She looked away, suddenly unable to focus on the drying clothing that had been stored in her trunk. The truth was, her reserve was as tattered as her ship, wherever it was. "Here's your shirt, sir. I'll have that drink now."

Placing the mended garment over her silent companion's arm, Rose retreated into the hanging maze toward the desk in the center of the room. How could Dillon Mackay understand what she was feeling? He was a man, used to getting what he wanted. He wasn't hampered by the restraints of a woman's world. No one thought it the least odd that he coveted his own ship. He had no concept of what the *Border Rose* meant to her. It was her dream.

Rose took a sip of the heavy amber wine and shuddered as it went down. She believed her father called it fortified and could well see why. It smacked of authority, meant to dominate, not compliment. No wonder Dillon favored it.

Rose had nearly finished the heady beverage by the time Dillon was dressed for the dinner being served in the officers' mess. Once again, to her chagrin, he'd tacked to an unexpected course. Anger no longer darkened his face. If anything, his expression bordered on apologetic.

"It's been a rough two days, Miss Beaujeu. Circumstances, I fear, have not nurtured our better natures."

Unable to argue that point, Rose remained silent, watching the handsome captain as he went on to help himself to the wine, as well as replenish her own glass.

"My only excuse is that I've been preoccupied with the welfare of my ship and crew, madame."

"It's mine as well, sir."

Dillon cleared his throat of what Rose was certain was an unsavory retort and then soothed it with the Madeira. "Perhaps we should, at least for the evening ahead, bury the proverbial hatchet, and indulge in some much-deserved relaxation. Since the island seems deserted, I think we can say we are on neutral ground. What say you, madame? Shall we drink to a truce?" He grinned. It was as pained and yet rakish an attempt as she'd ever seen. "At least until our next confrontation?"

Instead of an angry ogre, he was acting the Dillon she remembered, always able to coax a smile out of her, no matter how fair or foul her mood. At least he was trying. And so would she, for it suited her ultimate goal. Even as Rose touched her glass to his, however, she felt an odd sense of foreboding, as if approaching unknown waters.

"At least until then, sir," she agreed, "although it's

difficult to be at ease with my finery dripping dry on a line, while I gad about in your togs."

"Miss Beaujeu, I have never seen my clothes look so well. You do them honor."

Before Rose knew what he was about, he lifted her hand to his lips and brushed her knuckles. A gale of color swept to her face as he once again raised his glass. "To truce, madame."

How she ever was able to maneuver the clear purple glass to her mouth and back to the desk without spilling the brimming wine was beyond her. She swallowed the liquor with an effort. Despite the fact that she'd tied up her hair with ribbons, she knew she looked like she'd been dragged in by a press gang. He was probably making fun of her with his gallantry, she thought warily, although he seemed sincere enough.

"May I escort you to supper, Miss Beaujeu? Much as I'm enjoying your company, I dread to keep Captain Malone and my officers waiting."

"N-Nate's dining with you?" Rose stammered as Dillon helped her up from his chair and placed her hand on his arm as though she were clad in her finest silk and taffeta.

"The truce is ship-wide, madame. Even as we speak, your crew sups with mine forward. Necessity sometimes breeds allies of the worst enemies."

The fact that her men were no longer locked behind bars was too good to believe. With that freedom . . . *Enemies!* The term jolted all thought of mutiny from Rose's mind with a start. She looked up at Dillon as though he'd suddenly grown horns.

"Madame?"

"What?"

Dillon swept his arm toward the yawning space before the door he'd opened, where the men there leapt to their feet with benches scraping. "I believe we are keeping these gentlemen waiting."

Not Dillon Mackay! she argued with the monstrous idea, somehow moving one foot ahead of the other in response to his request. She'd fancied Dillon as her husband as a child and he'd be perfect for her, if not for the fact that he'd taken her ship. Wars came and went, but the *Border Rose* could never be replaced.

There was just something about him, even though I knew he was my enemy. How often had she heard Grandmother Tamson and Aunt Arissa say that about the men in their lives?

How can this Beaujeu love her enemy if she never gets to meet him? The defiant words she'd tossed at her family in order to make the voyage rushed in, draining her face of its color. God forbid, was this her destiny as a Beaujeu?

"Rosie, are you all right?" her cousin inquired, rushing to take her other arm as a concerned Dillon helped her to her chair at the table. "I might look like a ghost, but I assure you, I'm not!"

Nate's voice dangled like a lifeline in front of her and Rose seized at it lamely. "Nate! You . . ." She had to keep her eyes on her cousin, lest she plunge into that hopeless panic again. "You're looking well. I'm so glad to see you up and about!"

Rose took a seat amidst her admiring company and the remainder of the evening ensued quite pleasantly. The table had been set with china, and silver graced either end of it. Surrounding them were covered dishes, steaming in the chilly dampness left by the departed storm.

The men, of course, talked ships. Occasionally Rose participated, drawn in from politeness, although Dillon's officers did not have to listen to her long to realize that she knew her way about a vessel. After a while, she lost count of the number of times her glass had been filled, just as she'd lost track of the conversation from time to time. Between the possibility of Dillon Mackay being destined for her and the fact that the *Border Rose* had yet to be sighted, she was extraordinarily distracted.

The subject of the navy surfaced after some awkward small talk, during which a heavenly dessert of rice and raisin pudding, dashed with a liqueur-laced sauce, was served. Rose, however, only picked at hers, struggling to maintain reason, lest her real hunger for revenge and the recovery of her ship carry her away. As for this startling revelation about Dillon . . .

If he'd only give her back her ship, if this really was her fate, why, she could be all the woman he'd ever need. At least, she *thought* she could. He could teach her. She twirled the glass absently, the flickering lights from the candles dancing off it like the confusion in her mind—flashing here and there, with no order or logic. About her, a lively conversation of the navy versus the privateer was batted back and forth across the table, the latter naturally winning all favor. Neither Yanks nor bluenoses cared for their military counterparts, who were rivals in taking prizes.

"I've treated many a man rowed from ship to ship in the convoy to receive punishment on each and lost more than a decent share," the retired naval surgeon said. " 'Tis why I retired to a private practice in Halifax when my enlistment was up. I've no taste for flogging."

"That and a fetching Halifax merchant's daughter," Dillon reminded the elderly gentleman.

"Milady still cuts a fine figure," her husband agreed, lifting a toast to his wife. "And has the patience of a saint."

"A seaman's wife has little choice, if she's worth her salt."

"Well, I'd never stay landlocked while my husband

was off having all the fun in life!" Rose didn't realize she'd spoken her thought aloud until all heads turned toward her. The only face she saw, however, was Dillon's mocking one.

"Fun, madame? Do you call war fun?"

"Don't be telling me you're out here solely out of patriotic duty, Dillon! If that were the case, why were you so bloody anxious to while away your time at sea before that? Why weren't you tucked cozily in that fancy mansion of your father's and practicing some noteworthy profession?"

"The sea is no place for a woman, particularly in wartime! By God, Rosie . . ."

"Miss Beaujeu!"

"Miss Beaujeu," Dillon continued, undaunted. "Ask your cousin! I'd hesitate to wager the number of times he's regretted taking you aboard the *Border Rose* . . . and God only knows how much I've regretted it!"

"And you'll regret it even more if I have my way, Dillon Mackay!"

Rose bit her tongue, but it was too late. She'd blundered and blundered badly, she thought, not daring to steal a glance at her cousin.

"I—I can't reason with the likes of you! Either of you," she declared brokenly, dragging Nathan into the picture as well. "The fact is, I've outsmarted you both. I bought Nathan time to put up an honorable fight by holding you off with a pink petticoat and you can't bear that a woman did that."

"That was underhanded, Rosie."

"Miss . . ."

"By God, I'm captain of this ship and I'll call you by any damned name I please! Believe me, underhanded is complimentary compared to some of the words you've brought to mind."

"And *you* weren't underhanded when you approached us with guns hidden under painted canvas?"

"It's accepted practice, not a hysterical impulse."

Rose threw up her hands. "It's fine if a man does it, but not a woman! I'm not allowed to be canny, only hysterical!"

"What the devil are you doing?"

"Leaving this narrow-minded company, sir!" Seizing the new bottle of Madeira the steward had just refreshed their drinks with, she started around the table when Dillon rose to block her way to the main hatch.

"You've had more than enough to drink, madame, and it brings out a belligerence unbecoming a lady."

Dillon was uncommonly tall, which made him all the more imposing. He'd always looked down at her, come to think of it. Rose met his gaze equally, her chin tilted in defiance. Yes, he was bigger and stronger, but then, he'd always been that and it hadn't stopped her before. With a soft and devious curl of her lips, she held out the open bottle, as if to surrender it.

"Pardon my hysteria, Dillon," Rose averred, a slight purr infecting her voice as she placed tentative fingers on the lapel of his jacket. "I just can't seem to help it, my being a mere *woman.*"

She heard Nathan's startled "Rose!" as she upended the bottle, but it was too late for her to stop. The demon within her host had been cut loose, its bonds washed away by the liquor drenching Dillon's chest. She could see it breathing fire behind the smoldering ebony of his gaze as he reached out for her. Instinctively, Rose stepped back and threw the bottle at one of the captain's arrogantly planted boots, striking the instep with unerring aim.

Whether it was a howl or a curse which erupted from him, she did not take time to make out. The moment he grabbed his throbbing foot, she elbowed him sharply in the ribs, knocking him into the table, and then ran for the cabin as though Satan himself were on her heels.

"Easy, man, you know how Rose is," she heard Nathan Malone counsel as she hurried through the maze of clothing toward the safety of her cabin.

"By God, the girl doesn't know the meaning of discipline!"

"Sir, she's had an upsetting time . . ."

"Dismissed, Mr. Hanson! You *all* are dismissed!"

"I apologize for her, Mackay," Nathan spoke up again. "I hope you will remember that you are a gentleman."

Rose strained to hear Dillon's answer, but it seemed more of a chewed-up growl than a reply. Or maybe it was her heartbeat that muddled her hearing, for it was surely pounding in her ears and against her chest, beating the breath out of her in the process. She leaned against the door, which, to her dismay, lacked a lock of any sort. What on earth had come over her? She closed her eyes and tried to moisten her lips again, but her mouth had gone dry. Perhaps she'd gone a bit too far this time.

Six

An eternity passed before Dillon came to the cabin. Rose measured it in the furious footsteps that echoed overhead as the captain paced the deck. The closing of the outer compartment door and the deliberate progress of booted feet toward her tenuous sanctuary seized heartbeat and breath from her, as well as the fog generated from the liquor. Desperate, Rose implemented her feeble plan of defense, her fingers crossed at her sides that it would work. She closed her eyes and forced herself to breathe peacefully, while every nerve was poised at riot's edge.

The latch clicked, betraying Dillon's entry into her scant quarters. By now he blocked all hope of escape with sheer size, for there was not room for two to stand abreast of each other. The scent of his soap and talc was faint beneath that of the spilled Madeira as he paused by her berth. Rose could hear his breathing and it sounded normal, not as if it were being dragged from the depths of hell and forced with billows through his nostrils.

Perhaps the agitated walk on the quarterdeck had calmed him. Perhaps he'd think her asleep and go on his way. Perhaps . . .

Rose gasped as the front of her borrowed shirt was lifted away from her skin and liquid splashed on it,

streaming lukewarm in every direction, embracing her
throat and circling her breasts to dribble down her side.

"You idiot!" she screeched, coming up from the
berth to wrestle the offending bottle away from him.
"You're soaking your own cl—" Her voice was drowned
in the sweet burning nectar that found its way down
her throat, up her nose, in her eyes, and over her hair.
Much as she tried to push the seemingly endless stream
away from her, she was unable to do so until the last
drop struck the hollow of her throat.

She couldn't see Dillon's face, for the moon was ha-
loed behind him, but she knew his vital presence with
every other sense. He was sprawled atop her in a scandalous manner, his long, lean legs entangled with her
own. Every breath he took crushed her breasts and
filled her nostrils with the sweet scent of the liquor he'd
been evidently drinking.

"So you want to be treated like a man, eh, Rosie?"

"Aye . . ." she answered warily. He was laying a trap
for her, she knew, but she couldn't quite make out his
course.

"Do you know what I'd do to a man who'd taken my
clothes without asking and then had the audacity to
pour good drinking wine over me?"

Her eyes widened as she felt herself plunging helpless
toward some unknown fate. He wouldn't dare strike
her! Besides, he was too close at the moment, even if
that were his plan.

"I . . ." Rose jerked her head to the side as her lips
moved inadvertently against the still ones poised above
her. "No," she managed weakly.

"Because you aren't a man, I'll treat you with the
lesser of the fates such a fellow would have in store."
He leaned over so that his words rushed warm in her
ear. "I'll take back my clothes."

The bottle with which he'd assaulted her dropped to

the floor at the same time her heart struck her throat. "You wouldn't dare!" she choked out, her bravado washing away with the blood she felt draining from her face. "Because you're a gentleman," she reminded him, recalling Nate's subtle threat upon Dillon's earlier anger.

His weight held her pinned to the berth. If she were to escape his vengeance, it would have to be by wit alone. Yet, when he sought to work her shirt from her trousers, the touch of his fingers rendered thinking difficult, particularly now that they'd found the warm flesh of her waist. No man had ever touched her in such a threatening, yet strangely intriguing way.

"I needn't be a gentleman . . ." He splayed his hand out against the small of her back, as if he'd momentarily forgotten his dastardly intent, as well as his train of thought, and was mesmerized by the curve of her body. ". . . if you'd be treated as a man."

In drawing away from the unnerving exploration, Rose felt an uncommon swelling in the fore of his trousers, one she could not mimic. It steeled even as she pressed against it, making its bold presence inescapable to any but a dead woman. A decadent heat radiated from the double onslaught, unraveling her senses like furled canvas loosed in a gale.

Her childhood fancy about him never encompassed this wild vulnerability she was experiencing. Seizing his head between her hands, she pushed him far enough away to speak without sparking yet another sensual assault. She couldn't bear it if their lips should touch, if her sense of taste should be engaged as well in this battle of wills.

"Good God, Dillon, you'd have to be affected to do this to another man!"

For a moment, Rose thought she'd found her way out. Dillon pushed away from her, as though scalded by her suggestion. Instead of abandoning her completely, however, he merely shifted his weight so that he straddled her waist, still holding her fast to the narrow berth. With the moon catching the taut outline of his square jaw, Rose could see it bulging and twitching, a small sign of what she knew to be a fearsome retribution held barely in check at her absurd suggestion.

With no way to retreat, Rose reached boldly for the front of his trousers and seized him with a bravado she was far from feeling. "What's this, a belaying pin to flay me with?"

"By God, touch me like that again, madame, and I'll show you soon enough!"

She drew her hand away as though scalded by his threat. In a single fluid movement, Dillon sprang off the berth to land like an agile cat at its side.

"Now hand over my clothes."

"You . . . you'll turn your back?"

"One fair assessment deserves another, madame . . . and give me no more about acting the gentleman," Dillon added in a surly manner. "I'm not in a lady's company and am under no obligation to do so."

She'd avoided physical harm, but he'd not be moved again, not this time, damn him. Rose reached angrily for the hem of the shirt he'd tugged out earlier and yanked it over her head, daring color to rise to her face.

"There, you damned herring choker!"

She slung it at his face. Her bare breasts quivered ripe with her fury as she slid off the bunk and unbuttoned the trousers. They hung on her feet as she tried to stomp her way out of them and, when they finally came free, she kicked them at Dillon as well.

"I hope you're satisfied!"

Damnation, where did that tremor in her voice come from? Maintaining the glassy glare she directed at her silent and still companion, she reached for the blanket on the mussed berth and tugged it about her like a queen donning a royal stole. She'd be damned before she'd let him know she burned to the bone with humiliation.

"But hear me now, Dillon Mackay! Someday, I vow, I'll have the upper hand and see you pay dearly!"

A line had been drawn and a gauntlet thrown, yet for the life of him, Dillon was not certain which of them had done the drawing or the throwing. He was satisfied with one thing and one thing only. Rose Beaujeu had no idea she'd already made her vow good.

The night passed as hellishly as he'd anticipated. Like a starved man with a feast dangled before him, Dillon knew a hunger the nature of which he'd never known before. He'd lost count of the times he'd awakened from removing with his lips and tongue the sweet wine from her nubile breasts, turning her fire to passion and making love to the enigmatic creature until she begged for mercy. His aching desire knew no reprieve. Instead, it coiled inside him, poisoning his mood as Dillon strode the quarterdeck at dawn, eager to put his mind to something constructive.

Thankfully, the celebrated truce worked out better for the two crews than it had between him and Rose. With the low tide, the ship listed heavily to the starboard, exposing the streaks of lumber that rode under the waterline on the port. The smell of the heated tar with which they encased the hemp to make the oakum caulk filled the air along with that of the bread baking in the galley.

As the morning sun ascended, Dillon's breakfast of biscuits and gravy, served topside on his order, was interrupted when the *Thorne*'s carpenter climbed over the rail. The rudder was split beyond the hinges. That was the bad news. The good was that there was timber which

could be cut and put to use by the next tide, not a
moment too soon, to Dillon's way of thinking. He wondered which was worse, being grounded and helpless
to deal with the possibility of an enemy attack, or having
to deal a moment longer than necessary with Rose
Beaujeu, who was looking positively radiant this morning.

The morning breeze playfully teased her neatly up-
swept hair and ribbons as she stared from the main
deck at the crew loading on the longboat to go ashore.
What a perfect silhouette she'd make with her turned-
up nose and dimpled chin! The Orientals believed such
an indentation in a woman's chin signified she was
headstrong and, therefore, hard to manage. Dillon continued to stare at her profile. But if a man could handle
her, what a prize he'd have.

"Could I go ashore, too?"

"What?" he asked, startled from his speculation.

"Could I go ashore, too?" she repeated, approaching
him with all the innocence of an angel.

It was hard to believe this was the spitfire who'd
grabbed him in such a startling manner that he'd nearly
lost control, something Dillon had never done in his
life.

"Please, Dillon."

Please, Dillon. That pout had always worked with him,
but it had never crossed his mind to answer its call by
kissing it away until now. Dillon blinked away the idea
and concentrated on the men readying to shove away
from the ship. He needed no distraction from the serious business at hand. There were a few from the captive crew among them with bandages over superficial
wounds, but his own men were armed and would take
no chances in switching positions of authority. Besides,
the *Border Rose*'s men had proven themselves worthy of

a degree of trust, even if their mistress was another matter.

"I think not, madame. You could very well stir a mutiny against me, ravishing as you look."

Ah, now that was more like it. Displeasure surfaced to narrow her limpid gaze and trim the pout he'd found so beguiling. "But you have the freedom of the berth, main, and quarterdecks."

Dillon watched the battle of emotions blazing between thick dark lashes that reminded him of Spanish fringe, wondering whether it was a storm or merely threatening weather stirring in the cerulean sea.

"Anywhere on those decks?" the girl asked at last.

Threatening, he decided, taking measure of her suddenly sharp calculation. He took a cautious mental inventory of the territory, but could think of nothing she could use to do him harm. The weapons were locked away, save those manned by his own men.

He made a sweeping gesture with his arm. "Anywhere, madame. Now if you'll excuse me, I have work to see to."

So did she, Rose thought, with a smug tilt of her lips. Or at least there was some groundwork to be laid, if a chance to snatch Dillon's ship right out from under his own nose should occur. With all the men turned out to repair and refit the ship, her task should be easier.

"I suppose I'll go below and see to my other clothes," she said with a sigh of resignation. "Would you have me wash yours?"

Dillon cocked a suspicious brow. "Thank you, no. My steward has already seen to it."

The shirt he wore boasted more than its share of patches and repair. Rose couldn't help but wonder if they were from the fights at sea, at which he and his men seemed so adept. Perhaps scars lay strategically beneath each one. Although she'd had the opportunity, she hadn't allowed herself to dwell overlong on Dillon's magnificent torso, even when she and the doctor had stripped him to get him into a dry bed during the storm. In fact, she'd held a sheet over him for modesty's sake, while the physician did the actual undressing. Even then, the speculation that invaded her mind based on what glimpses she had had of the manly form managed to disconcert her no end. Then there was last night . . .

Rose dead-ended the memory before she lost the ability to think at all. She'd made an utter fool of herself, both in word and deed! He was just so . . .

An unladylike oath hissed through her set teeth as she took to the rungs of the hatchway. The only thing she wanted from Dillon Mackay was her ship, or at least his, and a healthy dose of revenge.

Instead of going to her cabin to fetch her clothes, she meandered about the officers' ward and paused to peep inside the door from which the master-at-arms had emerged earlier that morning. She'd seen the man climb into the boat to go ashore with the crew. Although he'd worn a pea coat, she hadn't noticed the jingle of the keys that usually accompanied his presence.

That being the case, they *had* to be in his room. With the keys to the armory in her possession, she could take enough weapons and ammunition to give her men a better edge when the time came to take the *Thorne*. All she had to do was stash them and tell her crew where they were, which, with the freedom Dillon so gallantly had given them, would be easy play.

Except the keys were not there. Rose was frantic as she hurriedly went through the four sea chests of the men who shared the compartment, but the large key ring worn at the waist of the master-at-arms was not to be found. As she sorted through the last of the chests, booted footsteps echoed on the deck above her. In a moment of panic, she shoved the chest back into its tight storage area and jumped to her feet, only to discover her skirt had been wedged by it. With a sharp tug, she freed it, tearing the hem, and rushed out of the cabin just as Dillon's feet appeared in the above hatchway.

Dashing to a bench reserved for his men, Rose sat down and tried to restore her breathing to normal as the captain of the *Thorne* reached the lower deck with a nimble leap, skipping the bottom two rungs. As he landed, a jingle of metal drew Rose's attention to his waist, where hung the key ring she'd sought. Mentally cursing him, she smiled at Dillon as he walked past her toward his cabin.

"Thought you were going to freshen your clothes, not that you need wear any in my presence. My word, how you've . . ." He hesitated long enough for a grin to rake his lips. "Matured, Miss Beaujeu."

"What did you do, swallow the whole block of sugar this morning?" Rose shot back hotly. *"Ravishing as you look,"* she mimicked. "Flattery of that sort will not make me like you, Dillon. Only the return of my ship will gain you the slightest favor."

He filled the open doorway of the cabin where he'd paused to take in her appearance from head to toe. If Rose hadn't known better, she'd have sworn her clothes still hung on the line inside, the way his dark gaze took on a strange glow. A response to it registered somewhere in her abdomen, unbidden and unnerving. Once again, she felt that curious sense of intrigue, seasoned with danger.

"You've torn your dress."

The man saw too much. "I stepped on the hem coming down the steps. I'll fix it later. Not being accustomed to sharing quarters with anyone, especially a man, I just wanted some quiet time to myself."

"I can't believe you've mastered the needle, but I could hardly tell where you'd repaired my shirt."

She'd hated sewing as a child, dodging her mother at every opportunity to avoid the boring lessons. She still found it tedious, but it was something a woman had to do.

"Who repaired that one, your sailmaker?"

"Aye, I had no lovely wench to do it for me."

"Oh, please, Dillon!" Rose averred, jumping to her feet. "That silver tongue of yours may slay other feminine hearts, but not this one. I find it annoying!"

"So you've said, but I've never seen a rosier glow on the horizon than that radiating from your face." He moved from the cabin entrance back into the ward room. "My experience with women tells me your lips are lying, Rosie."

Rose stepped back warily as Dillon purposefully closed the distance between them.

"Go away, Dillon, before I get sick!"

"Lips like those always protest too much, Rosie, when, in fact, they are begging to be kissed."

"Oh, puh-leez!" she enunciated, dodging to the side as he attempted to capture her between him and the wall.

Anticipating her hasty retreat, Dillon caught her by the waist and used her own momentum to swing her around so that her back rested against the rise of the hatchway bulkhead. "But they're afraid, aren't they, Rosie."

"No!"

"Liar!"

"I've kissed men before and it's disgusting!" Of course, they were peach-faced boys, mostly her age and spoiled with a life of ease, not men tempered by battle and the elements. Her family had kept her away from such experienced suitors.

"Maybe you've had the wrong partner," Dillon suggested. He lifted her chin with the crook of his finger, his attention totally absorbed with her lips, which had dried so that they started to quiver, even as she moistened them to stop it.

"They're afraid, Rosie, and so are you. You're trembling like a leaf."

"I always do that before I lose my breakfast!" Her head pressed against the steps. "Damn it, Dillon, I'm hot all over! I'm warning you! I . . ."

Dillon's lips were cool to hers at first contact, but as he gently coaxed her own, a spark of heat ignited and gradually seeped through Rose's jaw until her clenched defense melted away, slackening enough that his tongue was able to slip scandalously between her teeth. Rendered ineffective by its sweet assault, her hands gripped his taut biceps. She held her breath, as if waiting to discover the full extent of the havoc it was beginning to wreak with her senses.

Her knees felt as though they'd been robbed of substance, so that only Dillon's body, pressing her own to the partial bulkhead, kept her from collapsing in a breathless heap at his feet.

She had to breathe or die of this heady suffocation right here in Dillon Mackay's arms. The idea was not so repulsive, but instinct forced her to try to escape, at least long enough to get some air. Although his lips finally left hers, their imprint remained, unable to be cooled as she gasped with her cheek pressed against his. The scent of his shaving soap filled her nostrils, intoxicating as the shivers sent by the eager mouth that had found an ear to toy with.

Rose shuddered against him, her fingers still biting into his upper arms as though holding on to the last shreds of her sanity. She felt the rumble of his voice generated from his chest with her breasts, which had reached an acute degree of sensitivity, enough to pummel her brain with cravings for more than this stirring crush.

"I think I've made my point, eh, Rosie?"

Rose's eyes flew open to see Dillon's mocking expression hovering over hers. As he stepped away from her, she had to grab at the steps for support.

"I . . . if I don't get air, I'll be making mine, too, you slobbering herring choker!"

She rallied and stiffened, although where she found the strength, she had no idea. She wiped her mouth with the back of her hand in distaste, knowing full well she'd never be able to erase the feel of Dillon's heady plunder. He was dangerous, so dangerous she was torn as to where to run—topside or straight back into his arms.

"Confound it, Dillon, you damned near suffocated me!" she accused, seizing on the first option. Her feet were unsteady and she missed the first step. As Dillon reached for her, however, she found her footing and sprang up the companionway as though his mere touch was fire. "I don't think I've ever felt so sick!"

Sick with humiliation for not fighting him, and worse, she bemoaned silently, sick with a longing for more. The only mutiny on the *Thorne* this day had been that of her own traitorous body. Good God, she *was* sick!

Seven

The farthest place Rose could go from Dillon Mackay without jumping over the side was the top mast. She'd hoisted her back skirt through her legs, tucked it into her waistband in Turkish fashion, and made short work of the ropes, her kid slippers abandoned at the foot of the towering pine pole. That high up, the salt breeze fortified her as it whipped her hair, now undone by Dillon's unprovoked insanity, about her face. The gentle rocking of the ship at high tide served to soothe her rattled nerves. After her recent encounters with Dillon Mackay, it was no wonder that she was exhausted of emotion and energy.

The truth was, she hadn't slept well the night before, either. Every time she heard a movement in Dillon's cabin, she jerked into wakefulness, wondering if he'd come back into her room. Despicably enough, there was an element of her being that almost wanted that. Like her reaction this morning, there was something that drew her beyond reason to see just what he'd do next.

Annoyed and perplexed, she propped her elbows on the rail and her chin on her hands as she scanned the sandy beachhead where the longboat had been dragged ashore. The air was warmer this close to land and scented with the evergreen of spruce and pine. Most likely, the island was overrun with fresh game, but she doubted Dillon would allow time for a hunt to offer a change in their mostly salted diet.

Rose's thoughts were silenced by a movement in the periphery of her vision. It was on the other side of the natural breakwater of rocks that made the cove a safe place to moor. She blinked twice before her heart tripped with excitement. Two boats of fifty feet or so, both loaded with men and guns, were slipping around the jut of moss-covered blue-gray rock!

She glanced nervously down at the quarterdeck, where Dillon had reappeared with his sextant, and then to the foremast, where the watch she'd displaced was engrossed in the loading of fresh water barrels on the longboat. Neither of the men were aware of the approaching vessels! Rose reached for the leather sling containing the telescope ordinarily used by the lookout at that post.

Shaving mills! she thought excitedly. The long hair and beards the occupants of the large open rowboat couldn't be denied. They were one of the bands of raiders that privateered out of northern Maine and attacked small seaside harbors for plunder and profit, called *shavers,* she supposed, because they didn't bother to shave or groom their wild hair.

A smile spread upon Rose's lips, the first since their searing encounter with Dillon. This wasn't exactly the help she'd prayed for, but they *were* allies. Mayhap, she could even entice some of them to take the *Thorne* and sail after the *Border Rose.* Surely they'd jump at the chance to improve their lot with a seaworthy ship capable of preying upon the ocean sea lanes, rather than limited coastal ones.

By the time the first of the vessels rounded the point of extended rock and sent a roaring shot of warning across the bow of the *Thorne,* two more had appeared, indicating to Rose that their camp had to be close by. Such men usually kept supplies ashore, taking only what they needed for a single raid. Instead of sail, they manned sweeps or oars, giving them excellent maneuverability.

When the air burst with their cannon fire, all but the carpenters and hunters had returned to the ship with the barrels of fresh water and, along with the watch, were engaged in lowering them into the hold. Although she anticipated the shot, Rose started. She saw Dillon fairly leap in two bounds to the port rail, while others were frozen in shock where they stood.

"Shavers to the port! All men to stations! Strike a light, lads!"

His command echoed across the deck while the crew below her scurried to follow it. A shot from the second boat, which had navigated around the rock breakwater, streaked past the mainmast so close, Rose felt the breath of its deadly scream. She hastily started to climb down the ropes and met the ship's marines on their way up, their rifles strapped to their backs.

"In the name o' ballyhoo and blazes, woman, get ye below!" one called out.

Rose tried to spot Nate as she found solid footing on the deck. A number of men were streaming topside now, armed with cutlasses and pistols. Much as she hated to, she had to admire the training of Dillon's crew. They'd been set into motion by his command like a well-oiled machine.

But it was *her* crew that interested her at the moment. Since she'd seen none of them above deck, they had to be below. Rose rushed toward the forward hatch and went below deck.

The gun ports were already open and crews worked furiously to the gravelly bark of the gunners. Rose felt certain some of the men were her own, but was at a loss to identify them in the scramble. But Nate would know each and every one, if she could find him.

"Up with you, lads, and stand ready to assist!"

Rose turned to see her cousin cheering the men from the *Border Rose* up from the lower deck. None were armed, but none were supervised either, except by their own captain. It was too wonderful to be true. They could easily get weapons in all the turmoil.

"Nate!"

Rose's shout was lost in the thunder of the first port gun. The blast nearly burst her eardrums in the enclosed space. Before she could recover, the entire ship rocked with the impact of the shaver's shot. The hail of deadly metal exacted a toll of screams and splintering wood. Clinging to one of the support posts, Rose watched in horror as a member of the gun crew nearest her was dragged, bleeding and moaning, away from the track. In a second, one of the *Border Rose*'s men took his place, while Nate and another carried the man toward the hatch to the lower deck, where Rose was certain the *Thorne*'s physician was hurriedly laying out his equipment.

As they neared the steps, however, Nate spotted her and turned the wounded man over to another of his crew. "Hell's bells, Rose! Get to your quarters and stay there!"

"But Nate . . ."

In no humor to hear her out, Nathan Malone seized her elbow and shoved her to the lower deck behind his men.

"Nate, they're *shavers!* Friends!"

"So they appear," he answered, urging her relentlessly further down into the hold.

Instead of ushering her into the brig as Rose thought certain he was about to do, he pushed onward along the grated walk surrounding the storage area toward the stern of the ship. Rose realized he'd chosen the safer passage through the bottom of the vessel to access the stern quarters to which he was taking her.

"They're friends!" she reiterated in a loud whisper, thinking her cousin had gone daft.

"That's a matter of opinion, Rosie. I've heard tell of the same sort out of Scotia. But even if they are Maine boys, they and their shot don't know friend from foe on this ship and she's boasting Halifax on the stern counter. Now up you go!"

Rose climbed the ladder, considering Nate's words. It was true many in the New England states considered the raids of the shavers unsavory and their methods dishonorable, but no one refused the goods they took from the enemy shores and sold at home. Rumors of their taking belongings of innocent women and children, of pointless murder, were just that, rumors.

As she and Nate emerged in the officers' ward, she replied, "Then let's take the *Thorne* from within and raise the Stars and Stripes before they blow us to kingdom come."

By now, she'd prepared herself for the domino blasts from the guns at the waist of the ship and barely lost her step when she turned so that she might measure Nate's silence. Instead of contemplation, however, she saw only anger!

"We gave our word, Rosie! The captain's honored his and, by God, we'll honor ours."

"But this is war and they *forced* you to give your word. You had no choice!"

"That's why women have no place on a ship or in war!" Dillon Mackay swore behind her.

Where a closed door had been only a moment before, the unsavory pirate captain who'd taken the *Border Rose* stood, stripped of his shirt. In its place were strung leather straps holding twin pistols, ammunition pouches, and powder. At his lean waist hung the deadly saber he'd worn the first time she'd seen him.

"Your gender has disrupted man's peace since Eden!" he declared, seizing her arm and forcing her into the room. "Now get in there, bolt the door, and keep your head low, or so help me I'll turn you over to the shavers, though God help them!"

"Listen to him, Rosie, or by heaven, I'll do the same!"

Speechless at his vehement betrayal, Rose stared at Nate, until Dillon pulled the door to between them.

"The bolt, madame!"

With little alternative save fight the two of them, she obeyed. They had no idea what it felt like to be at the mercy of a man's world. They could live comfortably within the realm of their rules, because they were not subordinated by them. Even now, they could fight as they so chose, but not she. She was expected to cower alone while her fate rested in the hands of others.

Well, she wouldn't . . . cower at least. She might be frightened, she conceded, but she wouldn't cower. If only there were some way of letting the shavers know Americans were aboard, there might be hope yet. Only a miracle would save the *Thorne* from the attackers.

As if the answer to her particular quandary lay somewhere in the room, Rose scanned it until her gaze came to rest on the trunk holding the assortment of flags the *Thorne* used for its subterfuge. Spirit soaring as her idea took root, she hurried to it and threw it open. By heaven, she'd found a way after all!

The mooring lines had been cut as the shavers circled their prey, swift and deadly with the sweeps manned in each boat. They had it all, guns, men, and, above all, speed, Rose thought as she leaned out the stern counter casement and waved the American flag boldly. Even if Dillon could catch the wind, his rudder was split. Like vultures, all the shavers had to wait for was the *Thorne* to die in the water.

There were four boats in all. That would make two hundred or so men to the estimated fifty fighting bravely to escape. The shavers would surely try to board soon, for Rose had noticed the increasing lags in the *Thorne*'s attempt to return fire, indicating some of its guns had been blown up by the enemy fire. There was also fire on the ship, for she could smell it.

Even as she considered an outright charge, one of the ships broke away from the circle and started in with unerring speed. With Nate's grim observation that the shavers did not know friend from foe in mind, she waved the Stars and Stripes from the window all the harder. Surely it would at least give the attackers pause.

She watched the oncoming boat until she could no longer see it, but heard the shout of its men and the thud of grappling hooks assailing the *Thorne*'s rail. A crack of pistol fire from the upper deck soon enveloped the ship in a gray-black fog, driving Rose back inside. Splashes, thunder, shouts, and shudders blended with the clash of steel, telling her the final struggle had ensued. Rose took a deep breath and in desperation, leaned out the window again with her country's flag.

"Here now, missy, toss that line to a fellow countryman!"

Rose stretched out further over the slanted transom to see a man swimming in the water, a cutlass strapped to his back. He must have been knocked overboard during the fray. Eagerly, she let the flag, line and all over.

"Several of our crew is American, taken from the *Border Rose* of Castine! You've got to stop your men before they kill everyone. Ours are being forced to fight!"

"Tie it fast to something, *ma chérie*, and be quick!"

"Tie the wounded to something that will float and get them over the side!"

The urgency of Dillon's hoarse command from above spurred Rose even faster than her prospective rescuer's demand. Some of her crew were wounded and could not fight the current to make it to shore. She deftly knotted the rope about one of the support beams in the cabin.

"All right!"

The rope tightened at her clearing cry and within moments the wet long-haired privateer climbed through the stern window, his filthy, tattered clothes clinging to a lanky frame. Flashing a snaggle-toothed grin at her, he withdrew his cutlass from its sheath.

"But isn't this a *bonne* surprise! I suppose His Lordship will wish us to save you for his pleasure."

Lordship? The reference, delivered with a decidedly French accent, stunned Rose, but the words in its wake nearly took her knees out from under her. There were no lordships in Maine.

"You're an Acadian herring choker?" Her voice had lost its life. It had drained away with the blood in her face. "But you're attacking your own ship," she said, backing away as the man approached her, a lecherous flame now gleaming in his beady eyes.

"If ye're a good girl, François will be good to you."

Good God, would he take her right here at the point of his cutlass? Rose pressed against the closed door separating her quarters from Dillon's, unable to open it and retreat. She had to think, to thaw her frozen mind. There was no time for hysterics.

"Get me off this ship, sir, and you'll be astonished at how good I can be."

His smile widened to reveal more gaping holes between the blackened and yellowed remnants of his teeth. Her fingers slipping about the shaving mirror behind her, Rose felt her lips twitch in return. The silent reply must have been convincing, for the man lowered his cutlass to his side and stepped toward her.

"So you are kept by the famous Capitaine Mackay, eh? Then you would know how to please a stallion, *non?*" He straightened proudly to his full height, which was no more than enough to look Rose straight in the eye.

Dillon a stallion? Rose let the thought fly and waited until the man reached for her cheek before bringing the mirror off its anchor and slamming it into his face. The shatter of glass combined with a sharp beating on the door.

"Miss Beaujeu, let me in!"

Rose brought her knee up sharply between the swearing privateer's legs and then dodged the blind lash of his cutlass to race for the door.

"Help!" she managed as the bolt slammed back to permit the welcome intruder in. "He's got a cutlass!"

She only saw her rescuer's nicked and bleeding back as he stepped squarely into the room and unloaded his pistol at the staggering pirate, for Rose knew now, that was exactly what Dillon and their crews were against. French, Canadian, or English, they were pirates or wreckers, either of which was equally bad. The unkempt man sprawled back against the bulkhead, a startled look frozen on his bloodied face.

First Officer Hanson shook her from her horrified stance. "Come, milady! We're abandoning ship! She's going down!"

"What? Where's Dillon?"

"He's gone below to set off the powder magazine! I'm to take you over the side."

The powder magazine, she processed mentally. No, it wouldn't do to hand over more ammunition to cutthroats without honor. She'd sooner blow up the *Border Rose* than give her up, except she'd not had the chance.

"And Nate, what . . . Ohh!" Rose screamed at the sight of yet another pirate coming in through the passage she'd so conveniently provided for them.

His only weapon discharged, Hanson drew his sword to take on the cutlass-swinging fiend that came shrieking like a banshee at him. While Hanson possessed the grace of a formally tutored man of the blade, his opponent danced about like an organ grinder's pet, almost silly in appearance, yet deadly in effect. It was as though Hanson's well-polished blade could not make its mark. Unfortunately that was not the case for his murderous contender, a bluenose of English persuasion judging by his taunting oaths.

Realizing Dillon's young second officer was no match for the wretch, Rose seized up the cutlass from the slackened grip of the dead man and warily approached the other two men, whose blades were now locked to the hilt. Hanson's trembling muscles bulged with effort, as he held off his and stronger foe. With painful slowness, the pirate maneuvered the razor-sharp edge of his weapon closer and closer to the throbbing pulse in the lieutenant's throat.

If she were to do anything, she had to do it soon. The enemy's back was to her, an easy target. Drive a blade in and up to miss the bone and strike a vital organ, she'd heard her father once say. It sounded so easy, but why was bile rising in the back of her throat at the prospect? Why was she flailing like a spineless banner in the wind?

"Ye're bleedin', mate!"

The bloodthirsty innuendo carried the weight of threat more than her collection, forcing her to thrust the cutlass forward and up with all the strength she had left. Instead of dying outright, however, the pirate roared in astonishment and whirled with the blade protruding from his back with the most ominous and horrid expression she'd ever seen. She looked outraged death in the face, but it would not surrender.

Try as she would, Rose could not move. She could only see those awful bloodshot eyes bulging at her. She could only hear the jolting drag of feet sounding nearer and nearer. She could only feel the painful bite of filthy fingernails digging into her arms, deeper and deeper as the man jerked to his full height before her. He appeared frozen in time and then, without warning, fell away with a thud that shook the floor beneath her.

"Many thanks, milady. But we must go."

As her vision cleared, it was First Officer Hanson's face that replaced the hideous one. Rose was vaguely aware of being towed to the open window by his gentle, but firm hand.

"It's clear," the young man declared in relief, going on to lift her without ceremony to the sill. "Sorry, milady, but it's over you go. Just grab onto the line until I join you."

"I—I can swim," Rose informed him, although she wondered where she'd find the resources to do so. They were going to die anyway. It was just a matter of how they'd go, with merciful drowning or torturous murder.

She preferred drowning, but instinct refused to let her give in, even when she thought her arms were going numb from treading water in the cover of a floating piece of wreckage Hanson had secured for them. But for it, her skirts would have dragged her under long ago.

"Don't look back, milady! Just think about making it to that stretch of wood on the beach." Hanson managed a teeth-clattering laugh. "That is, if we don't freeze first."

The water was cold, as the Atlantic was prone to be in the spring. Fortunately, land was not much farther.

Then they'd have to thaw their stiff legs sufficiently to reach the woods. Then . . .

Thinking requiring too much effort, Rose did exactly as she was told. It was easier all the way around.

Although she stumbled over her skirts, she managed to keep up with her rescuer. That they'd gotten that far and arrived on the sandy, rock-stubbled shore, was encouragement enough to persevere, when it was more inviting to collapse on the edge of the water and let fate take its course. Her brief inspiration, however, disintegrated with the shock of the explosion on the *Thorne* in the distance. The very ground upon which she stood shook and the towering trees of their cover rustled with the shock wave above them.

"Dillon!"

Rose's strangled cry lasted longer than it took for the ship to literally disappear in a cloud of billowing smoke and flame. She watched the debris striking the water with a knifelike certainty that no one aboard could possibly have survived. No one, not even Dillon Mackay.

Eight

The moon streaked the littered waters with shimmering fingers, so that that debris which had not yet sunk or washed up on the beach stood out. Rose could see all clearly from her vantage on the rocky leeward point of the island. There was a hollow in the rock, high enough to escape the outgoing tide which frothed over shoals that had kept the shavers from searching that part of the shoreline.

Having been denied their prey and lost the two boats which had been lashed to it in the process, they'd begun rowing about in a frenzy, shooting anything that moved on the water. It hadn't mattered that many of the struggling seamen were wounded and tied to debris to keep afloat. Neither did it matter that they were bluenose or Yankee. The cast of the green water had turned red before they'd beached their crafts and gone ashore after the victims who'd made it that far.

The isolated shots and shouts continued throughout the entire afternoon, until Rose no longer flinched at the sounds. Only one terrible explosion in the distance that shook the very rock beneath her brought her to her feet with a short strangled shriek, but she was too close to the trees to see where it had taken place. Once her heart dropped from her throat to resume its normal place in her chest, she settled in her cover, and scanned the floating rubble from the *Thorne* on the off chance that someone had escaped the savage raid. That fragile hope was all that kept her from losing her last shred of self-control and bawling like a baby in Mr. Hanson's arms.

He'd told her he was proud of her when they'd reached the isolated and rocky area from which there was no escape, at least not by water. Inhospitable to man and vessel, it was too rock infested and shallow. That was what Dillon counted on the shavers believing when he'd given the young man orders to take Rose there at all costs.

The last Hanson had seen of Dillon, he'd been holding off the shavers at the rail with his marines, while the wounded were put over in the protection of the other side of the ship. "I'll be along after the men are off and the magazine charge set." That was Dillon's promise. He was fighting like a fiend from hell determined to take as many of the shavers back there as possible, so the first officer relayed to Rose with nothing short of worship in his gaze for his captain, once they were out of danger.

Although he didn't say so, Rose was certain Mr. Hanson did not think Dillon had made it to shore to rendezvous with them as he'd planned. So was she, even though she kept watching the floating wreckage, as if it might support the weak and most likely wounded captain of the *Thorne*.

How she wished she were in Dillon's warm embrace! Not even the lieutenant was there to share his warmth with her now, for once the pirates had given up their bloody hunt at sunset and shoved off with their remaining two boats, he'd left her to see if he might find any other survivors of the massacre hiding out in the thick inland forest.

"With luck, our hunters and carpenters may have

been able to find cover and they have guns," Mr. Hanson had said hopefully.

None to match the number sported by the shavers, Rose wanted to reply. Instead, she kept the discouraging thought to herself. She was certain Mr. Hanson, too, had heard the murderers vowing to come back to hunt down survivors in the morning and laughing that there was no escape for anyone from the small island. She supposed he was simply trying to cheer her.

The dear didn't realize it was an impossible task any more than he knew that she was at least partially responsible for all this. If she'd warned Dillon of the approaching ships, the *Thorne's* men would have had more time to prepare.

Nate and Dillon had put their men's lives ahead of their ship. They'd overlooked their differences for the mutual welfare of their men. On the other hand, *she* hadn't put aside anything, especially her personal vendetta against Dillon. It wasn't politics or war that had brought her so low. Patriotism had nothing to do with it. It was because he'd taken her ship. He'd done his captain's duty and remained loyal to his men, rather than win her personal favor by returning it.

Rose buried her face in the arms she folded on drawn knee and sobbed. Dillon was right. A ship in war was no place for a woman. Everything she'd done had wrought catastrophe. She had no rightful place in this world. She pulled her skirts about her, miserable in spirit as well as body, for, although they were no longer dripping wet, they were still damp and held the chill of the night air.

She was cold, cold as the dead men floating facedown in the water or washed up on the beach along with bits of wreckage. Rose almost envied them. They could feel nothing, not the chill, nor the guilt which would never give her a moment's peace again.

"Damn you, Dillon Mackay!" she cried out softly. "How could you blow yourself up and leave me to such an end!"

"Your grandmother!" an incredulous voice swore from the darkness. "Don't tell me you're blaming me for this as well!"

The wry admonition from out of nowhere abruptly choked off Rose's tears. She looked up from the cradle of her folded arms to see Dillon Mackay standing at the edge of her rocky hideaway.

Her limbs were stiff from her crouch in the cover of the rocky precipice, but she forced them to take her into the open arms awaiting her. As she wrapped her own about Dillon's waist and felt his body heat reaching out to vanquish the chill causing her to tremble as she pressed against him, she knew a burst of joy like none before. He was as real as she, and from the way he hugged her back and showered the top of her head with kisses, was just as happy to see her.

Dozens of questions flitted through her mind as to how he'd escaped the fiery ship and the pirates' wrath, but at that point she didn't care about the particulars. All that mattered was that Dillon was here, holding her as though he'd never let her go.

"I was afraid you'd disobeyed Mr. Hanson's orders and set out to find the others on your own. For once, it appears, you listened."

"I—I couldn't. I thought you were dead . . ." Rose stopped before the *because of me* on her lips tumbled out. "Oh, Dillon, I've never known such torment! It was worse than our battle and the burial of our dead. It . . ." She drew in a shaky breath while attempting to sort her scattered thoughts and emotions, until the un-forgettable face of the pirate she'd run through appeared and would not go away. "I killed a man, Dillon!"

Her voice was fraught with the desperation and fear

of that horrid moment. She knew it was a matter of survival, kill or be killed, but she'd never forget the feel of the blade forcing its way through living flesh.

There was no *I told you so* in Dillon's answer. If anything, there was a degree of praise. "Just in the nick of time, so Mr. Hanson reported." He pulled away long enough to wrap a dry woolen blanket about her, and Rose was too confounded by circumstances to ask how he came by it.

The officer could not have told Dillon about her letting the murderers in through the stern counter window, or she'd never have received such an enthusiastic greeting.

"Where's Mr. Hanson?" she asked. It was better to steer away from that subject.

"He and what remains of our men are setting up an encampment about two miles from here."

What remains. The words gave Rose's stomach a wretched twist.

"Nate?" Somehow she couldn't form an entire question, for there was little doubt in her mind that Nate had remained with the guns until the last.

"He's there in charge. I wanted to come for you myself," Dillon admitted, embracing her once again with fervor. "You don't know how badly I wanted to take you ashore myself, to see that you were safe."

"I guess the captain doesn't always get what he wants," Rose reflected softly. Like giving her back her ship. She was grateful for the protection of Dillon's shoulder, not only from the cold, but from revealing the guilt flushing her face. He was the better man, the better captain. Heaven knew she didn't deserve any of this. "How did you get away from the ship in time?"

"The last of us shut ourselves up in the armory. I set the powder charge while the men widened a hole in the side of the ship at the waterline. We left together."

"And how did you get to shore? Those animals were shooting anything that moved!"

Dillon and the few marines that were left had escaped under the cover of empty powder kegs, swimming around the breakwater to escape the vengeful fire of the remaining pirates. Equally amazing was that the crew which had been stranded ashore, helpless to assist them, had found the shavers' encampment, taken all the supplies they could carry, and blown up that which they could not. The tremendous explosion which had startled Rose earlier now had an explanation.

"So, compliments of our unsolicited hosts, we've a boat of sorts, which our men are repairing at the moment. It isn't much, but it's enough to get us to an inhabited island. According to the calculation I'd made before we were attacked, we're just south of the Grand Manan. If we head due north, we're bound to hit it or one of the settled islands about it."

"Thank God! I'd given up all hope. I kept hearing shouts and gunshots. I even feared Mr. Hanson might have met with some awful fate."

Dillon herded Rose toward the inner curve of the rock shelter. "Perhaps we should sit down before we both collapse. I've hiked the long way around the island to get to you."

"Aren't we going to join the others?" Rose asked.

"Not for a few hours. As I made my way here, I came across some armed scouts from the shavers' camp. They're carrying lanterns and working over the island like stirred hornets about their nest." Dillon added on a wry note, "They hadn't expected to be robbed themselves."

"So we're going to take the bastards in the morning?"

This time Dillon actually grinned. Rose had never seen him more handsome, despite the soot and powder smudging his bronzed skin and the brown hair hanging undone from its customary queue.

"How much did your father pay to send you to that ladies' school?" he asked.

She smiled back impishly and snuggled against his shoulder again. "Too much, to my notion."

A short while ago, Rose flailed in the depths of cold despair. Now, although she had no right to be when the damp chill of the night was considered, she was warm and looking forward to escaping the island with the man she . . .

On the precipice of finishing her thought, Rose glanced sharply at Dillon. She hadn't believed in Grandpère Alain's theory of fate compelling a Beaujeu to fall in love with his or her enemy. Now she wasn't so certain that it was just a coincidence. Could that be why, no matter how annoyed with Dillon she was, she could not deny the primitive stirrings he evoked within her. Was it really dizzying arousal she'd passed off as sickness this morning when he'd kissed her so thoroughly.

"If you're hungry, I have some beef jerky, again compliments of our unsavory hosts, and some wine of questionable vintage in this canteen."

Rose shook her head. "I'm fine now that you're here." How ironic that this morning she'd tried her best to get as far from him as possible. Since she'd nearly lost him, she couldn't get close enough.

"I insist you drink some wine. It'll warm you from the inside, while the blankets take care of the outside."

Rose took a sip from the canteen he offered her. The man had no clue that he was doing both better than any blanket might. "Have you ever been in love, Dillon?"

His chest moved with a short chuckle. "That's one sticky wicket I've managed to avoid. The sea—"

"Is your mistress," Rose completed for him. "That's

what Papa always said, even after he'd married Mama. If I were allowed to have a mistress, I'd be the same way."

"You know . . ." Dillon offered her another sample of the semisweet nectar. "If you devoted a minuscule portion of the effort you put toward wanting to live a man's life in accepting the fact that you are a woman, and a remarkable one at that," he inserted, "you'd be astonished at the resulting satisfaction."

"How would you know? You've never been a woman."

Dillon leaned against the top of her head and nuzzled her hair lightly. "I've known many women contented and fulfilled with their lot as wives and mothers. Your mother, for one."

She could be content with a lot like her mother's, wife and partner with the captain of their own ship. Rose listened to the strong beat of Dillon's heart, her ear pressed to his chest as she lost herself to the idea. She traced a circle in the furred mat which rose and fell with quickening breath. But for the war, Dillon Mackay was the perfect man for her, so much like her father in so many ways. As though turned loose on their own, her fingers broke away from the pattern to follow the faint trail of hair which narrowed to a line bound for his waist.

"Are you certain you don't want something to eat?" Dillon removed her exploring hand and shoved the canteen into it, startling Rose with his annoyed tone.

How could he think about food when the most amazing thing was happening to them, Rose wondered. Unless he didn't feel it. She shook her head. "I'm not hungry . . . and I don't want to fight anymore, Dillon."

"That makes two of us."

"I'd rather you kiss me like you did this morning." She felt him stiffen next to her.

"I was under the impression that you were not impressed."

"That was before I thought I'd lost you." Rose pulled away and looked up at him. "The truth is, I was overwhelmingly impressed, sir. I'd have withstood more if I hadn't been so undone by what I was feeling." Embarrassed by her own candor, Rose glanced away. "I've been kissed before, Dillon, but never like that, so . . . so, if you wouldn't mind, I'd like to see if it still works."

"I kissed you to prove a point, Rosie, to show you that you are a woman and, as such, can enjoy being one."

"So you didn't enjoy it?"

"That's not what I said. My motivation was to show you wrong, not seduce you."

"So you *do* like kissing me."

"We're talking about motivation here."

"No, we're talking about kissing!" Rose shot back shortly. "Now did you like it or not?"

"Yes, damn it!"

"Then let's do it."

"Do what?"

Ignoring the wariness in Dillon's tone, Rose removed the canteen from Dillon's lap and perched in its place. He was rigid as she tucked the blanket in at the shoulders of her dress to keep it up and then threw her arms about his neck.

"This, you thick-witted herring choker!"

Rose planted her lips upon Dillon's, drawing his head closer with the fingers she ran through his hair. At first, it was like kissing the rock which sheltered them, cold and ungiving, but it wasn't long before his mouth softened and little by little began to answer her fumbling attempt. Then, once its appetite was whetted, it grew hungry for something more than her inexperienced one knew to give. Dillon began to tutor her lips and tongue with his own in such a manner as to demand her attention as none of her former academy teachers had done. The intimate enlightenment bathed her every sense with delight and a yearning to know more.

"Good God, woman, you are a single-minded creature!" Dillon managed in a throaty whisper upon tearing away from the enticing union of their lips. Then, as if unable to stand complete withdrawal, he sought the flesh of Rose's neck, his words rumbling against it. "Do you know what you're doing to me?"

"The same as you're doing to me, I hope."

There was only one way to know for certain. Rose slipped her hand between them where the front of Dillon's breeches swelled, substantial as the rest of him.

"Whoa, Rosebud!" Dillon swallowed hard. He pulled her to him tightly. "If we keep on like this, there'll be no stopping."

"But I don't want to stop."

What was the point? Neither Aunt Arissa nor Grandmother Tamson had been able to stop the inevitable where their lifemates were concerned. Rose worked her fingers about the outline of Dillon's manhood and felt him shudder in response. Wriggling out of the weakening restraint of his hold, she moved so that she sat astride his outstretched legs.

He'd carried her that way many a time when she was little, but now there was something phenomenal happening between them, even aside from his obvious arousal, that made her more aware of Dillon. It was a natural way to embrace him. As she did so, she met his gaze and knew that his reticence was superficial, for there burned a passion hotter than any anger might evoke.

Eyes widening with a guileless seductive glow, she asked, "Do you want to stop, Dillon . . . *really?*"

His silence was as loud as any answer he might have said.

"We've fought this long enough, don't you think?" she went on, running her hands up his chest. "I've been so angry with you, I could have physically choked you, but . . . but to get close enough to do so blew away the smoke and revealed the fire. And it's not angry fire, Dillon. It's a ravenous fire! It makes me want to be a woman, when my head tells me otherwise. Oh, Dillon!" Rose averred fervently, "I think my brains have dropped to my breeches, too!" She frowned, momentarily stymied. "If I had breeches, that is."

The simple observation fanned yet another outbreak of wildfire in Dillon's fevered brain. Like Rose's, it seemed to have dropped below his waist. Yet there still was remnant enough in his head to know that they walked a dangerous tightrope, which, if snapped, threatened to take them past the point of no return. Yet her guileless description of her feelings these last few days mirrored his own. Anger had only served as a smokescreen for something far more powerful.

"I didn't believe it until now," the girl went on, absorbed with the tautened circles of his pectorals. "But it was fate that brought us together again."

Dillon clenched his hands about the smallness of Rose's waist as though it were the safest place for them. Yet the motion only brought to mind how she'd felt beneath him the night before.

He didn't attempt to refute her story about the Beaujeus marrying their enemies. He didn't dare, for to so much as loosen his tongue threatened to unravel his last grasp of control. He wanted Rose more than any woman he'd ever met, but because he cared for her . . .

The work of her deft fingers upon the buttons of his trousers blasted away the last of his wavering reserve. "Rosie . . ."

"For heaven's sake, Dillon, I know what I'm talking about! Let's get this over with before I die of . . . of wanting it!"

Her candor might have proved amusing, were his mind not so bombarded with the burning impact of its suggestion, nay, *mandate*. His passion, undaunted by the chill of the night, burst free as Rose peeled away the final barrier of his drawers. "Ah, Rosie!" he gasped.

"Make me glad I'm a woman, Dillon!" Rose pleaded in a voice as velvet and stirring as her touch, for it had grown thick with her newfound passion. "You're the only man who can."

Dillon had no answer. Rose was right, although fate had nothing to do with it. Their course had been charted from the moment he'd laid eyes upon her by the acute awareness of each other as man and woman. He was as stunned by the adult Rose as she had been by him.

As for his being the only man who could teach her the mysteries of love, he bristled at the idea that it should be anyone else. No other should touch, much less undo the loops which held the high stomacher front of her dress. As it fell away, the anxious buds of her breasts peeped through the thin batiste of her chemise, another thrill Dillon alone should experience. Their pert roundness was breathtakingly natural, rather than conjured by a corset, a bond of womanhood Rose evidently disdained. Somehow Dillon could not hold that against her. Why alter perfection?

And it was perfection revealed when the ribbon which held her chemise was undone and he was able to draw aside its tantalizing veil. The malleable flesh that filled his cupped hands just right, combined with Rose's curious touch along the length of his arousal, nearly cost him the moment. He was ready now, but that was not his purpose, nor her request. There were things she needed to experience, pleasures, he felt certain, were heretofore unthought of, much less enjoyed.

"Oh, Dillon!" she gasped, saving him the trouble of removing her delectable torture by reaching up to grab his face.

Her gaze melded with his for one short moment before she closed her eyes in an ecstatic rush. When he proceeded to attend to her desire-swollen breasts with his mouth and fingers, however, they flew open wide with a mixture of wonder and surprise.

"Heavens, I feel like a gale's about to bust my freeboard!"

Only Rosie Beaujeu would describe it like that, but Dillon knew exactly what she meant. "Let's just tack a little, Rosebud," he cajoled huskily, scrambling as best he could to ease her back on the blanket.

"I want you to lie down on me, like you did last night! I nearly lost my mind with distraction!"

Even as Dillon rose to his knees between her legs, she was hiking up her skirts and petticoats in eager anticipation. At the sight of the pink batiste, he smiled.

"Does this mean you surrender your petticoats, madame?"

Rose struggled with the laces of the delicately embroidered drawers which offered the last barrier between them and ecstasy. "And the drawers, if the blasted things'll come off!"

"Allow me, you little vixen."

As he reached behind her, the quivering spread of her breasts drew his lips to first one and then the other. Rose arched, making it easier to loosen the cords behind her. Still nipping and flaying her with his teeth and tongue, Dillon eased the drawers down over the silken curve of her hips and then ceased his play to remove the troublesome garment altogether.

He paused long enough to enjoy the vision before

him. Rose's raven hair was flung wild and untamed by brush or comb, spreading on the blanket beneath her in soft waves. Then there were her breasts, as nicely formed as the rounded hips and shapely legs brushing against his thighs with impatience. Last, but not least, his gaze was drawn to the dark triangle that was the ultimate quest in this carnal voyage. Homage was due all, but time was running out for him. Dillon leaned over her and concentrated on the small navel indented on the flat plane of her stomach. Only the tip of his tongue would fit, but that was enough to set off a rippling of flesh that robbed the girl of her breath and exacted his name in a conflict of astonished reprimand and plea.

He couldn't hold out much longer, not with Rose trembling with eagerness for him. Nuzzling her stomach, Dillon sought out the warm, passion-flooded haven at the juncture of her thighs and found it as inviting as the rest of her. It shouldn't have surprised him. Rose always caught on quickly, no matter what it was she applied herself to.

"For heaven's sake, Dillon, let's be done with it!"

And was always impatient when he was too slow for her, he mused, this particular time relieved, rather than annoyed. Her erotic challenge sparkled in eyes that shone brighter than the stars overhead with anticipation. If only there were time, he'd see her naked again, stripped of the cumbersome garments and bathed in moonlight.

Yet he needed no reminder of what she looked like in all Mother Nature's glory. As long as he breathed, Dillon couldn't forget the way she'd shed her clothing in proud defiance, exacting a toll she never suspected.

"Such a moment is for savoring, Rosebud," he answered, wondering even as he positioned himself against her if he were capable of granting it to her.

"Don't tease me, Dillon! I can't bear much more."

Nor could he. Dillon took the plunge, swift and sure, but instead of crying out as her innocence was torn asunder, Rose embraced him with her legs and hugged him to her.

"My word!" she whispered, dark lashes fluttering against her cheeks. "You're right, Dillon. This *is* something to savor." She demonstrated as much with the tightening of her virginal muscles about him.

"It doesn't hurt anything like the girls at the academy said it would." She wriggled beneath him in experimentation, relishing the moment, like a connoisseur might a rare wine.

"Rosebud," he managed, passion rising with the playful toes skimming up the back of his legs. "I've never met anyone like you." God help him, he meant it. Vixen and virgin, hellfire and heaven—she was a living bundle of intriguing paradoxes, packaged without flaw.

She smiled up at him. "And you never will again, Dillon Mackay. That's because this was meant to be."

Reason stood little chance against the provocative way she worked her hands up his arms to his shoulders and drew him down until their lips met.

"Love me, Dillon Mackay."

Despite the best of intentions, there was no way for Dillon to gentle the storm of desire that consumed them. It made the one which had grounded the *Thorne* seem pale in comparison. No wind drove the ship harder than their labored breaths and racing blood drove them. No wave tossed it higher than the heights they reached, entwined in passion's embrace.

Dillon stalwartly strove to remain at the helm until Rose, shuddering and rocking beneath him, threatened to faint. Then, not weak at all, she seized his upper arms until her nails had dug into his skin and bore, not only full impact of his lusty fulfillment, but the thrusting weight of his body. Dillon succumbed to the lovestorm, until explosive rapture rendering him spent of energy and thought.

His face buried against Rose's neck, he roused enough to kiss the erratic pulse there until it began to slow. This afternoon, when he'd given Hanson the orders to take Rose ashore at all costs, he had been stricken with the thought that he'd never see her again. A short hour ago, he'd suffered hellish torment, praying the girl had remained where Hanson had left her, that she'd not fallen into the hands of the murderous thieves. Now he lay in the arms of an angel, one, it dawned on him slowly, that he surely was crushing the life out of.

Yet, as Dillon moved to relieve Rose of his weight, she tightened her thighs about him and mumbled in groggy protest. "Don't take it away yet!"

Well, *almost* an angel.

Nine

Rose glowed like a morning sunrise as she hurried in the predawn darkness to follow Dillon around the island in search of their crews' campsite. He'd permitted her to sleep awhile in his arms, their legs entwined in a remnant of their earlier intimacy, before shaking her into wakefulness to make the rendezvous with his men. Now his manner had become somewhat distant, as hard to keep up with as his long strides, but Rose paid it no heed. He had to be captain to his men first.

Besides, the memories of their fiery interlude offset the chill generated by both Dillon and the early-morning darkness. She replayed the rapturous scenes over and over in her mind, as though even now she wasn't certain that they'd not been a dream.

"You *are* rather like a stallion," she whispered impishly as Dillon held back a low pine branch for her. They'd moved from the beach a good distance inland by now.

"What?" Preoccupied with his own thoughts, he hadn't heard her.

"That shaver was right. You're right much of a stallion. I'd never known the like!"

"It was your first time, Rosie." The reminder was terse, as if he'd have the subject ended right there.

Dillon was right, of course, Rose thought, falling in

once again behind him. He needed to concentrate on commanding his crew, not their lovemaking. It was just that it was so new and wonderful for her! Why, she was still feeling the aftereffects, those little internal quivers that seemed to flare up like rebellious embers in a banked fire.

"The shaver said I was a stallion?" Rose nearly collided with him as Dillon stopped abruptly and turned, his brow knit with a frown.

" 'So you are kept by the famous Capitaine Mackay,' " Rose quoted. She doubted she'd ever forget a detail of that horrible episode. " 'No doubt you know how to please a stallion, *non?*' That's what he said."

"He was French? And how'd the blackguard know who I was?"

As great a lover as he'd been, it wouldn't surprise Rose if Dillon had earned his reputation in the boudoir. It wouldn't surprise her, but it didn't set well. "How many women have you made love to, Dillon?"

Dillon reluctantly withdrew from the introspection which had evidently deafened him. "Hmm . . . what?"

"How many women have you made love to?"

"None like you, Rosebud."

"But . . ."

"Think now, Rosie. Did the man tell you anything else?"

"You're evading the issue, Dillon Mackay!"

"There will be no issue worth discussing if we don't make it off this island!" he lashed out.

"But you said . . ."

"The men took what they could carry and destroyed the rest. If the shavers have supplies elsewhere . . ." Upon seeing alarm register on Rose's face, Dillon softened his voice. "That's why we're counting on getting away, before a confrontation. But if we don't, Rosie, I need to know all I can find out about our enemy."

Rose nodded, sobered by the hard dash of reality. "Well," she began, replaying the scene in her mind. "He said they were going to save me for His Lordship, which made me think they were bluenose shavers, not American. Americans have no lordships anymore."

"They may have been manning a shaving mill, but they were pirates, not even privateers of the worst lot! From what you just said, it appears they're backed or led by an Englishman."

"Or a Canadian. Since your kind won't fight with us, you're not much different."

"I thought you said you didn't want to argue anymore," Dillon reminded her.

"You're right, no politics." Rose stepped up to him and raised up on tiptoe. "Agreed?" she asked, puckering her lips in a comic but irresistible fashion.

Dillon purposely responded with measured tenderness. He'd lost control once and did not want to risk it again. Even as it was, Rose was reading too much into what had happened and it made him damnably uncomfortable. Besides, he needed no distraction, not now when their lives were at stake.

"Now let's get moving. We've work to do."

"And we won't talk about ships anymore, either," Rose decided aloud as she picked up her step behind him once again. "Except to say, I'm really sorry about the *Thorne*. I know how it must feel to have your ship taken away."

"Damnation, Rosie, have you swallowed a magpie's tongue?"

"Damnation, Dillon," she mocked, "What ill wind blew up your hawse hole?" Her chin began to quiver, but she would not let it have its way, even though it affected her voice. She marched across the distance between them and poked at his chest with accusation. "I've just had one of the most glorious experiences a girl could have, but, damn your blustering breath, it wasn't so great as to carry me through this. I'm trying to bury the hatchet and you're pulling it back up as fast as you can!"

Dillon turned away from her before she could witness the full scale of the battle waging on his face. He waited until it was resolved before swinging back to her and taking her into his arms.

"I'm sorry, Rosie, but I've got bigger things on my mind at the moment." He brushed the top of her head with his lips and squeezed her even tighter until their bodies, remembering the ecstasy each held for the other, melded in an eager crush. "And you're making it hard to keep my mind on them when I'd much rather be—"

"Who goes there?"

The demand of the watch broke Dillon away from Rose abruptly and not a moment too soon. Already his body was responding as though hungry again for that which it had already received in a most satisfying manner.

Dillon cleared his throat, hoping it would work on his mind as well. "The *Border Rose,*" he replied, using the agreed-upon password.

With a rustle of bushes, a shadowy figure emerged into the clearing carrying a musket. "Damn, Cap'n, we was just about to come lookin' for ye! What took ye so long?"

"There were shavers searching the woods with lanterns near that side of the island," Dillon explained. "We had to wait them out, rather than risk an encounter."

Dillon repeated the facts again when they arrived at the makeshift campsite. It was evident that the crew had not spent much time resting. The guns they'd taken lay spread, cleaned, and loaded on a blanket, while the longboat the men had stolen was rolled bottom up and patched with tar.

"She's fit as we can make, sir," the carpenter announced proudly. "We can shove off at sunrise before things get too hot around here."

"Excellent, Mr. Gunderson, but I'd know what you're talking about."

"It's the shore lookout, sir," Mr. Hanson explained. "He sighted two sets of sail by the moon making way toward the shavers' side of the island."

"You all right, Rosie?"

Rose turned away from the grim conversation as her cousin emerged from the cluster and squeezed her shoulders with affection.

"Never better, Nate."

It felt as if the flames from the small campfire they'd built for warmth and to melt the tar had singed her cheeks. Not until Nate followed her inadvertent glance at Dillon Mackay did she realize what she'd done. Yet, she could think of no way to diffuse the suspicion that sparked in her cousin's gaze.

"I'm just thankful you survived. How many did we lose?"

"All the seriously wounded and better than half both crews. Aside from two watches, we're all here."

Rose counted fifteen present. All that remained of her crew was Nate, one of his gunners, and two men who'd gone ashore to help the *Thorne's* carpenters. A more haggard lot she'd never seen. Nate was putting up a good front, but she could see blood on his shirt from where the splinter had impaled it. Evidently, the wound had opened under the strain of escape.

Sinking numbly to a log which had been felled near the fire, Rose permitted Nate to tuck the blanket serving as her cloak about her shoulders. Seventeen men from a crew of forty or so? She didn't want to know any more. Instead of asking more questions, she sipped from a cup of rum handed her by a member of Dillon's crew and coughed spasmodically.

"Dillon will save us, Nate," she managed, despite the biting liquor. "I know he will."

That comforting thought and the rum made it possible for Rose to drift off to sleep after eating a biscuit from a tin lifted from the pirate stores. Curled in her blanket by the fire, she could hear men talking and working to load the boat. Occasionally she heard Dillon's voice, which suited the visions of them together sailing the *Border Rose* in a time where war could not come between them.

Now she knew what Aunt Arissa and Grandmother Tamson had spoken of. That unknown something which drew them to their husbands-to-be was the fate Grandpère Alain said drew the Beaujeus to love their enemy.

When thunder roared on the other side of the island and shook the ground on which she lay, Rose was startled into wakefulness. In the blink of an eye, she realized she was not the only one struck with alarm, for the crew abandoned their assigned tasks to take up the muskets and pistols they'd stolen.

"What do you think, sir?"

Dillon stood motionless, head cocked as he listened to the chaos erupting from the direction of the shavers' camp. "I'd say," he ventured with a smile that flashed white over his bristled chin, "that you spotted British warships last night."

"Certainly doesn't sound like a friendly greeting," Nate agreed with him.

A loud whoop arose from those who remained of the *Thorne*'s crew, while those from the *Border Rose* held their tongues with mixed emotions. A quick glance at her cousin intensified the alarm climbing Rose's spine. What would become of him and his men now?

"Dillon!" She ran over to where the captain stood. "Dillon, what about us? You made a promise!"

"And I'll keep it. Captain Malone and his crew have fought enough with us to become our own as far as I'm concerned."

Nate broke away from his cluster of men and held out his hand. "You're an honorable man in war, Dillon Mackay. I hope your character remains such in other aspects."

"What a silly thing to say, Nate! Of course he is! You were right when you said we were fortunate to have been taken by a captain like Dillon. He's all you said and more," she admitted, color bursting on her face. "I see that now." She stepped between the two men and locked arms with each with an emphatic squeeze. "We're all in this together now."

The chorus of cheers from both crews allowed no room for contest from the silent captains. Nate finally broke the glaze of ice he'd created and turned to Dillon.

"So what do we do now, Captain?"

Rose caught the flash of relief in Dillon's gaze before he answered smoothly, "Time to square the yards, lads. If the British are attacking the pirates' camp, the blackguards may try to escape from this side of the island. I'd suggest we move inland and form a line in the trees to keep them at bay until the marines land to assume control."

Some of the pirates did exactly as Dillon predicted. While only one of the *Thorne*'s sharpshooters had survived, the others made a considerable showing, so that by midmorning, the skirmish was over. For the last time, Rose's petticoat went under fire. This time it was rent in strips and tied to the muzzles of their guns to indicate surrender to the marines who charged toward them, unaware that Dillon and his men were not pirates as well. That they'd collected six of the brigands and turned them over for arrest, however, was the convincing factor.

It wasn't until they arrived at the pirate's seaside encampment that Rose realized only one of the ships was British. The second one flew the red jack, but there was no mistaking the red freeboard and black railing, much less the yellow-clad figurehead with raven hair and eyes the color of sapphire. She grabbed Dillon's arm and pointed to where the ship was moored.

"Dillon, look! It's my . . . our ship!" she amended with a bright blush. "It's the *Border Rose!*"

"You're Captain Mackay?"

An officer, resplendent in the royal blue of the British Navy, moved forward to greet Dillon.

"Aye, and yon ship is my prize, captained by my first officer, James Green."

"So the man *said* when we overtook the ship. I'm First Lieutenant Mott, sir, of His Majesty's Ship *Demand.*"

"So you *say,* sir," Dillon answered in kind.

The lieutenant was clearly taken aback by Dillon's audacity. Unfolding was the classic mutual dislike of the navy toward the privateer. That the navy was British made them all the more condescending in attitude, for anyone else in its eye was inferior, be they ally or foe.

"Yes, well . . . Captain Bernard will certainly wish to speak to you immediately." Mott motioned toward one of the boats beached on the shore. "If you will accompany me, sir."

"I would like to see to the lady's establishment on

the *Border Rose* first," Dillon objected. "This has been an ordeal for her, to say the least."

"My men will see her and your crew . . ." The officer halted with second thought. "Are there any American prisoners among the survivors—aside from the lady, that is?"

Rose held her breath beneath the man's disdainful appraisal. She resisted the urge to brush her hair away from her face. She'd not move one wild curl to win this one's approval, although she was certain she was a bedraggled sight.

"None. The bastards killed everyone when my ship went down, regardless of nationality."

Instinct told Rose the officer didn't believe Dillon, not the way he kept looking from her to Nate. Suddenly it dawned on her that she still linked arms with her cousin.

"The captain will want to know every detail." Thankfully the man returned his appraisal to Dillon and motioned toward the boat awaiting them. "Shall we, Captain Mackay?"

"I'll be fine," Rose assured Dillon, thrilling in the concerned look he gave her as she casually moved away from her cousin. "I'll be able to change into dry clothes and make myself fit to look at again."

"Madame, it would take a sore eye to take offense at you, no matter what you wore." As though she were clad in the finest of silk, Dillon took up her hand and brushed her knuckles with his lips. "Until later."

Rose couldn't help it. She flushed scarlet as the uniforms of the Royal Marines putting the prisoners in chains for transport to the brig of the warship. Even after the boat with Dillon had pulled away and she sat in another bound for the *Border Rose,* a strong hint of it remained. That was how he made her feel, warm inside and out.

Mr. Green was on deck to welcome them aboard and so were a number of Royal Marines. As he showed Rose to her quarters, he briefly recapped the story of how the British ship had overtaken them and refused to believe that he was a prize captain from the *Thorne* because he'd had no papers substantiating his claim. Rose winced inwardly at the guilty thrust the man unwittingly inflicted, but held her tongue as he went on.

"But now that Captain Mackay is here, he'll surely straighten things out, although, greedy as Captain Bernard is, he's likely to still demand we pay for the shot."

"Sounds more like a shore saint and sea devil than an honorable captain of the Royal Navy," Rose observed wryly.

"Is the *Thorne* on the other side of the island?"

"The pirates destroyed it. They killed everyone except those you saw come aboard. That any of us are alive is a miracle."

"The captain wasn't able to save his papers, was he?" Rose shook her head as the gravity of Dillon's situation deepened.

"Well, as far as Bernard knows, there are no American prisoners aside from you. I told him everyone aboard was part of the *Thorne*'s prize crew. The way they fought that storm with us, I couldn't say anything else."

By the time the first officer left her, Rose knew just what she had to do. She wanted nothing else to come between her and Dillon. First, however, she needed to get out of her tattered clothing and make herself civilized again.

Her remaining trunk on the *Border Rose* had been packed with her winter wardrobe, but she was able to find a suitable weight vermilion pinstripe dress that would serve her well enough. Its three-quarter sleeves boasted small black bows at the cuff to match the sash at its high waist and the ribbon adorning its neckline.

A silk rose nestled in black lace was the perfect coordinate for her freshly washed hair, which she pulled artfully to one side in a modest cascade of natural curls.

Rose was in the midst of choosing appropriate jewelry from the casket she'd surreptitiously fetched, along with the ship's manifest, from the hidden compartment in the rudder case of the captain's cabin, when Mr. Hanson knocked at her door. In a rush, she tucked the papers in her garter.

"Captain Bernard has sent you an invitation to dine with him and Captain Mackay on the *Demand*, Miss Beaujeu," the young officer informed her. "A boat is waiting, whenever you are ready."

"Dillon hasn't come aboard yet?"

Mr. Green shook his head in denial. Why hadn't Dillon been allowed to come back to the *Border Rose*? She repeated the question aloud.

"The captain sent a note that he'd been given water to bathe and clean clothing on the *Demand* and was accepting its captain's hospitality for supper. That's all I know."

"So nothing is wrong?"

Mr. Green shrugged. "It doesn't seem so. When we arrive in Halifax, Captain Mackay can verify he is who he says. Perhaps the British captain is simply exercising caution, what with the *Thorne*'s and the *Border Rose*'s papers in Davy Jones's locker."

Only the *Thorne*'s, Rose thought to herself, anxious to put the last of the obstacles between her and Dillon behind them.

The sun hung low in the west when the longboat shoved away from the *Border Rose* to take her to the *Demand*. Now every bit the lady from corset to crinolines, she'd used the sling to board the smaller craft and to debark at her destination.

With brass buttons glistening in the setting sunlight

and elegant plume swaying with his walk, the whisker-
jowled Bernard moved forward to take Rose's arm. Her
attention, however, was diverted by a stone-faced Dillon
Mackay.

"Welcome aboard the *HMS Demand,* Miss Beaujeu. I
am Captain Homer Bernard, at your service."

"Are you really, Captain, or are you merely being polite?" Rose replied with just the right amount of mischief.

It was time Dillon saw she could be a lady if she chose
and still speak her mind. The one surprised brow which
cocked of its own accord told her he'd noticed as much
as the appreciative gleam that settled in his gaze as he
took her in from head to toe and back again.

"I must say, your charm exceeds my expectation,"
Captain Bernard countered.

Rose batted her eyes. "Am I to think, sir, that you
consider American women somewhat lacking?"

"Indeed no, madame. Forgive me if I gave you that
impression! I merely meant that, considering the ordeal
you've just survived, I did not expect to find you as
radiant and, I might add, spirited."

"Then I forgive you, sir," Rose conceded, placing her
arm on that offered by the man. "Being from New England . . . Captain Mackay did tell you I was from
Castine, didn't he?"

"Yes, of course."

"Then, sir, you know how we feel about this damnable
war. We've done our utmost to remain neutral in spite
of Mr. Madison's warmongers."

"We've many friends in New England, I believe that,
but, if you will, madame, I would continue our conversation over a cordial glass of spirits," the captain said,
escorting her to the stern hatchway with the utmost de-
corum.

The warship was larger than either of Dillon's or

Rose's ships. The captain's dining room was forward of his cabin with windows to its starboard and larboard. The table had been elaborately set with as much silver as there was brass on Bernard's uniform. Rose had only seen such elegance on the most formal of occasions in New York and never on a ship. Although John Beaujeu could have afforded it, he, like his late wife, enjoyed a simple life.

Nonetheless, she had attended the school for young ladies of substance and therefore knew which of the many eating utensils embellished with ornate design to use first. She was seated at the captain's left, across from the uncomfortably silent Dillon. Knowing that he was upset because his word was being questioned, Rose wanted to reach across the linen-swathed table and squeeze his hand in reassurance. With her glass brimming with golden sherry, she instead acted the courtly dame during the introductions to Bernard's other officers, among them First Lieutenant Mott, and suffered an unbearable eagerness for the conversation to abandon amenities and move on to more relevant manners.

It wasn't until after a lavish meal, however, that that was to be. The gracious facade had worn Rose's nerves to the point of screaming, while the men made small talk about the various ports and popular commodities from liquor to lace. But for the sherry, which the steward made certain she was never without, and the subject of the *Demand*'s assignment to wipe out the pirate haven, she couldn't have stood it.

Captain Bernard had been sent specifically for that purpose after an informant betrayed the location of the pirate's nest to the Royal Navy. While the threat to neighboring maritime settlements and shipping had been eliminated, however, the man Rose had heard referred to as His Lordship had not been on the island at the time and had, hence, escaped justice. Even as they supped, the prisoners were being interrogated.

"I regret the complete loss of the *Border Rose*'s crew, Miss Beaujeu. Such is the way of outright murderers and thieves."

"I can only say that we were fortunate that it was Captain Mackay who took the *Border Rose.*"

A hint of a smile played on Dillon's thinned lips at that remark. Rose could well imagine what he was thinking and returned it before resuming the conversation.

"My men and I were treated most honorably. When the pirates attacked, Dillon . . . I mean Captain Mackay," she said to quickly amend the faux pas, "well, he and his crew risked their own lives to save us. Because I alone survive is no blemish on their effort. I have never seen such a bloodfest!"

"It's sinful that you did," Bernard agreed. "I regret requiring you to discuss such a matter, but I must be thorough in my report. What you've told us confirms Captain Mackay's testimony."

"Oh, but I've more than that to confirm Dillon's story."

Not only the captain, but Dillon was looking at her with undeniable curiosity. Despite the wary cloud in the latter's gaze, Rose was unable to restrain herself a moment more. It was time to erase distrust between them forever. She reached beneath her skirt and produced the bundle of ship's papers, having left the specie and other items in the hiding place for the time being. What she handed over to the Captain Bernard was the most important. Among other things, it certified the registered port of the ship, its owners, captain, and the contents of its cargo.

"Here are the *Border Rose*'s papers," she announced.

"What?" Dillon nearly came out of his chair, but his long legs bumped the table. The rattling finery on it forced him back to his seat before he upended the entire affair.

"I'm sorry, Captain Mackay. I lied in the beginning because I didn't trust you. After all we've been through, I do now."

Her apology gained no reprieve in Dillon's damning gaze.

"Well, well, this is very interesting."

Rose couldn't bring herself to look at Captain Bernard. She kept resisting the silent stream of accusation Dillon directed at her, searching it for a dawning of appreciation for what she'd just done. He'd wanted the papers, hadn't he? They'd been at the root of all their confrontations. So why wasn't he relieved that she still had them and had backed his story?

"Gentlemen, follow me, if you will," Bernard went on, oblivious of the troubled waters between his two dinner guests. "We took an American vessel adrift from storm damage. It had no papers. The captain who claims it as his prize not only does not have its papers but has no ship of his, much less papers for that. Hence, we have only his word and that of his crew that the *Border Rose* is his rightful prize, while we have in our hands the ship's papers, just surrendered by the ship's owner to me."

" 'Twould bear up well enough at a prize court, I'd say," one of his officers remarked.

Drawn from the singe of Dillon's harsh glare, Rose stared at Captain Bernard as though he'd lost every ounce of his wit.

"I did not surrender them, sir! I showed them to you to back up Dillon's word! He told the truth and so do I. What you are suggesting is a black lie!"

Looking like the cat who made off with the fish, Captain Bernard tutted in reproof, "I have eight eyewitnesses who saw you hand the papers over to me of your own free will.''

"Then they'll also witness this!"

Rose lunged for the papers in the man's hand. Unlike Dillon, she ignored the lift of the table she struck in order to do so. Startled, Bernard yanked the papers away so that she was forced to seize his wrist below them instead. That she did, and with such a vengeance that her momentum carried both her and the captain over with his chair.

"They're ours, you potbellied dandy!" she growled, holding tight even as they struck the floor. "Get 'em, Dillon!"

"Damn it, Rose!" Rather than claim the papers, Dillon grabbed her by the waist and hauled her, kicking and grunting, away from the blustering captain.

"What are you doing?" Rose shrieked in outrage. "They're ours!"

Dillon jerked punishing arms about her, cutting off her wind with a hissed, "Quiet, girl!"

Helpless to do otherwise, Rose fell limp against him as the officers helped Captain Bernard to his feet. Blood mottled his face as much as it did her own. He straightened his uniform jacket with indignant snatches, while raising the hand with the papers at her.

"Madame, you may thank me for overlooking this travesty of an attack on my person!"

Even as she bristled to respond, Dillon cut off her breath again with his viselike grip.

"Captain Mackay, you may return your hysterical mistress to the *Border Rose*. This matter is best resolved in a prize court. Set your course for Halifax, sir. The *Demand* will accompany you, and, lest you be tempted to cross us, the detachment of my marines on the ship will remain with you. Am I understood?"

"Quite, Captain Bernard. This will be settled in prize

court where you cannot take advantage of a naive girl as you have this evening."

Ignoring the ominous threat in Dillon's voice, Bernard turned away. "Mr. Mott, have the press gang accompany you and our guests to the *Border Rose* and have a good look at her crew."

"By God, man!" Dillon swore, shoving Rose behind him. "Those are loyal Nova Scotia men pledged to privateer for the Crown! You can't impress your own allies! Privateers are exempt!"

Bernard took his time in answering. Waiting for the steward, he held out the wineglass that had spilled when Rose attacked him until it was refilled. After taking a sip, he handed it back to the steward.

"My dear captain, I can do anything I wish until I have proof that you are indeed Dillon Mackay of Halifax and that these men have indeed signed such articles. The way you and the girl have been exchanging glances throughout the meal gives me just cause to suspect at least the latter is not the case."

For a second, Rose thought Dillon would lose his tenuous restraint. Every muscle in his body was primed for attack. Even the officers saw it. Their hands rested on the hilts of their blades, ready to intervene between the dark thundercloud and their unaffected captain.

This time it was Rose who dissuaded violence. "Let's go, Dillon. When we're through with him in court, he'll think a whirlwind's blown up his hawsehole."

Ten

Three men were taken from the *Border Rose* by the press gang, including Mr. Hanson. Ironically, they were all from Dillon's crew, although the rough-looking recruiters had studied Nate for a good while before passing him by. If not for his bloodied shoulder, Rose was certain he'd have been impressed into Captain Bernard's service as well. Instead, they'd threatened to whip Nate if she didn't tell where the remaining papers and specie were hidden. Never would she forget Dillon's accusing glare as she revealed the secret compartment in the carved rudder case.

She'd lied worse than Tom Pepper. There had to be a way to set things right. She had to think, to sort out this ballyhoo of blazes, not just for the sake of saving her ship from the British Navy's clutches, but for her and Dillon's future.

Rose had no more touched her pillow when she sat bolt upright. Of course! That was it! Their future together was the key. All she had to do was convince Dillon Mackay of it.

She found him in the low room under the forecastle with Nate, and Doc Ames. Speaking in low tones, they shared a pot of steaming coffee at the crew's mess table, which, nestled between two of the ship's carronades, afforded a measure of privacy. Ointment applied by the minister-turned-doctor glistened in the low lamplight, highlighting the bloody stripes cut by the pressman's cat on Nate's bare back by Mott's threatening lash.

Rose hesitated at the bottom of the steps, staggered by another guilty rush, and then approached them. "I'm sorry, Nate. I know I've made a mess of everything, but I meant well." She glanced over at Dillon and was dashed to see no hint of the forgiveness Nate voiced.

"At least I'm a step farther from taking a walk up ladder lane."

It was true. If Nate had been taken aboard the *Demand*, his chances of going to the gallows were increased. As it was, no one suspected he was not part of the bluenose crew. Therefore, Dillon still had the chance to arrange for passage from Halifax to a neutral port as he promised.

"I thought I was helping, Dillon."

"Then you're more dangerous on my side than against me."

"I never thought the captain would take the papers the way he did."

"That's the problem, Rosie. You don't think, you act!" Dillon shoved his empty coffee mug away from him and started to rise.

"But I've *been* thinking and I think I have a solution to our problems! At least to some of them," she amended. "Just hear me out . . . please, Dillon."

Dillon glanced at the small hand Rose placed on his arm. He could easily throw it off, but something in her voice cut through his outrage. He knew her motive had been good when she handed over the *Border Rose*'s manifest, but that did not lessen his urge to choke her slender neck. The truth be known, he was angrier at his helplessness in the nasty turn of fate than at Rose.

"Here, let me pour you some more coffee," the girl offered in a transparent effort to appease him.

Dillon sat back to be served. "So what is this magnificent idea?"

Rose handed him the steaming cup and glanced over her shoulder to be certain they were still alone before turning back to the table. Chewing her bottom lip as if to squeeze courage from it, she braced herself with a breath that drew Dillon's inadvertent attention to the modest cleavage of her dress.

"I've been thinking . . ."

He blew the steam away from the cup he raised to his lips.

"And I think the best way to keep the *Border Rose* out of the hands of that uniformed brigand is for you and I to get married."

The tentative sip of coffee Dillon had taken seemed to explode in the recesses of his mouth, exacting a spasm that sent it everywhere but his stomach.

"Oh, Dillon, you've scalded yourself!" Rose cried in dismay, hurriedly taking the sloshing cup before it spilled onto his lap and putting it on the table.

Only after clearing his throat repeatedly of the shock-induced reaction was he able to throw off the feminine hand patting his back and exclaim, "By God, woman, have you been nipping at the cable?"

"I've been too upset to drink liquor, Dillon!" Rose replied indignantly. "I've needed all my concentration to think this through and it will work. Just hear me out." A remnant of the renegade coffee tickled Dillon's throat, and as he cleared it away, she went on.

"If you and I are married, the *Border Rose* becomes yours as my husband, so the prize court wouldn't ever take the ship of one of Halifax's grandest citizens away! That bastard Bernard will snap his buttons!"

Dillon would have laughed if he hadn't seen that the lovely lunatic was serious. "I don't think we need take any quite so drastic a measure, Rose."

"I would hardly call it drastic, considering we love each other."

Dillon groaned inwardly, well aware of the speculative attention of his companions. He could see her course was set on that fate nonsense again. "Maybe we should continue this conversation in private, madame."

As he rose from his bench, however, Rose backed away, crossing her arms in an obstinate manner he'd witnessed too many times to count. "I have nothing to hide from these gentlemen. We'll talk right here or not at all."

"Fine, then we won't discuss this insanity any further." Stepping around her, Dillon started for the steps when he was seized by the back of his belt and hauled to a stop.

"Oh no you don't, Dillon Mackay. You're going to own up to last night!" Rose dropped away from him as he pivoted to face her. The blaze of the lantern over the table flared in her eyes as she continued hotly. "I thought our . . . that what we did meant you loved me, but I guess I was wrong!"

"You sonovabitch!" Nathan Malone came up from the table with a start, but Doc Ames grabbed one arm in restraint, while Rose took the other.

"No, Nate! This is between Dillon and me. I can fight my own battles!"

Dillon swore beneath his breath.

"I tried to tell you, Rosie, but you wouldn't listen. You were so damned enamored with that fate nonsense—"

"That I was whistling up the wind? Is that what you're saying, Dillon? That it's all whimsy?"

Her voice quivered as she stepped up to him and placed an unsteady hand on his chest. Dillon dared not look into her gaze or he'd drown, he'd lose himself to her crazy notion when marriage was the last thing on his mind.

"Then see if this is whimsy, Dillon Mackay!"

Before Dillon realized what she was about, her small fist drove into his abdomen just below the sternum. Delicate creature that she appeared, her well-placed blow was as breath-robbing as that of any man, doubling him over as she quickly jumped back.

"Damnation, Rosie . . ." he rasped.

"Go to hell, Dillon Mackay, and don't come back till you've come to your senses!"

Fair weather pressed in to speed the journey to Halifax, but Dillon had to choke the sail in order to stay within sight of the *HMS Demand,* which followed them like an overgrown fledgling. For Rose, the scant two-day journey couldn't end soon enough. It was hard to avoid Dillon in the confines of the ship, but she hadn't had to speak to him.

It was one thing to have given in to this damnable attraction she'd felt toward him. That she could live with. The unbearable part was that it had meant nothing to him, nothing at all! Even doxies got a coin in appreciation of their effort.

Except she wasn't a doxy! She'd just been a naive girl who'd done what Dillon accused her of—whistling up the wind, acting the fool before she thought it through. He'd taught her a hard lesson, but she'd not make that mistake again.

Rose didn't know how yet, but she was more determined to snatch the *Border Rose* from Dillon Mackay than ever. Once again she resumed her charade of acquiescence, waiting and watching for any opportunity that might present itself to work toward that goal. She was very good at it by day, acting the charmer, not only to Dillon, but to their marine guards.

The first resulted in wary appraisal, hardly an improvement over the alternatives of indifference or anger. The latter, she discovered, annoyed the captain no end, which only encouraged Rose further toward playing the coquette. As far as she was concerned, the marines were the lesser of the evils and at least did their gallant best to make her smile. Besides, she knew where the Englishmen stood in the order of things, which was more than she could say about Dillon.

Nights were another story. That was when her real feelings surfaced, raw and wounded. Rose hated being the fool and awakened more often than not during the two long nocturnal ordeals with eyes red and swollen from the anguish. All that assuaged her was the prospect of revenge, of showing Dillon Mackay she was not such a naive little ninny after all.

When the *Border Rose* sailed into Chebucto Bay through the west passage of the Halifax Harbor, the huge green hill which flanked the city was bathed in the golden glow of the dawn. Already awake and dressed after a fitful night, Rose stood at the rail on the main deck and stared at the rooflines which reflected the hodgepodge makeup of the town. Interspersed between the Dutch gambrel, French hip, and sharp-pitched roofs of English design were church steeples and block houses forming a backdrop for the sea of masts which dominated the waterfront.

There were ships of every description with bumboats carrying their hands back and forth from their moorings to the shore. From the sound of the hooplah, some were returning from leave and bringing their equally intoxicated wenches back to the men-of-war. The dismal opposites of the fighting ships were the prison hulks, floating in disrepair at the far end of the harbor.

Rose took it all in with a mixture of anticipation and anxiety until the sight of the bodies hanging from chains along Mauger's Beach wiped away all semblance of the first emotion, replacing it with a sick dread. Behind her she could hear the British marines jesting as to which they thought were deserters as opposed to pirates and other sundry criminals. They guessed according to the tattered rags which, in some cases, fluttered from bleached white bones and in others, still clung to the dead men's flesh, tarred black to keep the crows away.

Her hands shook so conspicuously that she folded them, steeling herself with prayer. So far Nate and his men had passed for Nova Scotians. Whether it was to keep Dillon's promise of protection and delivery or the fact that they disliked their Royal Marine guards more than their captives, the *Thorne*'s crew had made the *Rose*'s its own. If for no other reason, Rose had to continue to be nice to Dillon, no matter how much she longed to choke his luff.

When she finally did gain the upper hand, she'd wipe that smile off his face and be quick about it, she vowed. Someday Dillon Mackay would be the puppet and *she* the master.

"Take a look to the starboard, about ten degrees."

Once she recovered her breath from the start her cousin gave her, Rose did as she was told.

"You don't see anything," Nate reminded her as she gasped in surprise.

Rose schooled her face to indifference, but it was difficult. She hadn't expected her prayer to be answered quite so soon. Once again, it was not in the way she expected. Yet there was her brother's ship, big as Billy-be-damned and moored right in the enemy harbor!

It resembled the *Border Rose* in design, but the detail was Johnnie's own. The freeboard was dark gray and the trim black and gilt. The golden-haired sea nymph that was its figurehead, another of the Wilson brother's masterpieces, bobbed up and down gracefully with the tide. They'd made it in the image of Johnnie's fiancée, Amelia Bowers. However, once they'd moved beyond the vessel and could view it, the name on the stern counter read the *Nancy*, registered in Digby, not Castine.

Had Johnnie's ship been taken as well? The thought made Rose physically weak. She grasped the rail as though it were all that kept her from sinking to the deck. "Oh, Nate!"

"Easy, girl. We'll find out the meat of it."

Nate was right. She couldn't let on that she recognized the boat. There were too many eyes upon her. Yet the sleepless night made the burden twice as hard to bear. Her nerves frayed beyond weathering the demand of them, Rose pivoted away from Nate and the rail and abandoned the deck.

Her eyes stung as she flew down the hatchway with floating skirts and sought the solace of her room, the one her father had had built with her in mind. Her porcelain washbowl set having gone down with the *Thorne*, she poured water into the replacement copper basin and soaked a linen cloth in it. Red swollen eyes simply would not do, she told herself, pressing it to them as if to extinguish the fire there.

"Rosie?"

Rose dropped the cloth, disconcerted by Dillon's sudden presence. "Do you consider yourself above knocking when entering a lady's room, Captain, or don't you consider me a lady anymore?"

Dillon let the barb slide. "Are you all right?"

She sniffed and picked up the wet linen. "Oh, I'm just fine! I enjoy being taken against my will into an enemy port, where they flaunt the prisoners they murdered like hideous banners along their beaches."

"Damn!"

In the fleeting moment it took to say the word, Rose was engulfed in Dillon's arms, her face pressed against the warmth of his chest.

"What the ballyhoo of blazes are you doing!" Summoning all her will, she wriggled away from him. "If it's feminine company you want, there's plenty ashore more willing than I! I don't make the same mistake twice."

"Rose, I wouldn't hurt you for the world. You're . . . very special to me," Dillon finished awkwardly. If she didn't know.better, she'd think he was on the brink of an apology. "I promise I'll see you and your men safely bound for Maine as soon as it can be arranged."

"The sooner the better." Rose crossed her arms tightly, as if to punish her breasts for responding to Dillon's embrace. She was special all right, special enough to send away at the first opportunity.

"Except that you may have to remain behind awhile, to testify at the prize court."

So that was the motive behind this sudden break in the iceberg! "You want me to testify that my ship is rightfully yours? When pigs fly!" she swore indignantly.

"Well, if you prefer it go to Captain Bernard . . ."

It was like choosing one's poison and, unfortunately, Dillon was the easier of the two to take. And damn the man, he was counting on that.

"I'll testify on one condition." There wasn't any point in giving him total victory.

"Rose, I don't think marriage . . ."

"Not that, you idiot! I've thought it through, you see. I'd rather be chained in hell than be accountable to your beck and call, much less saddled with your brats."

"What then?"

"I wish to remain on the *Border Rose* until her fate's decided."

"Don't be absurd! You'll have far better accommodations at the Pontac."

"I don't think I'm being unreasonable, Dillon. It's the least you can do. The *Rose* is all I have."

Her emotion was real enough. She didn't want to leave her ship. It was all that was familiar in a strange and enemy port. Perhaps it was that which caused the wavering of Dillon's set countenance, that or the tremor in her voice. "And I only have her for a while."

"I'll speak to the authorities on your behalf."

Or maybe she'd stirred a flicker of guilt. Rose hoped so. She'd hate to think she was the only one suffering.

Eleven

Dillon walked from his solicitor's office on George Street along the boarded walks which served the business district. They saved trekking through muddy streets to the house his father had built with the fat profits the last war with the Colonials had provided. Three stories high, the white flat-roofed mansion with its belvedere commanded the block on Argyle Street as well as a good view of the harbor below, but it was the black crepe on the door which only confirmed what his attorney had told him. *He was supposed to be dead.*

Still, he was unprepared for the pandemonium which broke loose when he stepped inside. His sister's wild offspring thought for sure he was a ghost. Poor Henry, a longtime family servant, welcomed his reinforcement against the troublesome duo, regardless. It was only his stalwart stepmother, Amanda Mackay, who kept a steady course through the children's shrieks and doorman's praises.

Steady as she was, though, Dillon could see the strain of his sister's visit had taken its toll on the robust Scotswoman who'd taken to him like her own son. Her hands shook as she shared good whiskey with him in the gentleman's parlor, where she was as at home as Dillon himself. As she told him how her shiftless son-in-law had tried to take over the family business the moment word of Dillon's death had reached George Street; she took on fresh wind, fortified by her Scot's temper. Ellis Harrison had gravely underestimated his mother-in-law, who set him aright in short order as to who was still in charge.

"So he up and leaves your poor sick sister and the bairns to go back to his work withoot so much as a fare-thee-well!" the woman sniffed, adjusting a dust bonnet on her faded red hair like an officer setting his cap for a course.

Evidently Audra's coach had been attacked by brigands. The coachman had made a valiant effort to outrun the men, but the vehicle overturned on a sharp bend. His sister was thrown from it and down a rocky incline. That the children survived uninjured aside from a few bruises was a miracle.

They were the only witnesses. The driver had broken his neck and Audra recalled nothing, not of the incident nor of her past life. The frightened babes' testimony was meager. The long hair and beards they described led authorities to believe the Harrison coach had been attacked by a stray band of shavers on an inland raid, since one of the villages between the site of the attack and the shore had been looted as well. The men evidently had been lured to the coach by its load of trunks fastened to the roof and back.

"Shavers on *horseback?*" Dillon queried skeptically.

His stepmother shrugged. "I'll be buggered if it made sense to me, either. They might have stolen them, I suppose."

Some local vessels which supplied the English *HMS Demand* with fresh fish before sailing on to Halifax brought in the tale of his alleged death, although Dillon wondered if there could be a connection.

"It bowled me over for a' that," Amanda Mackay admitted, "but I wasn't aboot to let his high and mighty

come and take over like he was of a mind to do. That's
when he up and left, just this mornin'. Not that I'm
fond of his company, but I'm sorely sorry he's not here
now. I'd love to ha' seen the pompous dandy's face
when ye walked in hale and hearty."

Dillon was relieved Ellis Harrison was not present.
He was in no humor to be the gracious brother-in-law.

"I ne'er believed, o'course, about ye dying and such.
Call it the *da-shealadh* or the old second sight, I dinna
know." His stepmother chuckled. "Even our Joeli's
bones said 'twasn't so. Mastah Dillon, he out takin' ships
plump and plenty, she says. Nae that I believe in all that
voodoo nonsense of hers, either."

Joeli was one of the Maroons brought to Halifax some
years earlier by the English in another one of their in-
famous relocations of undesirable ethnic groups.
Amanda Mackay took the young black woman in as a
house servant upon finding her begging in the streets
and had had a loyal friend as well as employee ever
since. Joeli was a marvel of a cook and had an uncanny
knack with herbs and medicines handed down from
her mother.

"I'll have Henry take down the crepe right now,"
Amanda said. "Things'll be better, now that you're here
to take command." She smiled and squeezed Dillon's
hand firmly. "Glad to have ye aboard, Dillon. You'll be
aboot for a while, I'll wager, what with havin' to outfit
another ship."

Dillon nodded, his suspicion that Amanda Mackay
was wearing thin under this new strain once again confirmed. She was always glad when Dillon came home,
but this was the first time she'd alluded to the fact that
she needed him here. Even after his father died, she'd
been quick to see Dillon off to sea again. She believed
the sooner life got on, the better it would be for them
all.

"I'm hoping to buy my prize at auction."

"That's *three* this time!" Amanda exclaimed in satisfaction. "What is she?"

"The *Border Rose,* Castine-built schooner."

"Not by the Beaujeus!" In earlier days the Beaujeus and Mackays entertained one another. Amanda had been fond of Rose's parents, although she wasn't as familiar with Rose, who'd been allowed to remain aboard ship.

"The same."

Over a second glass of whiskey, Dillon told the story of the capture of the *Border Rose.* He left little out, except for the fact that he'd seduced John Beaujeu's daughter. He was still trying to deal with that careless interlude himself.

"Ooch, nay wonder the lass is peeved at ye, takin' her ship. But I dinna see a thing ye could ha' done different. War is a sad thing."

"I thought I'd bring her here until the hearing at the prize court. She can't stay aboard ship once they take it to the dockyards for repair. It's taking on a little water," he explained.

"Then bring the lass here tonight, lad!"

"I'd sooner move a tiger with my bare hands." Dillon shook his head. "She's where she wants to be. There's a marine guard and a few of my own men on duty, so she'll be in no danger on the water."

"So she's a free spirit like her mama?" There was admiration in his stepmother's voice, although Amanda swore she suffered *mal de mer* at the mere mention of a storm. Her one trip from Liverpool to Nova Scotia had put an end to all her sea travel, and the fact that she married a captain always struck her as one of life's ironies. "What does the lassie look like now, lad?"

"Wild black hair and blue eyes that can change shades quick as her mood. Hellfire blue seems to be reserved for me." As much as that disturbed him, Dillon found it fascinating. Rose was like a storm, dangerous and intriguing at the same time.

"Am I to believe this wild rose has blossomed into a pretty young lady?"

"Pretty hard to deal with," Dillon evaded smoothly. Upon Amanda Mackay's arched brow, he confessed. "And pretty to look at."

The blasted marines from the *Demand* practically fawned over her and she was so caught up in flirting just to aggravate him that she failed to see the unsavory fires her reckless behavior stirred. It was a wonder the men he'd assigned to keep an eye on her hadn't had to jump to duty and protect her from some crude advance from the Englishmen.

As for himself, Dillon was torn between shaking her for her rebellion and holding her when that frightened vulnerable look haunted her eyes. How the same pair of lips that could singe a man's ears could also pout in such need of a kiss was beyond him. No woman had ever disrupted his life in such a confounding manner.

"Well, from what ye've said, a nice hot bath and a plump bed would do her more good than stayin' on a ship! Poor thing's probably scared out of her wits."

Dillon shook off the pang of guilt raised by the woman's remark. He didn't want Rose to be frightened, not like she'd been when he'd left her earlier, but the two of them were better off apart, just the way she wanted it.

"Amanda, I offered our hospitality and she refused. My obligations as a gentleman are met. Mine as a businessman are not, and I've no time to waste," Dillon averred grimly, banishing Rose's haunting desolation from his mind. "I'm not about to let the navy snatch the *Border Rose* out from under my nose!"

His stepmother studied him, as if seeing something

in his manner or declaration that surprised her. But she brushed it aside in a moment and pushed herself up from the chair she'd taken by the hearth.

"Show them they can't hoodwink a Mackay then!"

She swayed a little as she found her footing and Dillon reached out to steady her. Amanda was hardly in shape to handle his stepsister and her children, much less a houseguest, he realized once again.

"What happened to the children's nurse? I specifically recall sending funds to retain one."

"I doot they've ever had a guiding hand, save Audra's. Like as not, his high and mighty dribbled that away on his own. Whatever the case, none came with them and I've had no time to look for one."

Dillon glanced toward the staircase. "From what I've seen, Henry'd best lock them in a room until you do."

"Ooch, listen to ye, Dillon Mackay! Spoken truly by a man who's nay been aboot bairns before. They're full of life and nay more. Would I had more time to see to them myself," the woman added wistfully, adding with a renewed breath, "But that will come."

"Then give them some of that Scotch whiskey and put them to bed." Dillon put his arm about his stepmother's shoulders and grinned. "I'm going up to see Audra before I return downtown."

He left Amanda Mackay chuckling and scolding all in the same breath and climbed the steps two at a time. From what he'd seen so far, he was going to be stranded ashore for a while, at least until the Mackay household was put back in shape.

As for Rose Beaujeu, other accommodations would have to be found. All the Mackay home needed was her knack for inciting riot. It must have been a fleeting madness that made him even consider it. Dillon froze as a combined gong and crash from the far end of the hall was followed by Henry's decided wail.

"Dear God, Master John's father's clock! Give me those weapons instantly!"

The man was backing out of one of the guest rooms, two small sticks with what appeared to be bandannas tied at one end in his arms.

"They're our swords!" came an outraged protest.

"We saving Mama!" a second shriller one echoed.

"Master Dillon is here now, children. Your mama is utterly safe and you'd best save her by taking a nap. Now I shall close this door and when I open it again, you will be in your beds or . . ." Henry stalled in his threat, but upon catching sight of Dillon, rallied. "Or I shall send Master Dillon in to put this ship in order!"

There was a mad scramble from within the room even as Henry pulled the door to behind him, indicating the decision was still out as to whether Dillon Mackay was man or ghost. The weary servant motioned toward the large grandfather clock sitting in the hall. The glass-paneled door in the front boasted a long crack running from corner to corner.

"Sword-fighting hellions, sir! Neither you nor Miss Audra were ever so wild. It's their father's blood, I'll wager. There's not one ounce of discipline in them, not one!"

"We'll begin interviewing nurses immediately."

Henry sank on one of the upholstered side chairs along the hall wall. "We'll need a strong-willed soul and quick to boot. One who can run a tight ship, as it were, sir."

Dillon immediately banished the vision of Rose Beaujeu standing over the two tow-headed hellions dashing out orders in short, stern fashion. Much as the match of hellion versus hellions amused him, he wasn't certain even Satan would entertain such a plan.

* * *

Keelhauling. Rose could think of no better discipline for the ill-mannered boy who'd skipped ahead of his parents as they paraded through the decks of the *Border Rose* sightseeing. The stream of curiosity seekers had not stopped since the unloading of the cargo had begun upon docking at the King's Wharf. It had driven Rose into the privacy of her cabin.

First there were naval officers and their clerks. Then came a group of merchants, each taking note of the damage done to the ship. Rose took them to be prospective buyers for the *Border Rose,* which would surely be auctioned, regardless of how the proceeds were split from the sale. Yet, it was the citizens who gloated over every bloodstain or sign that a Yank had suffered under the bluenose victory that had made it unbearable.

The most obnoxious of the lot accompanied a man from the governor's office, evidently to advise him as to the seaworthiness of the ship. Rose could hear his words clearly through the bulkhead separating the captain's cabin they were inspecting from her own abode.

"The ship's fit enough, but such gaudy taste I've never seen, even for Americans. I'd do away with this fancified rudder case as well as the name. Too feminine, to my notion." The man snickered. "No doubt the *Border Rose* was the name of some colonial draggletail."

Having stepped into the washroom which connected the two cabins, Rose flushed hot with indignation at the insinuation. Draggletail indeed!

"Pock-faced and potbellied to boot, eh?" the self-appointed critic went on to the raucous amusement of his companion. The latch of the connecting door clicked, drawing Rose's attention to it. "But enough to make a man's blood burn, what, fellows? Imagine the panting and wallowing that commenced within these walls."

The other man bellowed as the door started to open,

but Rose could not retreat, not with the washbowl still brimming with her morning bathwater. The cabin boy had forgotten it in the hectic activity following their docking. The light that flooded the small space from Nate's cabin gave her a perfect view of the crude tour guide. She saw his dark hair, lightly powdered and brushed straight back in a queue, the superior smirk of his curled lips, and the impeccable cut of his dark-brown suit. It all became a wet blur as she slung the basin of water in his face, but not before she noticed the striking color of his startled gaze.

"What the ballyhoo . . . ?"

"Just cooling your blood, good sir!" Rose announced, her bravado faltering with recognition. She didn't believe her eyes, even after the water had fallen away to reveal astonished ones the same Beaujeu blue as her own. Lifting her chin high, despite the exclamations echoing about her, she held out her hand. "I am Rose Beaujeu, owner and namesake of this fine vessel."

It was Jack Beaujeu, although how and why her brother came to be here and why was still beyond her. Regardless, his blustering outrage was sure indication that he did not wish for her to acknowledge him. Relief flowed through her, nearly undermining the indignation she mustered.

"And I further resent your insinuations as to my reputation and taste."

At that moment the guard who'd been assigned to her outside cabin door burst into the room and looked from Rose to the drenched businessman and back again, clearly at a loss as to what to do.

"This man entered the washroom without knocking, Corporal, and I dissuaded him with the only defense I had left."

"It was . . . I am . . ." Jack took a towel from the shelf on the bulkhead and wiped his face and sleeves. "I offer my apologies, madame. I meant no disrespect. I had no idea a woman was aboard this ship. That is to say, she ... the ship was reported to be a prize, about to have the broom put to the masthead."

"Until she is auctioned off, sir, I am still owner and prisoner on my own ship," Rose declared smugly. "Am I not, Corporal?"

"That's the way of it, Mr. Andrews. Least for the time bein', sir. Cap'n Mackay got her permission to stay on a bit."

"Mackay?" The other man, until now, had remained silent. "Captain Dillon Mackay?"

"The same, sir."

"But word is he was killed in a battle with shavers off the Grand Manan, lost the *Thorne* in the process."

"The ship was lost, sir, but not the captain. This here is his prize, or so he says," the corporal added, inadvertently letting his own feelings on the matter slip. Even one of the *Demand*'s own recognized injustice when they saw it.

"At least you were taken prisoner by a gentleman, Miss Beaujeu, which accounts for your obvious well being." Jack gave Rose a sweeping appraisal. "I am Jack Andrews, one of the Governor's Sea Fencibles and unofficial advisor to the governor's agent, Mr. Thomson. He hopes to make the *Border Rose*, or some like ship, a profitable private investment."

The second man, equally young and clearly embarrassed by the situation, gave a reserved nod as Rose's brother went on. "My humblest apologies, madame. Never would I stoop so low as to insult such a lovely and spirited lady. You must allow me to make amends."

Rose quirked a fine-lined brow at her brother. Whatever was he up to, posing as one of the Americans who placed purse above country and continued to trade openly with Nova Scotia? They did so under the protection of a letter from the Royal Governor from press gangs and seizure by the British Navy and Canadian privateers. It was hard to imagine Jack running illegal trade, even if he hadn't agreed with Mr. Madison's trade embargo, but his belonging to the Governor's Sea Fencibles was nothing short of incredible. It was practically enlisting in the enemy's forces by supplying them.

"You must accompany us to dinner tonight. Where better to find out the fine points of a ship than from its owner?"

"I'm a prisoner, sir," Rose reminded them.

"Then we'll bring supper to you. There should be no problem with that, should there, Corporal?" Jack asked. "Naturally, we would bring enough for you as well."

"Sorry, Jack, but I've got to be at the Governor's Lodge this evening," her brother's companion spoke up, clearly uncomfortable with the idea. "I'll check with you before you sail tomorrow as to what you think of the ship."

"Good, then it's settled. I'll meet you here at seven this evening," her brother told her.

Sail tomorrow? She ventured a glance at the corporal, who appeared as discomfited as she about the arrangement. Of course she wanted to see Jack, but was it safe for either of them? It appeared he was deeply involved in something which, by coming to her rescue, might lead to his discovery.

"Do you see a problem, sir?" her brother asked. Even as he spoke, he slipped something into the guard's hand, a generous coin by the brightening of the latter's face.

"No, sir. There'll be two of us on duty tonight . . . to ensure the lady's safety," the corporal explained, stiffening proudly. "Cap'n Mackay don't want nothing happenin' to her."

"It's good to know the lady's in such responsible

hands." Jack turned back to Rose and bowed slightly. "Until this evening, madame."

Rose didn't answer. She wasn't certain what to say and didn't want to appear too anxious. Besides, her mind was awash with speculation.

Twelve

Jack did not come to supper as he'd promised. When a servant from one of the city's elite hotels came aboard with a sumptuous meal of roast pheasant with all the trimmings, Rose thought she'd surely scream in frustration. How could her brother do this to her? It was bad enough that she hadn't heard a word from Nate, but this was the final straw.

She was so upset, she hardly tasted the spread the servant put out for her in the captain's quarters, and it wasn't until after the hotel servant had cleared the table and packed the dishes for his return that he remembered an envelope with the regrets of her benefactor. Rose thanked him and sent him on his way. Only then did she read the missive from Jack.

Nate had indeed contacted him! Her cousin and the remaining crew of the *Border Rose* had been assigned to his ship, since Jack Andrews would be sailing into American waters to allegedly transfer English cargo to ships which would carry them into Boston. The war had merely made it more difficult for New England and Nova Scotia to continue their mutual trade, but it was carried on nonetheless.

Although her brother did not elaborate, Rose could only assume he was involved in some degree of espionage and acting as a contraband captain to avoid sus-

picion. It was the only reason Jack would change his
ship's name and registry voluntarily and trade with the
British. Nothing else made sense.

When the *Border Rose* was transferred to the shipyard
as scheduled the following morning, her own crew and
enough of Jack's crew to man her would, posing as men
from the dockyard, take her out to sea instead. Provisions would be scarce, but since the ship bore no cargo,
she would fly toward Castine on ballast alone. That
Jack's ship sailed on the same day would raise no brow,
since the harbormaster had already cleared it. All she
had to do was wait aboard until the men fetched her,
a task simple enough on paper, but unbearable in execution.

Upon burning the missive in the small stove in the
captain's cabin, she set about her assigned task with
razor-edge nerves. Most of the night she spent at the
stern counter, staring through the heavy fog rolling in
with the tide at the ghostly lanterns hailing the presence
of the moored ships in the harbor. After working out
a dozen possibilities to fill in the blanks of the sketchy
plan her brother had outlined, the straining of the
ship's lines and the rock of the tide, punctuated by the
monotone call of the night watch, eventually lured her
into restless sleep.

After a long night in a favorite tavern on Water Street,
Dillon Mackay found her there when he entered the
cabin in the dark hours before dawn. Many of his men
had also gathered at the Crowing Hen to celebrate their
return and, from the grand nature of the merriment,
it was just as well he was in no hurry to refit and put
out the next day.

Approaching the bed where he'd caught scant little
rest in the previous nights, he studied the sleeping
source of his restlessness. It was beyond him how such
a charming, angelic exterior could hide a temper to

match old Jimmy Squarefoot. But then, if his recollection of the Bible were correct, Satan had once been an angel.

Although Rose Beaujeu wasn't really evil, he admitted with a pang of tenderness. He tugged a folded blanket from the head of the bunk and shook it out. She was simply mule stubborn and aggravating.

Dillon scowled, realizing he'd digressed to the same subject he'd spent the better part of the night discussing with Nell. Instead of sweeping the owner of the waterfront tavern into the back apartment where she lived and entertained when the right man caught her eye, they'd toasted his return from the dead and talked about Rose Beaujeu.

Dillon wanted to shake the beguiling little waif for robbing him of his usual home-from-the-sea entertainment, but another softer side led him to gently wrap the blanket about her and ease her away from the early-morning dampness at the open window.

Still clad in the fetching dress she'd worn the day before, the girl shivered with arms crossed and nuzzled against him. What had she been doing at the window? Waving the American flag in hopes of rallying a rebellion in the midst of English warships and a host of Red Jack privateers?

Her cheek was like ice, he thought, smothering an oath at his procrastination in taking her to suitable quarters uptown. She needed looking after, being too headstrong to do it herself. As he eased her back on the pillow, she began to stir, her dark lashes batting away slumber and her lips poked out in childlike protest.

"Dillon!" Her slumber-thick voice echoed in recognition. "Is it time yet?"

"Time to warm you up, Rosebud. What were you

thinking, falling asleep with your head nearly out of the window?"

His arm still trapped beneath her shoulders, he used his free one to tuck the blanket about her. She smelled of a modest citrus bouquet tinged with the fresh scent of sea salt. No doubt Rose still scrubbed with the soap her mother had used on her as a child, for it was familiar. Dillon used to enjoy holding her as a child squirming in his lap and sniff her raven hair as he ventured to do now, reveling in the silken feel of its unbound tresses.

Smitten, Nell had said. It sounded plain and simple to her that Dillon was smitten by this Yankee rose. What was it every seaman dreamed of? A woman as wild and unpredictable as the sea, not some fire-burnt house maid who swayed at the thought of a rolling deck beneath her. Worse, the woman had said, he'd been smitten since Rose was a wee thing scampering about her father's deck and defying her mother's precautions.

But men were smitten by other things, Dillon mused as Rose closed her eyes again and buried her cold cheek against the crook of his arm. Lunacy came to mind, for he had to be crazy to actually be considering taking the girl as his wife.

That afternoon his attorney had watered the marriage seed Rose herself had planted, stating it was the simplest, most viable means of retaining the *Border Rose* as his prize, especially if Rose refused to testify in his behalf. Signing wedding papers didn't require the public coercion going to court did. After all, marriage was the girl's own suggestion. Nell cultivated it.

After spending six hours and at least that many tankards of spirit at the proprietess's table in the back, he'd begun to warm to the idea. Even Henry's suggestion that Amanda Mackay needed a stalwart second in command to handle the new crew brought aboard the Argyle Street residence by his stepsister started making sense.

If a hellion was put to the task of taming two miniatures of her own bent, why, she'd hardly have time to make mischief on her own. Kill two birds with one stone! he thought.

Then there was the fact that, so help him, he wanted Rose Beaujeu in his bed more than he'd ever wanted any woman. That brief taste of her passion on the secluded breakwater had stirred a fire that would not die, much less give him rest. His gaze dropped to the vee of her bodice, where her breasts rose and fell, inviting his touch with each breath.

Marriage. Dillon's hand froze in its journey to the warm beckoning valley. He shook away his inborn panic at the idea with reason. Aside from the obvious benefits suggested by his lawyer and servant, there was one other very important one. It would end this merciless guilt that had plagued him since he'd first given in to his lust for the girl. It would allow both peace of mind and body, something neither had known since he'd seen that pink petticoat flying from the mast top.

His body was demanding satisfaction now, but he'd learned Rose would not be rushed on anything that wasn't her idea. When she awakened later, he'd have her things packed and moved to the Queen Anne. There he'd shower her with luxury and summon his every charm to win her attention and favor.

Ordinarily, he'd take her to the Mackay home on Argyle, but considering the state of things there at the moment, he feared that would send her running back to the harbor. The inn was the best and most private choice. Instead of talking theater and literature as most females seemed to prefer, however, he would speak of ships and the benefits of a feminine hand aboard.

He'd laid out this plan carefully with Nell's approval.

The thought of it had made his palms sweat and tightened his throat like a hemp cravat. However, with Rose next to him, seeking his warmth in blissful slumber, the tightening was affecting him elsewhere. God help him, he'd never have another night's rest until Rose Beaujeu was his and he had every right in the eye of the law and of God to be lying next to her.

The sound of a boat scraping against the side of the *Border Rose* and the heavy scent of rum and tobacco were the first elements of the new day to penetrate Rose's warm, comfortable sleep. Dillon had come to her in her dreams and begged forgiveness for his hurtful behavior. He'd promised to marry her and give her the *Border Rose* as a wedding gift.

How could she refuse when he was so humble and penitent? She'd loved Dillon Mackay all her life. Besides, she'd been so cold without him. His was the warmth she needed, fired by his fierce passion. What glorious love they'd made, entwined in each other's arms!

Rose was reluctant to give it all up and go back to the chilling reality knocking at her consciousness, but the movement of men on the deck forced her out of her sweet lethargy. She began to disentangle herself from the arms and legs of her dream lover, but found them terribly confining. It was as though they had transcended the netherworld of sleep to the now and present.

"Wake up, sleepyhead! I've got to get you off this ship before she goes to the dockyard."

And the voice was certainly as real as the breath brushing hot against her ear. Startled, Rose swatted at it with her hand as though it were an annoying mosquito and opened her eyes wide with astonishment upon striking a rough-shaven jaw.

"Dillon, what the devil are you doing here?"

"It's my bed."

Rose bolted upright on the mattress and looked about in confusion. Quickly it all came back to her. She'd been at the window, whiling away the night in anticipation of the arrival of Nate and Jack's men. But Dillon had come in a dream! She cut her eyes at the man watching her intently, a lazy, satisfied smile on his face. Her dream about him had been so real! A weak sensation curled in her abdomen.

"You didn't . . . we didn't . . ."

Dillon laughed as she frantically felt her clothing as though to reassure she was properly dressed, even if improperly placed. "We both have our clothes on, Rosie. I only held you because you'd fallen asleep at the stern counter and gotten yourself chilled. Scoundrel that I may be, I don't take advantage of sleeping beauties."

"Beauties?" Rose echoed, still uncertain that this laughing, boyish Dillon was not part of a dream. "Did you swallow a sugar loaf with all that rum you reek of?"

"No, but it brought me to my senses."

The sudden solemnity that claimed Dillon's face and voice made Rose more wary than ever. Still, curiosity would not let his statement pass. "About what?"

"About you, Rosie . . . about us."

Dillon put his arm about her and pulled her back down to the mattress, so that they lay eye to eye. "I left this ship yesterday, eager to put as much distance between you and me as possible, Rose Beaujeu, but I found I was more miserable away from you than with you."

A confounding, sinking feeling registered in her stomach while Rose basked in the glowing whiskey-gaze fixed upon her. Dillon Mackay could not be here, not now, and certainly not saying this!

"If that's a compliment, sir, it needs sound polishing."

"Then allow me, Rosebud."

The arm that had rested over her waist grew as possessive as the hand behind her head, which drew it toward him. Their lips met in a tender instant that gradually grew to a long and hungry intensity, wreaking havoc with her senses when she needed them most.

She should have been kicking him away, not permitting his legs to entwine with her own. Her fists should have pummeled his back instead of splaying wide over his shoulders in wanton worship.

The hours of misery since he'd first introduced her to the intoxicating intimacy between man and woman were banished by the shameful eagerness to drink of its forbidden nectar again. Rose's need was intensified by the inborn knowledge that Dillon's was as desperate as her own. He devoured her lips, her neck, and then pressed on to the breasts he'd rousted from her bodice with devious fingers.

The rasp of their breathing, the thunder of their racing pulses drowned out all sense of awareness, except that which they shared for each other. Neither of them heard the knock on the cabin door, nor did they hear the latch as it gave entrance to Nathan Malone. It was his bellowing oath that tore them apart, cooling their passion like a shower of icy hail.

"You bastard herring choker, you've played this tune one too many times!"

"What the . . ."

Dillon rolled off the bunk to his feet instinctively, but his desire-dazed reflexes were not sufficiently recovered to avoid the smash of Nate Malone's fist against his jaw. Shards of lightning flashed painfully white through his consciousness, and then blackness fell like a heavy curtain.

"Dillon!" Rose gasped, reeling forward to peer at the floor where the young captain sprawled, limp as a dead man.

"For God's sake, cover yourself, Rose!" Nate barked, stepping over Dillon's still figure and tossing a blanket to the shocked girl. "What the blazes was he doing in your bed?"

Pulling the cover over her disarrayed bodice, Rose glanced uneasily at Doc Ames, who stood silent in the doorway, eyes averted in respect. "I . . . it's his bed," she answered lamely.

"Tie the man up, Doc, and then ready yourself for a wedding."

"A what?"

"You heard me, Rosie. I'll not be taking chances on bringing you home to your father with child and unwed." Nate pulled Dillon's arms behind his back, while Doc Ames made quick work of binding them with hemp. "You can thank your stars I didn't let on to Jack what's happened between the two of you, or you'd be a widow to boot."

Dillon groaned as he was hauled up between the two men and ushered to a chair, his head lolling about as though his neck were broken.

"He should have spent the rest of the night with his doxie instead of returning duty bound to his ship," Nate observed dourly. "I thought when he went in the back with Nell, he would be engaged for the night. Seems she wasn't enough for our randy goat here."

"Nell?" Rose echoed in disbelief. "You mean he came to me from a whorehouse!" And she'd thought her dream was coming true!

Suddenly as sick as she was infuriated, she slid off the bunk, her blanket held modestly in front of her. "Well,

to hell with him and Nell! I'll see him there first before
I'll wed his likes."

Nate was not moved by her outburst. "You've no
choice in the matter now, Rosie. I can't say from what
I just saw that this was all his fault."

Rose clenched her jaw, unable to repudiate Nate's
accusation. No, Dillon had treated her nice for a few
moments and the next thing she knew, she was melting
beneath his lying lips. She'd not been the fool once,
but twice! Heaven help her, what if she *were* carrying
his child? It was only one time, but from the talk she'd
overheard, that was all it took. No, she'd not bring a
bastard into the world. She'd not let Dillon off so easily
with his free ways.

"What'll we do with him after the wedding?" Rose
turned her back to Nate to rearrange her bodice and
assemble her composure before the sob aching within
her chest burst free.

"You can take him with us, if that's your wish. Otherwise, he'll return to Halifax in the longboat with the
rest of the men we captured."

"I certainly don't want the likes of him about," she
declared, anger at last sufficing to overcome her embarrassment and humiliation. Dillon Mackay had had
his way with her for the last time. Now the tide had
turned. It was she who was in control.

Her dress fastened primly, she stepped into the washroom between the two stern cabins and emerged with
a basin of water, now cool from sitting overnight. With
an angry sling, she doused the dazed man bound to
the captain's chair.

"Wake up, sir! You've charmed your way into a wedding and then I'm sending you packing back to your
Halifax whore!"

Dillon shook his head, his wet sandy-brown hair darkened by the soaking, but his mind was still too fog

bound to reply. He seemed more preoccupied with flexing his jaw to see if it would work.

Rose turned and stomped through the connecting room, dropping off the empty basin as she did so. "Call me when he's regained his wits. I want him fully aware of the depth of the hole he's dug for himself this time."

Doc Ames, now donning his former role of minister, made quick work of the ceremony, while the nameplate on the *Border Rose* was changed to that of a ship which had been cleared for departure from the port, confirming Rose's faith in her brother's plan. Dillon was unbound long enough to sign the paper proclaiming Rose his wife, a task he undertook with a glare hot enough to burn right through her. He was furious beyond measure and pulled at the cords about his wrists until they were chafed.

"I thought you said you'd come to your senses," Rose taunted with bitterness after the others abandoned the newlyweds in order to carry on with the escape plan.

She laughed without humor, her gaze dancing with pure hellfire. Whatever purpose had been behind Dillon's initial change of heart had vanished now. Bloodlust throbbed in the veins standing out on his temples. It delighted Rose to see him suffer a taste of his own medicine.

"Although I thought wallowing with cheap tavern sluts weakened a man's senses."

Unable to understand Dillon's muffled reply, she removed the gag from his mouth.

"I had to be weak in the head to consider marrying the likes of you!"

"Oh, Dillon," Rose tutted in admonishment. "You don't like the fit of the shoe now that it's on the other foot, do you?" She ran a teasing finger along his twitching jawline. "But I will give you an out, at least with this marriage nonsense. If I find I'm not with child, I'll tear up the wedding contract. If I am, then all I want from you is your name. Either way, you'll be free to whore about as much as you like"

She paced away from his seething silence to monitor the ship's progress along the channel. Mauger's Beach was to the starboard with its sun-bleached skeletons and tarred corpses spotlighted by the morning sun. Rose swallowed the bile that threatened the back of her throat and turned abruptly with forced brightness. They still had to pass the guns at the battery on the point. Then they were home free.

They would be putting Dillon off with the few men taken captive on one of the forested islands beyond. There the men could hail a fishing vessel and gain return to Halifax. Then Dillon would out of her life forever. She'd no longer be tempted by those lips which had left hers swollen with promised passion. Nor would the muscled planes of his chest serve as her pillow, beating with reassurance and strength. As for the talented hands bound behind his back, they'd no longer wreak havoc with her senses.

Yet, as if they'd somehow been loosed, Rose felt a warm tide flush through her. Damn her memory, she'd have to learn to block it out, something that would be easier when the man in the flesh was no longer present. Still, it plagued her, what had changed his mind about her earlier and brought him to his senses? Was it his need for her testimony as his wife or could it be possible that he truly had realized some feelings for her?

"Why did you come back here, Dillon, after bedding your whore? Are you such a manjack that one woman was not enough or did you have ulterior motives, like claiming the *Border Rose* by marriage?"

"I was drunk and needed sleep. You were in my bed and too heavy to move."

Heat rushed to Rose's face as though her cheeks had been slapped. He'd reeked of rum, and hence his admission reeked of the truth. Yet his kiss had been so earnest. If he were drunk, could he have been such an accomplished actor?

"So you felt absolutely nothing when you kissed me?"

"A woman's lips and a soft willing body, no more than I left behind on Water Street."

"How the hell many women have you kept locked up in your cabin, you swabbing bastard?"

He was lying. He had to have known it was her. She stared into his cinnamon dark gaze until she saw it—a glimmer of satisfaction. Damn his eyes, she let him score a hit! With decided effort, she gentled her voice and smiled.

"So you weren't really attracted to me, is that what you're saying?"

Suspicion surfaced to Dillon's face. He chose not to answer.

Rose brushed her shoulder-length raven locks behind her ears and cocked her head in a curious manner as she approached the wary man. "But you know who I am now, don't you, Dillon Mackay?"

"Jimmy Squarefoot's own daughter, I'll vow!"

"So if I were to kiss you, there'd be no mistaking me for another woman, would there?" Rose went on, ignoring the insult. All trace of Dillon's momentary satisfaction had disappeared.

His jaw grew more angular with the struggle to maintain his silence against an overwhelming barrage of curses.

So the tide had turned again. Lifting her skirt, she straddled his chair and ran toying fingers through his hair, brushing it up and over his ears and down along the corded taper of his neck. Wriggling her hips, she settled in the cradle of his thighs, perfectly designed by nature to accept her.

Her breasts brushed the flesh bared by the opening of his shirt, tingling with such a ferocity that it startled her. Rose steadied herself. This time she was in control. No runaway sensations were allowed, unless they were Dillon's. Ignoring her body's rebellious response, she focused on Dillon's mouth, all the while very much aware of the outrage smoking like a thousand rush lights in his eyes.

She sought his lips in a brushing, tentative manner. They neither responded nor drew away, but Dillon's iron control did not extend sufficiently to squelch the involuntary twitching of his leg muscles. They responded with complete candor to the silken softness of her embracing thighs.

Again, Rose refused to let go the shudder the telltale reaction exacted, at least on the exterior. The molten riot in her abdomen was beyond reach of her conscious restraint, but he needn't know. She sought his lips again, this time tracing them with the tip of her tongue. The bulge of his jaw grew and his white, even teeth bared, not in the surrender his lips demanded of hers, but in a snarl. Deep within his throat it echoed, low and thunderous.

He wouldn't frighten her. Bound as he was, he was like a toothless dog struggling at the end of a short leash. She mastered the sudden leap of her fluttering heart against her chest. He deserved to be as taunted as she had been with frustration and anger. Splaying her hands against his chest, she began to trace the pattern of muscle through the soft sandy bristle, narrowing her circular motion each time until the nipples were drawn like dark hemp.

As she bent down to tease them with her tongue, as

he'd done well enough to her, Dillon caught his breath. His flat abdomen constricted, as though seeking to escape her and the waistband of his trousers, and the narrowing of sun-bleached hair that dipped below the line of his trousers hailed Rose's attention.

Ever so slowly, she let her fingers trip down the downy trail until they disappeared into forbidden territory. Dillon arched against the back of the chair, his escape barred, and swore beneath his breath.

"You bloody vixen, you're likely to find more than you've gambled on, if you don't retreat in short order!"

His warning came too late. Already Rose had discovered the wet, velvet head of his rock-hard arousal. She withdrew one finger and raised it to her nose. It bore a musky scent, decidedly male and strikingly compelling. As if entranced, she lightly touched it with her tongue. Salty, she mused, not all unpleasant.

But where had it been? Repulsion flooding her face, Rose pushed away from Dillon as if scorched by the thought and slapped his face.

"You hoary bastard!" she cursed, all the while trying to wipe her tongue on her sleeve. "It's still wet with your draggletail's drippings!"

Dillon was half tempted to let the girl think she was right, but damn her beguiling hide, he was about to burst with want of her. He'd remember the wonder on her face till his dying day, the sheer enchantment of awakening sexuality. Never had he witnessed anything so stirring to the blood.

"I've had no woman since you, Rosebud," he confessed in a voice thick with want, yet tinged with anger at it. "And I've been tortured with wanting you again ever since. What you're trying to rid your sweet tongue of was stirred by you and you alone."

"So you say!"

"Why would I leave a warm and willing bed to seek a cold one?" Dillon challenged.

The disdain on Rose's face wavered with doubt. Her eyes dropped inadvertently to the swollen member.

"So that's for me?"

"Aye, Rosebud. Untie me and I'll show you."

Rose's features harshened. "When pigs fly! If it's really for me, you needn't be untied."

She might be naive, but she was no idiot. Rose ran her hand down the bulging length of Dillon's admission of desire. He gasped and closed his eyes, bringing a small smile of gratification to her lips. Maybe he hadn't been lying, at least about his longing for her, she mused, working at the fastens of his trousers to reveal the meat of his confession in all its primitive splendor.

It was warm and pulsed in her hand with eagerness. Her tongue poised between her lips, she squeezed it gently, intrigued by its mercurial properties.

"For the love of God, woman, take it one way or the other!"

Dillon's teeth were clenched as though he were in agony. Rose leaned over and tasted the dampness in the indenture of his whisker-shadowed chin with her tongue before moving it up to his lips. Dillon strained against his bindings and met her mouth with his own, drawing her to him.

Rose hiked up her skirts and settled once more in Dillon's lap. She thrust herself against the iron spike of his desire and opened her mouth as Dillon's kiss deepened. Her very soul was being drawn out of her chest along with her breath and she was savoring every moment of it.

Suddenly Dillon tore away, his breath as urgent as his warning. "Tarry no more, woman, or 'twill all be spent between us, rather than as intended for a man his wife."

As though a practiced courtesan, Rose knew exactly

what Dillon meant. Her body cried out with equal desperation to set things right. Grasping his shoulders, Rose eased up the length of his passion and paused.

The ship had begun to rock as it cleared the channel, caught in the crossfire of ocean and estuary currents, so that the exact positioning for the union required her to concentrate on mounting the savage beast. Rose descended in a fierce marriage of hungry flesh, her gasp of pleasure blending with Dillon's, united as were their bodies in the bucking of the tide.

The plunder and pillage, accentuated by the tossing of the ship as it struggled to right itself in the crosscurrents, grew to unbearable proportion. In the background, the excited shouts of the crew working in the riggings escalated with the frenzy to a mindboggling pitch. Dillon arched against the bonds tying him to the rocking chair beneath him. They cut into his chest as they cut into his wrists, but that was as far as their restraint held him.

Just then, the mains caught the wind and the *Border Rose* lurched forward. Rose fell hard against Dillon as he filled her with his passion. The spiraling high which had borne her upward and upward suddenly gave way and she felt as though she'd faint from the euphoric whirlpool that pulled her into its glorious depths.

The slam of the deck as her knees struck it barely registered until the shivers which claimed her began to subside. Only then did she feel the burn of smooth wood against her flesh and realize that the chair holding them both had overturned.

With a shocked "Ow!" she struggled to her feet, her wide gaze traveling over Dillon in disbelief of what had just transpired between them. Her color burned its way from head to toe without mercy as she backed away.

"Either untie me or put me upright! Someone's coming!"

Dillon's words penetrated her daze and she hurriedly tried to lift the chair. His weight, however, was too much for her and all she succeeded in doing was rolling him to one side. She looked at his still-swollen member and reached for a blanket. Tossing it over his lap, she hurriedly rearranged her skirts and then pulled Dillon's gag back in place to smother the string of oaths that poured forth.

As Nate opened the door, she grabbed the back of the chair and struggled with it.

"Nate, lend a hand. Dillon's tipped over."

Nate looked from Rose to the man on the floor and back to Rose before walking over to Dillon. Accusation was rich in his gray gaze.

"I didn't hit him, I swear it!" Rose blurted out, hoping to divert his obvious thoughts. "And leave that on him!" she added as her cousin moved to snatch away the blanket. "He was chilled."

Try as she might to hold the blanket in place, it slipped when Nate heaved Dillon into an upright position.

"No wonder you were blushin' to shame a ripe rose."

"Well, we're married honest enough and I thought I'd have a look at the goods. You've a filthy mind, Nate Malone!" she blurted out in a heated fluster.

Unable to look at her cousin, much less Dillon, Rose fled the cabin to the top deck. There she remained until a longboat had been put over the side for the release of the prisoners. Just as Nate had said, the *Border Rose* had heaved to off one of the uninhabited patches of land beyond the channel to Halifax Harbor and the reach of its guns.

When Dillon and Nate joined the others on deck, Rose avoided acknowledging their direct scrutiny, although she could feel it well enough. She moved away from the place where lines had been put over for the men to lower themselves into the longboat and pretended to study another far-off deserted stretch of rock, sand, and forest.

"Are you sure you want to turn him loose?"

Rose started at the proximity of Nate's voice. She shook her head. "Over the side with him. I'll have none of his noose about my neck."

"I'd like to say good-bye to my wife, if you don't mind, Captain."

Rose stiffened. Her ripe color fled her face as Dillon approached her and put his hands at her waist. After a short, tender kiss, he whispered fiercely for her ears alone as he backed away, "We're not through yet, Rosebud. Not by a long shot."

Unable to respond, she watched as he lowered himself over the side, one powerful arm under the other until his booted feet touched the bottom of the rocking boat. His men, who had preceded him, had already taken up the sweeps and waited as he smiled grandly up at her and bowed with sturdy, braced legs spread cockily against the precariously rolling deck.

"Until we meet again, milady."

Thirteen

Castine, Maine—September 1814

The wind was working on the dunes bordering the south end of her father's property. Rose left the low gray cottage with its adjoining tower, glad that she was heading in the same direction as the blow toward the dockyards on the north creek. She wrapped her canvas coat about her and hastened down the pine-covered slope, aware that her father anxiously watched her from the leeward side of the lofty observatory. Perched atop a pine knoll, it was a peculiar sight, like an inland lighthouse or a pitiful attempt to give the cottage a medieval flair. John Beaujeu had built it after he retired to land with his right leg amputated at the knee. It had been crushed between a longboat and his ship in a rough sea and was no longer stable on the pitching deck of his beloved ship.

The handicap hadn't grounded others and would never have grounded him had her mother lived. As it was, not even Rose was there to share his sea voyages, for he'd sent her off to school to become a proper lady. So he'd built an office on the lower level of the wooden tower and an observatory above with hinged windows three hundred sixty degrees round that could be opened for an unobstructed view. Designed much wider

at the bottom than the top, it allowed the man less rise
on the steps, making the climb easier to cope with on
his wooden leg.

That was where he'd been when he spied the approach of a British warship moving upriver toward the
Malone dockyards and sent Rose to warn the men. The
damned Lobsterbacks had already occupied Castine
proper and used it as a base to launch their forays farther upriver and inland. Many of the Maine boys had
burned their own ships sooner than have them taken
or torched by the enemy.

Rose hastened along the well-trodden path, thankful
that it was downhill. She sped through the towering
pines, hoping the men had noticed the warning signal
of a pink petticoat on the tower, which could be seen
from below. That would give them more time to make
the preparations practiced for just such an event as that
about to take place.

At least the *Border Rose* was out of her cradle and in
the water again, she thought. No British official would
hold it ransom as they had many of the crafts being
repaired or built along the river. The curs had confiscated large sums of moneys from the shipyard owners
and promised to give them back only when the finished
vessels were delivered as prizes of war. Rose doubted if
the poor souls would ever see their capital.

Most of the Beaujeu fleet had been at sea when the
British took the town in the heat of August. Only the
Border Rose had been hemmed in, high on dry dock for
repairs to damage from her last privateering voyage.
Since then, the English navy, freed from Europe by Wa-
terloo and Napoleon's exile to Elba, had set up a naval
blockade that tightened along the coastline of the states
like a hangman's noose, choking off trade. Men wealth-
ier than her father had gone to soup kitchens, their
fortunes either burned or confiscated before their eyes.

Except for the vessels still afloat and unable to break the blockade, John Beaujeu's assets had dwindled like the rest. It was impossible to profit from them within the enemy's yoke. Rose herself would rather die than put herself at the mercy of British charity, but her father had grown increasingly ill, weakened by another spell with his heart. So she carried on small talk with the dashing red-coated officers when they intercepted her on her way to and from the charity lines, all the while silently cursing their spit-polished boots for daring to expect her to be cordial.

Meanwhile, her brother Jack was running the business from one of the Caribbean island branches. Nate had a ship of his own now, taken on the venture that had momentarily crippled the *Border Rose*, and, like Jack, had been doing well the last report they'd heard. The only Maine trade going on was with Boston by Mud Marine, as the coastal folks called the overland freight wagons.

Until now, the Malone shipyard had been too far off the beaten path for the British to sniff out. The *Border Rose* was repaired and freshly painted stem to stern and Rose was damned if they were going to take her ship now.

Tom Raite, the dockyard foreman who married one of Rose's Malone cousins, had seen the signal on the bluff, waving pink above the evergreen of the swaying pines. Already his men were loading into armed boats, much like those of the shavers. Nowhere in sight was any trace of the *Border Rose,* which had been towed farther upstream and hidden around a sharp bend in the silver streak of water which cut through the pine. No ship with any amount of ballast could navigate that far upstream and the woods hid her from sight by land.

"Rose, ye'd best be gettin' back up to the house! 'Tis likely to get a might fierce here pretty soon."

"Where away, Tom?"

One of the rough alleys from the town, a dockyard castaway, left jobless by the blockade stopped in midrun to await instruction. That particular soul could curse till his lips turned blue and the ears of anyone within earshot red. Tom pointed toward one of the boats taking on some of his cronies, who'd also seen the flying pink signal, and the burly figure of a man took off for it like a loping bear.

Now there was a crew to be reckoned with, Rose mused. It was hard to tell how many British ships they'd plagued with fireboats. They knew the way of the tide better than the fish and could set a boat loaded with explosives on course for another with deadly accuracy.

Ordinarily the shipyard workers didn't associate with these rough and often shiftless men, but war made strange bedfellows. The Malone men had hidden them once after they'd blown up a British supply ship, and the rough alleys had promised to come to the aid of the shipyard when the time came.

"Rosie, head up to the house!" Tom barked, distracting her from her curious observation of the men as they tied on another smaller craft behind them, loaded to the waist with kegs of gunpowder. "If the Bloody-backs follow us back here, 'tis no place for a girl, much less one in your condition."

Rose needed no reminder of her condition. Her belly was distended far beyond what was normal for a woman nearly six months gone, although with her loose-fitting dress it was hard to detect unless the wind plastered it to her blossoming figure. Aggie, their cook, vowed it was more than one babe got by her short, clandestine marriage. Whether that was so, or nay, however many little ones she carried, anything she'd put in her mouth for eight long weeks had been rejected. She'd cursed and gagged on Dillon Mackay's name more often than she cared to remember.

Now she only cursed him. Every time she had to bend over, she swore an oath on his grave. Whenever she put on her clothes and found they had to be let out even more, she expostulated fierce enough to hold her own with the rough alleys from town. If he'd only known how true his parting words had been about it not being done between them yet!

Rose rubbed her round stomach as though generating strength and started away from the dockyard, her skirts whipping about her legs in the stiff breeze carried inland from the ocean and filtered by the pine. Instead of heading up the path toward the house, however, she turned into the trees to follow the creek. She'd remain with her ship until the fighting was over, and if the British found their way upstream to the *Border Rose*, she'd light a torch to it herself.

Her life had come to naught but waiting, it seemed. She waited in the food lines for supplies with which to supplement the meager stores from their garden. She felt as though she'd waited a full nine months plus for the end to this pregnancy and had a good nine more to go. Now she'd wait again, wondering if this time she really would lose her beloved ship.

Dillon paced the *Byron*'s deck back and forth as the banks of the river thickened with trees and then grew thin in places with rock-strafed sands. Ahead the salt-water scent grew sweet with the marshland at the northern edge of the Beaujeu property. Unless he missed his guess, the wide creek leading inland to the dockyard was just beyond the towering pines ahead, easily missed if one didn't know where it was.

He, however, knew exactly where the crooked estuary

was. He'd spent many a shore leave exploring the cays and coves and hunting on the marsh. He also knew that the *Border Rose* had slipped into port a month earlier and not been seen since. Therefore, the ship had to be there, and with it, his lovely high-spirited and equally infuriating wife.

"Up there, sir, around the bend!"

The captain of the sloop shouted orders to prepare for a change in course, setting the masts working with white-uniformed seamen, their red sashes flying in the stiff wind as they moved leeward of the billowing canvas.

Dillon wasn't particularly fond of working with the Royal Navy, but his new ship had not been refitted and he'd been delayed in port long enough by the turn of bad luck that had begun the moment he'd first seen a pink petticoat waving in the wind. It was much like the one now fluttering over the tower on Malone Hill.

Two of his ships had been lost less than a day out of port with no survivors. According to word of mouth along the waterfront at Digby, the closest port to where the attack had taken place, Lieutenant Green and First Officer Hanson, for whom Dillon had negotiated release from his impressment and incurred the wrath of the *Demand*'s captain, had gone down with the vessels. Only floating debris had been found by local fishermen, who blamed a renegade French privateer they'd been forced to trade with. Others reported the dubious ship was Yankee.

The investigation was dubious at best and left Dillon far from satisfied. First, the war with France was over. Besides, what crew out for profit would sink a good ship, unless they'd already taken more prizes than they'd had crew to man. Judging from the reported debris, they weren't practiced enough to take a ship without blowing it to bits, cargo and all. Even pirates were a cut above that lot. Instinct told Dillon his ships were in another port, repainted and renamed, and that the debris was scattered to make people think the vessels had gone down.

The captain of the *Byron* had been assigned to patrol the waters in search of the mysterious privateer and, with the governor's permission, Dillon had accompanied them. To date there'd been no sign of the ship.

"By the stars, I would never have seen it!" Captain Stevenson exclaimed at his side. "The way the water curves, it appears a shallow cove rather than an estuary."

"It made a good spot for smuggling during the war with the colonies," Dillon acknowledged, his gaze darting to a floating log drifting toward them with the tide. Something wasn't right about it. "What do you make of that, Captain?"

Stevenson squinted in the bright sun. "A log, what?"

"Maybe," Dillon acknowledged. "But if I were you, I'd have my marines fire a few shots at it from the mast tops."

"And give away our approach?" The officer was clearly astonished at Dillon's suggestion.

"Believe me, Captain, they know we're coming. I've seen that pink petticoat before and it means trouble."

Stevenson lifted his spyglass and swung it from the tower on the top of the pine knoll to the approaching driftwood. With an oath, he lowered it again. "Can't see a thing for the sun's glare."

"I'm certain that's what the men swimming beside it are counting on."

"Captain Mackay, I yield to your uncanny instinct for survival. Your brother-in-law vows you're first cousin to Davy Jones."

"The sharpshooters, sir?" Dillon reminded the congenial officer, taking no satisfaction in Ellis Harrison's high esteem.

If the sniveling bastard thought Dillon was God Himself, it wouldn't matter, especially after abandoning his wife and children as he had. He hadn't even had the decency to ask after them, when Dillon arrived at Annapolis Royal after the reports of his lost ships reached him. Despite his eagerness to help Dillon with his investigation, Dillon could barely stomach the man. Ellis Harrison did nothing for anyone without a price.

The marines climbed the ropes to the top masts and, once adjusted to its sway in the current, aimed and fired at the slow-approaching log. With the first rifle cracks, part of the log thrashed away, confirming Dillon's suspicion. There were men guiding it in the cover of branches, branches tied, no doubt, to a canoe or small boat.

The next round set off an ear-shattering explosion, a black cloudburst against the western sky. Dillon ducked behind the ship's rail and then rose to the triumphant shout of the crew in time to see the smoke being disposed of by the brisk wind. Just as he suspected. If that log had gotten within a few yards of the *Byron*, it would have blown a hole in her side big enough to offload a full cargo.

"I didn't think the shipyard would simply roll over and play possum," Dillon commented, glancing back at the pink banner over the tower. "Surrender doesn't flow well in the Beaujeu or Malone blood."

Rose Beaujeu Mackay should be at the house. From what he'd been able to find out in the town, she'd been taking care of her father since her return, although it wouldn't surprise Dillon to find her dug in at the shipyard ready to fight to the last.

Dillon's contemplation was interrupted by hellish shrieks erupting from a small branch overgrown with rushes. In the time it took him to turn, a longboat with a dozen men shot forth toward the *Byron*. The marines already in place fired a new round into it as another came at them from the opposite side.

All hands piped to quarters, Captain Stevenson ordered the gunners on deck to set their sights on the smaller crafts, but before the *Byron* got its first shot off, a four pounder sprayed shot across the deck. Dillon dove for the planking, taking the captain down with him as he did so.

The tattered mainsail and the confusion in the mast top told that their attackers were no novices. Dillon helped the shaken captain to his feet, grinding out orders automatically in a low voice.

"Gunners fire at will!"

To his frustration, the captain shook him away and countermanded the command. "Belay that! We've a certain way of doing things in His Majesty's Navy, Mackay," he chided Dillon. "Fire number one!"

The number one gun's shot went far over the enemy's stern.

"For God's sake, have faith in your gunners, Captain! Let them fire when they're certain of their aim!"

A cannonade split the port rail on the quarterdeck. They were caught in a deadly crossfire.

"Fire number two and three!"

The *Byron* shuddered with the report of her guns, but once again the men manning the sweeps of the longboats had moved out of range before the order to fire.

"Captain, focus all guns on the bloody bastards and fire at will! You're not dealing with trained naval officers! We're sitting like fat ducks in the water, unable to maneuver!"

Captain Stevenson scanned the splintered deck and grabbed the aft mast as the *Byron* rocked with a second round at the starboard. Blood streaked his left temple as he turned to Dillon and nodded.

"All gunners fire at will!"

"A brigade men!" Dillon shouted, upon seeing another equally urgent problem light on the mainsail. "Choke the sail aloft." Seeing the confusion on the second officer's face, he reiterated above the roar of the cannonade, "Furl it, damn it! All canvas down and wet!"

Noise carried easily over the water, even as far upstream as where Rose waited anxiously. Black smoke billowed and dissipated. She watched it as it moved closer and closer. They were surely to the shipyard by now, if she was her father's daughter and any judge of distance. With that much fire, she could only come to the conclusion that the yard was ablaze. What little work there had been for the employees was now going up in smoke and ashes.

A knot tightened in her chest. John Beaujeu hadn't authorized an outright battle, only a diversion. The shipyard carpenters and caulkers, plankers and dubbers were just that, not soldiers. They were to try to distract the British sloop and run for their homes to safety, nothing more.

Her father had been right about the rough alleys. He'd warned they would hinder more than help, but Tom and Rose had heard of their successes and were excited about giving the British a taste of Yankee fire.

Rose blinked away the glaze from her eyes. Even though the tree cover lay between her and the battle, the wind had shifted and the smoke now blew her way. So many men, family men, she fretted, immune to the cannon fire that had made her jerk and start at the onset.

Except that it was more rifle fire now, that and the loud cracking of the seasoned timber burning at the shipyard. The southern sky was aglow with its light, upstaging the sunset to the west. She could feel heat and so could the mosquitoes that flocked farther upstream to bite her flesh and fly about her head in a whining frenzy.

Choosing to risk being drained of blood rather than suffocating in her slicker, she'd put the coat aside. Four with one slap, she mused, squinting in the dusk to count the squashed pests on her palm. Suddenly the task was made easier by a brilliant flash of lightning over the south side of the river. An earth-shaking thunderclap followed.

Rose exhaled in relief. At last, she thought. The wind had surely been the forerunner of a storm, and a downpour was the only hope for the shipyard.

The waiting grew to an unbearable proportion, for Rose could see the dark cloud of driving rain moving ever so slowly, too slowly, toward them. There'd be nothing left but cinders if it didn't hurry. Such was her concentration on the sky that she didn't see the armed group of men who made their way around the bend of trees which hid the *Border Rose* from the sight of the shipyard.

"We done all we could, little lady!" one of them shouted. It was the burly one who'd been last to join the longboats. "Best we torch this ship before they lay their Limey hands on't."

Rose's heart seized even tighter. "How do they know it's here?"

"They's on our heels like hounds on a fresh scent!"

To Rose's horror, three of the men tossed burning torches on the brush camouflage of the *Border Rose*.

"C'mon down and hightail it up the hill. We'll lead 'em into the marsh!"

Rose couldn't respond. All that commanded her attention were the torches, which sent out flaming forays to the tree branches, now dry from having been cut some time before and tied to the bow of her ship. The moment of truth had come and she could not bear it!

"No!"

Burly raced up the narrow board which served as a gangway from the grassy bank to the quarterdeck to fetch her as Rose leapt to the main and, after nearly falling to her knees, raced forward. "Come back h'yere, gal! We ain't lettin' 'em take a good ship!"

Rose ignored the man's outrage and seized a grappling iron from its rack beneath the rail. The dry evergreen was burning hot, its needles glowing embers eager to melt the fresh paint and chew into the wood of her precious ship. Already the figurehead's face had blackened dark as its hair, a silhouette against the hungry blaze.

Shoving the wooden-handled iron between the fiery brush and the freeboard, Rose tried to pry it away so that it would fall into the river. Smoke rushed up in her face, stinging her eyes as intensely as the heat singed her cheeks, but she would not back away. Not until the demon brush was floating downstream toward the shipyard.

But the flames had yet to eat through the lines holding it flush against the ship. Rose threw down the hook and reached beneath her skirt for the dagger she'd worn there ever since the British occupation. As she withdrew it, thick-fingered hands tried to lock about her burgeoning waist to draw her away.

"Get away from me!" Rose swung the finely hewn, narrow blade at her assailant. She'd only meant to warn him, but misjudged the distance between them and slashed his shirt open across his potbelly. "I'm sorry, but I have to save my ship!"

For a moment, she thought the man would lunge at her and toss her into the fire, such was the fierceness of his narrowed gaze as he fingered the bleeding cut across his midriff. The simultaneous crack of several British muskets from the bend in the creek, however, saved her. He backed away, swearing fit enough to strike another fire between his teeth.

His retreating words fell on deaf ears, for Rose was working at the lines looped through the decoration on the rail. She sawed through the newly tarred hemp, her lungs aching. One cluster of evergreen had fallen away and was sizzling in the water, welcome sound to her frantic ears. Now if only those few drops of rain, which heralded the approach of the thundercloud would bring it on!

Armed with sword and pistols, Dillon rounded the curve of the creek and stopped as if struck in the chest by a four pounder. Ahead loomed the trim hull of the *Border Rose*, marred only by the burning pine of her disguise. Above her decks, her masts loomed tall, blending in with the trees from which they'd been cut and trimmed. The new and freshly tarred hemp forming the network of her lines were now aglow with creeping flames, inching their way to the tops.

Yet it was not concern for the ship that froze blood in his veins and breath in his chest. It was the sight of the single figure fighting furiously to keep the flames at bay on the foredeck, while they ate along the sides. Didn't the little fool, with her dark hair and flailing skirts whipping about her, see she was being surrounded!

His answer came as instantly as the question crossed his mind, thawing his limbs into action. With enough men, they could cut away the brush as Rose was doing and save the ship and the reckless girl. The breath which had been lodged painfully in him came out with his hoarse command.

"To the ship and help the lady save her!"

Rose saw the men running aft where the single plank of a gangway accessed the ship and a sob escaped her smoke-seared throat. Yes, they were the enemy, but there was no chance of recovering ashes. Her father had been right about knowing when to fight. Now was not the time.

Now they would save her ship out of greed, not nobility, and she'd get it back another day.

"Hellfire and damnation, woman, are you trying to kill yourself!"

Rose turned abruptly. She couldn't make out the face of the man who wrapped his arms about her, but she knew that voice anywhere. "Dillon!"

"Merciful Father!" the man exclaimed as his embrace tightened over the swell of Rose's belly.

"Aye, you're to be a father, but, for the love of God, Dillon, help me save my ship!"

Above there was a loud whoosh, like that of a giant bird sweeping down on them with beating wings. In the background someone yelled, "Duck, lads!"

Rose glanced over Dillon's shoulder in time to see one of the shrouds, which had been lashed to the channel on the outside of the hull, break loose. It flew like a smoldering net toward them.

"Dillon!"

Rose jumped at the man, practically mounting his waist as her forward momentum carried him backward for two steps in eternity. Overhead the sky hurled another lightning bolt so close that it sizzled in the marsh to the north of them. Almost immediately, a clap of thunder exploded white as the pain that registered in the back of Rose's head, where one of the oak pulleys struck her.

Such light. Such brilliant, agonizing light. Then there was cold, wet rain, stinging her cheeks, soaking her clothes and sweeping her along toward a place where neither light, nor sound, nor smoke, nor touch could reach her.

Fourteen

Dillon had been prepared to shake the life out of Rose when he found her again. His anger over their forced marriage and the wanton humiliation that followed had obsessed him almost as much as the longing she'd left him with.

When he'd seen her on the burning ship, his heart had stopped in his chest. An eternity had passed in the time it took him to reach her, once again torn between wanting to strangle her and protect her. But when his hands had come to rest on her thick waist, his mind had gone blank with shock. He'd no doubt it was his seed she carried.

A pregnant woman, however, had no place fighting a fire in the midst of a battle. She'd had no business inhaling all that smoke, nor bearing the brunt of a flying block of solid oak on the end of a burning whip, not for his sake. He'd never seen a living being bleed so much. Her neck and shoulders were soaked in gore, as well as her skirts.

And lifeless! He'd felt no pulse at all before making that seemingly endless race up the pine knoll with her, silent and deathly pale, in his arms, her rag doll limbs flailing without feeling against the low branches of pine that parted for them.

He'd burst into John Beaujeu's low gray cottage,

drenched by the downpour of the storm and streaked with soot. He'd once cut a man's leg off and seared and tarred the bloody stump to keep him from bleeding to death. Not once had he panicked or grown sick from the gore, but his insane fear for Rose had pierced him with a blade so cold, he'd yet to stop shivering.

But for Aggie Prichart's disciplined orders, Dillon would have sobbed then and there upon depositing the girl on the bed the housekeeper had turned back in anticipation of their arrival. She'd been warned by John Beaujeu, who'd watched the melee from the knoll, that Rose was hurt and being brought up the hill. There'd even been time for her to fetch bandages and put water on to boil.

Watching it, that was Dillon's assigned task. When it boiled, he was to take the pot into Rose's bedchamber. Never had he known such a process to be so agonizingly slow.

John Beaujeu spoke to him there in front of the stone cooking fireplace for the first time since he'd arrived. Dillon fully expected a fist to his jaw or stomach, at the least to receive the full blast of the man's scorn and temper, but the older gentleman offered neither. Instead, he handed Dillon a full snifter of French brandy and draped a dry blanket over the younger man's shoulders.

"I knew you'd come, son," he said, as though pleased to see him. "The physician will be here within the hour, so there's naught to do but wait."

Dillon would have preferred to be flogged round the fleet than suffer the grim appraisal of his father-in-law. Hell, he'd hand the man the cat to do it. The small act of hospitality, worse, the compassion burning blue in his mentor's gaze was like adding salt to a raw and open wound. A wedge cut fiercely at Dillon's throat, blocking any semblance of the apology he wanted to scream out.

" 'Tis no doubt, you love her. Only love for a woman can break men like ourselves." He swallowed with an emotion Dillon had rarely seen in the man. "She's your very breath. You don't want to live without her."

It was true. Life with Rose had been annoying as hell at times, but he'd never felt more alive. It was like life on his beloved sea, unpredictable, never boring. She'd ruined him for other women! If she didn't it make it . . .

Dillon downed the rest of the brandy and turned in time to see the water boiling. Carefully he removed it from the trammel and started for the bedchamber extended under the catslide that ran off the roof at the rear of the cottage. In the doorway, he paused and blanched at the sight of the blood-soaked rags on the floor where Aggie had discarded them.

"Here now, don't ye go faintin' on me!" The housekeeper left the still figure on the bed and took the water from him.

"I'll do anything to help." Dillon steeled himself and looked over at Rose. He wasn't certain exactly what needed doing, but he was prepared for it.

"The best ye can do is see that her papa takes his medication! 'Twouldn't do to have two patients, now, would it?"

"Took it, Aggie," John Beaujeu said at Dillon's back. "How bad's the head wound?"

" 'Twas a nasty crack, and there's the truth, but there's other matters that worry me as much and more." Aggie sniffed abruptly and turned back to Rose. "I'll not be lyin' to ye, sir," she said shortly. "Neither Mama nor the babes may make it, 'specially if the doctor don't get here."

"I'll drag him up here if I have to!" Dillon swore, pushing away from the doorway to do just that.

The sound of approaching horses brought Dillon even faster to the front door. A curricle drawn by a matched team came to a halt in front of the door and a short, stocky man with spectacles perched on the edge of a bulbous nose jumped down with greater agility than his white mustache suggested. He gave Dillon a cursory glance as he brushed by him with a "See to the team, lad."

At least he'd had something to do, Dillon mused hours later. The time it had taken to put the doctor's curricle in the carriage house and the team in the stable had provided some distraction from his concern for Rose, which was more than he had now. The doctor had come out once after his initial examination and confirmed the serious risk Agatha Prichart had feared.

Rose had yet to regain consciousness and was having difficulty breathing. The blood loss and the blow to the head tripled the trauma her body had to deal with. Her youth and good general health was all that lay in her favor—that and prayer.

The rain had stopped and dawn broke over the eastern part of the peninsula when the physician emerged the second time from the bedchamber. Dillon rose from his chair, dreading the grim news behind the man's grim spectacled gaze but having to know.

"Well?"

"She's stopped bleeding, but only time will tell."

"What about her breathing?" John Beaujeu asked from his wing-back chair near the hearth where he'd spent the night, sleeping off and on under the effects of his medication.

Dillon had almost envied him it, for he'd not been able to close his eyes, even for a moment. He'd stared at the closed door to Rose's chamber as if sheer will would make things right beyond it.

"Weak, but steadier. The smoke didn't do her any good."

The doctor helped himself to a chair at the porringer table the family used for their informal meals.

"I'm going to have a bite to eat and then get some sleep. I'd suggest you all do the same."

"I'll sit with Rose while Mrs. Prichart cooks breakfast," Dillon announced, as though daring anyone to object.

"Go ahead, young man. You're young and I doubt this isn't the first night you've spent without sleep and reported for duty the next morning." The doctor looked at John. "It's you I'm worried about."

"Save your worry for Rose, Doc."

"Nonetheless," Agatha Prichart interrupted, bustling out of Rose's room with a basinload of soiled bandages and linens, "I'd see you at least take a nap in your room. The guest room's ready for the doctor."

"I took the liberty of asking Moss Hill's widow to come by this morning in case we need her. Aggie's going to need a spell herself," the doctor announced, raising an admonishing finger at the housekeeper when she started to protest. "Take your own advice, woman!"

Dillon never heard Agatha's tart reply. The way cleared, he was already making tracks for Rose's chamber. He couldn't eat or sleep until he saw for himself that she was all right.

As he approached her bedside, however, he could tell his wait might be a long one. Agatha had washed the girl's blood-matted hair and bandaged the swelling at the back of her head. The woman had even put her in a clean nightgown of crisp cotton with red silk ribbons.

No semblance of color was anywhere on her face or lips. She looked like a corpse. Dillon folded her hand in his. God help him, she even felt like one, cold and waxen. He could barely make out the rise and fall of her breast beneath the light coverlet.

He closed his eyes to thwart the stinging wetness that

dampened his golden-brown lashes. In a moment he'd blinked it away, but he couldn't rid himself of the cutting knife in his throat. Dropping to the edge of the bed, still holding her hand in his, he reached out with his other to touch the round swell of her abdomen.

How far along was she? He counted. Five, six months?

Slowly he let Rose's hand go to splay both of his on her belly. If his child was moving at all, he intended to feel it. Children, he corrected himself. John had told him the women in the village suspected Rose carried twins. If there were two babies, surely they'd get cramped and shift position.

He cleared this throat huskily. "I love you, Rosebud." There, he'd said it. He'd taken that final step, made the commitment with his heart, rather than with the forced hand and word that had made up their marriage ceremony. He only wished she'd heard it.

Three days later, Dillon stood at the graves of his twin sons. Rose had been wrenched out of her deathlike state by the painful constricting of her abdomen, startling him from his catnap by her agonized gasp. After six more hours of the ungodly torture, the babies emerged, blue and still as the death that had claimed them.

Not once had he left Rose's side. With each gut-wrenching contraction, he'd held her hand and coaxed her through it. He'd sweated as profusely as she and his own flat stomach muscles had knotted in sympathy. The marks where her nails had dug into the flesh of his arms had barely healed.

Hardly noticing what Aggie had done with the first-born, he'd been in a state of shock and relief when the second came. Then and only then did he realize the first had yet to cry. He'd stood like a statue while a teary-eyed Aggie Prichart put brother next to brother and then wrapped the blanket about them with all the tenderness which might have been expected had the little ones been alive.

The sob tearing at his chest remained with him, renting at his insides without mercy. Unable to watch the sad bundle anymore, he focused on Rose, who, for the first time since regaining consciousness, had been given reprieve of, at least, physical pain.

When her body had been ripped apart to deliver his children, she'd made neither whimper nor tear, but bore it as brave as any gravely wounded man Dillon had seen on a battle-bloodied deck. Now, however, tears spilled in a glassy stream down her ashen cheeks and a small, terrible sound struggled from her bloodless lips.

He envied her her freedom to cry unashamed, to vent her grief. When she squeezed his hand weakly and uttered a strangled apology, he'd dropped to his knees at her side.

"No, *I'm* sorry, Rosebud. I should have come for you sooner."

"I killed our babies. I tried to save my ship and I killed our babies."

"The *Border Rose* wasn't lost," Dillon somehow managed. "And you didn't kill the babies. This is just one of those damnable things, Rosebud."

"Ashes to ashes and dust to dust . . ."

He prayed that God would spare Rose's life, which hung in the balance even as the minister sprinkled dirt on the tiny little boxes too small for the bier. They had to place boards across it to keep them from falling into the deep and open grave below it.

There were dozens of people present, but their faces were all a blur as they offered John Beaujeu their condolences. Most were reluctant to approach Dillon, not that he could blame them. He was one of the enemy.

He'd led the British to the well-concealed shipyard. They even blamed him for the loss of Rose's babes with every ill-concealed stare.

Somehow he couldn't deny the accusation in the disparaging looks cast his way. Yet, when John Beaujeu introduced him, forcing their handshakes, his grip remained firm as that which barely held his emotions in check.

"He saved Rose's life twice," his father-in-law informed them. "But for his quick thinking, there'd be a third grave here today."

Dillon knew the excessive praise was the result of selfish desperation, nothing more. There'd been no more valor in his frantic attempt to fill Rose's still lungs as there'd been in snatching her from the burning ship. He hadn't known what he was doing any more than the astonished physician had when, cursing life itself for leaving her, he'd seized Rose's still, breathless form up in his arms and blown his own breath into her mouth. There was no thinking to it, except for the fervent prayer echoing over and over in his mind. *Give her back!*

When the girl began to gag and finally heaved up the soot-blackened fluid which had contaminated her lungs and filled her throat, Aggie Prichart threw up her hands and praised every saint in the heavens. And Dillon's prayers had been answered. Somehow, Rose had come back to him from death's own stronghold and had mostly slept from the arduous journey since.

"Not many would stand by a woman like yourself, Dillon Mackay," the housekeeper swore later, when a few of the mourners left the cottage after the graveside service. "Pay 'em no mind! Them British were here long a'fore yerself. Besides, ye had no way of keepin' them what came to the funeral from it."

Despite his encompassing grief, Dillon had been

aware of the two sides which squared off with the tiny graves between them. Captain Stevenson and his officers on one side and the townsfolk on the other. A knife could have cut through the air, for the men Stevenson's crew had fought and put out of work were among them.

Dillon had managed to intervene on their behalf by pointing out to Stevenson that these men had not been the ones firing cannon at the ship. They'd been waiting in an attempt to divert the *Byron,* but the rough alleys had preempted the plan with that of their own. When the battle ensued, the shipyard workers had disappeared into the forest and marsh, just as John Beaujeu had instructed them to do if diversion failed.

His intervention hadn't won him many friends, although that was not his motive. Dillon simply wanted to right a wrong for those who had been arrested. As for the rough alleys, a few had been caught, but most, like the muck of humanity that they were, merged into the marsh.

"Is Rose still sleeping?" Dillon asked, not wanting to dwell on that disastrous encounter.

At least the good fortune of the storm had saved the shipyard and the *Border Rose,* which was now under repair by the men he'd seen paroled by the British on their own oath not to raise arms against the king. As soon as it was completed, he intended to take it and his wife back to Halifax, away from the British occupation and the accompanying guerrilla warfare. He had other plans as well.

"Like a . . . well . . ." Aggie caught herself, but not before her eyes brightened with the grief they all felt. She resigned her answer to a sigh. "Aye."

Dillon went into the bedchamber which had been his home of the last few days. It was there he'd taken his meals and there he'd finally shaved and bathed for the double funeral. He hesitated at the open door and held his breath until he was certain he saw the gentle rise and fall of Rose's own. The doctor's warning that Rose might not survive still haunted him each time he left her side.

The creak of the planking under Dillon's booted feet alerted Rose to the presence of someone in the room. The desolation of her grief had stung her eyes so badly, she'd finally closed them in an attempt for relief.

She recognized Dillon's crisp, purposeful walk. How attentive his guilt had made him! Aggie ran on about how he loved her so much, he'd snatched her from the hands of death, but Rose knew his real motive. He'd come for his revenge and he'd not be cheated of it. He'd no more saved her life without an ulterior motive than he'd saved her ship without one.

Still, she thought, he was a consummate actor. If she didn't know him well as she did, she'd think he really cared, the way he picked up her hand and tenderly folded it between his. Rose blinked open her eyes and peered at the grim and contrite ones fixed on her face.

"It's you," she said flatly, trying to ignore the comfort he offered, all part of this grand act.

It was hard to do, for she needed it desperately. The alternating swing between grief and her own guilt would give her no peace, not even in the weak slumber that frequently claimed her. She'd not wanted the babies or any part of Dillon. She'd wished them away and her horrible wish had been granted. Her only solace came from the notion that perhaps God had seen she was no more fit a mother than a captain of her ship. She'd failed miserably at both.

"Mrs. Prichart is warming broth for you. Can I interest you in some?"

"Do I have a choice?"

He smiled in a crooked, but utterly charming manner. "Not with your Aggie."

More like *his* Aggie. He'd fooled the Beaujeu cook as completely as he had her father. If she weren't careful in her weakened state, he'd do the same to her. God knew there was a part of her that wanted him to. The grief was so hard to bear alone.

"Why do you insist on torturing me so!" Rose was instantly dismayed that she'd voiced her thought, but Dillon misinterpreted it.

"Because we all want you back to your old self."

"I wish you'd let me die."

"You're too much of a fighter to mean that, Rose-bud."

She meant it all right, but at the moment was too tired to argue. Death had been such a wonderful escape and that had to be what had happened to her. Rose tried to tell Aggie about it, how bright and beautiful it had been, not dark and cold like the grave, but the woman said she'd been dreaming.

She hoped her babies had followed that light. The notion helped alleviate some of her remorse, for Rose knew in her soul if they had, they were in a better world now, not beneath the loose blanket of dirt being packed by the shower pattering on the roof.

"I don't want to fight. I want to be left alone."

"If you're suggesting that I go away again, you know I won't."

It was like talking to a plague. "Then *I* will," she said, closing her eyes again to shut out Dillon's face. She'd been blinded by his charms and lies before. She wouldn't make the same mistake again.

The battle ended in a stalemate. Instead of arguing, Dillon remained with her awhile, and when she awakened from yet another arrest of fatigue, he was gone. Agatha Prichart occupied the chair Rose had seen him sleeping in during the brief periods of lethargic wakefulness. Her mixed responses of disappointment and relief served to add to her general confusion, where night and day were often difficult to separate.

To spite the confounding man and, admittedly, to give in to the despondency which smothered her will to do any more than fade away, Rose thought to refuse food and brave Aggie's wrath. Dillon, however, nearly choked her to force the clam and chicken broths prepared by Aggie.

The final defeat came when her father joined the opposing forces. John Beaujeu looked as bad as Rose. His black hair, shot with gray, was as dark as his complexion was waxen. He dropped with a tired grunt into the chair beside her bed. At his dispassionate "I'll eat again when you do," Rose took up the cup of broth Aggie placed on a mahogany-and-walnut inlaid bedtray in front of her and sipped it of her own accord.

There was no choice in the matter now. Aggie had bemoaned the fact that her father wasn't eating either, but they'd kept secret the spell with his heart which had robbed his face of color and his voice of life. Her stubbornness had cost the lives of men and her babies and now threatened the only man she'd ever loved, whom she could trust with heart and soul. She could not let death take her father.

" 'Tis black gum against thunder, but it's workin'!" Agatha Prichart observed beneath her breath to Dillon a week later.

The two conspirators watched from the hall, just out of sight of the two recuperating patients, lest they give themselves away. John Beaujeu was telling Rose about the work Dillon reported being done in the shipyard and the repairs on the *Border Rose*.

"The shears weren't damaged, thanks to the storm, though we didn't need to hoist the ship out of the water. The most of her repair will be replacing the lines and riggings. The fire took to the newly tarred hemp like bees to honey. Our riggers and hawsers stores are working away while the carpenters replace the roof. This sunshine is as much a blessing as the storm!" the older man observed, nodding toward the small window which opened on the east side of the house. "There's more work for the men than before we were found out, what with the rebuilding."

"But where's the money coming from?"

Most women would have been content with the outcome, but not Rose. She had her father's business sense.

"Dillon, where else?" John Beaujeu answered.

"I'll not take the traitor's charity! I'd crawl to the soup kitchen first! At least the men there make no pretenses about their being the victor and we the spoil."

"It's not charity, child. It's a loan."

"The collateral?"

"The shipyard, of course. The *Border Rose* is already his as your husband."

Dillon winced at the torrid oath escaping the mouth of the angellike creature clad in dainty ruffled and bowed muslin. The only way Rose had accepted the gown and matching robe was because she thought the women of the village had made it for her. If she'd known Dillon purchased it, she'd have worn the hopelessly stained ones which had seen her through the loss of the babies.

"Rosie, I spent good money and my relatives spent a trying time to teach you how to act and speak like a lady. It's an insult to all of us when you act anything but."

Rose grew silent at her father's stern reprimand and turned away to stare out the window. After a moment to compose herself, she spoke again. "He'll have it all, just watch him. He's no privateer, he's a black-hearted pirate with a thirst for revenge."

"Do you think me a fool, girl?" her father challenged impatiently.

Dillon held his ground as Aggie, appalled by Rose's accusation, tried to pull him away from the door.

"Well, I'll hear no more of it, good as ye've been to us all!" the cook whispered, the burr in her speech prevalent despite her effort to keep her voice down.

As she shuffled off, chest puffed like an angry hen, the rattle of paper being unfolded drew Dillon's attention back to the room. Much as Rose's suspicions of him wounded him, at least he knew the reason behind her silent treatment of him. She'd not so much as given him that much advantage, always retreating into sleep, either feigned or real, sooner than speak. He'd feared so much for her health that he'd not challenged it.

"It's from Jack," John Beaujeu told the girl. "The British aren't on the top everywhere. Your brother and his fleet of privateers have collected fortune enough to buy every shipyard on the river."

Dillon hadn't known Jack Beaujeu well. They'd only met on the odd occasion when the respective ships on which they'd apprenticed were in port at the same time. Like Dillon's own father, John Beaujeu did not want his son to learn the ropes and ways of the sea on a family-owned vessel. There was too much risk of favor, and the captains wanted their sons treated like any other apprentice, so that the lads' resulting respect and knowledge was earned with wit and muscle as their fathers' had been. The lessons had served all four well.

"I can't believe it!" Rose exclaimed, excitement rising in her voice for the first time since she'd come back to them from death's door. "Two ships at once and one a slaver, of all things!"

Jack Beaujeu had overtaken two ships sailing for Jamaica, one a heavily laden merchant ship and the other a slave ship from the African coast. It was a privateer's dream. The first carried too much cargo to do more than waddle in the water like a drunken duck and the latter was hardly armed at all. He'd found twelve casks of gold coin disguised in nail barrels among the other valuable commodities.

Both were stout ships, taken with no more than a warning shot. After fumigating the slaver with vinegar, tar, and brimstone, it and the merchant vessel were incorporated into the Beaujeu fleet. The blacks were given a choice of remaining in the islands or training under the seasoned crews assigned to the newest additions to the fleet.

" 'Now Moab, there to the spoil!' " Rose read with glee. "I can't believe Jack has started quoting the salvagers' Bible.

"He and his men were salvagers to a degree," John Beaujeu conceded. "At any rate, as you can see, we're more than holding our own and, fair-minded man that he is, Dillon has agreed to see those of us trapped in Castine through this hellish occupation."

"He's blinded you with his purity of heart, hasn't he?"

Stung by the bitter remark, Dillon clenched his hands at his side. Damnation, what more could he do to prove he was not their enemy, that the circumstances of war plagued him as much as them? It wasn't his fault he was born on the side which was at present victor.

Besides, being on the winning side hadn't brought him the fortune it had the Beaujeus of late. His ships weren't even clearing the harbors before being destroyed. He needed the *Border Rose* and another ship yet to replace them. He'd found them both in Castine and was paying for them handsomely.

"Dillon Mackay isn't being so kind for nothing, Papa. He has his reasons."

"Such as?"

"Expanding his fleet, just like Jack."

"He didn't have to rebuild our shipyard or intervene on the behalf of our men with the authorities so that they could continue to work and provide income for their families."

"He has ulterior motives, I know it!" the girl insisted with characteristic obstinacy.

"Then what are they?"

John Beaujeu's challenge was infected with the increasing annoyance and frustration Dillon also felt.

"He hates me. I have been a thorn in his side since he took my ship. When I took it back and left him the jilted husband, he became obsessed with getting even." Her voice broke and the bed creaked as Rose threw herself back on her pillows. "He didn't know he already had."

"That's a lie, Rosebud, and you know it!"

Unable to remain silent a moment longer, Dillon burst into the room like a cloud of thunder. Rose's eyes widened with shock and then narrowed with calculating recovery.

"Is it, Dillon?" she rallied. "Then leave my ship and get you back to hell and Halifax where you came from."

"I can't do that."

"You won't do it, more likely."

"I can't. You are my wife. I love you and . . . and, by God, I'm taking you away from this place, back where you'll be safe and not forced to live on broth and dried beans handed out in a food line."

Rose shook her head. "I'll not go anywhere with you, Dillon Mackay! Father needs me here."

"No, I don't," John Beaujeu objected. "Aggie took good care of me before you returned and I'd have more peace of mind knowing you were in Halifax. It's fairly bustling with good fortune . . ."

"And the enemy!"

"But for the British compassion, we'd be starving now."

"But for their ships, we wouldn't be."

"That's war, Rose," her father pointed out. "Just because they are the enemy doesn't mean as men they are all bad. We'd do the same to them had we the naval power."

Coming to a dead end, Rose shifted course toward Dillon. "Love," she derided. "What do you know about love?"

"As much as you, I daresay." There was no point in arguing. The girl's mind was clearly haunted by this insane idea that he wanted revenge. Maybe he'd given her reason, but that was before he'd nearly lost her. "Regardless, you've nothing to fear from me."

"And you'd trust your only daughter to this scalawag?"

"I would," her father answered glibly. "I think this scalawag is the only man who has a chance at making a suitable wife and mo—" He winced at his painful slip of the tongue.

"Forgive me for my eavesdroppin'," Agatha Prichart said from the doorway, "but s'help me, I agree with your papa. Ye need a strong young hand, Rosie lass, lest ye run straight to hell with that recklessness of yours."

Straight to hell. The words echoed ominously in Rose's beleaguered mind as she glanced from her father to Aggie and back. Didn't they realize that was where they were sending her?

Fifteen

A high-pitched wail distracted Rose from her study of the street below at the windowseat of the master suite in the Argyle Street mansion. It was one of those loud, unmanageable children of Dillon's sister's, the little girl of four. Rose had seen her poke her tow-haired head into the room from time to time when that strange black servant with the French accent entered to attend her.

It had been this way for the entire four weeks since she'd arrived. Children shouting and adults shouting louder. No wonder Dillon preferred to work late hours at his George Street office. She'd go with him were they on speaking terms. The only balm the chaos had provided was to assuage some of the pain Rose felt over the loss of her own babes. Heaven apparently knew she wasn't cut out of the same cloth as her mother had been. Motherhood wasn't meant for her any more than childcare was intended for the new nanny the children's father had sent from Digby.

Rose had only seen the woman once, but that single glimpse was enough for anyone to see Mavis Adams was naught but a high-class doxie with her heavily painted face and none too confining bodice. Her bosom swelled over it like Yorkshire pudding over a pan too small to contain it. And her perfume. What she needed was a good scrubbing to tone it down!

As for her temper, Rose had seen shorter fuse on a grenade in midbattle. She argued with as much as she corrected her rebellious charges. Often the loud shouting matches had to be silenced by Dillon, his imposing stepmother Amanda, or the Haitian maid Joeli. The little ones were in awe of the first, warily respectful of the second, and spooked by the third, especially when she threatened to summon the devil to take them where they belonged as she was doing at the moment.

"I git de blackheart hisself after you! Hisss!" the maid demonstrated with a snakelike rush of air between her two large front teeth.

"I'll cut off his head and feed him to the dog!" the boy called James rallied bravely.

"Hissss!"

Joeli must have moved toward the children, for the two erupted in a unified shriek and a stampede of little steps followed, growing louder outside Rose's door and then fading down the hall leading to the wing of the house opposite it where they resided with their invalid mother.

"Hissss!" Joeli called after them.

"Don't hiss at me, you heathen!" Rose heard Mavis Adams warn.

"Cap'n Dillon, he say keep dis house quiet for his bride and Joeli, she do! Dat quiet mean fo' you too, Miss Nanny."

The handle on the door to Rose's room turned, admitting the colorfully dressed servant. Joeli had a particular fondness for bright red and yellow. It was exemplified in the red skirt and yellow blouse she wore beneath a black-and-red fringed shawl of the same print as the bandanna wrapped about her coal-black hair. She saw Rose rise from the window and motioned her back down.

"You sit, you rest! You too white and Joeli too black, Missy Rose. When de papa come for his wife and dem younguns, maybe we bof pink up some, yes?"

When Rose didn't answer, Joeli went on to make up the large thick-postered bed in the center of the room. " 'Course, I dear dread dat," the servant went on. "He one evil man, dat one. Poor Miss Audra, she not r'ember, but dem younguns do."

"Why would he come for them now?" As far as Rose could discern, neither wife nor children had seen their father since the assault which robbed Audra Mackay Harrison of her memory.

" 'Cause dat's where his money come from. He know Cap'n Dillon no let his sister or dem younguns go hungry. Den he no go hungry, too."

No one in the household liked Ellis Harrison. References to the man were made with disdain, if not outright contempt. Even the even-keeled Amanda Mackay took on an added edge to her characteristic Scottish sharpness at the mention of his name. She steered away from any discussion of him, instead confining the stiff chitchat of her obligatory daily visit with Rose to the family business.

"Now that you're a Mackay, it's your duty to know your husband's affairs," she'd told Rose.

Dillon suspected someone within his confidence of making known his ships' destinations and cargoes. Other merchants had suffered the same misfortune as well, and the British naval command was inundated with complaints as to their ineffectiveness in protecting Canadian ships.

Having been seaworthy enough to sail them to Halifax after her lines and riggings had been replaced in the Castine, the *Border Rose* was in the shipyard for painting and minor repairs after the fire, leaving Dillon free to begin his own investigation of the recent plague of bad luck striking maritime merchants. Those ships that left as privateers were never bothered with similar bad fortune. The cargo ships were overtaken within two days of leaving both Halifax and Digby, reportedly by a French or Yankee privateer. After the attack on the *Thorne* by fellow countrymen, Dillon was not so certain there was not an enemy within driven by greed alone, a pirate not a privateersman.

Rose was intrigued by the mystery herself, and counted on her new mother-in-law to keep her posted as to the developments. Although the woman was not given to affection as Rose's mother had been, Rose liked Amanda Mackay. For one thing, she hadn't taken sides in the silent dispute between her son and his bride.

As for her command of the household, it was jeopardized more by concern for her daughter than the disorder brought about by her precocious grandchildren. The youngsters heeded her will. There was no argument between them, merely quiet discussion, whereby the woman could exact proper behavior by means of shame or, push come to shove, bribery.

Amanda herself had undertaken to reintroduce Audra Mackay Harrison into Halifax society. Like Rose, Audra had been a recluse in her room until recent weeks. Unlike Rose, Audra hadn't the will to resist the household's gentle persuasion to rejoin the living. Her days were spent with visitations and charity work. Amanda was doing everything and anything that might help jar her daughter's lost memory, or at least renew her interest in life.

That morning, Rose had watched mother and daughter making their way to the neighbor's home for dance lessons given by a French officer who was a paroled prisoner of war from Melville Island. That afternoon, yet another was to tutor a group of young ladies in French.

Although the war was basically over with France, the exchange of prisoners had not begun. Still, enemy officers were allowed in and about the town within certain limitations, and some made money by teaching French and dance. Others, like the ordinary soldiers and sailors beneath their station, sought income from their crafts and wares at the prisoners' market. Audra and her mother made a weekly trip to the island for the affair, which was a favored outing for the aristocracy as well as the common citizen.

"Po' babies, got a papa dat doan wan 'em and a mama dat doan know 'em," Joeli muttered under her breath. "Dat's enuff to make 'em on'ry. What make you so on'ry, missy?"

Rose was drawn back to the present upon hearing Joeli's mumbling. The maid looked up at her with her usual disapproval, all the while making up the sofa where Dillon had spent his nights since their arrival. Unlike her mistress, the maid clearly stood behind her "Cap'n Dillon."

"I'm too tired to be ornery," Rose quipped, dreading the inquisition she sensed coming.

"You gone wear one 'o dem new dresses yor lovin' husban' done bought you, *non?*"

Joeli had asked that every day since the trunk with Rose's new wardrobe arrived, a belated wedding gift from her husband. It was the best that Halifax, a city literally bursting at its boundaries with fortunes from the war, had to offer. The Oriental silks, Irish linen, and Spanish lace worked into smuggled French designs were enough to steal a woman's breath away, especially when compared to Rose's own dresses, which had been realtered to fit her slender and now childless figure.

"My blue one will do, the embroidered one," Rose answered.

Audra had been so enthralled with the finery that Rose had offered the girl her choice from the lot, much to Dillon's outrage.

"De hem is frayed out," Joeli pointed out in disapproval, not for the first time. Most of Rose's dresses were worn from the many treks she'd made from the Beaujeu cottage to the shipyard and back. "An' it's gettin' too tight. Whedder you likes it or not, Missy Rose, you is better. Dey ain't no tired in dem blue eyes o' yors."

It was best to let Joeli have the last word if Rose wanted to be left in peace. Much as she hated to admit it, the Maroon was right. She was better and, because of that, she was getting restless.

But she'd wanted to die rather than be transplanted in her enemy's home. What did it matter to Dillon where his wife was, as long as the *Border Rose* was legally his? Why did he go out of his way to control that fiendish temper of his and indulge her, when it was apparent he wanted to strangle her? If it was the love he'd proclaimed in Castine, why had he never broached the subject of sharing the oversize bed Rose felt so lost in?

Not that she wanted him there, she told herself. She'd never forgive him for forcing her to leave her father, knowing that, considering the man's condition, she might never see John Beaujeu alive again. He'd been so pale and wan the day he and Aggie saw them off from the small harbor. Rose knew the cook would take good care of him, but Aggie still wasn't his daughter.

It appeared, regardless of her will, that Rose was not to have her way in any case, either in living where she wanted to or in living at all. The days at sea filled her lungs with rejuvenating salt air and the roll of the ship beneath her was as nourishing to her spirit as a mother's own arms. Except when another ship was sighted and posed possible threat, she was allowed the full run of the decks, making it impossible to stay sequestered in her cabin.

Upon their arrival in Halifax, Rose had walked off the gangway without Dillon's assistance, her upturned nose and cheeks ruddied by exposure to the cooling autumn breezes. At the Argyle Street residence, she'd disembarked from the coach, refusing her husband's arm and marched straight into the door being held open by the manservant Henry. From there, she stopped only to acknowledge Dillon's curious family and then followed Amanda Mackay to the master suite reserved for the newlyweds. She'd not left it since, not for meals, nor to meet the many visitors who came to make the acquaintance of Dillon's Yankee bride.

Now she was going stir crazy. It wasn't like her to stay abed half the morning, and, while she liked to read, she'd depleted the selection of books Amanda Mackay had brought up to her from the library on the first floor. She'd even altered and sewn her dresses until the seams, rent from wear, stood out like those of a ragamuffin in hand-me-downs.

Although not accustomed to having a personal maid, Rose allowed Joeli to help her dress and then took a late breakfast at the table near a window which overlooked the busy street. A myriad of curricles and coaches moved both ways on the caked and rutted thoroughfare, while men and women dressed in finery strolled along its cobbled walks with aristocratic indifference to the magnificence of the houses towering on both sides.

Occasionally wagon vendors ventured into the district with fresh wares. Rose liked to watch the parade of their horses, which invariably wore decorated halters or distinctive hats with adornments reflective of its owner's business. One wearing a bouquet of autumn flowers and greens attached to its halter drew a cart laden with baskets of cabbages and other late fruits of the harvest into the side drive of the Mackay home. Its driver was not nearly so gaily bedecked in his tattered coat and lap blanket.

Rose wondered if the black man was one of slaves newly arrived after escaping from the Chesapeake Bay area with the British fleet. She'd heard the city was becoming as inundated with them as it had been with the Maroons years earlier. As the vehicle disappeared around the back of the house, a commotion at an intersection farther up the street brought traffic and pedestrians to a stop.

Pressing her face to the glass. Rose spied a fire engine race with bells ringing and dogs barking across Argyle. It was headed for the waterfront. Following it was a brigade of soldiers and citizens, all outfitted with leather hats and buckets.

A few men ran from the elegant houses along Argyle Street to join the firefighters, volunteers, she guessed, fitted like their counterparts with hats and buckets which were kept in their homes for such occasions. It was quite fashionable for gentlemen to belong to such organizations, providing a manner of excitement which could not be found at the gaming tables or the lavish balls which were increasing in numbers as the holiday season approached. As Rose peered over the rooftops down toward the harbor for a sign of smoke, she was distracted by another movement, not of adults, but of children—two to be exact.

Without cloak or coat, a small boy led his smaller sister by the hand, running down the sidewalk toward the intersection where the fire engine had disappeared. Their pale flaxen hair whipped about their cherubic faces as they glanced over their shoulders at the house they left behind like escaping thieves. Although she'd heard more than she had seen Audra Mackay Harrison's offspring, Rose knew instantly the meat of the situation.

She shoved away from the window, nearly overturning her breakfast dishes as she bumped the table. All the while she kept an eye on the retreating figures, hoping to catch sight of Mavis Adams on their heels. The woman was probably in the kitchen flirting with the vegetable man, she thought, recalling a one of Joeli's comments about Mavis's interest in anything wearing trousers.

"Joeli!" she shouted, when the little girl tripped and fell, momentarily halting the flight below.

Damned worthless nanny! There was no telling what might happen to the youngsters in streets overrun by drunken soldiers from the Citadel and equally intoxicated sailors from the docks. Fights were as common as the thieves and pickpockets along Water and Barracks streets, which ironically hemmed in the fashionable Argyle.

"Joeli!"

Rose rushed out into the hall and down one of the graceful sweeps of steps that approached from each of the two wings of the mansion to a landing in the central hall before merging into one. By the time Rose struck the landing, the Maroon maidservant came rushing up from the back of the house.

"The children, they've run away!" she answered the question in the black woman's alarmed gaze. "Get that shiftless nanny of theirs. I'm going after them! That way!" she said, pointing to the direction she was about to take, not knowing the street name.

Rose didn't realize how her self-imposed confinement had handicapped her until she reached the corner of the street and held on to a lamppost until she could catch her breath. At least on the ship, she'd walked the decks daily. It felt now as if each icy breath was cutting into her chest like burning daggers. Her pulse pounded so loud in her ears that she could barely hear the roar of excitement generating from farther down the street where smoke billowed against the bright blue sky.

She scanned the crowd ahead, which thickened toward the fire, for any sign of the two runaways. Nowhere did she see the two troublesome towheads. With little option but to charge ahead if she were to catch them, Rose did so.

At least the run was downhill toward the burning building. Still, she was flushed and perspiring, despite the chilly November air. Rubbing her arms, she paused to look around, but if the children were in the mob of onlookers, they'd been completely swallowed by it.

"Excuse me, have you seen two children with flaxen hair, almost white?" She held her hand out at waist height to indicate their size. "A boy and a girl," she explained to the curious group surrounding her.

Upon receiving a denying round of shaking heads, Rose shoved deeper into the crowd, repeating the questions to man, woman, soldier, and sailor. A fire was an exciting thing, she reasoned frantically, so it made sense that the little ones would push like their larger counterparts toward the burning building to get a better look. Still tossing her queries over her shoulder, Rose squeezed through broad shoulders and wide hips.

The little devils were likely peering at the spectacle from under the wheels of the fire engine, she thought. For a moment, she dropped to her knees and considered crawling through the sea of legs, skirts, and the occasional sword.

"Pardonnez-moi, mademoiselle, but are you ill?"

Startled by the French apology, Rose did not resist

when a man standing next to her grasped her arm to help her to her feet. Her breath was ragged and the little bit of smoke carried toward them by the offshore breeze had begun to assault her recently recovered lungs. Rose wondered if she'd ever be able to breathe normally again, without tasting the fiery heat of the smoke she'd inhaled while trying to save the *Border Rose.*

"J'ai essoufle, monsieur!" she responded automatically, French a second language at the Beaujeu homes. "I'm breathless, that's all."

A dark brow raised in surprise. "You are Acadian, *non?*"

Rose glanced in dismay at the distance she still had to go to reach the front of the crowd. "My grandfather was. But tell me, monsieur, have you seen two fair-haired children, a boy about six and a girl four?"

"You have lost your babies, *non?*"

Rose shook her head and quelled the sharp pang of despair his inadvertent reminder evoked in her breast. *"Non,* they are not mine. They're my . . . my niece and nephew," she explained, stepping around him. "I must find them before they get hurt!"

"C'est bon, then I will help you." With a flourish of his arm, he cleared a path in front of her. "Excuse us, please. The lady has lost her children in the crowd. Excuse us."

Rose was too astonished by the sudden disappearance of his accent to do anything but take advantage of his help. He had to be French, she thought. His slip of the tongue when she'd surprised him by dropping to the ground was as telling as his coiffure, which was cropped short on the sides and tied in a queue in the back in the dashing style of the defeated French emperor.

The stranger soon had her along the edge of the on-lookers, who were being held back by a line of scarlet-jacketed soldiers. The smoke was thicker there and

Rose's eyes stung as much as her lungs, but she continued to search the surrounding area, all the while keeping close to her escort.

"Over there, madame! Is that them?"

Rose looked in the direction her companion pointed. There, standing on the roof of a tinker's wagon, were the blond escapees, watching the firefighters containing the blaze to the one structure in wide-eyed fascination.

"Yes. Thank you so much!"

Once again, the curious stranger cleared the way for her with his broad shoulders, clad in a coarse woven serge of bright peacock. The jacket, though patched on the sleeves, was as impeccably tailored, nonetheless, as his nankeen trousers. Whatever he was, he was a gentleman and a godsend.

"Ho, little ones, your aunt is near collapse with worry!" he chided upon reaching the wagon.

Instead of fleeing as Rose feared they might, the two runaways stared down at her with wary eyes, the boy's the same cinnamon color as his uncle's and the girl's her mother's pale green.

"Did Unca Dillon let you out of your room?" the youngest ventured at last.

Rose ignored her helpful companion's shocked expression. "No, I came out because I saw you leave the house and was afraid something might happen to you. You should never leave without an adult or without your cloaks in this chill."

"It's warm here," the boy pointed out.

Rose couldn't argue there. The heat from the burning cottage, which had now collapsed into smoldering rubble, was comforting, even if the smoke was debilitating.

"You don't have a coat ei'ver."

"I didn't have time to fetch one, Alison." Yes, that was the little girl's name. Jerome was the boy's.

"Neither did we," Jerome countered with a stubborn set of his jaw. "Not and see the best of the fire, that is."

Rose rubbed her arms, but the cold was not what bothered her. She could taste the charred wood, like blackened bile in the back of her throat, and her head felt light.

"Here, madame. Forgive my negligence!" In an instant, the stranger wrapped his bright jacket about Rose's shoulders. "You are not well," he chided, brushing her now colorless cheeks with the back of his hand.

"I need some air," Rose conceded. "Fresh air."

The man lifted the children down from the top of the wagon. With Alison perched on his hip, he turned to Jerome. "Your aunt is ill. Are you man enough to hold her hand and lead her through the crowd after me?"

In answer, Jerome took Rose's fingers in his sooty ones with burgeoning pride. How gifted this man was with children, Rose thought, falling once again in the Frenchman's wake. Dillon, on the other hand, thundered through the house like a Norse god, threatening to lower the hammer of his anger on them.

"Watch your skirts, madame."

Rose lifted her frayed hem as they stepped into an alley littered with household cast-off, which would have had a ripe stench were the weather warmer. She was glad it wasn't, although now that they'd gotten away from the blaze and in the shadows of the buildings on either side of them, the cold was becoming more noticeable despite her newfound friend's jacket.

"There is a coffee house around the corner. Perhaps we might step inside to warm ourselves. Then I shall see you home."

"Oh, that's not necessary, Monsieur . . ." Rose broke off. She didn't even know his name.

"Benet . . . Claude Benet at your service, Madame . . ."

"Beaujeu. I mean Mackay," Rose added hastily. The color rushing to her face was the only warmth she felt.

"Mackay, you say?" The Frenchman, whose accent had surfaced once again, glanced at the children. "*Quele coïncidence!* Then these children, your niece and nephew, they belong to Madame Harrison, *non?*"

Jerome pressed against Rose in an effort to gain some of the protection of the jacket Monsieur Benet had loaned her.

"Madame Mackay, I must insist you come into the coffee house until I can find some wraps for the children and yourself. Perhaps the proprietess has some blankets, *non?*" Benet held up his hand to prevent further protest. "You have my word, my motives are of the purest nature. You are a lovely lady, but what man in his right mind would try to charm a woman with two children under tow? Besides, I have a tutoring appointment this afternoon with their mama."

So this was the French officer Audra Harrison had observed to be such a handsome gentleman! She had to agree with her sister-in-law's observation. With three pairs of expectant eyes upon her, she at last conceded.

"Since you are a family acquaintance, monsieur, we shall stay just long enough to warm by the fire and find wraps for us. We can't have Jerome and Alison taking a chill."

"You're the one who's sick all the time," Jerome observed indignantly.

"I think Unca Dillon keeps her locked up in her room like a pwinccss," Alison protested. "He stoled her from the enemy and won't let her go home. He's gonna lock us all up now."

"No one is going to lock anyone up," Rose spoke up, ushering Jerome in ahead of her while Claude Benet held open the door. Whatever must the man be thinking!

The coffee house was beginning to crowd with patrons from the businesses on George Street, although the bang of the noonday guns at the Citadel had not yet been heard. At Monsieur Benet's request, they were given a table near one of the two large stone fireplaces which were built back to back, splitting the building into separate rooms. The larger was reserved for the serving of food and the smaller for both business and social gatherings over the variety of drinks served from the taproom.

As Monsieur Benet finished ordering warm milk for the children and a mild flip for Rose and himself, a serving woman placed a steaming meat pudding on the small table behind them where a single gentleman dined alone. Alison climbed to her feet on the bench beside Rose and stared at the dish with longing.

"That looks good!"

"We'll just have the warm milk," Rose informed the hopeful child. "Joeli will have our luncheon ready by the time we get home." If the poor woman wasn't out searching the streets for them at that very moment.

Alison's high wail raked across Rose's spine like a nail on metal. Instead of shouting at the child, however, Rose crossed her arms and waited with a reproving glare.

"She must like to eat at taverns," she whispered aside to Jerome, so low that the other child immediately dropped her voice to a whine.

"We do."

"It's a shame she doesn't know how to behave in one like you do. I'd like to bring her back sometime, but not if she acts like this."

"You can bring me!" the boy suggested brightly.

"Me, too!" Alison whimpered.

"You don't know how to act," her brother reminded her smugly. "You're a crybaby."

At this Alison started to increase the volume and pitch of her objection. Rose knew every eye in the tavern was fixed on their table.

"See! You are!"

There was no need for her to say anything derogatory. Jerome was handling the situation nicely for her.

"But I would bet that your sister could act like a big girl if she wanted," Claude Benet suggested, picking up on Rose's strategy. "It is a shame that she does not."

"I do!" Alison informed him with an indignant sniff.

"A big girl does not shout. Do you see your aunt shouting, even though I am sure she is sorry she brought you in here. You are making all the people stare at her."

"I do!" the small girl averred, dropping to the seat beside Benet in a huff of ruffles.

Rose afforded the man a grateful glance. "So you *can* whisper, Alison! You know," she said to her conspirator, "I'll wager she can act like a lady. If she would, I wouldn't mind spending some time with her, you know, reading and maybe going on an outing or two."

"And me," Jerome interjected, not about to be left out. "I haven't cried once. Men don't, you know," he added with a degree of authority.

"Well, you certainly know how to speak in a low voice, which is what one does in a public place," Rose admitted with an encouraging smile.

By the time their refreshments were brought and the serving woman went into the back apartment to check with the proprietess about the loan of some blankets, Rose had promised to read a book to them, starting that very afternoon. Then the next day, they were to come back for a full luncheon, providing it was all right with their mother. Although the children invited Monsieur Benet and it was clear that the idea was appealing to the man, he declined.

"I fear I have presumed too much already."

"Your presumption has been our rescue, monsieur, although I am curious." Rose took a sip of the hot flip. It was wonderfully warming and light on the rum content, just as her companion had ordered.

"About what, madame?"

"Your accent. It comes and goes."

Claude Benet smiled widely. "Madame, if one is trying to get through an English crowd in these times without attracting attention which would detain them, one does not do it with a French accent. Fortunately, my English is without accent when I apply myself to that end."

"Well, Mrs. Harrison thinks you to be a fine teacher."

"She is a fine student. I find no fault with her memory when it comes to her study. It is sinful, this thing which happened to her."

"She doesn't remember us," Jerome spoke up solemnly. "But I think she still loves us."

"Of course she does!" Rose assured him, pulling him to her. "A mother never forgets her children in her heart. Never!"

Her eyes blurred with the sudden and unexpected anguish that surfaced in them. Two baby boys, so tiny, so still. She swallowed hard and buried her face in Jerome's wind-ruffled hair.

"Rose? Is that you?"

Rose blinked furiously to clear her vision, for she was certain her ears were deceiving her until she heard Alison gasp in sheer horror.

"Unca Dillon!"

Sixteen

The coach ride back to the elegant Argyle residence was cold and it had nothing to do with the temperature. Thanks to Claude Benet, who went on his way, Rose and the children each had a blanket. Rose pretended to be interested in the passing vehicles and pedestrians, but she could feel Dillon's icy gaze on her.

Admittedly, the situation he found her in did look somewhat scandalous. After refusing to speak to her husband and sequestering herself in their bedchamber for over a month, she was found in another man's company, in his coat no less! She'd watched Dillon's jaw square off sharply as she explained, a solo voice in a chorus of help from the children. At his explosive "Enough!," not to mention the drilling look he gave each of the little ones, they quieted so that Rose alone was left to sort the confusion.

"So you say these two are the cause of this?" her husband had asked, his gaze lashing out in reproval of the two wide-eyed youngsters staring up at him.

"They've been cooped up in the house, Dillon, with no diversion save shouts of reprimand. I can see where the prospect of a fire might induce them to seek some excitement."

"I can see where you would, madame."

"They weren't really thinking about the consequences . . ."

"Why does that not come as a surprise from either of you?"

"And we were going straight home as soon as we took off the chill," Rose went on, letting the gibe slide.

Dillon gave no more than a polite thank you to Claude Benet, insisted on paying the bill, and then herded them out to a hired coach with blankets wrapped about their shoulders like street beggars. It hadn't helped at all that she'd explained Benet was Audra's French tutor. He was clearly in a stew, about to boil over. The tension inside the cab of the coach was enough to expand its sides.

Although the trip was a short few blocks, moving amidst the traffic just beginning to thaw from the chaos created by the fire seemed to stretch out forever. When they finally came to a halt before the Mackay mansion, the children bolted for the door leaving Rose behind with her grim companion.

"They're not really bad children, Dillon. They're just full of life and misunderstood."

The dour look he cast at her before climbing out of the vehicle was the only objection to her observation he made.

Distracted by the grand welcome the youngsters were receiving at the door by servant and family alike, Rose accepted his hand as she stepped down to the cobbled walk leading to the front steps. Amanda and Audra had come home for the midday meal in the midst of the search for Rose and the youngsters and were beside themselves with worry. Henry was still out looking.

"I'll go see if I can spot him," Dillon offered, once Rose was delivered safely inside. "I'll deal with you later."

Before Rose could react, he bussed her on the cheek

with cold lips and exited to the waiting coach. Was that affection or a threat?

A threat, she decided with certainty, even though his whiskey-colored gaze had lost some of its hostility. Aside from Dillon's material generosity and polite inquiries as to her health, he'd really shown no interest in her since leaving Castine. Although the chaste kiss he'd left her with felt branded on her cheek despite his winter-chilled lips, it was just for show in front of his family, she was sure of it.

Rose hardly tasted the hot luncheon served in the long frescoed dining room a short while later. Even after Henry returned with the information that Master Dillon would join them for supper upon closing the office, the succulent pieces of pork tenderloin refused to go down. The children, who'd been permitted to join the table at Rose's request, however, were ravenous.

"They told me they knew how to behave in a tavern," she explained to Amanda and Audra. "I think this will be a good test for them. If they pass, I'd like to take them on an outing tomorrow."

"Do ye even know where to go, lassie?" Amanda Mackay asked skeptically.

"Monsieur Benet suggested Melville Island. He said there were lots of interesting wares there for youngsters."

"Isn't he wonderful?" Audra spoke up, her pale-green eyes dancing. "And he's absolutely right! It's amazing the things the prisoners make."

"You could go with us, Mama," Jerome suggested, his enthusiasm barely suppressed.

It was decided that Audra would accompany them, leaving Amanda Mackay a day of peace and quiet. By the time the meal was over, Rose was tired, but the children were too excited to be cajoled into taking a nap.

She'd promised to read to them and they'd not let her forget.

A leather-bound copy of *Aesop's Fables* was the book of choice. Rose talked the children into lying on her bed with her under a blanket, where, propped up against the pillows, she began the story of the dog and the manger. This led to a discussion of sharing and then another fable.

Rose had no idea when she drifted off to sleep, much less when Jerome and Alison did. When she awakened to see the light fading in the curtained window, neither of the children were in the bed. Evidently Joeli had moved them, just as she'd laid out one of the new, untried dresses Dillon had purchased for her.

Rose studied the white India muslin with its dark blue embroidery and adorning sash. There was a new chemise, too, trimmed in pale-blue ribbon and lace. She would wear it to supper, she decided, not because she feared annoying Dillon, but because she had nothing in her own trunk fit to be seen in public. If she was coming out of seclusion, it might as well be in style.

Joeli was so delighted that Rose had decided to dress and join the family for the evening meal that she flitted about the room like a hummingbird while her new mistress bathed in the citrus-scented water prepared for her. She chattered constantly, as much to herself as to anyone, and then set about fussing with Rose's freshly washed hair, brushing it to a dry sheen in front of the blazing hearth.

"Dat Cap'n Dillon, his eyes gonna jump right outta his head! I know'd you was de gal for 'im. It was in my bones."

"Your bones told you Dillon and I were meant to be together?" Rose queried skeptically. "Do they predict the weather, too?"

"Not deez bones, missy," the servant declared, pointing to herself. "Mah majick bones. Dey say it, den it's dest'ny. You make more babies, be real happy. Dat what Joeli see in de bones."

"I don't believe in magic," Rose replied, staring at her image in the mirror.

Although the transformation from the soot-stained urchin who'd undressed before it earlier did seem just that. She looked the elegant lady, even if that were not case. Like her marriage, it was a facade. Joeli's magic bones were no more reliable than all her grandfather's talk about the Beaujeu destiny to fall in love with the enemy.

Dillon wanted her because he wanted her ship. He treated her to all she could ask for because he owed that much to her father for his wicked deceit. His was a man's conscience, obliged only to men. The rest was a grand show.

Although he shared the master bedroom with her, he came to bed only after she was settled in for the night. There were stilted requests that she join the family for supper, but he'd made no sincere attempt to convince her to give up her seclusion. All he cared about was his fortune, his business, and catching the greedy hand in his pocket.

"Now doan you go downstairs yet. I promised dat little gal she kin see you in your new dress first." Joeli chuckled. "You done made yourself two leetle friends, dem two."

"I've discovered I have more in common with them than I thought."

It was true. They were in a strange home with no one who really wanted them. Like caged animals, they longed to be free. Together, the three of them might, at least, escape the physical confines of the house. As for being wanted . . .

Rose dismissed the rising doubt that shook her more

than she cared to admit. No, she certainly didn't want Dillon to want her! And she didn't want his attention, either, she told herself sternly.

After Joeli left the room, she sat down before the dressing table and concentrated on arranging her hair in the simple fashion she preferred. Those tightly curled styles which dangled over one's ears like bobbing springs involved burning her hair into submission, not the least appealing to Rose. Instead, she tied a blue ribbon the same shade as her sash around her head to keep her unbound tresses out of her face and then arranged the shorter pieces around her forehead, where they curled of their own rebellious accord in silken wisps.

She was in the process of choosing the right accessories from her casket of jewelry, which had miraculously remained with her through all her tribulation, when the door opened and Dillon Mackay stepped into the chamber. At the sight of Rose seated still at the dressing table he stopped short in his long stride toward the sofa at the opposite side of the room, where Joeli had put out an evening coat for the more formal meal being readied in the basement kitchen.

Rose met his gaze through the mirror, but could tell no more of his humor from it than she could that of his staring ancestors, whose portraits hung in gilded frames around the ball gallery. All she knew was that it missed no detail, not of her dress, nor her soul. She rose from the polished bench in a rustle of skirts, the cameo necklace she'd been considering clasped in her hand.

Damn him, he had no right to make her feel like this! She'd done nothing wrong. In fact, she'd saved his niece and nephew from God only knew what trouble. If he thought to intimidate her, then he'd best think again.

"I am not the least bit sorry for what I did today. I did it in the interest of the children!" she announced, lifting her chin in defiance. "So if you are going to deal with something, deal with that, Dillon Mackay!"

Still nothing in his expression or manner to betray what he was thinking, she fretted, holding her ground as he silently approached her, tossing the russet coat he'd pulled off on his way up the stairs over the foot rail of the bed.

"You should be bloody grateful! In case you hadn't noticed, this household is ashamble with disorder! That nanny is too absorbed in herself to care what happens to those children!"

He was close now, too close to maintain the assault of her flashing blue gaze without crooking her neck upward. His lawn shirt still carried the scent of a closed-in office meeting tinged with a sweet tobacco smoke. Then there was that spice talc he applied to the rippling flesh beneath it that morning in front of his shaving mirror, unaware that she watched him from beneath half-lidded eyes.

She wouldn't back down, no matter what he did, Rose averred silently. She'd been right in everything she'd done and, by thunder, if there was any dealing to be done, *she'd* do it!

"And I think you owe Monsieur Benet and myself an apology for your scandalous suspicions. Oh, you didn't say a word, but your behavior was ample insult!"

There, she thought, catching sight of a brief flicker of something in that unfathomable expression. At his side his fists clenched and then unleashed with painful slowness. At least she was getting some reaction.

"Well?" Rose demanded.

The way he grasped the bare flesh of her arm exposed by the puffed sleeves of her garment bore no resemblance to the anger which she suspected had drawn his fists taut but a moment before. Instead of biting into her soft skin, his fingers skimmed over it, leaving a trail of gooseflesh in their wake.

"Dillon!" As she started to pull away, his grasp tightened, gentle, but nonetheless restraining. Her mouth went dry as his body moved to contain her in the curve of the dressing table."Wh-what are you doing?"

"Apologizing."

Rose's eyes widened as he ran his tongue over his lips in a titillating manner and lowered them, moist and warm to her own. The kiss was not hard with passion, but possessed of a tender sensuality. Such was its captivation that it never once occurred to Rose to withdraw from it. It was all she could do to deal with the ballyhoo of blazes that infected her with each earnest swell of pressure, each heady brush, each cajoling taste he took of her mouth.

She'd prepared to do battle, but not this kind. When he drew away, she could barely stand.

"You . . . you're not angry?"

Now that was an effective rebuff! Rose tried to summon another, but Dillon's arms, now wrapped around her, made it exceedingly difficult. She started to try again, but the lopsided curl of his lip stopped her.

"Welcome back to the world of the living, Rosebud."

"What?"

Rather than repeating himself, Dillon kissed her again, long and thoroughly. A thousand responses leapt to life, proving his word that she had rejoined the living. She was alive, every part of her, and hungry for that which she'd only been introduced to. The realization only deepened her disappointment when he at last released her and backed away.

Was this what she'd really wanted all along? She stared up at him in disbelief.

His own breath as ragged as hers, he took another

step back, as though he needed that distance to restore himself. When he spoke, his voice was strained. "My apologies for my zeal, madame. Suffice it to say, I was beginning to think you would waste away in this room."

Although Rose was not certain she knew whom he sounded like, she knew it wasn't Dillon Mackay. Dillon was driven by passion, not propriety. What had starched his drawers? Whatever it was, it thankfully had the same cooling effect on her. A moment more in his arms and she'd have . . .

"A less demonstrative apology would have been acceptable."

"But not nearly as enjoyable." He bent down and picked up the necklace she'd dropped.

Rose turned away, only to realize the mirror betrayed the scarlet flush of her cheeks. Staring straight ahead, she waited while Dillon fastened the chain about her neck. She tried not to flinch at the contact of his warm fingers on flesh that had become so sensitive. Impulsively, she reached for a vial of expensive perfume and, all too aware that he stood no more than a heartbeat away from her back, proceeded to dab a modest measure on the aroused spot, to rub out the lingering sensation of his touch.

"I like that about you, Rosebud. I never did care for women who bathed in perfume. You always smack of soap and fresh air."

When had he noticed that, Rose wondered, meeting that impenetrable gaze in the mirror uncertainly. It occurred to her that she was not the only one surreptitiously watching the other.

"Like a lye-scrubbed deck, eh?"

Her chuckle was nervous as she replaced the vial and moved away. He didn't try to stop her. For that she was grateful. At a loss as to what to do, she picked up his discarded jacket and exchanged it for the more elegant one she'd seen him wear in the evening, an Egyptian-brown affair with black collar and cuff. Upon handing it to him, she turned to close the door of the mahogany clothes press.

"You do remind me of a ship," he acknowledged, "although you could stand a bit more tumblehome."

"I've been ill," she admitted grudgingly.

"Well, now that you've made up your mind to leave this room, I'm sure you'll fill out in no time at all." Dillon shrugged on the jacket with affection and held out his arm expectantly. "Well, madame?"

Rose tried to consider what possible commitment or concession could there be in accepting it. All she could discern was that it would be rude to do otherwise. After all, he'd apologized, quite thoroughly, she mused, still aglow, both inside and out, from the encounter. He'd even given her a compliment, though most women would not have thought so. To be compared to a ship was considerable recognition in the eyes of a man like Dillon Mackay.

Supper that night was an enjoyable affair. The meat pasties accompanied by winter greens, turnips, and fresh breads were ample and thrifty as well, considering they made use of the leftover pork served that day at noon. Since Dillon had coaxed Rose out of their room before Alison had the chance to see her, Rose cajoled him into letting the little ones join them again for supper.

Jerome, determined not to allow this rare privilege be the last, sat at Dillon's left and mimicked his behavior to the point that Rose had to contain herself to keep from laughing. She even thought she saw Dillon crack a smile when the boy asked Henry to refill his milk after the servant had topped off Dillon's wineglass. As for Alison, her only transgression was picking at the dark blue flowers on Rose's dress. After a reminder that adults ate at the supper table rather than played with their clothes, however, the tow-haired cherub finished her portion with an endearing vengeance.

"I'm glad you got to meet Monsieur Benet before he leaves us, Dillon," Amanda spoke up when the conversation turned from the progress of the work on the *Border Rose* to the fire.

"He's going back to France?"

"Nay, Audra's friend is leaving for the West Indies to meet her fiancé's family and will nae be havin' more lessons."

"Monsieur Benet said nothing about it today," Rose remarked in surprise.

"He didn't find out until we did, this afternoon."

So that was why Dillon's sister had pulled such a long face during the entire meal. At the tavern earlier, Rose could have sworn she'd seen the same curious glow in Claude Benet's eye at the mention of Audra Mackay Harrison's name she'd seen in Audra's when the young woman discovered the rescuer of Rose and her children had been her French teacher. More certain than ever that her suspicions were not completely unfounded, Rose turned to Dillon.

"Perhaps we could have Monsieur Benet continue the French lessons here," she suggested. "Six is not too early to begin studying the language."

"I don't need to speak French!" Jerome protested.

"And if it's French Audra enjoys so much," Dillon added to the boy's argument, "you can teach her."

Dillon knew she spoke fluent French. She used to teach him choice curses when her father wasn't about. "But my French isn't as proper as that of an educated gentleman to whom the language is native. Why, I could use some lessons, too."

Her husband cleared his throat. She'd made her point. "So, am I to understand that Monsieur Benet would teach, not just Audra and the reluctant Jerome here, but you as well?"

Rose nodded, uncertain as to what exactly was going through Dillon's mind. Was that amusement flickering in the russet hues of his searching gaze? Or was it annoyance?

Next to him, Jerome squirmed in his seat, a look of the damned on his face. The boy clearly thought he was on the sacrificial block, yet he did his best to act the adult about it.

Rose waited expectantly for the verdict Dillon mulled over in his mind. He was being maneuvered and he knew it.

"Very well, if Amanda will make the arrangements, I'll see to the financing."

Jerome practically deflated, sinking in his chair until his dismayed eyes were table level.

"And we can see if Monsieur Benet feels Jerome ready to learn a new language," Rose offered out of sympathy.

"He talks like the men who attacked us. Maybe he's a bad man."

"What's that?" Dillon asked the boy in surprise. "You say the men who attacked your mother's coach were French?"

"Some, I guess."

Dillon's reaction had been so fervent, Jerome shrank down even further, as if to avoid his gaze. Seeing this, the man softened his voice.

"That's very important to know for sure, Jerome."

"They talk funny!" Alison chirped, not one to let attention pass her by.

"Not the man in charge," her brother contradicted.

"So he was English?"

"He was dirty," Jerome answered. "He had a long beard and long hair."

"I don't give a damn if he bathed, I just want to know if he spoke English or French!"

At the snap of Dillon's patience, both children stiffened against their chair backs.

"Children," Rose spoke up, diverting their attention and, at the same time, soothing them with her voice. "Uncle Dillon isn't angry at you. He's angry because he wants to catch the bad men who hurt your mama and the ones who are sinking his ships. He needs your help."

With a wary glance at Dillon, Jerome exhaled heavily. It was clear that whatever had been on the child's mind had been blown away by the blast of frustration.

"Maybe if I tell you what I know," Dillon ventured, mimicking Rose's manner. "Some of the people who have traded with these pirate crews thought some of the members might be French. I find it curious that this might be the case . . ."

Not the least interested in the conversation, Alison turned to Rose. "He don't like us, does he?"

Tiny as the child's whisper was, it struck Dillon dumb. Never had Rose seen such a confounded look on his face. He opened his mouth to deny the accusation, but nothing came out.

"And if he don't like us, he won't like his own children, either," the child went on with prim indignation.

"Here now, child, ye've said enough!" Amanda Mackay snatched the little girl up in her arms as she rose from the table. "Henry, take the children to Mavis!"

Dillon had gone white as he watched his stepmother hand Alison over to the manservant. The scrape of Jerome's chair beside him failed to distract him from the little girl's sad, accusing look, which seemed to hold him with unrelenting bonds. Only when the boy put a small hand on his arm did they break.

"I'll help you catch those bad men, sir."

Dillon took the child's hand in his own and shook it. His voice was strained tight as the cords standing out on his neck as he answered. "Thank you, lad, later. We'll discuss it later, I promise."

Seventeen

After a thick butter rum pudding for dessert, the ladies retired to the back parlor, while Dillon retreated to his office. Oddly, Rose felt an urge to join him, to tell him Alison had meant nothing by what she said. He stated that he had notes to compile and would not be much company.

It was at his desk that Rose found him later, after the children came downstairs to say good night. The two skipped into the parlor where the women chatted quietly by the hearth. They begged Rose to read them another story before they had to go to sleep. She agreed, but only after they bade their uncle good night as well.

If this was the family she had to be part of, then by heaven, it would be a cohesive one. Innocent as it may have been, putting the fear of Dillon in the children as a means to intimidate them into proper behavior was absurd. Fear had no place in a home, only respect and love. While Amanda Mackay represented that, the aging matron was overwhelmed by all the that had befallen the family. Rose intended to become an ally in the restoration of respect, order, and love.

Dillon obviously heard her charges' rambunctious approach, for he'd put aside the bottle of liquor he'd been sampling without a glass when they entered the room and sat watching the door as they entered. Rose de-

tected the smell of Scotch whiskey. She'd noticed the
same smell some nights when Dillon came to their
room, but she said nothing about it or the uncommon
strain that showed in his eyes.

Had she been so wrapped up in her own suffering
that she'd missed his? She'd pictured Dillon stalking
about Halifax like an angry god, ready to exact a pound
of flesh for the attacks on his family and business. Now
it was plain that this was not the case. Circumstances
must be worse than Amanda had let on, for Dillon
wasn't the sort given to drink when faced with a quandary.

"The man in charge of the bad men didn't speak like
Monsieur Benet. He was kind'a like us," Jerome told
him. "An' he had a blue mark on his arm."

"A tattoo," Dillon observed. "What kind of picture
was it?"

"I can't remember. It wasn't a flower, but it wasn't . . .
I don't know what it was."

"That's all right, Jerome. I know you must have been
scared."

Jerome stood a little taller. "I was with Mama. Her
head was bleeding and I held it off the dirt."

Dillon grimaced in an attempt to smile and glanced
uncertainly at Rose as he weighed his words. "Well, I'm
glad she had a man with her."

Jerome cleared his throat, drawing Dillon's attention
back to his small, extended hand, which the latter took
and shook firmly.

"I thank you, lad, and I apologize for getting angry
earlier. I've a lot on my mind of late."

"I don't mind. You just find the bad men so Mama
will be safe." The boy dropped his head and backed
away. "Good night, sir."

Standing off to the side, Alison twisted her nightdress

in front of her and looked up at Dillon with wary green eyes.

"I cwied," she admitted candidly. "I thought Mama was dead."

"I don't blame you, Alison. There are times when even grown men wish they could cry, you know." The anguished slip Dillon hastily swallowed tugged at Rose's chest.

Once Alison decided Dillon approved of her behavior as well, she walked forward and held open her arms. "Girls hug nighty-night," she informed him with a prim purse of rosy lips, which she brushed across his cheek when he leaned down and followed her lead.

"Where does that come from?" she asked, reaching for the slight stubble which had abraded her soft skin. With pinching fingers, she tried to gain a hold on it in wonder.

"The same place your hair comes from." Dillon cut a pleading glance at Rose, as if afraid to move and frighten the little girl away.

"My hair is soft. This is hard."

"It gets that way when a boy grows into a man," Rose suggested. She'd never really given the matter much thought. She ran the back of her hand along Dillon's cheek experimentally.

This time he did jerk away, startling both Rose and Alison. "I have work to do, ladies . . . and gentleman," he added for the benefit of the boy staring at a small brass compass which rested in a case on the corner of the desk.

"Dillon's right!"

Rose immediately set about herding the children toward the door. Whatever had possessed her to touch him like that? With one fleeting dart of insanity, she'd been tempted to gather his head to her breast and offer him comfort—Dillon Mackay, the beast that had cruelly spurned her love and torn her from her home to bring her to enemy soil!

"Off to bed with you," she said, patting Alison on the bottom as she skipped out after her brother. "I'll be up to read you your story once you're tucked in."

She waited at the door until the retreating stampede faded overhead, indicating they'd gone into the opposite wing of the house. What kept her, she wasn't sure. More insanity?

Perhaps it was the raw pain she'd glimpsed earlier on Dillon's face, inflicted by an innocent child's observation. Or maybe it was the panic on his face when Alison had hugged him. It was the first sign of vulnerability she'd ever witnessed in the man she thought she knew so well. Or maybe, it occurred to her, this was the first sign that he really needed her, if for no other reason than to act the intermediary and settle his household into a semblance of order.

"I don't dislike those children," he said tersely, reaching again for the bottle. "But I can't say I like them, either. They're too . . ." He searched for a word as he pulled the cork. "Too undisciplined."

"Like green apprentices not used to discipline or the ways of a ship."

"Precisely!"

"And what do you do with those raw swabs? Do you turn them loose with your ship and expect them to know what to do?"

Dillon took a swig of the liquor and winced as he swallowed. "Never, they need . . ."

"Training," Rose provided for him. "Children aren't so different. Considering what I've heard, these two have had precious little of it."

"And their mother was spoiled beyond measure. Maybe even I was to blame for that. Audra's such a sweet pretty girl. Father and I denied her nothing."

Although touched by the spark of affection when he spoke of his younger stepsister, Rose drew him back on course. "And what happens when you've a crew that's been at sea under strict discipline for a long while and you put into port?"

"The bloody bastards go berserk! Can't get them back to the ship for all the gold on the seven seas!"

Rose smiled, watching her point sink in. "Precisely." Turning, she started for the door.

"Where are you off to?"

"To read a bedtime story."

"Ah!" Dillon nodded, all the while looking into her eyes as though searching for more of an answer.

Rose smiled shyly. "They were very sweet today and seemed so interested. I enjoyed being needed."

Rose thought he was going to rise and approach her, the way he set aside the Scotch and placed his hands on the desk in front of him. She held her breath at the off chance that Dillon might recognize just how much *he* needed her, that he might admit it. Instead, he moved his chair back and reached for a ledger behind him, which he laid on the desk.

"Then I shall join you later."

The idea bolstered her heart momentarily until she realized the reply was no more than a figure of speech, a dismissal. Before she left the room, Dillon opened a ledger in front of him and began to study it, as though he'd already forgotten her.

Why that was so disturbing was beyond her. She'd done such a good job of convincing herself that she wanted nothing to do with Dillon Mackay and, after one simple kiss—no, two, she reminded herself—her carefully erected defenses were breaking at the seams.

Alison and Jerome were waiting in the big guest bed when Rose went to the makeshift nursery. Mavis Adams had started one of the stories in an impatient monotone, her brightly painted nails tapping on the back of the book as if to hasten its end. The nanny rose from the upholstered rocker reserved for that purpose and handed the book over to Rose.

"Shall I come back when you're finished?" she asked, her manner implying that it would be an ordeal, but she would do it.

"I'll stay with them until they're asleep, but I would think you'd look in on them before you retired next door."

"Oh, yes. Of course I will." She yawned. "I think I need a nice rum toddy to tuck me in. Shall I fix you one, Mrs. Mackay? I always do one for Miss Audra. Helps her sleep, you know."

"Thank you, no. I'll sleep just fine after today's excitement and so, I think, will these two."

Although Rose started right where Mavis had left off, Jerome was more interested in what his uncle Dillon was going to do to the bad men when he caught them. After much gory speculation, which his sister found distasteful enough to make little retching sounds, he finally settled down under the covers to hear the true story of how the *Thorne* was taken by shavers who were eventually captured.

"When I get bigger, do you think Uncle Dillon will let me sail on one of his ships? I could grow up to be the best gunner he ever saw." The boy's opinion of Dillon had grown to great proportion after hearing how the captain had outwitted the pirates and blown up his ship, taking two of the pirate vessels with him.

"He'll yell at you," Alison mumbled sleepily.

"That's what captains do, Ally."

"Jerome has a point," Rose chimed in. "Dillon is used to commanding a ship and giving orders. He punishes his men strictly for not following them, but he also cares for them enough to risk his life so that they might escape."

Rose waited for Ally to pop another perplexing question at her, but the little girl had drifted off to sleep, her rag doll clutched to her chest. A glance at Jerome told her that he was not far from doing the same himself.

"I'm gonna be like Uncle Dillon when I grow up," he told Rose, blinking furiously to hold his eyes open. "I might get mad and yell sometimes, but I'd never drink too many flips like Papa and hit Mama or Ally. I'd just fight with men who needed to be taught a lesson."

Leaning over his bed, Rose kissed his cheek, her heart twisting in her chest at the pained confession the little boy made. She could think of no comforting words to assuage the raised furrows on his brow. Instead, she gently brushed them away with her fingers.

"I don't want Papa to come for Christmas. He always loses his money and drinks too much rum and gets mean to us."

"Well, he'll not do that with Uncle Dillon around . . . or me, for that matter. I promise!"

What manner of beast had Audra married, Rose wondered, kissing the child once again. One last glance at his face, illuminated by a low-burning lamp kept on the dresser in the nursery, showed his pale lashes had settled like golden down upon round cheeks.

Beautiful, she thought, closing the door quietly behind her. They were beautiful children, like small angels laying there in their beds. All they needed was love and attention, a showing of the ropes, she thought with a grin.

Rose crossed the upstairs hall to the master wing, all the while trying to ignore the unbidden vision of two dark-haired babies wrapped in a linen sheet, still and blue. They'd been beautiful, too, in their own way. Had the breath of life flushed color to their skin, the little boys might have been miniature cherubs. Well that's what they truly were now.

Below, the tall grandfather clock struck on the hour, startling Rose from her troubled thought. Her hand on her chest, she paused at the gallery rail and stared down the beautiful cascade of steps. It was such a grand affair, like something she'd pictured in a castle, not a house, although, she had to admit, this was no ordinary house.

It was hard to believe she was the mistress of such a place, she thought, testing the smoothness of the polished wood with her finger. The enormity of such a task made Rose glad that Amanda Mackay was still in control. Although the girl had seen her grandmother run *Annanbrae,* seeing was one thing, knowing was another. She'd be content to try to help with the children. Maybe someday her own would fill the halls with laughter. The idea jolted her. It had only materialized because the doctor had told her she was made for having babies.

"Here we go, Master Dillon! Two hot rum toddies, one for you and one for me."

Mavis Adams's distinct voice drifted up the stairwell to where Rose stood, banishing any further consideration of the matter of motherhood. Why was Mavis waiting on Dillon? Where was Henry?

Above the muffled fall of Mavis's slippered feet across the carpet, the nanny spoke again. "A hardworking man like yourself needs a bit of relaxation, especially what with things as they are with your wife. Do you want me to rub that neck and shoulders like I did last night?"

Rose strained to hear Dillon's answer, but it was cut off by the click of the library door closing. Mavis and Dillon? Pulling a wretched face, she spun away from the balcony and marched straight to the master bedchamber.

It was absurd. Surely Dillon could see what sort of woman Mavis Adams was. Rose worked at the fastenings on the back of her dress and swore in frustration. She never needed help with her old clothes, but her new dresses were designed for an affluent wearer, one with a maid who could fasten the back closing for her.

In a huff, Rose pulled the cord next to the large bed to summon Joeli and then plopped on the edge of the mattress in annoyance. She'd never get used to this lifestyle, especially if it included keeping the likes of Mavis Adams about.

"The hell with it!"

Rose jumped back to her feet and stormed out of the room. Upon meeting Joeli at the top of the stairs, she dismissed the puzzled maid with a sharp, "Never mind!" and took to the steps with billowing skirts. If she was going to manage Dillon's household, the least he could do was unfasten the back of her bloody dress!

"Mrs. Mackay!" Mavis Adams gasped as Rose barged into the library, slamming the double doors back against the bookcases to either side of them.

Rose stopped in front of the desk and took in Dillon's loosened shirt, not to mention the painted fingers which were frozen beneath it.

"Do you need something, Rose?" Dillon asked, unaffected by her sudden intrusion.

"Mavis, I'd suggest you take your toddy to your room and check on the children before you drink it."

Mavis slowly withdrew her hands from Dillon's shoulders and took up one of the steaming cups from the desk. "Maybe I should fix you one, madame. You seem to have your skirts in a twist."

She'd like to twist them around Mavis Adams's neck, but instead of saying so, Rose smiled. "Nothing my husband can't help me with, I assure you." She drilled

Mavis with a challenging look which followed the grudgingly silent nanny to the door.

"May I inquire as to what that was about?" Dillon tilted his chair back and crossed his arms. "One day I can't get you out of your room and the next, you want to take over the house!"

Rose stepped up to the desk and shoved the long legs propping him backward to the floor, uprighting him abruptly. "I'll tell you what it's about!" she blurted out hotly. "It's . . ." Her mind blanked out as Dillon rose to his feet, so that she had to look up at him. "It's about this damned dress!" she rallied in relief. "I'd need arms long as my legs to unfasten it!"

"So you want me to unfasten your dress for you?"

Rose bristled at Dillon's mocking manner.

"Hell, no! You might hurt your neck and shoulders."

One corner of his mouth pulled to the side in mild amusement. "You haven't spoken of your own accord to me since leaving Castine and now you're jealous! My God, but you're a mercurial creature!"

"Jealous!" Rose echoed incredulously. She pivoted, stepped away, and then turned back. "If there was any jealousy this day, sir, it was yours at the coffee house. I was appalled for Monsieur Benet!"

"I'll say one thing for you, when your wind shifts, there's no sign of it coming. Turn around, Rosebud."

"All my other dresses fasten up the front where a girl can dress herself. This fashion nonsense is absurd!" Rose fumed, pulling at her skirt self-consciously. "Why couldn't you have these dresses made like them?"

The chuckle at her back did nothing to improve her indignation. "I will have to pay more attention to your likes and dislikes, now that you've decided to act my wife as opposed to my prisoner."

"I'm stuck with it, so I might as well make the most of a bad situation! Remember, you could be footloose and fancy free if you hadn't brought me back with you!" she said, glaring over her shoulder. "Mavis could rub anything you wanted her to!"

Dillon laughed outright this time, a rich pealing sound Rose had not heard in a long time. Her chest swelling with pique, she turned with a stomp, only to have her dress drop in a swirl at her feet as she did so. Belatedly, she went after it with one of the fists she'd raised to pommel him, while setting the other to its original course.

She was successful in neither attempt. The material which skimmed down over the silken weave of her chemise and petticoats was too fast, as fast as the hand which grasped her assaulting wrist in midair and wrestled it behind her.

"Green is a becoming color on you, Rosebud. I've never seen you wear it so boldly. As long as I know you, life will never be boring."

Rose tried to wriggle out of Dillon's militant hold, but her twisted arm felt as though it were ready to pop from her shoulder. "You're hurting me!"

He released her instantly, permitting her to back away. The tangle of her dress, however, hung in her feet, and in a moment, Rose was in the strong circle of Dillon's arms. All trace of his earlier humor had disappeared as he stared down at her earnestly.

"I'd never intentionally hurt you, Rosebud, though God knows I've inadvertently caused you enough agony to last a lifetime. Believe it, if you can, but I suffered with you, like nothing I've ever been through before."

The hands at her back seemed to caress as though reluctant to give her up, yet they did. With a deep breath, Dillon stepped back, the light in his gaze snuffed like the expression on his face.

"Our marriage isn't what either of us envisioned, but perhaps we might renew some of the friendship we knew before this blasted war. Consider the house a ship and the people its crew. If we do that, we might make it a tolerable place to exist."

Although her skin still burned from the confinement of Dillon's brief embrace, Rose reached down and drew up the plaguing dress over her shoulders. A ship and a crew, she thought, recalling the voyage from Castine to Halifax where the barrier of noncommunication had kept them apart. She supposed the involvement in the Mackay household wouldn't be much different, though now she and Dillon were speaking, even more, touching. As she nodded and turned to leave, she found herself wondering which situation was worse.

The quandary robbed her of sleep that night, at least enough to notice that Dillon never came to their room. The green streak her husband outrageously accused her of possessing would not give up the suspicion that he might have gone to Mavis's room.

So the restless night had passed, leaving Rose less than bright the following morning when the children burst into her room. They'd had their breakfast, she was informed, and had put on their very best clothes to go to the prison market. With a glance at Dillon's undisturbed bed on the sofa, Rose crawled out of her own to start the day.

Bedecked in a high day dress of peony-red corded muslin topped with a woolen fur-lined cloak to fend off the winter chill, she later climbed into the family coach with Audra and her two excited charges for the adventure to Melville Island. Amanda had suggested they take Henry with them, but Rose assured them their driver was all the escort they would need.

Signs of the most recent snowfall glistened in the sunlight which filtered through the buildings along the eastern side of Barracks Street. To her right, Rose could see the Citadel, a formidable presence that was as much a reminder of the war at hand as the multitude of uniformed men in red coats who filled the streets.

All Rose could think of was the island she knew to lie in the harbor beyond, the one with the hanging bodies, savagely torn by the wildlife and the elements. Rather than dwell on the gruesome sight which had first welcomed her to Halifax, she concentrated on the passing scenery, which, as they left the town, became denser and denser with trees. They followed a fjord, Audra informed her, called the Northwest Arm, at the end of which, they would find Melville Island floating in a round cove on its western side.

Eventually, Rose saw it for herself, a small green swatch of land surrounded by saltwater, its only approach a wooden bridge which crossed the creek separating it from the shoreline. There was a plain wooden dwelling at one end for the British officers' quarters. A distance away was another for the common soldiers. All the way to the back of the island was the prison itself, an old converted fish house according to Audra. It was surrounded by tall, spiked fences with sentry boxes here and there about its circumference.

"You certainly know a lot about this place."

Audra blushed. "Monsieur Benet spent a lot of time here before he was paroled. He told my friend and me about it. And of course, Mother has brought me here," she added hastily. "Most of the prisoners now are . . ."

"Americans," Rose supplied when the young woman broke off with another rush of embarrassment. "It's not your fault our countries are at war, any more than it's mine."

Audra reached over and squeezed Rose's hand. "I can see why Dillon fell in love with you. You're not only pretty, but understanding, too."

Understanding? Rose could hardly accept credit for being that. Evidently her husband had done a good job in convincing his family he loved her, as he had her own.

The market ran the length of the long, narrow building which housed the prisoners. It reminded Rose of an Oriental bazaar, with the tradesmen squatting at the end of their hammocks, their wares spread before them in the gangway. While most sold their crafts, others added the spice of gambling with a wheel-of-fortune where the patron paid a sixpence for a spin. The prizes ranged from a bone toothpick with case to small busts carved of famous personages from King George to Napoleon, to George Washington.

Jerome and Alison were mesmerized by the assortment of toys made from wood and bone, including small replicas of boats, a wide variety of games, and dolls with jointed arms and legs clad in neatly sewn clothes made from material scraps. There were knitted hats and embroidered garters, as well as fine needlework of every description. Gold and silversmiths sold rings, lockets, and brooches made from melted-down coins.

Allowed to choose one item each, the children shopped long and hard through the rows of wares. Rose found it difficult to keep up, not only with the little ones, but with their mother, who was constantly wandering off, staring at the crowds with that blank look she often wore. Jerome finally chose an exquisite replica of a corvette, rigged with human hair. Alison, torn between a doll and a pair of small painted slippers, opted for the doll after much deliberation and discussion with its maker, an Irish woodcarver who spun an intriguing yarn about its name and heritage. His fellow prison mate had done the needlework on its petticoat, he revealed.

Rose made some purchases of her own. Her favorite was a boat-shaped music box, which, when the small hatch was lifted, played a halting yet melodic rendition of a sweet ballad about a lost love. Given the chance to name it herself, she naturally asked the vendor to paint *Border Rose* across its stern. After all, it did have a lady figurehead, although her features were indistinct.

Outside the long buildings were peddlers from Halifax who plied their trade in hopes of garnering some of the moneys the prisoners made. Makeshift canopies were set up where shaves and haircuts were being offered for a fee, while others represented the stalls of tailors, who took orders for suits and gowns. Rose, Audra, and the children stopped at one of the stalls near the exit to watch a crude adaptation of a Punch and Judy puppet show.

"In this one, the Americans may triumph if none of the guards are watching too closely."

Rose glanced over her shoulder in surprise to see Claude Benet standing behind them. He extended his hand to her in greeting and then turned to offer the same to Audra. No longer was the young woman off in some other world. Instead, she literally glowed with the awareness of this one, and, in particular, the presence of her tall, dark tutor.

"Monsieur Benet, how wonderful to see you!" she exclaimed. "I have the most wonderful news! Dillon has asked Mother to arrange for you to resume my lessons, as well as take on my sister-in-law and my son as students!"

"*Alors,* that *is* good news!" Claude Benet nodded at Rose and then looked down at Jerome. "So you wish to learn to speak French, eh?"

"No, Mama says I need to."

"Honesty becomes you, young man. Perhaps I can find a way to make it interesting."

Jerome obviously didn't think so, but, rather than disagree, he turned back to the show as the group gathered around it broke into laughter over the absurd antics of the puppets.

"So you've decided not to return to France with your fellow countrymen, monsieur?" Rose inquired politely.

"I fear I have fallen in love with this cold and blustery country of yours, Madame Mackay. I have lived here in this one place longer than I have lived anywhere else. I've made many friends whom I should miss, were I even lucky enough to secure passage back to France."

"So you've no family?"

"None of any consequence. Distant relatives, I believe you call them, none concerned with my whereabouts or activities. It is my hope to obtain a full-time teaching position here."

"You have my best wishes for success, sir," Rose told the man sincerely.

"And mine as well," Audra concurred, going so far as to grasp the gentleman's hand in her own.

Upon realizing her zeal, she dropped it and blushed. Pale as Dillon's sister was, Rose found it curious that even the mention of her tutor's name could rouse a healthy color to her cheeks.

Pretending not to notice, Rose stifled a sudden yawn behind a gloved hand and glanced up at the bright sun overhead. "Heavens, it must be noon!" As if on cue, the faint thunder of the guns from the Citadel echoed in the distance.

"Such a sense of timing, madame," Claude Benet teased. "I am impressed!"

"I'm hungry!" Alison announced, turning as the curtain to the makeshift stage dropped to end the show.

"We'll need to hurry to travel to the tavern and still have the children home in time for their naps," Rose fretted. She'd promised Joeli and Amanda she'd not make a whole day of it, since they did not consider her or the children up to such an endeavor their first time out together.

"Perhaps Monsieur Benet would like to accompany us? Or did you hire a coach?"

Claude Benet smiled. "In these days, mesdames, I walk. At least until I find regular employment."

"Then you must ride with us!" Audra insisted. "It will give you a chance to get to know Jerome!"

For a young lady who never seemed to care what she did or where she went, Dillon's sister had suddenly developed more than her share of will. However, Rose was not averse to offering their future tutor a ride.

"By all means, Monsieur Benet. You must join us. We owe you that much for finding the children yesterday."

"But your husband . . ." Benet hesitated awkwardly.

"Won't mind at all," Rose finished. "He didn't yesterday, either. He was simply preoccupied with other matters and taken aback when he saw me and the children at the coffee house. He . . . umm . . . apologized last night, as a matter of fact."

"Bien, then I will be glad to accept your kind offer."

When Mr. Tibbet saw them emerge from the stockade, he pulled the coach out of the line of vehicles belonging to those who were also visiting the island prison. Some of the groups had even brought along picnic lunches, which they ate within the confines of their carriages, while others made meals of the meat and fruit pies sold by the town vendors.

"Look, there's Uncle Dillon!" Jerome shouted, pointing to a group of gentlemen approaching the bridge from the direction of the attendant's cottage.

Most of the men were in uniform, all red except for one. As they came closer, engaged in conversation, Rose recognized Captain Stevenson from the *Byron* in the one blue jacket. The others, she assumed, aside from her husband, were officers in charge of the prison, although what business Dillon had with them was a puzzle. Was he checking on Claude Benet?

"Unca Dillon, come see my doll!" Alison shouted.

Or was Dillon following her? Rose wondered, raising her hand to wave as her husband looked in their direction. It was certainly no secret that she and Audra planned a visit to the island.

Alison ran to meet Dillon as he excused himself from the company. He tucked a packet of some sort within his coat and leaned down to examine her treasured purchase with a strained grin.

"I don't know much about dolls, Alison," he admitted, "but this appears to be a good one."

"It is! Her name is Erin. That means Ireland, 'cause that's where the man said she was born. Her stockings are painted on, so I can't lose them. They're green, like her eyes and mine."

Dillon pretended to compare those of the doll to Alison's dancing ones. "So they are. I suppose you could be sisters."

"I'm going to be her mama," Alison patiently corrected him. "But you can hold her."

"Well, actually I'm busy at the moment." Dillon rose from the squatting position he'd assumed to examine the doll. "Captain Stevenson is waiting for me."

"I got a ship. A corvette, Aunt Rose called it," Jerome spoke up, holding it up for his uncle to see.

"I'd like to take a closer look at that later if you don't mind, lad. Right now, I'm working on that information you gave me last night about the men who attacked your mother's coach speaking like Frenchmen."

The young boy's chest swelled with pride at his uncle's acknowledgment, but Claude Benet was astonished.

"*Mon Dieu,* tell me this is not so! No gentleman of

France would attack a coach with women and children. They must be Romans, these fiends!"

"So we meet again, sir." Dillon extended his hand to the man. His manner was like yesterday, polite and no more.

"But what you say, it is incredible!" Benet went on, accepting the handshake.

"I don't think we are speaking of gentlemen of any nationality, Monsieur Benet, nor do we speak of privateers."

"They're bloodthirsty pirates!" Jerome announced with excitement. "And Uncle Dillon is going to catch them and put them on Hangman's Beach!"

"You were transferred overland from Annapolis Royal yourself, weren't you, monsieur?"

So he *had* been checking on Claude Benet! Rose looked at Dillon in alarm. Surely he wasn't suggesting the tutor was even remotely associated with the likes of the scoundrels they spoke of.

"I believe you already know that, Captain Mackay," Benet answered with a slight smile.

"I'd be interested in speaking to you about your transfer in greater detail, but, as I said before, I am keeping the Royal Navy waiting at the moment."

"Perhaps Monsieur Benet could be our guest for supper this evening. The two of you could speak then," Audra suggested brightly. "That would also give Mother the opportunity to make the arrangements for his tutoring position without her having to go out in this cold."

There was an awkward moment of silence before Dillon conceded. "Very well, if it suits the gentleman."

"But of course!" Benet replied.

Rose put her hand on Dillon's arm. "We've offered to give the monsieur a ride back to town. It's the least we can do after he came to my rescue yesterday with the children."

"The least!" Audra concurred. "I am ever so grateful!"

"I look forward to seeing you all later then," Dillon said, backing away and bowing slightly. "Especially you!" he added, pointing to Jerome. "That's a smart-looking vessel, lad! We'll see if you know your sails."

Eighteen

Instead of the frigid evening Rose expected, she was relieved to find Dillon a charming host. He arrived home in time to help her into her dinner dress—a yellow muslin over a colored silk slip. Disconcerted by her husband's dutiful attentions, Rose toyed with her hair before the dressing table, all too aware of the smooth muscles exposed while Dillon changed his shirt and coat.

Although their conversation had been mostly idle talk about the weather and Rose's impression of Melville Island, she sensed a charged atmosphere between them. It crossed her mind that Dillon might still harbor suspicions about Monsieur Benet, but if he did, they were surely connected with his sister and not her. She was tempted to ask if he'd found out what he wanted from the commandant of the prison, but decided it best to stick to the stilted small talk.

Claude Benet arrived at the agreed-upon hour. While Dillon entertained him in his office, Rose went, summoned by Audra, to the woman's room in the guest wing of the manor. There she found her sister-in-law in a dither about having chosen the right dress and Joeli in an equal quandary over the prospect that Audra might change her mind and have her press another at the last moment. Final preparations for the dinner were going on in the kitchen, and the servant needed to be there. All the while, Alison sat on her mother's plump bed and made her doll dance to the music she hummed.

"I think we need that dash of spring," Rose suggested, complimenting the green hue of her sister-in-law's draped sleeve gown. "Perhaps it will make us think it's warmer than it really is. Dillon said there were a few stray flakes of snow about earlier when he walked home. The soldiers were piling the cressets high with wood for the night watch."

"Dere, you see, missy! Joeli done pick de right dress! She ain' no fool, yes?"

"Do Frenchwomen wear much makeup? All I've ever seen are the Acadians and they're plain as corn husk dolls."

Rose ignored the disdain toward her French ancestors. If Audra knew of Rose's past, she most likely would not have made the remark. "I think modest makeup is the best choice. Too much and you might appear more the courtesan than the lady."

"I got to git down to de kitchen! You gals have to git prettied up wid'out Joeli."

"I'm sorry I kept you so long, Joeli," Audra apologized as the black woman started for the door. "I shouldn't have slept all afternoon."

"You needs your sleep, missy, more'n you needs pretty up for a teacher man!" The outspoken maid closed the door before she could incur her young mistress's wrath. Audra thinned her lips and waved at Alison.

"Ally, go to the nursery. Mavis should be seeing to your supper soon."

"I hope Erin likes what we got to eat. I know she doesn't like Mavis."

"She's just a doll, for heaven's sake, child. Now stop being cross and do as I say!"

"Maybe if you eat a good supper, you'll be allowed to join us for a while in the parlor before you go to bed." Rose shrugged as Audra gave her a questioning look. "There's more flies to be won with honey than vinegar."

Alison made a retching sound as she slipped through the door. "Yuck, I don't want flies in my honey!"

"You do have a way with my children," Audra complimented when they were at last alone. "You make them want to behave correctly. With me or Mavis, they always have a ready answer."

Rose thought of using the comparison of a captain and his untrained recruits, but thought better of it. It would be lost on Audra. Although adult in age, the woman was hardly more than a child herself, an immature twenty-two. Amanda said she'd married Ellis Harrison on her sixteenth birthday.

"About what Joeli said," Audra spoke up, drawing Rose's full attention. "She's right, you know. I am trying to look my best for Monsieur Benet. He's such a gentleman and makes me feel a lady, respected, even revered."

"How you choose to dress is up to you, Audra."

"But you do find it odd, considering I'm a married woman."

"Well, yes, I suppose," Rose admitted.

"I don't even know my husband!" Audra folded her hands and twisted them like the features of her fair, doll-like face. "I'm . . . I don't like what I've seen of him! There's something sinister about him, despite his charming manner and good looks."

It appeared that Audra, while losing her memory, had come to her senses where Ellis Harrison was concerned.

"I wish I had some words of comfort for you, Audra,

but, as you know, my marriage to Dillon isn't exactly a model. I'd like to be a couple in love, but I fear too much bitterness has passed between us." A sudden heaviness settled in Rose's chest over the admission.

"But Dillon is a good man. He has a ripe temper, but, when you get to know him, he's more bark than bite. I can't say that about Mr. Harrison."

Rose put her hands on Audra's shoulders to quell the sudden shiver that assaulted them. "I don't know what to say, Audra, except that it appears we both are in difficult situations. I'll do my best to be your friend, but I warn you, for your sake, as well as the children's, try not to show so much interest in Claude Benet. People will talk and the stains of scandal, real or imagined, are hard to erase."

Audra was not comforted. If anything, she seemed more despondent. "It doesn't seem fair, Rose. I know in my heart that Claude Benet would be a wonderful father to my children and a good husband to me. Ellis Harrison makes me fear for all three of us."

"Perhaps if you give the man a chance."

"He dropped me here months ago and, short of sending that incompetent nanny, I've heard nothing from him since. The journey is not so far nor difficult between here and Annapolis Royal."

So Audra was not oblivious to her husband's distant behavior. "I understand he's been trying to find new lodgings for you and the children."

"He gambled away my dowry," Audra told her flatly. "From what I'm told, it was a considerable fortune. Now I live on my children's allowance and my brother's generosity."

"As for that nanny," Rose went on, declining to comment on the man's character, at least before she had a chance to judge him for herself, "if you are displeased with her, send her on her way. We'll manage with the children somehow."

"Oh, I daren't!" Audra hurriedly arranged her skirts before the mirror on the back of the door. "We'd best go. The men will wonder what's keeping us."

Rose didn't know whether Ellis Harrison deserved it or not, but his wife was terrified of him. She hugged her sister-in-law with genuine sympathy. After helping Audra on with a shawl interspersed with golden thread, the two left the bedchamber and hurried down the grand staircase.

At least with Dillon, Rose knew there were some saving graces. He had an admirable character, which was respected by his peers and which would make him a devoted husband to a woman he'd chosen, rather than been forced to wed.

"Well, it's aboot time the two of ye came down to join us," Amanda Mackay declared when they entered the parlor where the men had joined her a moment before. Her glass was brimming with the trusty Scotch whiskey, and her round rosy cheeks suggested this was not her first.

"Now that the men have gotten their business oot of the way, we can have a civilized dinner without talk of this blasted war."

Instead of the war, an equally troubling subject surfaced; the outbreak of smallpox in Irish Town. It had also spread to the fort and waterfronts. Precautions were being taken and hospitals and alms houses were asking for more volunteers to handle the influx of patients.

"Thank heaven the children have been inoculated," Audra averred as a brandied fruit dessert was placed before her.

"Are ye certain they have been?"

Audra's face went blank for a moment, as though she

strained to recall more than that one slip of the past which continued to elude her and then nodded uncertainly. "I believe so. They've the scars on their arms."

"Ma pauvre madame! How terrible this must be for you, to have no memory of your past!" Claude Benet sympathized. "How horrible it must have been."

"I am afraid to remember, monsieur." As though his sympathy were a balm she desperately needed, Audra placed her hand on Benet's arm.

Rose caught the quick exchange of glances between Amanda Mackay and Dillon and once again was engulfed in concern for the distraught young woman. Had Ellis Harrison given her reason to fear him? As far as Rose knew, he wasn't present at the time the coach was attacked. He was preparing for the transfer of a group of American prisoners to Melville Island.

For all his weakness where gambling was concerned, it appeared the man was dedicated to his work. Audra felt she had reason to fear him, but didn't know why, while the remainder of her family didn't care for him because of his greed and lack of responsibility to his family. Rose wondered how the children felt about their father. Perhaps that was where she might get the least biased answer of all.

After supper, Jerome and Alison were once again allowed to join the adults in the parlor for a short while before having to go to bed. Mavis sat on a chair in the corner and watched grudgingly while Audra held her audience transfixed with a classical number on the harpsichord.

"Like an angel!" Claude Benet exclaimed, joining in the round of applause that followed the end of her selection. "Why, it makes me want to dance!" He turned to Amanda Mackay. "Madame, if your daughter would be so kind as to play another tune, I would be honored if you would dance with me. After all, who has not heard how light you Scots are on your feet?"

With a flustered, "Listen to the man!" Amanda Mackay came to her feet.

"Can I dance, too?"

"Why not?" Rose took Alison by the hand and led her to the center of the parlor floor.

"Do you think it would be gentlemanly of us to let the women do this alone?" Dillon asked his smaller companion, with whom he inspected the hand-crafted corvette now mounted on the table beside them.

Jerome was honest. "I'd rather you finish showing me what the sails are."

"If I tell you, too many, you may get them confused," Dillon pointed out thoughtfully. "A man can't learn everything at once."

"I don't know how to dance."

"I can show you," Rose offered. "And Dillon can show Alison."

She grinned as Dillon brushed past her and picked up his miniature partner. "This wasn't what I had in mind," he whispered in a low, devilish tone.

There it was again, that suggestive manner which set her nerves on end in anticipation. Yet, when they were alone, there was no hint of it. What transpired between them was at arm's length, or room's length more likely. She gave him a puzzled look, but he'd already swept a giggling Alison away to the music her mother played.

Jerome was reluctant at first to move his feet, but the more playful Rose became in hopping first on one foot and then the other, the more he began to loosen up. Soon they were sashaying and skipping in a large circle around the others.

"He's a smooth one, that," Amanda Mackay laughingly observed, when, winded by the exertion of the dance, she took over at the harpsichord, turning Audra over to Monsieur Benet.

The tune the woman played was a Scottish fling, normally accompanied by the pipes, but nonetheless lively. Again, each of the couples did their own interpretation of the dance. By its end, the six of them were in a circle and took turns swinging the dancers on either side of them, as well as creating a step or two of their own.

Rose stumbled for a chair, only to be caught in Dillon's capable arms. "You're going to have to build up your strength for the Newtons' Christmas Ball next week. Something tells me you'll have more than your share of partners."

"Including my husband?" Rose asked breathlessly. Two could play this game, except that, in her heart, she wasn't playing. Whether he intended to or not, Dillon Mackay was making her feel a woman again, alive and very much aware of him as a man.

"Indubitably. I'm keen to see if you've learned to dance to more than the jigs you used to do on the decks for the crew."

"I've had my share of partners, Dillon Mackay. I can match your step and then some!" she challenged playfully.

When had she last seen Dillon this relaxed, this cheerful? Here was a different side of him, one she'd not shared since she was that young girl dancing on the deck of her father's ship and he an apprentice seaman. Rose was reluctant for him to let her go when Jerome drew him back to the study of the model ship.

She was far from lonely, however, for Alison solicited her help to dress the doll Erin, whose smock had been removed earlier so that the child might see the fine needlework on its petticoat. Audra, once again at the harpsichord, was playing a familiar French tune and singing with Monsieur Benet, while Rose hummed along.

"They sound silly!" Alison observed, glancing at her mother and the Frenchman.

"That is another language. Those words have meaning just like the words you know," Rose explained. "Let me show you."

Slowly, she translated the French ballad into English, embellishing it to keep the little girl's attention. Alison was amazed when she finished.

"It didn't sound like that!"

"Maybe you would like to learn some French, too," Claude Benet suggested. "I would charge no more for such a pretty little student."

"I look like Mama," Alison announced, producing an affectionate and snaggle-toothed smile at her mother.

"Indeed you do, mademoiselle. But I can only offer my complimentary tutelage to one lovely lady at a time. A man has to earn a living, *non?*"

"Now that's a slick way o' makin' a point," Amanda Mackay observed good-naturedly. "Ye've a business head on your shoulders, Monsieur Benet. I can see that."

"There's only one thing that concerns me about retaining Monsieur Benet as a tutor."

Everyone turned to Dillon, who, for all appearances, hadn't even been listening to the conversation. Apprehension seized the air as he grimly went on to explain.

"Monsieur Benet's apartment is in Irish Town."

"But, as I said earlier, Monsieur Mackay, I am seeking other lodgings. I have no wish to be exposed to this smallpox, even though I have been inoculated."

"I hesitate to have you coming here daily, increasing the risk of exposing my family to the pestilence."

Audra's face was crestfallen, yet she did not protest. Dillon's point was well made.

Taking in his sister's reaction with impassive scrutiny, Dillon turned back to Claude Benet. "There is a small room on the third floor in the north wing above what used to be my schoolroom. My own tutor was assigned to it when I was small, but now it's being used for storage."

"But, of course!" Amanda Mackay chimed in, catching her stepson's drift. "We could clean it out and there's a back staircase so ye can go to the kitchen for your food. It's nae big, like Dillon says, but it has a small stove for warmth."

Claude Benet sat in quiet astonishment. It was clear that he'd expected Dillon to have changed his mind, as had the rest of the group.

"Why, Dillon, that's wonderful! It would solve all our problems!" Audra slid off the music bench and rushed over to hug her brother.

"You can move in whenever you wish, if that is acceptable," Dillon told Benet when Audra backed away. "Your room and board will cover the tutelage of this household and you will be free for the remaining hours of the day to teach in others."

"Can you teach us those silly songs?" Alison asked, rushing over to the stunned Frenchman.

"Especially the songs," Benet told her, pulling her and her doll into his lap. "Perhaps, even though your Erin is Irish, she'd like to hear you sing to her in French, *non?*"

"Erin likes singing," the little girl averred certainly.

"And I shall teach Jerome the language of the sea in French."

"Uncle Dillon is teaching me that in English," Jerome stated, not so easily swayed toward the idea of studying French as his sister.

"Then you will have something that you can teach your Uncle Dillon, *non?*"

"I *am* a little foggy on my French," Dillon admitted in such a way as to flood Rose's heart with pride.

She'd misjudged him in so many ways. Given the chance, he'd make a wonderful father. Like herself, he'd not been exposed to children and had to learn to deal with them. His response kindled the first real sign of enthusiasm in the little boy at his side.

"Then I'll learn it and teach you back! I can learn fast," the child went on. "These lines here are standard rigging and those are the running, because they are supposed to be able to move. And that's a halyard and a lift and braces and . . ."

Dillon laughed. "At this rate, lad, you'll be a captain by the time you're old enough to leave home."

"Do you really think so?"

"Well, you'll still need the actual experience, but I'd wager you'll be one of the youngest captains on the sea."

Jerome fairly beamed under Dillon's encouragement. He looked at the man with nothing short of worship, this from a child who, but a few days ago had been afraid to address the man directly. He now saw beyond Dillon's intimidating exterior to the congenial and compassionate man beneath.

Compassionate. The word jolted Rose to recall Dillon's devotion to her when she'd been at death's door. She'd seen her own pain reflected in his eyes. She'd felt it until she'd sunk beyond feeling and shock took over. When that began to lose its hold on her, bitterness swept in, and mistrust, and . . .

A knock on the front door stilled her ponderings as well as the conversation that had faded into the background of them. She glanced at the sliding paneled doors partially opened in time to see Henry pass the parlor on his way to answer it. Dillon rose from the excited Jerome's side, listening as Henry opened the door. The question on his face was the same that reflected on everyone else's. Who would be calling at this hour?

"What took you so long, old man? Show the driver where my bags go."

Whoever it was, they were quite impudent, Rose mused.

Dillon swore beneath his breath and walked toward the paneled doors. Behind him, Audra moved from the music bench as though stung by Claude Benet's proximity and reached for Amanda Mackay's hand. Alison peeked around the paneled door and then jerked back inside, her pale complexion growing even whiter.

"It's Papa!" Clutching her doll tightly to her, she hurried over to her mother and grandmother.

Rose fully expected to see an ogre with horns enter the room with her husband instead of the handsome gentleman who did so. Ellis Harrison was indeed a man to turn a lady's head. His golden hair flowed in waves toward a queue in the back and his facial structure and complexion were as flawless as an Italian master's sculpture. He paused just inside the room with a practiced grace.

"Tah, how fortunate that I arrived before my family retired for the evening! Particularly my lovely wife."

Straightening his impeccable cuffs, he walked straight to Audra and placed a chaste kiss on her ashen cheek. "Your new frock becomes you, my dear. A gift from your generous brother?"

"Thank you, sir. Yes, it is."

Audra followed her husband's gaze to Claude Benet, who now stood uncomfortably beside the harpsichord. Amanda Mackay quickly snapped out of her shock and assumed the role of hostess.

"Mr. Harrison, I'd like ye to meet our guest, Monsieur Benet. He has just agreed to accept the position of tutor for the children and the ladies."

"Another prisoner who has found the provinces more to his liking than his native France, eh?" Harrison extended his hand to the Frenchman. "How fortunate you are to have found employment, Monsieur Benet."

"Indeed, sir."

"Unfortunately, once our new home in the valley is complete, we shall no longer need your services."

"The man is not limited to employment by this household, Harrison," Dillon informed his brother-in-law tersely. "He's to earn his room and board here and his income elsewhere. If he's half the tutor he's reputed to be, he'll have no problem. I'd be more concerned with your own prospects. What's this about a new home in the valley?"

Ellis Harrison answered with a shallow smile. "While some may say gambling is my downfall, it is also my salvation. Lady Luck is once again favoring me. As she appears to be you as well," the man finished, glancing meaningfully at Rose. "You must be the new Mrs. Mackay I've heard about."

"This is my wife, Rose." Dillon put a possessive hand at Rose's back. "Rose, this is Ellis Harrison, Audra's husband."

"Your name does you justice, madame. I can see why it's so easy to love thine enemy in my brother-in-law's case."

Rose had to resist the temptation to pull her hand away when the man smoothly lifted it to his lips and brushed her knuckles.

"My decided pleasure, madame."

Instead, she moved closer to Dillon and managed an acknowledging smile.

"A shy Yankee rose with a blush to inspire poets."

And a polished scalawag with a tongue to gag a maggot! The reply hung on Rose's lips until later when she'd retired and Dillon at last came to their room. They were the first words out of her mouth as her husband quietly closed the door behind him, thinking her to be asleep.

"Not you, silly," Rose giggled as Dillon straightened with wounded indignation. "Ellis Harrison!"

"I thought you would be sleeping by now." He was obviously sorry she was not. Rose felt as if a chill had crept into the room, rather than her husband.

"I couldn't. All I could think of was that bragging saccharin jackass. He didn't even speak to his children until Mavis told them it was their bedtime! All he did was run on and on about his newly won fortune. And when he looked at Audra, he was cold as Arctic ice for all that devoted husband blow he made. You're much more convincing!"

Dillon tossed his jacket across the back of the sofa and swung about abruptly. "What the devil does that mean?"

Rose wanted to shrink beneath the covers. How on earth had that slipped out? She met Dillon's provoked gaze and groaned inwardly. Things had been so good between them tonight, even if it had been only on the surface. She'd actually felt protected when he'd put his arm about her upon introducing Ellis Harrison.

But there was no longer any audience. Dillon had shed his convincing charm and glared at her as though she'd insulted him.

"It means that your charade as the devoted husband is more convincing than Ellis Harrison's," she reiterated stiffly. "Oh, for heaven's sake, Dillon, there's no one to impress now. Don't look at me like that! I know you didn't want to marry me. All you wanted was my ship. I'm not a fool!"

Dillon yanked off his cravat and began to unfasten his shirt. "Don't flatter yourself, Rosebud."

Rose threw herself in exasperation against the pillows at her back. She hadn't meant to start an argument. She'd only meant to establish some common ground between them, their dislike of Ellis Harrison.

"All I'm trying to say, Dillon, is that I know you're trying to make the best of this situation. You didn't want me, but you thought enough of my father to take me home as your wife. You've shown more honor than I gave you credit for. You've been very generous and thoughtful of me." She blew her frustration through her lips and turned toward him. "For God's sake, you simple swab, I was complimenting you!"

Barefoot and bare-chested, Dillon bolted up from the sofa where he'd sat to take off his boots and stockings. "Well, pardon the hell out of me, if I don't see it that way! Strike me, Rose, I . . ."

He stopped at the edge of the bed and ran frustrated fingers through his hair, unwarily ridding it of the neatly tied black ribbon that had held it in place at his neck in the process. When he dropped his hands to his sides, they were clenched taut as his jaw, as though wrestling with the urge to shake her.

Rose blinked up at him in confusion. Dillon was like fire, welcome when controlled and dangerous when not. All she wanted was warmth, some common bond between them that would hold in private as well as public. She'd been alone in her despair for so long.

"I'm sorry." Damn her eyes. Hadn't the loss of her babies dried them forever? She closed them lest they betray her further and wiped away a tear that escaped one corner before it could streak down her cheek and find its way to her ear.

"Rose, Rose!" Dillon swore huskily, grabbing her face

between his hands. The bed swayed with his weight as he leaned over her. "What am I to do with you?"

Somehow Dillon had read her innermost thoughts, for he answered his own question with a kiss. His mouth covered hers, breathing life into her body as Agatha Prichart had claimed he'd done once before, when he'd snatched her from the hands of death. Except this time it was with assurance, not demand.

Rose returned his kiss, matching his fervor with her own until she felt the dominating weight of his body upon hers. She writhed beneath him, lifting her head and shoulders to receive his heady worship. Somehow she disentangled her arms from the covers trapped between them to treat her fingers to the warm, living feel of his back, moving with a sensual flow beneath them.

How her gown or the covers removed themselves amidst the tantalizing seduction of Dillon's lips, Rose didn't know. She only knew one moment of reprieve. Then he was back, flesh to hungry flesh.

His hands were everywhere at once, caressing, kneading, cherishing. Splayed against her back, they lifted her so that her breasts were served to ravenous lips and reduced to quivering taut and hot beneath his flaying tongue. Working down to her buttocks, he lifted her once again for his next course, the contracting skin of her stomach, the sensitive crease of her thighs, which merged of a sudden to the place where desire mounted to an unbearable proportion.

"No, Dillon!"

Her protest sounded no more like her than it reflected her body's true longing. Rose raised up on her elbows, shaking her head in breathless horror as her knees drew up in wanton surrender to Dillon's reason-shattering kiss. A coil of carnal desire began to unravel, shaking Rose from the core. Shuddering, gasping, she pulled a pillow over her face, lest she scream in the sweeping, sweet anguish that robbed her of all sensation but that which Dillon impressed upon her.

She thrashed beneath him, yet he would not give up his assault until she lay spent and helpless. The only objection she could make when Dillon rolled away from her and began to cover her with the layers of blankets, so inadequate in warmth compared to him, was an imploring, "No!"

Heedless to her wishes, he tucked her in, tender as a babe and then brushed her forehead gently. "That was no act, Rosebud."

Wasn't it? she thought foggily as he straightened and returned to the sofa. Hadn't the pleasure been one-sided? She blinked at him as he slipped beneath the coverlet and settled on the protesting cushions. Yes, it had been, although had she enjoyed her side any more, she'd have fainted dead away. As it was, she fell asleep, clinging to a pillow, rather than the man she longed for.

Nineteen

" 'Tis nae joy in this Christmas, save that of the innocents," Amanda Mackay observed matter-of-factly as she helped Rose into a lavish, embroidered silk gown.

Joeli was helping Audra dress for the neighbor's Christmas ball and the older woman insisted on doing the same for Rose.

Rose could think of nothing to say to argue the point. Ellis Harrison's arrival had fallen like a heavy cloud over the warm and lively spirit of the household. Audra rarely ventured from her room except for the brief hours she spent with her children in the schoolroom. There she changed, like a corpse come to life, basking in the approval and encouragement of Claude Benet.

When the adult lessons were over, Audra remained to watch the man with the children. Rose lingered also, enjoying the little ones' spontaneity and the easy rapport Monsieur Benet built with them. He truly was a gifted teacher with the ability to take the mundane and make it interesting.

When the lessons were over and Monsieur Benet left the house to teach his other clients, however, Dillon's sister once again took on that haunted, absent look and returned to her room where she'd been taking all her meals. It appeared Amanda's previous efforts to bring her daughter out had come to no avail.

"Well, at least Audra's going to the party tonight. Perhaps she'll enjoy it so, she'll come out of her seclusion again," Rose said hopefully.

"That's only because Monsieur Benet has been invited and ye weel know it, lassie." Amanda thinned her lips for a moment, as though weighing what she was about to say, and then went on. "The man is a gentleman's gentleman, but I fear his kindness where Audra is concerned has turned the lassie's head. It canna lead to good, I fear."

Again Rose was hard put to find something of comfort to say. After last evening, she doubted Ellis Harrison actually cared whether his wife was infatuated with her tutor or not. He hadn't chosen to sleep in the spare room across from Audra's out of consideration of his wife's frail state, but because it left him free to entertain Mavis Adams.

Rose had seen the nanny slip into Harrison's bedchamber shortly after the hall clock struck one. Caught in a ballyhoo of blazes over Dillon's absence from her own bedroom, she'd not yet closed her eyes, so that when the hour rang, she'd bolted from her bed, donned a robe, and gone looking for him. As she started for the staircase, she spied Mavis tiptoeing down the north corridor to Ellis Harrison's door.

Startled at nearly being caught sulking about, Rose gave up on her own quest and returned to her room with the sole satisfaction that at least Dillon was not spending the night with Mavis Adams. He was likely still in the library, judging from the sliver of light she'd seen in the hall below. Had Rose sought him out, she no doubt would have interrupted whatever work he found so necessary as to rob him of sleep.

Or was it merely convenient? That consideration was more wounding than Rose cared to admit, but before it could wring its full damage to her troubled mind, the door to the bedchamber burst open and the subject of her distress rushed into the room, tugging at the tie and collar of his shirt.

"Sorry I'm late, Rosebud, but . . ."

Dillon broke off at the sight of Amanda Mackay working at the tedious fastenings of Rose's gown. "Amanda, hadn't you best be dressing yourself?"

"I am dressed, ye tardy simpleton! 'Tis your wife ye'd best be speakin' to," his stepmother tutted in admonishment. "She'd need two nimble-fingered handmaids to dress her in the likes o' this fancy! Pretty it is, laddie, but nae practical."

"Perhaps Rose will choose her own dresses from now on," Dillon replied, his gaze lingering appreciatively on the low bodice, where the design of the silk had been enhanced by the stitching of tiny seed pearls. "Although I will not apologize for this." He walked up and brushed his lips across Rose's cheek. "You are a vision of loveliness."

"Tah!" Amanda snorted, retreating toward the open door. "Just like a man to try to flatter his way out of a blunder!"

"Any men with eyesight will be lining up to dance with you. Just remember, the first and last are mine," Dillon told her, taking over closing the small looped fastens where his stepmother had left off. "On second thought," he added, glancing over her shoulder with a rakish grin, "I don't think I'll want to let you out of my sight."

Rose didn't suppose he would in public. In private was another account altogether. His flattery was as shallow as his stepmother had indicated.

"Why are you avoiding me, Dillon?" she asked bluntly.

She saw him stiffen in the mirror and then force himself to relax, once again tackling the last of the pearled buttons. "I'm not avoiding you, Rosebud. I've been busy at the office and with the investigation. We're close to something, I believe."

"To finding the enemy's inside source?" she asked, momentarily distracted.

"These men are not enemy, my sweet, they are vermin of the lowest sort. Jerome's revelation has led to the discovery of a conspiracy that has shaken boots all the way to the Crown."

"Who are they then?"

Dillon backed away to admire his handiwork. "I'm not at liberty to discuss it, Rose, not even with my family. Suffice it to say there are governor's people in Digby, Annapolis Royal, and Halifax who are involved. The governor himself is on the verge of apoplexy! I was with him earlier, which is why I'm so late." Dillon folded his arms across his chest and abandoned the subject. "My God, you're beautiful!"

"You sound surprised," Rose quipped. She carefully arranged her skirts so that she might sit on the bench and place the cluster silk rosettes on the dressing table in her hair.

"I am continually surprised by you, Rosebud."

Rose sighed as he turned away from the mirror to change. If Dillon Mackay were as light on his feet on the dance floor as he was at evasion, she would be stepping on air. She watched as he stripped off his clothes and strode to the hearth in nature's magnificence where the small porcelain tub Henry had filled for her earlier stood.

"I didn't know you were going to bathe, Dillon. I used scented soap." Rose hoped her embarrassment didn't show in her voice.

"I noticed," he said, lowering himself into the water. "I always did favor this scent. It's not overly sweet. Just clean and pleasing to the senses. You've used it since you were a babe on your father's ship.''

Struck dumb that Dillon had noticed such a thing at all, much less been aware of it since she was a child, Rose continued to watch her husband as he set about scrubbing his broad back with a brush. His long legs pressed against his chest, he looked overgrown and out of place in the small enclosure, which had been designed, complete with painted flowers, for a woman.

After the bang of his elbow on the close metal rim evoked a pained grunt, Rose was tempted to offer help, but dared not risk spotting the exquisite pale-blue silk. Besides, she thought, breaking away from the intriguing spectacle when Dillon rose to his feet and reached for a towel, she had to finish getting ready herself. Even as she picked up the tiny roses, however, her eyes were drawn to where Dillon rubbed the linen briskly over ridge and taper of glistening manly flesh.

As though he sensed he was being watched, Dillon suddenly shook out the towel and wrapped it about his waist. But not before Rose saw that the crew's observation about certain male body parts shrinking in cold water was completely unfounded.

Shocked at her outright immodesty, she tried the silk adornment on one side of her head and then the other, all too aware that her face was now as bright as her gown was pale. How could someone so decidedly virile deny himself a woman's bed?

Rose threw the floral adornment aside. He was seeing someone else during the day, she stewed silently. He had to be!

"Who is she, Dillon?"

Dillon glanced up from fastening his trousers, a blank look on his face. "She?"

"If you're not warming my bed, you must be warming another woman's. Now I want to know who the . . ."

Rose bit off the *bitch* that nearly slipped off her tongue. "Who she is," she stated primly, lest her voice betray the hurt behind it.

"I am a married man, Rose, and I'd appreciate it if you'd stop comparing me to Ellis Harrison. Unlike my brother-in-law, I do not subscribe to adultery."

"You don't subscribe to the marriage bed, either!"

Rose couldn't believe what she'd said and, from the look on his face, neither could Dillon. Yet there was more than disbelief agitating him. It was something stronger, more explosive smoldering in the whiskey depths of his gaze.

Indignation? Outright anger? Whatever it was drove him to yank the ends of the new tie about his neck as though he wished it were hers in the noose. He made three attempts before it hung correctly about his starched collar and reached for a wine velvet coat with contrasting hunter cuffs the color of his snugly fit trousers.

"Are you ready to go downstairs?"

Dillon's question cut like a whip through the tension in the room, undeniably ending the discussion he'd found so annoying.

Though aching with confusion and frustration, Rose pointed out with cool indifference, "Your hair is still wet."

Hissing a short unintelligible oath, Dillon tossed aside the coat, took up a discarded towel, and began to work it over the straight shoulder-length locks.

How true were Amanda Mackay's words about there being no joy this holiday season! Rose stood up and, fingering the single sapphire on the otherwise plain silver locket that had been her mother's, exited the room without donning the matching earrings, leaving her companion to vent his wrath alone.

As Henry helped her on with her woolen cloak, Dillon came down the steps and picked up his own wrap from the chair where the manservant had left it. Although he was the picture of the handsome gentleman ready to step out, there was something about his brooding demeanor which suggested that the elegant trappings made him uncomfortable.

In a deep moss-green brocade evening coat no less elegant than his host's, Ellis Harrison stood next to his wife with the ease of a prince in his own court.

"La, but aren't we the royal group!" Harrison remarked, setting down the snifter of imported brandy he'd been nursing while waiting for everyone to assemble. "Only those involved in the sea trade have access to such finery these days."

"Actually, everyone of means has the same access here in Halifax, Harrison, because of our success on the high seas," Dillon contradicted him shortly. "Even the street vendors have improved their lot since the outbreak of the war with the United States. I believe I saw a pieman just yesterday with coat of that same cut."

Harrison pulled an indignant face. "Just because you've had a bad run of luck lately is no cause to be so trite, Mackay. A pieman never saw the day he could afford my tailor!"

"Please, we're going to a party! I can't bear unpleasantries!"

Audra, resembling a winter angel in ecru velvet with sable and gold trim, appeared on the verge of tears. She looked imploringly at Dillon, whose set jaw Rose was certain held back the ready reply he had for his brother-in-law.

His sister's dismay, however, effectively dampened his sullen play. "Far be it for me to distress such lovely company," he conceded with a stilted bow to first Audra and then Rose. "My apologies, ladies."

"Isn't Mrs. Mackay coming with us?" Rose asked glancing up at the gallery above.

"I think not, madame. Joeli said that Mrs. Mackay was going to retire early. She isn't feeling well."

"Perhaps I should stay with her then."

As Rose started to unfasten her wrap, Dillon stopped her. "Nonsense! All that would accomplish would be to keep her awake longer entertaining you. Besides, I guarantee she's in the best possible hands with Joeli."

Rose glanced toward the staircase as Dillon ushered her toward the front door. "I thought the children were going to see us off. Alison wanted to see our dresses."

"Mavis is getting them ready for bed, madame," Ellis Harrison informed her from behind. "Much as I appreciate your interest in Jerome and Alison, you do have a knack for spoiling them. I still can't believe they've actually taken meals in the dining room!"

The little ones had been kept cooped up in the nursery and schoolroom like prisoners since their father's arrival. Not even they, rambunctious as they were, dared incur their father's wrath. Like Audra, they appeared afraid of him. Rose, however, was not so easily intimidated.

"They're people with feelings and the need for company, just like you are, Mr. Harrison. If they behave properly, I see no reason . . ."

"When you become a mother, you'll understand, madame. Until then, I'd suggest you leave the parenting of my children to me."

"Why you pompous . . ."

"Rose!"

"Rose, please!" Audra's faint appeal blended in with Dillon's more forceful one.

With a glare as hot as the oath that choked her, Rose turned and marched out into the cold night air. What was she doing here? She wasn't a wife and she certainly wasn't a lady! She was a ship out of water, drying up at the seams with choked sails longing to be unfurled.

Nothing was as it appeared on the surface, not the carol Audra suggested they sing as they walked across the street to the neighbor's home, nor the care Dillon took in escorting her over the stone walk, now lightly glazed with the snow which had begun to fall that afternoon. The sounds of the music and laughter coming from the mansion, aglow with lights in every window and evergreen boughs tied with ribbons and fruit draped over its entrance, bespoke the holiday spirit. The cold air permeated with the smoke from the cressets burning along the street and the tempting smells of the baking going on in the kitchens of the fine homes added to that end. Yet, for all appearances, it didn't feel like Christmas, not to Rose, not in her heart.

Inside, however, there was at least distraction from her inner despair. Dillon's neighbors and associates went out of their way to meet the Yankee bride who had remained sequestered in his home. Some were motivated by curiosity, while others were genuinely interested in the woman Dillon Mackay had chosen as wife.

Uncertain as to what to speak about, politics being tactfully avoided in her presence, Rose was plagued with finding the correct comment or reply for the multitude of compliments and questions that came her way. The names of the men and women who bombarded her with attention seemed to fly in one ear and out the other, leaving her on edge with frustration. Never was she more grateful when the buffet in the dining room was opened and she had the excuse of eating.

The financial success of the Halifax businessmen Dillon mentioned earlier was evident in the lavish assortment of platters on the table. Seafood, fowl, and game of every description were set out among puddings and vegetables. Sauces to meet the most critical taste were seasoned and prepared to perfection with fresh imported spices, Rose was informed by a particularly proud kitchen maid, rather than the bottled ones being experimented with in England.

"We're fortunate to be stationed here in the provinces," a British colonel concurred on the subject concerning the abundance and quality of the spread. "My wife writes that such as this is still sparse in London due to the war, while your populace has seen no better times."

"If one calls dealing with drunken sailors and soldiers infesting our streets better times," one of the women ventured in obvious disdain. "They come from the fort to the waterfront and from the waterfront to the fort, and here we sit, caught in the midst!"

"Good fortune has its price, madame," the colonel reminded her. "Where would the merchants of the city be without the demand for their goods from the troops stationed here?"

"Nonetheless, it does seem your officers could exercise better control of your troops or crews . . . or whatever," the lady insisted. "The streets aren't safe!"

"If you're looking for safety, madame, perhaps you should consider moving to Pleasant Point or in the country," Dillon suggested at Rose's side. "I've just purchased a farm a few miles inland with that very thought in mind."

"A farm?" Rose queried under her breath.

"It has estate potential. The land is good, and the house, while not as extravagant as our current one, is sound. I'm having an architect draw up plans for expanding it and improving the landscaping."

"Am I to assume I'll be living there?"

"Of course, what a thing to say!"

"What a thing to do!" Rose shot back, rising from

the row of chairs which had been placed along the perimeter of the room for the guests. "I'm beginning to feel I have as much a part in this marriage as Alison's bloody doll!"

"Rose . . ."

Dillon took the plate his wife shoved at him sooner than let it drop to the floor and stared at her retreating figure in frustration. Everything he did, he did with Rose's welfare in mind. He'd promised John Beaujeu to cherish his daughter and meant to keep that promise, yet he felt as if he'd jumped overboard with his hands bound by circumstances he never asked for.

"Is Rose all right?"

Dillon grimaced. "I need to talk to her, Audra, but I'm damned if I know what to say."

"Tell her what's in your heart, Dillon. You've a wonderful one, you know, bigger than I ever gave you credit for. If . . . if anything ever happens to me, don't let Ellis Harrison take my children. I had one near miss with death," the young woman reminded him. "I want you and Rose to take Jerome and Alison . . . if anything should happen."

"What are you afraid of, Audra?" Dillon asked softly. "Have you remembered something?"

"Oh, I'm sure Rose is fine! She just went upstairs to freshen up."

Dillon's puzzlement over his sister's unrelated answer was solved at the sound of Ellis Harrison's voice behind him. "The music has started again, my love. Do you think you remember how to dance?"

Watching as his brother-in-law led the girl away, Dillon handed the dinner plates over to one of the servants and started toward the group of men gathered about the table laden with fine wines and stronger but equally extravagant spirits. The sooner this intrigue was resolved, the easier life would be for them all. Then, somehow, he'd deal with Rose and convince her that she was wrong about him.

The dancing was lively. From the stairwell, the parlor looked like a swirling flower bed of vibrant colors and smiling faces. Ordinarily it would have been as inviting as the music, but all Rose wanted to do was go home, home to Castine.

"That dress, is it blue or silver? It's hard to tell the way the chandeliers set it aglow," Claude Benet said at her shoulder.

"Blue."

"As madame seems to be?"

Rose didn't answer. If she admitted it, she might cry. "Isn't Audra lovely tonight?" Instantly, she regretted her spontaneous grasp at small talk. Now, she was not the only one who wore a heavy face.

"Like an angel in a cathedral, beckoning yet beyond reach."

So Audra's attraction was not one-sided. There was a certain light in Claude Benet's gray gaze that shone especially for Dillon's sister and her children. Since Ellis Harrison's arrival, Audra had basked in it only during their morning lessons and her depravation had waxened her complexion, as well as her manner.

"I suspect that you know such a feeling yourself, although I can not imagine why."

Rose stared at Benet in astonishment. She shouldn't be so shocked, she told herself. It was common knowledge in the Mackay household that Dillon kept late hours and slept on a sofa in their bedchamber.

"Forgive me, madame, I presume too much. Your husband has been too generous with me for me to cast such aspersion against him."

"I can't hold the truth against you, sir."

Rose blinked with consternation at the sudden haze that formed in her eyes and hurried back up the steps.

Upon reaching the second-floor hall, she looked back to see an apologetic Claude Benet on her heels.

"Madame Mackay," he averred, taking her hand between his. "For nothing would I see you so distraught! I am a cur, *non*, worse than that! How can I make this up to you?"

Rose's answer came in an imploring rush. "Take me home, Monsieur Benet! I can't bear this charade. I'll send word to the hostess that I am ill and . . ."

"But the scandal! It is your husband who should accompany you, not I."

"You asked what you could do, sir, and this is it. Or do you wish to stand here and watch me as well as Mrs. Harrison suffer? And we needn't tell anyone. We can simply go!"

"I cannot leave without offering my thanks to the hostess for her hospitality!" Benet answered.

"Well, I can. She didn't invite me, she invited Dillon and his wife, which I certain don't seem to be!"

"Madame . . ."

"Good night, Mr. Benet," Rose said, turning in a hushed whirl of silk to head for the servants' stairwell. "You may tell our hostess and my husband what you wish. I need air."

By the time Rose reached the bottom of the narrow, enclosed staircase, she heard Claude Benet's footsteps behind her. Not bothering to wait, she made her way through a startled kitchen staff to a back door. The walk across the street was short, and to stop and ask for her wrap would risk questions she was in no mood to answer.

"Madame, your husband will be furious at this!" Monsieur Benet called after her from the back stoop as she started around the corner of the house.

"The air out here is glorious, monsieur! Not nearly so suffocating!"

Benet caught up with Rose in the side garden. Rose slowed not a step, but kept on with her delicate silk skirts hiked scandalously to her knees.

"*Mon Dieu*, but you have put me at a disadvantage! If I remain, I am a cur, and if I go, I am no less!"

Ignoring the bewildered coachmen gathered around the cressets burning on either side of the vehicle-filled drive, Rose skipped recklessly into the street. "Aren't you tired of being a prisoner, Monsieur Benet?" she challenged. "Don't you long for the freedom of the open sea where you can swear to your heart's content and answer to no one but the gulls and the wind?"

"*Non*, I prefer a nice warm fire and a loving companion with whom I'd spend the rest of my life."

The charming image the tutor painted in Rose's mind brought her to an abrupt halt. She saw a laughing Dillon, like the one she'd adored since childhood, change to the brooding one who'd been annoyed with her wounded questions earlier. The upward swing of her reckless spirit took a downward turn toward renewed despair.

"Since that doesn't appear to be either of our destinies, will you settle for a warm fire and a hot rum toddy instead?"

Claude Benet glanced from Rose to the brightly lit house and back again. With a grim nod, he pulled off his jacket and draped it over her shoulders. "Against my better judgment, madame, I would be honored."

They started toward the Mackay home, a gray monument a block away sitting among geometrically landscaped trees. The draperies drawn, its only welcoming lights came from the front lanterns, which seemed to watch their approach with small glowing eyes.

Twenty

Not even the hot buttered rum a disconcerted Henry served them managed to faze Claude Benet's guarded demeanor. Only after the second drink in front of a blazing fire in the parlor hearth did he let down his guard enough to tell Rose about his life in France.

It was an unhappy one. Born late in his parents' lives, the third of three boys, there was no place for him to go to seek his fortune except the French military. It was only out of family obligation that his older brother, who inherited the Benet estate, saw to his education and secured him a lieutenancy in the navy. He'd not seen or written to his family in six years, nor had they attempted to contact him.

"I had a friend who had the most marvelous family. They were always doing things together, laughing and loving every moment. With my parents so old and my brothers away at school, we had nothing like that in our home. That family," he went on wistfully, "that is what I had hoped to have someday. That man, he has so much and yet he does not appreciate it."

Aware that he spoke of Ellis Harrison, Rose commiserated with Benet's anguish. What he wanted was as beyond his reach, as Dillon seemed to be hers.

"This friend, was it a she?"

"Madame, you have an incredible insight!" Benet

sighed, nonetheless keeping his back as straight as an arrow beneath the ancient burden he admitted to her. "It was a she, as you said, a beautiful, sensitive she, not unlike Madame Harrison. The madame reminds me much of her."

"She didn't marry your oldest brother!"

"And moved into that cold, lifeless manor! Perhaps that is why it grieves me to see your sister-in-law so, how do you say, caged, like a beautiful bird."

Benet grew silent for a moment and studied the remains of his drink. Suddenly, he looked directly at Rose.

"Like you, madame, if I may be so bold. When you left that house, you took to wing and now are right back in your prison. This I do not understand, especially when your husband shares the same confines, obviously in love with you and yet keeping a distance."

"What lies between my wife and me, Monsieur Benet, is none of your affair!"

"Dillon!" Rose gasped.

"Nor is it your responsibility to escort her home without my knowledge!" Dillon went on, blowing into the room like a storm cloud toward the disconcerted tutor.

"It's not his fault!" Rose wedged herself between the two men before Dillon took it into his mind to use the fists clenched white at his side. "I left and he had no choice but to follow me or leave me to find my way home alone. As a gentleman, he could not allow that!"

Although her words rang true, Dillon still trembled with the need to explode, to take the brunt of the panic that affected him as he searched his host's home room by room for Rose like a madman. When one of the kitchen staff said that a lady in blue silk had left by the servants' entrance with a Frenchman, Dillon had boiled into a green rage.

"What the lady says is true. I could not leave her to

her despair alone on the street," Benet said righ-
teously.

"Despair?" Dillon lowered an accusing gaze to Rose.
"Is that why you left, because I didn't tell you about the
farm?"

"I left, you swaggering fool, because I am not your
wife!"

The dregs of the drink she slung at Dillon before
shoving him aside were cold and sticky. He reached inside his coat for a handkerchief and wiped his face and
the front of his jacket with a marked, tedious effort.
Although he watched Rose's stomping retreat on the
staircase, he also saw Claude Benet lower his head and
step away in deference to the awkward confrontation.

"You French are supposed to know women, monsieur. If you can explain Rose, by God, you are a gen-
ius!"

Dillon walked to the liquor cabinet and helped himself to a healthy dose of Amanda's favorite whiskey. Biting and burning as it was, it was cool as spring water
compared to his present disposition.

"I am not so accomplished with the ladies myself,
monsieur, despite my countrymen's reputation. I think
they are like delicate flowers. One little slight and poof!
They wither."

"Or stick the hell out of you with their thorns!"

"Only when a man does not give them the attention
they deserve, monsieur," Benet replied solemnly. "The
confusion lies in what that attention is."

"I've given her every bloody thing a woman could
want!"

"I don't believe your wife is impressed by material
things, Monsieur Mackay."

"Then you haven't seen her with her ship!"

"She is a different flower, I must admit. However, I
do not think, even if you were to give her that, that she

would be happy. Those vibrant blue eyes, monsieur, they are always for you. Most husbands would pay and do pay fortunes for such . . . if you will forgive me my impertinence, such longing."

Dillon clenched the bottle in his hand. He knew the anguish of longing all too well. Yet, somehow he thought Rose could be pacified with dresses and a fine home. He'd even tried to assuage her physical need, although it was nearly his undoing.

"What she needs is her husband's time, his attentions, if you will."

But time alone with Rose was sheer torment. Dillon had taken to staying half the night in the library, so that when he came to their room, she would be asleep and he would be too tired to ache for her. Even that pitiful plan had failed him of late.

"But I have said enough. I am a stranger in this house with no right—"

"You are a friend in this house, Claude Benet. You have my apologies for my earlier behavior." Dillon offered an outstretched hand. "I'm glad Rose had someone to turn to."

"For her sake and yours, monsieur, I would rather that person be you."

"So would I."

"Then go to her, monsieur. Tell her what even I can see in your heart, then show her."

The Frenchman took his leave by the back servants' stairwell, leaving Dillon to a half-empty bottle and heavy heart. The adage about things being easier said than done couldn't apply more, he thought with disparagement.

After a good amount of pacing back and forth before the banked hearth and listening to be certain none of the violence that had threatened in her husband's demeanor came to fruition, Rose tackled the act of undressing for bed with a vengeance. Anger was so much easier to vent than the griping hurt she felt inside. If he cared the least for her, why hadn't he come after her?

Is that why you left, because I didn't tell you about the farm? Dillon's incredulous observation added fire to an already simmering stew. Her husband might be the smartest captain on the seven seas when it came to ships and sailing, but when it came to women, he was as dumb as any lubber who ever tripped in the scuppers!

Rose stopped the thrashing and twisting which had enabled her to get her dress down over her shoulders and took as deep a breath as the perilously stretched garment would allow. Now she could turn the fastenings around to the front where she could reach them.

Her stepmother and Joeli had both retired for the night and Rose would not bother them. She'd rather rip the garment to shreds, except that silk did not tear so easily and the seamstress had not been slack in her stitches. As it was, a few pearl buttons were already sacrificed on the floor.

Once the circulation had returned to her arms from reaching behind her head in her struggle to come out of it, she returned to the row of tiny loops stretched tightly over her bosom. Using her thumb, she shoved at one of the buttons, which seemed hopelessly ensnared by the tight fit. It came free with a pop and flew across the room, smacking into the opening door of their bedchamber.

Rose looked up to see Dillon jerk back into the hall in the midst of his silent entry and then peer around to seek the missile which had narrowly missed him. Spying it rolling toward the bed, he solemnly retrieved it and the others which had gone a similar route. She expected some admonishment or offhanded comment, but instead, saying nothing, he put the pearls on the dressing table next to her music box. To her astonishment, he lifted the hatch on the tiny ship's replica, starting the sweet plucking melody of the ballad.

Then, turning with a polite incline of his head, he held out his hand. "I believe you owe me a dance before you shed your silks for the evening, Mrs. Mackay."

Rose took a backward step as Dillon moved toward her. If only she knew this man with mercurial moods. A dance was the last thing she would expect him to offer.

"I don't feel like dancing."

"You're my wife, despite your notion to the contrary," he added wryly. He caught the train of her gown which was now twisted in front of her and wrapped it about his arm, all the while moving with her slow withdrawal. "You've decided you want to be treated as my wife." With his reeling in the length of her skirts, Rose had little choice but to reverse her step until she was close enough to him that her tightly bound breasts brushed the lapels of his coat ever so lightly. "So dance with me, wife."

Dillon's graceful backstep forced Rose's wooden legs to life. In the background, the metallic strains of the music box mingled with the sudden rush of blood to her ears. If he was still angry, he hid it as well as he hid any other emotion he might be feeling.

For all his show of formality, he was far from the proper dance partner. None of her admirers in New York had even been so bold. Both his hands were at her waist, holding her in such a manner as to make her senses scream for more of what they suggested. There was no ignoring his lead. Wrapped in her own skirts and bound by them to him, she'd no option but to sway with him in the bizarre confrontation while her will slowly bent of its own accord to his unspoken demand.

So compelling, so hypnotic was this Dillon that Rose dared not object when he coaxed her even closer to him. In one step, in two, their legs melded, even as their bodies, with single movement. When she could no longer stand the tickling of his tie against her nose or the suspense of what he was about, she raised her face to study his. To her astonishment, his lips moved down as though they'd been waiting for her.

He stole a kiss, short, yet no less impassioned, and pulled her to him tightly. They were no longer dancing, but holding together like a carving of entwined lovers, swaying side to side in a charged silence.

She was aware of his every breath, every beat of his heart. Her fingers measured the tension gnarling the muscles of his back. A hint of her citrus bathwater invaded the decidedly male scent of tobacco, good Scotch whiskey, and a wholesome spice talc which assaulted her nostrils. When he swallowed she felt the slide of his Adam's apple against her forehead, even its rumble when he finally spoke.

"I love you, Rosebud. So help me God, I don't mean to hurt you!"

Rose stiffened within his embrace, wondering if she'd heard correctly. Behind her, the melody of the music box haltingly died. Neither of them moved, as though each waited for the other to break the deafening stillness of the room.

"I don't know what I thought had happened to you," Dillon finally said after filling his lungs with air. "I was ready to go to the shipyard." His chest shook with an attempt to chuckle. "I wouldn't put it past you to try to take the *Border Rose* and head home."

"You'd only come after me."

"I wouldn't wait so long this time. I won't risk losing you again."

Losing her? Rose shook her forehead in the cradle of his neck in confusion. He didn't want her, but he didn't want to lose her. He said he loved her, but . . .

No, she told herself sternly. She'd been teased too many times by that idea, by his public affection, only to have her hopes dashed by a long, lonely night. Why should she think this sudden declaration was any different.

"I'm sorry, Dillon, but I don't believe you." She would have moved away, but he was not about to let her go. His grip tightened.

"Believe me, Rose!"

The hand wound in her skirt holding her captive, Dillon reached with the other for the fastens straining over her bodice and began to pop them, one by one. For him, they fell away with eagerness. Rose shrank away from the warm touch of his fingers, lest it add to the riot building within, but the resulting tug on the silk only facilitated his intended task, and the bodice finally fell away to her waist.

"Don't do this, Dillon! Don't make me want you and then leave me to a cold empty bed!"

She shoved her hand between them and pressed it against the hard evidence of his own need. Her boldness accomplished what her appeal could not. Dillon backed away as though she'd scalded him.

"Damn it, Rose, you don't understand!"

He rocked on his heels and then pivoted abruptly away. His mask of indifference dissolving in a wildfire of emotion, he tore off his coat in a single motion and threw himself into the winged chair by the hearth.

"But I do!" she argued, not nearly as certain as she sounded. She'd never seen Dillon so undone. "You don't love me! You want a figurehead for a wife, not a living breathing woman!" She shoved her gown down to her feet and stepped out of it. "This," she said, snatching it up in her hand and shaking it at him, "is show! Just like your words, pretty to look at, but empty!"

Dillon's gaze followed the shimmering dress when she flung it at the door. "I made a promise, Rose."

His voice was so low, she wasn't certain she'd heard him right. "A promise?" she echoed. "A promise to whom, Dillon? To your mistress? Is that it? Do you have a mistress somewhere in the city?"

There was no mistaking the bitterness in his laugh as he replied. "Mistress? Strike me, woman, you've ruined me for any other woman! And, believe me, I've had the opportunity!"

"Mavis Adams has been fairly panting after you!"

"And any man who catches her fancy," he sneered. "Give me credit for better taste than that, at least!"

Rose believed him, at least about Mavis. As for his claim that she'd ruined him for other women, she'd seen and felt proof that that was not the case. He'd covered his lap with his coat too late to disguise his male arousal.

"Then who is it you made this promise to?" she asked, walking over to where he sat.

He straightened warily as she dropped to her knees in front of him. Her corset presented an ample view of her bosom, drawing his attention in a way words could not. The game had changed dramatically between them, Rose realized. She leaned forward, her elbows resting on Dillon's knees. Now it was she who issued the demands, she who'd become the predator. If ever she was to find out the nature of the barrier that kept her and her husband apart, it was now.

"This doesn't feel as though you're ruined for women, Dillon." She ran her hand under his jacket and once again sought out the hardness straining against the front of his trousers.

"You're a brazen wench, Rose Beaujeu!"

Encouraged by the blaze of passion that fired behind the strange and sudden vulnerability which tortured Dillon's face, she ventured on. "I'm a woman, Dillon. You made me that. You introduced me to these damnable feelings! You came after me and kept me as your wife, when you could have gone free. You had the ship. Our babies . . ."

A flash of two small crosses marking the graves she'd visited just before boarding the *Border Rose* streaked across her mind and she choked. *God, don't let me cry now!* she prayed. She had to maintain control of this situation while Dillon was at the disadvantage. She cleared her throat and blinked away the wetness in her eyes.

"You had no obligation to them," she said flatly.

"John Beaujeu . . ."

"Or my father!" Rose snapped, annoyed at the way her life had been arranged by the two men. "What did you promise him, Dillon? I thought he was pleased that you took me as your wife. I—"

"Me, Rose!" Dillon grabbed her hand and forced it to the arm of the chair, so that he might speak without the considerable distraction of her blood-stirring hold. "I made the promise to myself!"

"That you would love me, but not in your bed?"

Rose snatched away from him. "That is the most ridiculous bag of wind to ever strike a sail!" she swore, crossing her arms stubbornly in front of her. "Why would any man make such a damned fool promise, especially one with a masthead the size of—"

"Damn you, Rosebud, I don't know whether to laugh at you or wash that salt tongue off with soap!"

"To hell with my choice of words, it's yours I'm waiting to hear!"

Her challenge wiped all trace of humor from his lips. Again he struggled with himself, but his features refused to hide his innermost feelings anymore.

"My promise wasn't so ridiculous, Rosebud, not when I held you in that bloody bed while you writhed in pain like I've never seen, nor wish to see again." He pressed against the arms of the chair, as though trying to back away from the vivid recollection assaulting him. The veins in his hands swelled with the effort. "Not when I saw my babies wrench the very breath out of you and leave you at death's door. You'll never go through that again on my account, Rosie, never!"

His voice broke with emotion and with it all the hurt that had been building within Rose found its way out.

"Oh, Dillon, they were my babies, too!"

The agony they'd suffered separately once again washed over them in a drowning tide, but this time, instead of bearing it alone, they faced it together. Dillon cradled Rose against him, holding on to her as though he feared he'd lose her again, while Rose cried softly against his chest, not just for the twins buried in the family cemetery at Castine, but for the time that had been lost between her and the man destiny had chosen for her, her enemy and her love.

She'd been so wrong about Dillon. His was a sacrifice few men would have made, and, caught up in her own grief and misery, she'd resented him for it. But he was wrong too, no matter how noble his intentions. He was a man and she was a woman. He was her husband and she his wife.

"I—I love you, you wonderful, sweet, silly man!" she whispered brokenly against his neck, when the pain subsided enough to let her speak.

"Silly?" Dillon sniffed. "You have a strange way of seeing things, Rosebud."

Rose seized his beleaguered face between her hands. "There are some things, Dillon, that just happen. You lost the *Thorne*, but it didn't keep you from going back out to sea."

"We're not speaking of a ship, we're talking about your life."

"And how many times have you nearly lost your own? Did it stop you from taking another risk?"

"It's not the same thing," he mumbled, turning so that he might kiss the inside of her palm. "I may have taken your ship, Rosebud, but you took more. My heart jumped out of my chest and into your pocket when that broken mast buried you in canvas and rigging. Damn your beautiful, troublesome hide, you've had it ever since! If anything should happen to you, I'd go with you, understand? A man can't live without a heart."

"And who is going to fill that house you've bought in the country? Where will our children come from?"

"You're all I need, Rose."

"Well, you're not all *I* need, Dillon Mackay. I want a baby, our baby. The doctor told me I was built to have a dozen more!"

Dillon drew his head back skeptically against the wing of the chair. "Is this the same girl who swore on a blue streak that she'd not be burdened with my brats?"

Rose wiped the scowl off his face with her fingers and drew the flat line of his lips into a smile. She knew she'd never heal completely from losing the baby boys until she had another child. Was that why the distance Dillon maintained between them had made her so desperate for his husbandly attentions or was it simply the destiny she'd tried to ignore?

"I'm a woman now in case you hadn't noticed, and I've changed my mind. A woman can do that, you know.

I want to make a baby with you and I want to start now, Dillon."

The sturdy thighs upon which she rested tensed as she slipped her hand between them with a devious tilt of her lips. Before she even touched him, she saw the burst of passion in his gaze and knew she'd won. His paltry attempt at further protest faded under her convincing arguments.

"Whoa, Rosebud!" Dillon caught her probing fingers and stilled their mischief. "It's been a long time." He managed a crooked, almost pained grin. "Besides, the last time I shared a chair with you, the result wasn't that fulfilling."

The picture Dillon's reminder called to mind broke the rising pace of Rose's heart with laughter. It hadn't been funny at the time, but now, with Dillon grinning at her and the barriers between them melting away by the moment, it was.

"I'm sorry I left you, Dillon, but . . ." Rose giggled and covered her face, as though that would stop the rush of heat that stung her cheeks. "But I was so embarrassed I didn't know what to do! The look on Nate's face . . ." She peeked at him through her fingers. "The look on your face!"

Rose cried out in surprise as Dillon pushed up from the chair and dumped her on the floor.

"It wasn't *that* funny!"

Her disgruntlement faded abruptly as he stripped off his shirt and threw it at her. "In fact, I've half a mind to toss you out on the street in your corset for the neighbors to gawk at. Except that I'm damned particular about who sees the charms of my wife."

He leaned over and, taking her hands, brought her to her feet. His fingers were equally nimble with the laces of her corset as they were at the loops of her dress.

"In fact, I've yet to see you in Mother Nature's full glory myself. Time has always been pressing us, Rosebud."

"I've nothing better to do tonight, do you?" Rose asked as the corset fell away.

It was followed by her chemise and petticoats. With the fire banked in the hearth, the room had cooled, but she hardly noticed. Dillon's at-long-last unbridled longing warmed her. Despite his professing that he wanted to savor this moment, his hands fairly shook with eagerness until all she wore was her mother's sapphire locket.

"That, too," he told her as she fingered it. "Such perfection needs no meager jewels."

As Rose reached behind her to take it off, Dillon cupped her lifted breasts, rubbing the impertinent peaks between his thumbs and forefingers. A quivering weakness erupted within her, tightening her abdomen and loins against the resulting flood, and her fingers failed to work.

"I can't!" she gasped.

"Then leave it," he whispered, seizing her about the waist and lifting her against him.

Rose shimmied up Dillon's rock-hard body, her legs wrapped about his waist and ground against him. The teasing contact only made her ache for more and increased her frustration when he dropped her on the bed.

"For the love of God, Dillon, take off your clothes!"

"Subtlety is not one of your strengths, Rosebud," Dillon taunted, dancing away from her reaching hands to see to the task himself. "Get under the covers before you take a chill."

"I'm so warm, my toes are about to burst!" Or something was, she thought, easing over to make room for Dillon, who stepped out of his trousers and kicked them aside.

"Maybe I should start on them then."

Rose curled her feet and shoved them beneath the blankets. "Dillon, right now my toes are the least of my worries!"

"Then where should I start?"

He was teasing her, damn him, when she was about to die of want. Indignation overcoming modesty, Rose placed her hands on the shadowy dark tuft at the apex of her thighs. "Here," she said.

"My God, you are a vixen!"

Dillon moistened his lips with his tongue like a beggar before a feast as he stepped up to the bed. His hands devoured her flesh, with long, tender caresses from her ankles to her inner thighs, round and round her stomach, and up to her breasts, so that each received its rightful due. They were followed by kisses, tiny little ones trailing here, long sensual ones lingering there, until Rose thought she'd explode.

Unable to stand his heady torture anymore, she grasped his aroused flesh in her hand and worked its length with her fingers. With a groan, Dillon came to the bed and covered her body with his. As he moved downward to position himself, she sighed in ready relief.

However, it was not that which she craved that brushed her contracting, desire-ridden flesh, but Dillon's kiss. Rose bolted upright and seized the startled man by the ears with a oath that would shame the saltiest of sailors.

"You're not going to get away with that again!" she averred. "You know what I want and I'll damned well settle for nothing less!"

Dillon moved up, forcing Rose back against the mattress. "Such sweet, tender words, Rosebud. They stir my soul!"

"Damn it, Dillon, I'm don't care about your bloody

soul at the moment!" Rose wrapped her legs, still tingling from the graze of the bristled muscle that slid up between them, about his waist.

"Rose, I may not be able to pleasure you as you deserve," he warned on a more serious note.

Her glare faltered as Dillon positioned himself against her. Much as he enjoyed seeing just how lusty this beguiling wife of his really was, he could hold back no more. When she'd grabbed him so brashly, she'd nearly cost him the moment then and there. Only by his mischievous distraction, had he managed control this long. Now, however, there was nothing to stop his avaricious thrust.

He neither saw Rose's eyes widen nor her perfect breasts flounder with its jolt. He was no longer a lover, but a male animal with raw craving, growling and demanding all nature had to offer him. So long he'd wanted this pagan release, so long he'd denied himself, and now there was nothing left but the abandon which overtook him, pummeling him within and without in sweet, molten desire.

When the remnants of his spent senses returned, he turned and whispered huskily in Rose's ear, "I'm sorry, Rosebud. I'll make it up to you." He squeezed her with what little strength he had left. "I love you, Rosebud, more than life itself."

He'd intended to pleasure her, to show his overwhelming gratitude for the way she'd absolved his guilt by turning it into a beautiful promise. She, the one who suffered the most, had healed him, the man who wasn't even aware he needed to.

He owed her more than he'd just given her, he thought, rolling to the side and pulling her into his arms. He nuzzled her neck, his nose brushing the chain of the locket there'd been no time to remove. Why had he been so afraid of this commitment to heaven? He'd need to apologize for that, too, for not believing in destiny. But that would have to wait until later. They had the night. God willing, they had a lifetime.

Twenty-one

Dillon loved her! Rose never knew so few words could bring such happiness. Nor could she have guessed the full extent of her lust, once he'd masterfully tapped it. They were well matched, he'd told her after he'd once again worshiped her body into a frenzied passion.

Afterward, as she lay in his arms, she recalled hearing Ellis Harrison return with Audra and guiltily sympathized with Dillon's sister and Claude Benet. She had no right to be so content.

"Why the frown, Rosebud?" Dillon whispered in her ear. "Good God, don't tell me you're wanting more! I wonder that I'll even be able to walk after last night."

"I was just thinking of Monsieur Benet and Audra."

"Why?"

Rose brushed Dillon away from her playfully. "Are you blind, Dillon. He adores your sister and the feeling is mutual."

"Frankly, you've monopolized my attention."

"Me and business, you mean."

Next to her, Dillon shifted, propping himself up on his elbow. "If not for that distraction, I'd have gone mad with want. Not that I fancy losing two ships. However," he said, leaning over to kiss away the blanket barely covering the tip of her breast, "I promise I shall devote at least equal time, if not more, to you, once I return."

"Return?" Rose cocked her head to stare at him. "Where are you going with Christmas only a day away?"

"I'm not leaving until after the New Year."

"For where . . . Digby?"

"Castine."

Rose let out a squeal of delight and threw her arms about him, drawing him down upon her. "Oh, Dillon! I can't believe it! I'm going with you," she averred.

"Not this time, Rosebud. I can't take you."

"Why?"

"Because it's too dangerous, what with these pirates about."

"I've dealt with pirates before." Rose couldn't believe Dillon would think of leaving her behind, especially now that they'd reconciled their differences.

"Rose, when the war is over, I promise you shall sail with me wherever you wish, but not until."

Rose pushed away from Dillon and slid off the mattress onto the cold floor. "You could take me if you wanted," she accused shortly, reaching for her robe on the chest at the foot of the bed. "You could leave in convoy."

"There aren't many ships leaving this time of year."

"Then why are you? I suppose you'll be taking my ship."

Dillon tossed back the covers and climbed out of the bed without thought to his own nakedness. "I'm taking *our* ship fully loaded with supplies for your father's warehouses. It's part of a deal we made. I provide the goods. He sells them. We both profit." At the skeptical arch of Rose's brow, he closed the distance between them. "Your family ships don't stand a chance of getting through the blockade! It's not worth the risk. And you know as well as I that Castine is bereft of adequate supplies for its inhabitants."

"They wouldn't be if it weren't for the bloodybacks and marauding bluenoses!" Rose shot back over her shoulder.

She concentrated on building the fire in the hearth, rather than the manly body braced behind her.

"This bluenose is trying to help, Rose."

As the kindling she'd added to the glowing embers caught up, Dillon grabbed her waist and pulled her against him. "Because he's in love with his enemy and wants to take care of her and hers."

No, Dillon had exaggerated about being worn out. He was as stiff as the log she tossed on the fire. Her buttocks tingled from the virile contact and, to her surprise, she grew warm from within. She leaned over, refusing to turn in his arms lest she lose her argument to go with him and placed another log on the fire. Dillon thrust himself against her.

"You make the most mundane task take on an entirely new fascination, madame!"

Rose gasped, reaching back for the hands which kept her from being shoved into the flames that had begun to lick the firewood hungrily. "Dillon, are you trying to burn me alive?"

"Nay, madame, only to make you burn."

Rose made a halfhearted effort to move away. Her lack of zeal did not go unnoticed by Dillon, who used her effort to turn her in his embrace. Her robe parted to allow that which made him man to slide against the contracting flesh of her stomach, while he kneaded her buttocks.

"Making me burn will not get you out of taking me with you," she said, unable to help the delighted curl of her lips.

"No, but it will make the debate much more agreeable."

Rose nearly laughed as he danced her over to the bed, not once breaking the intimate contact until she was pressed against the mattress. Then, with a brusk, "To my bed, you brazen wench, until you realize who is master here," he rolled her backward and threw open her robe.

"I know no master, Dillon Mackay!" She laughed as he made to tickle her ribs, but instead, he tugged the belt of her wrap out from under her.

"Twenty lashes for insubordination!" he went on.

The makeshift cat whipped across her breasts with satin tongue. Already hardened from the morning chill in the room, the peaks grew even tauter. As the second lash came down, Rose instinctively knocked it aside.

"So I can't even trust you to take your punishment like a . . ." Dillon gave her a dastardly grin. "A *woman.* I can see you require more discipline than most."

Before Rose knew what he was about, he was upon her, wrapping the silken belt of her robe around her wrists. She pulled against him, but seasoned as he was with ropes and knots, he secured her to the bedpost before she could muster serious resistance. "What manner of game is this, Dillon Mackay?"

A shudder ran through her at the devious rake of his gaze. She could almost feel it burning over her from her lips to her breasts, from her navel to the downy juncture of her legs.

"A far more merciful one than that you played with me, madame." He cupped her face in his hands, tracing her lips with his thumbs. "For one, I will not leave you beached with longing, nor awry with embarrassment. Your penance," he predicted huskily, "shall be for these eyes only and your lashes dealt with this."

Rose drew in a ragged breath as Dillon licked his lips

in a shamefully suggestive manner. Regardless of the outcome of her husband's wicked game, something told her she could not lose.

Such was the price of being married in body and soul to Dillon Mackay. As Nate once observed, he was a man of his word and left Rose little idle time throughout the holidays. When he was not with her, there were enough recent memories to keep her aglow with warmth until he was beside her again, fanning passion's fires.

As for his leaving for Castine without her, she finally coerced the entire truth out him. Dillon was sailing to Maine with goods for her father's warehouses. He was also acting as a decoy for the *HMS Byron* and carrying extra men and additional guns, which were being installed on the *Border Rose* the day he escorted her to the dockyard to see the handiwork of the craftsmen who had restored her.

The ship had put on her finery once again and looked fit as she had on her maiden journey. Now, however, aside from the cannonade on the main deck, there were six pounders at strategic points about the top. The sections of rail in front of them swung away on wide hinges which had been painted the same as the freeboard to disguise them. At her bow was the figurehead, its charred, fire-blistered features restored to perfection.

"Plucky as her mistress," Dillon observed wryly. "So will she pass?"

"I'd see what you've done to the cabins before I'll say, sir!"

Rose preceded Dillon down the stern hatch from which she'd exited weeks earlier no more alive than the wooden maid at the bow. What a difference love made! she mused, standing back for Dillon to open the door to the captain's cabin. To her delight, he swept her off her feet and, using his foot to spring the latch, carried her into the room.

"After all, this is where we were married!" he explained as he set her down.

Immediately, Rose saw that Dillon had not found the elaborately carved rudder case a threat to his masculinity. It remained just as the Wilson brothers had made it. Smiling, she walked over to the door which connected to her former quarters through the head. It, too, had not been changed.

"We can use that as a nursery someday," she said.

"It will do for the first mate in the meantime. So, what do you think . . . of the ship."

Rose followed Dillon's sweeping arm with her gaze to where the captain's bunk butted against the stern counter. She saw that it had been altered. It was almost as big as the poster bed at home. With a suddenly shy smile, she walked over to it.

"It appears the captain is expecting to have company."

"If we're to fill a nursery, he'd best have it," Dillon chuckled. "My children's mother will sleep here when she's not sorely vexed with me."

"Oh, you'd never vex your children's mother," Rose teased, wrapping her arms about his waist.

"Not intentionally." Dillon's voice had dropped to a lower octave. He pulled her to her feet and brushed her lips with a tender caress. In the background the noonday guns thundered from Citadel Hill. "So does this meet milady's approval?"

"I shan't say until I try it, sir," Rose replied, slipping past him playfully. "It's a shame we must wait until the war is over."

Dillon caught her wrist and tugged her back. "Who says we have to?"

"Dillon, the workers are topside!"

"It's time for the midday meal. They're leaving like rats from a sinking ship for the Split Crow."

"So we've the ship to ourselves?" The idea was as stirring as it was pleasing—she and Dillon alone in the cabin where so much had come between them.

"I thought it only fitting that we christen the new bed."

Her husband had produced a bottle of French champagne from a locker beneath the berth. "Henry must have forgotten the glasses," he remarked, giving away that this was a well-planned liaison.

"Who needs glasses," she quipped with a diabolical grin to match her husband's.

They spent the remainder of the afternoon sharing the nuptial bed the circumstances of their forced wedding had denied them. Rose still blushed, recalling the sly looks they'd received from the dockworkers upon emerging topside a few hours later. Of course, she and Dillon had every right to rock the ship on its keel in the privacy of the captain's bed. The *Border Rose* was theirs!

Since that time, three weeks ago, Dillon had left Rose with a sweet tide of memories with which to pass her time until he returned. He continued to unveil his plans for them with the excitement of a child at Christmas, from presenting the *Border Rose* in the harbor to showing her the isolated farm on the outskirts of the city, where he planned to spend his time ashore.

"Are you weady, Aunt Rose?" Alison asked from the hall, her r's still coming off as w's, despite Claude Benet's attempts to change them.

Rose was hesitant to let her reverie go just yet. Her husband had carried her like a new bride over that threshold, too, although without the amenities of a bed or fire, they'd decided to christen their bedroom in warmer weather. Besides, the caretaker had been there and was as anxious as Dillon for Rose to like the place.

She'd heard nothing from her husband or his ship in a week. All she could assume was that the pirates had not taken the bait and her ship was on its way to Maine with much-needed provisions. There was nothing to worry about, she told herself sternly. She addressed the expectant little girl standing in the open door of the master bedchamber.

"I'm getting my cloak now and I'll meet you in the front hall."

The trip to the farm would be a cold one, accented, not only by Dillon's absence, but by the latest snowfall. Drifts were piled high as the hedges growing at the edge of the manor grounds. Only if it were absolutely necessary did anyone leave the house. That, combined with the end of the holiday excitement, had the entire household suffering a bout of relentless doldrums.

Everyone except Ellis Harrison. Audra's husband claimed to be snowed in and had taken up residence in Dillon's office, which was within walking distance. With him strutting about the house like the rooster left in charge, no one, aside from Mavis, who was like a lusting second shadow to the man, ventured far from their rooms, except for meals and a short gathering after supper. Driven to distraction by the inactivity, which only made her long for Dillon more, Rose came up with the idea to hire a sleigh to take them out to the farm Dillon had shown her before he left.

Audra and Amanda were going to accompany her and the children. Rose was certain Dillon's sister agreed because Claude Benet was to act as their escort. Out of politeness, an invitation went out to her brother-in-law as well, but he claimed to have taken a chill and preferred to remain settled comfortably in the library with the fine selection of imported liquors Dillon kept. Everyone, including Rose, sighed with relief when he declined.

On the way back the adults promised to take the children skating on the arm near Melville Island to try out the new skates they'd gotten for Christmas. Alison and Jerome were fairly jumping with exhilaration when Rose descended to the central hall of the lavish Argyle Street mansion. Bundled in coats, gloves, and wool leggings, they reminded her of bouncing overstuffed dolls.

"This is a wonderful idea, Rose!" Amanda Mackay, who'd been sequestered throughout the holidays with a cold, told her as they walked out to the waiting sleigh. "It feels good to fill these lungs with fresh air!"

With footwarmers and blankets, Claude and the children huddled together on one of the seats, while the women, wrapped in cloaks with deep fur collars and black otter muffs, settled in the facing one. After going a few blocks to the Parade, they joined several turnouts, each with two horses in tandem boasting dozens of small bells jingling on the harness. All were bound for the trip along the North Arm for the skating.

Somewhere ahead of them, a man with a bugle played a few lines of "Rule Britannia," and away they went up the slope past Citadel Hill and across the white-blanketed common. The sunshine was blinding with brightness, giving the surroundings a fairylike appearance which was enhanced by the ethereal tinkling of the sleigh bells.

When the entourage sought the shadowed thoroughfare of the woods bordering the Northwest Arm, the Mackay sleigh veered off on another white road, its runners squeaking and squealing above the lively French song Monsieur Benet led the children in. The jingle of the silver-belled harness, now isolated from the indefinite ring of the multitudes, seemed to keep time just for them. Although Rose missed Dillon, she was enjoying herself.

She pictured the chart he'd spread on the desk in the captain's cabin. He'd be in Castine by now, she thought. He might even be sharing a warm brandy by the stone hearth in her father's kitchen, while Aggie and John Beaujeu plied him with questions.

Someday there would be such an inviting scene in the big kitchen attached to one end of the large two-story farmhouse that loomed over the next rise, she mused wistfully. The smaller building was decidedly French, with its hip roof, while the new addition boasted more Georgian lines. Dillon called it a bastard. Rose considered it a charming portrayal of their ancestry, both Acadian and English.

Not that she intended to remain there twelve months out of the year. She and Dillon agreed that they would settle for six months at sea and six at home. Their children, were they to be blessed with them, would accompany them and live the best of both lives.

"It's not as big as Grandmama's house," Jerome observed as they moved through the snow-crested orchards lining both sides of the approaching drive.

"It isn't," Rose agreed, "but it's all Uncle Dillon and I need for now."

"Do I have a room?" Alison queried.

"We'll make room for you when you visit," Rose assured them.

"Somebody's living there!" Jerome shouted, pointing to the single spiral of smoke wafting up from the attached cottage.

"That would be Mr. Givans. He's the caretaker who's supervising the repairs Dillon's ordered."

"It'll take forever, by the look of it," Amanda Mackay whistled skeptically.

The farm had been occupied by a family from Boston since the removal of the Acadians prior and during the French and Indian War in the Colonies. The last heir was a young woman who'd married an English officer and returned to his family home in Gloucester when his tour of duty was over. With no use for it, it had gone up for sale and now belonged to Rose and Dillon.

Large enough to be self-sustaining, the farm was the perfect home in the country. The lands offered field and forest for hunting and riding, as well as a large fish pond for summer and winter recreation.

Mr. Givans met them at the front door, which opened into a narrow hall. "Mrs. Mackay, this is a pleasant surprise! Shall I put on some tea for your guests?"

"Don't you dare go to such trouble!" Rose told him. "We're just taking a quick tour before going skating on the North Arm." She quickly made the introductions and then dismissed the older gentleman with a smile. "You go back to your warm fire. I'm going to show the family about."

The caretaker but nodded in agreement and made his way to the back of the hall. There he snagged the children's attention by disappearing under the straight set of steps, which rose unceremoniously to the second floor.

Alison, however, was more concerned with her own needs than where the servant went. "Is this my bedwoom, Aunt Rose?"

"Room," Claude Benet corrected, enunciating the "r" with a roll.

"Woo-oom," Alison mimicked with equal drama, causing them all to chuckle. "It won't wo . . . rk!" she said with a self-righteous stomp of her booted foot.

"This is the parlor, Alison," Rose informed the child. "The bedrooms are upstairs."

"Where's the servants' steps?" Jerome, who delighted in using the hidden stairwells to reach the forbidden belvedere atop the Argyle Street mansion, inquired. Unable to resist his curiosity any longer, he ran to where Mr. Givans had disappeared in search of a hidden door.

"There are none. This is a simple house."

"Look, you can run all the way around it!"

Jerome ran through the dining room in the back and returned by another door into the parlor. Alison, not to be outdone, took off on her own exploration.

"Alison, come back and listen to your aunt!" Audra called after the girl in a tone that wouldn't seize the attention of a well-trained hound.

"*Alors, ma petite.* To me this instant!" At Claude Benet's command, the patter of footsteps halted and then resumed in obedience. In a matter of seconds, Alison appeared in the hall looking sheepish.

Rose felt for the child, who'd hardly been allowed out of the nursery since her father's arrival. There was so much energy bundled in that little package and nowhere to expend it. "It's all right with me if the children wish to run downstairs, as long as they don't go up the steps."

"Tah, off with ye then, ye little heathens," her mother-in-law said with a wave. "Run yourselves ragged so the rest o' us will get some peace."

With a loud whoop, Jerome took off, Alison squealing after him.

By the time she showed the adults the other downstairs rooms—a living room, dining room, and bedroom, which Dillon intended for his office, the children had calmed sufficiently enough to accompany them upstairs, where the same symmetrical layout existed for four bedrooms. Alison claimed one of the front ones so she could see what company was coming, while Jerome chose a back one overlooking the frozen fishpond. They acted as though there were no question that they'd not move in with their aunt and uncle.

She again felt a pang of guilt that she should know such happiness when it was clear that Audra and Monsieur Benet knew no end to their misery. Although Rose talked with Amanda Mackay about the placement of certain furniture the matron offered freely, she did not miss the couple's wistful exchange of glances. Audra literally stared in adoration at Benet's back when the man carried the children downstairs, Jerome riding like an organ grinder's monkey on his shoulders, while Alison clung to his hip.

Mr. Givans called to them in a chipper voice from the back of the hall when they reached the first floor. "I made some hot chocolate while you were about your tour, Mrs. Mackay. I hope you don't mind. I don't get much company in this weather and I'd appreciate it if you and your guests would join me for a cup."

Scampering away from Monsieur Benet to their new-found friend, the children led the way for the others through the formal dining room to the attached kitchen cottage where a blazing fire in the stone hearth received them.

"That oven's been added on," Mr. Givans explained to Jerome, who asked why the stone was different in color. "In the old days, the folks who lived here did their bakin' outside." He pointed through a casement window to a mound next to the woodpile, glistening white in the sun.

"Who were they?" Alison asked.

"Habitants, they called 'em. Acadian farmers, they were. Had four children."

"Where'd they go?"

"How do you know?" a skeptical Jerome queried at the same time as his sister.

Thoroughly enjoying his enrapt audience, Mr. Givans walked over to a set of three small steps which rose to a narrow door. "They went everywhere, I suppose. Some went to the Colonies, some to Louisiana. Some even got as far as the Indies and England herself!"

"But where did this family go?" the little girl insisted, running her fingers over a smooth nobbin protruding from the stone face of the hearth wall before taking a seat on it.

Her host shrugged. "Only the walls can tell," he said mysteriously. "And all they say is that there were four children—a boy and three little girls."

"How?"

Mr. Givans motioned Jerome over to the door and opened it. "There, if you look real hard, are their names and how tall they were at the time they stood right where you are. See the marks?"

"I can see them, but I can't read 'em." Jerome glanced apologetically at Monsieur Benet. "Not yet anyway."

Intrigued as the children, Rose stepped forward. "Let me see if I can." The marks were on the door facing, while the names had been etched in the jamb. Two began with the letter A and two with L.

"Ala . . . Ali . . ."

"Alison?"

Rose shook her head at the little girl's hopeful suggestion. "Alain!" she announced, an eerie strangeness settling over her. She swallowed dryly and concentrated on the name of the shorter child. There were two N's and two T's crossed as one. Unmistakably it read Annette.

Her grandfather had told her about his family's little farm in Acadie, he called it. He'd painted a pretty picture of the outdoor stone oven smoking near a patch of wildflowers. His mother refused to clear them away, despite his father's complaint that they edged in on the garden.

"Liselle," she went on, hardly needing to focus so hard, now that she knew the names.

"That last one's the one I can't make out," Mr. Givans told her, holding a candlelamp over Rose's shoulder to help her see.

Somewhere within her chest was a burst of joy. "And Laurette, Laurette Beaujeu."

The older man snorted in surprise. "I never saw a family name. Where's that?"

Rose put her hand over her heart. "In here." Her calm manner broke with emotional excitement. "This was my grandfather's home! His name is Alain and his sisters are Annette, Liselle, and Laurette." Destiny had once again played its hand among the Beaujeus in a most unexpected manner. Rose believed more than ever in her love for Dillon and the Beaujeu fate to marry her enemy. By doing so, she had returned to claim the family lands seized by the British nearly sixty years before.

"Do you know where they are?"

The realization struck her dumb for a moment before she acknowledged Jerome's question. "Yes, I do. Grandpère Alain is in Albany, New York. His sister Annette married a farmer on the New York border. Liselle married a lieutenant in the British army and lives with his family in South Carolina."

"And Laurette?"

"Aunt Laurette lives in Philadelphia, I think. Her husband's a printer." Rose frowned at her uncertainty. But she would find out. Oh to see her grandfather's face when he learned a Beaujeu now owned the land that had been taken from his father! She laughed and blinked away her excitement. "It's my family," she explained to her companions. "I can't wait to tell Dillon!"

Twenty-two

Rose had acted adequately impressed when Dillon took her to the farm and tried to imagine it as home. The homestead had been quaint, but offered none of the allure that sailing with Dillon on the *Border Rose* had. Now she didn't have to imagine anything. It *was* her home, the place that would be the roots for the family she hoped to have. If only her husband were there to share this wonderful discovery!

They'd plan a family reunion soon as the war was over and invite all the Beaujeus. Of course, there was work to be done. The plaster walls needed mending and painting, perhaps even wallpaper in certain rooms. Then there were carpets. Naturally the floors would have to be done over to restore their original polish, but she'd not cover them completely. And she'd . . .

Not for the first time Rose laughed, forcing herself to stop her runaway plans as the sleigh turned onto Argyle Street. Her mother-in-law cut her a curious glance and then smiled.

"Ye canna know how glad it makes me to see ye laughin', lassie. Joeli swore ye and the lad would fill the house with life, but I was beginnin' to hae ma doubts. Not that I believe in them bones o' hers anyways. I'm only wishin' ye weren't such gallivanters, plannin' to sail here and there and movin' out to the country."

Amanda Mackay removed a hand from the otter muff which kept it warm and patted Rose's knee. "But I understand. A woman needs her own home, like a man his ship."

"We've neither sailed nor moved yet, Mrs. Mackay . . ."

"Amanda, dearie! You're one of me own now."

The sleigh drew up before the portico of the Mackay mansion and Henry opened the door almost before it came to a stop. Across from them, Claude Benet shook two sleeping children exhausted from their outing on ice. Next to Rose, Audra beamed with affection at the drowsy smiles he received from his charges.

Alison and Jerome enjoyed their uncle Dillon's company. He was prone to do the unexpected, which delighted them no end. However, they seemed to crave the attention that the more conventional Claude Benet gave them. The same need seemed true of Monsieur Benet toward them. The man without a family had found one. Sadly, it belonged to another, one who could care less about them.

"Henry, for heaven's sake, are ye tryin' to heat the whole out of doors?" Amanda chided as she hurried up the front steps and through the open door.

The servant looked past her to Rose with a stricken expression. " 'Tis bad news, madame. I can't bear to say it!"

Rose froze in midstep. Dillon! Like Henry, she couldn't bring herself to speak her worst fear.

"I told you to tell me as soon as the family arrived! Lud, man, is Mavis the only servant in this household who obeys orders?"

Ellis Harrison moved Henry aside with a contemptuous sling and strode straight to Rose. How she remained standing was beyond her. She wanted to hear nothing of what he had to tell her. Somehow she went inside under the unsolicited wing of Harrison's arm. Behind her followed Audra, Monsieur Benet, and the children, all uncharacteristically quiet, as though the silencing dread which afflicted Rose had touched them as well.

"My dear sister," Harrison began, once all were in the vestibule of the hall. His voice echoed with ominous tone all the way to the second-story ceiling.

Rose was neither his dear, nor his sister. What attention she'd received from him had come from a distance, which had suited her perfectly. She neither liked him, nor the way he looked at her, always scrutinizing with a mixture of crude interest and outright calculation.

"The *Border Rose* was brought into the harbor this morning by another vessel."

Rose let out a tentative sigh of relief. Dillon hadn't gone down with his ship, he'd been disabled. "Is Dillon hurt?" she managed against another swell of alarm. If he wasn't, he'd be here telling her the news in person and swearing fit to redden even Jimmy Squarefoot's ears.

With an impassive tone, Ellis Harrison added to her growing concern, "She was found adrift, stripped of her cargo, with no crew, at least alive."

"Dearest God!" Amanda Mackay whispered, sinking into one of the chairs lining the hall.

Rose had no chance to react further, for at that moment Audra Harrison collapsed on the floor in a dead faint. But for Monsieur Benet's quick reflexes in breaking the fall, she'd have struck her head on the parquet floor which shone at the edge of the round plush carpet in its center. As Alison began to cry, while Jerome did his best to assist the Frenchman, his small face whitening by the moment.

Claude Benet glanced from Rose to Amanda furtively, before settling his gaze upon Audra's rightful husband. "Your wife, monsieur . . ."

"Henry, take Audra up to her room and have that damned Maroon see to her!" Harrison barked.

Amanda Mackay, recuperating from the shock herself, intervened with consternation when Claude Benet started to hand Audra over to the manservant. "Nay, Monsieur Benet. I'd have you carry her, if you will. You're a younger man than Henry. Henry, ye fetch Joeli, while I stay with Rose and the children."

"Is mama going to die?" Jerome asked solemnly of his grandmother. Although he did his best to put up a brave front, his eyes were glazed to the point of spilling over.

"Nay, laddie. She's just had a fright." Amanda pulled the boy gently against her skirts. "Come now, Alison, there's no need for tears."

"You children go to the nursery! This is no place for two whining brats! Your aunt has had a terrible shock!"

Rose had watched the goings-on, but not really seen. She was aware of the commotion, but had not really heard. Suddenly, however, she became aware of Ellis Harrison's arm about her shoulder and drew away as though slapped.

"So have your children, sir!" she rallied indignantly. "And that worthless nanny is nothing more than a jailer!" Rose reached for Alison. "Hush now, Ally. Whatever has happened, we'll face it together," she averred against the little girl's velvet bonnet. "We must be brave!"

She had to be, Rose told herself. She wasn't like Audra. She was strong. She had to keep a clear head. "There, you see!" she challenged her disgruntled brother-in-law as Ally wiped her eyes and sniffed with ragged restraint. "Your son and daughter are brave as any adult." If the children could rein in their emotions, so could she. "Now, were you saying Captain Mackay was not among the dead on board?"

Robbed of his greedily assumed authority by Amanda and Rose, Harrison answered, clearly miffed, "So it seems."

Rose lifted her chin. "Then I must assume he is not dead. Is there a search among the islands for any who might have escaped to shore?" Even as she asked, she knew in her heart that if Dillon had survived, he'd never have abandoned the ship, at least not without setting fire to it as he had the *Thorne*. He'd have died first.

The thought ran her through, stilling her heart, but her mind refused to surrender. With painful slowness her blood began to pulse again. The *Border Rose* had been heavily armed. She'd been accompanied by the *Byron*, a British warship. Dillon's crew was ample for two ships and primed for a fight.

The only danger was to the pirates that dared attack them. There had to be more to this than her brother-in-law was telling her, more that, perhaps, he didn't even know.

"Alison," Rose said softly. "You go to your grandmother. Aunt Rose has some business to see to."

"Indeed, madame, I shall take care of business. It's only fitting as the only man in the house that I should spare you ladies that."

"But I don't wish to be spared, Mr. Harrison," Rose answered tersely.

Ellis Harrison puffed up like a blow toad in his green-and-black woven coat. With a thin mask of politeness, he objected. "Madame, I yield to your expertise where this house is concerned, but I must insist—"

"Mr. Harrison," Rose interrupted with equal determination. "I was raised in the shipping business. I cut my teeth on a belaying pin and learned to walk and climb in the riggings of my father's ship. I know ships from keel to top mast."

"But surely in your grievous state . . ."

"I am not grieving, sir, I am angry! And I will not grieve until I see my husband's body! Until that time, I intend to do everything I can to locate him."

"And how do you plan to do that?"

Rose ignored the man's cynicism. "First, I want to examine the ship. Depending on what I find there will determine my next move."

"You will not like what you see, madame. The fighting must have been severe."

For the first time, Rose realized someone other than the family was in the hall. Standing outside the library door was a swarthy man, clad in canvas trousers and a woolen pea jacket. A red knit hat covered just the top of a bushy head of dark hair, shorter on the sides, but greatly in need of scissors. A thick shadow, nearly a beard, indicated a razor was in order as well. As Rose took in his appearance, the man stepped forward in varnished knee boots and bowed slightly. "I am Captain Maitland, at your service."

"Captain Maitland was the one who found the *Border Rose* afloat off Petite Mouton."

He was a seaman, all right. His ruddied complexion and rough hands bespoke a life of handling ropes in the bitter elements. He was also French, although his accent was faint.

"How far away is Petite Mouton, Captain?"

"One . . . nearly two days from Halifax," the man answered. "I'd have taken her in at Liverpool, but Halifax was my destination and the *Border Rose*'s port of registry."

"You found her papers then?" Rose asked in surprise.

"In a nail barrel, but then, what would such a barrel be doing in the captain's cabin, except as a disguise for such things?"

Why indeed would Dillon have kept the papers in such an obvious place when there was the hidden compartment in the rudder case?

"Maybe ye'd best rest, Rose, rather than set off on a jaunt sure to upset ye even more," Amanda suggested, mistaking Rose's confusion for distress.

"I thank both you and Mr. Harrison for your concern, but were I to sequester myself in my room, my imagination would make any respite impossible. I'm best kept busy." Rose turned to Captain Maitland and extended her hand. "Captain, I thank you for bringing my ship home. Now if you will tell me where she's moored . . ."

"I must protest!" Ellis Harrison blurted out. "You've no business submitting yourself to this and you barely out of sequester yourself!"

"Then protest, sir. I intend to see the *Border Rose*. Captain?" Rose prompted, returning to her question of the stranger.

"She is in the harbor near the Mackay warehouses. But at least wait until tomorrow, madame. It will be nightfall before too long."

"I know how to light a lantern."

"But the waterfront is not the place for a lady."

"The captain is right, Rose. Please wait until the morning," Amanda Mackay pleaded.

Rose wrestled with the idea. Waiting would be torture, although there was no guarantee that she'd find anything to help her hold on to the belief that Dillon was still alive. The guns of the Citadel would be signaling the hour of six soon, she reasoned, judging by the shadowed street visible through the front windows.

"Very well," she conceded at last, "but only if Captain Maitland will stay for supper and tell me every detail he observed about the *Border Rose*."

"Don't be absurd! Captain Maitland has already gone far and above any obligation to us!" Ellis Harrison declared derisively. "Why, he's not even presentable!"

Rose smiled apologetically to the captain for Harrison's tactless observation. "I'm quite at home with men of the captain's bent and dress. I grew up with them and many are my dearest friends." She placed a plaintive hand on Captain Maitland's arm. "It would ease my mind, sir."

"So would a good dose of laudanum!" Harrison fumed. "Perhaps you might address the captain tomorrow."

Maitland wavered as Rose tightened her fingers on his arm, his dark eyes darting from her to Ellis Harrison and back. Rose seized the opportunity. "My husband keeps an excellent French brandy, one of the advantages of making a living at sea that I'm certain you're acquainted with."

"I've seen my share of contraband," Maitland admitted warily as Rose turned her back to him for him to help her off with her wrap.

She took the cloak and tossed it on a chair before engaging the disconcerted captain's arm again. "Have a brandy at least," she suggested, leading him toward the back parlor where a fire was always kept going. "I promise, I shan't keep you away from your first night ashore too long. The taverns should be ripe by the time you reach them."

"You've a keen appreciation of man's life at sea and ashore, madame."

"I said I was raised among sailors, didn't I?"

The captain compromised by spending an hour or so before supper with the family in the parlor. In the informal atmosphere, he relayed what information he could, although it was clear that he was not at ease.

Captain Maitland and his men had come across the *Border Rose*, and, upon hailing her and receiving no answer, boarded her. The evidence was there of a hard battle. Many of the sails had been rent by shot, the mainmast toppled, and the deck was mottled with blood and sand. They collected the discarded weapons, sewed the bodies in blankets, and put a skeleton crew aboard the vessel to take her to their destination of Halifax.

"You saw no British warships?" Rose inquired.

"There's plenty about when you don't need them, madame. I saw but one."

"And its name?"

"What possible interest is a British warship?" Ellis Harrison mumbled irritably at Rose. He'd given up his charade of the concerned brother-in-law and had not called her "dear" since.

"They may have seen something."

"If they had, they'd have claimed the ship for their own!"

Recalling the encounter with the avaricious captain of the *HMS Demand,* Rose realized he spoke the truth. Still, she was curious.

Maitland shifted beneath her expectant gaze. "It passed too far away to tell."

Possibilities of all sorts haunted Rose after her guest left. She could hardly eat, much less carry on any semblance of conversation at the dinner table, where Ellis Harrison had taken Dillon's customary seat without thought to the feelings of his female companions. Dillon had confided that he was sailing as a decoy. Perhaps he'd been on the British ship. But then, he'd not have left the *Border Rose* adrift.

When one solution came to a dead end, another quickly usurped its place. What if Dillon had set a charge to blow up the *Border Rose* and abandoned ship to be picked up by the *Byron?* The ship hadn't blown and . . .

A man couldn't last long in the water, not in the dead of winter. They could have put over in a longboat. She'd forgotten to ask the captain if any were still aboard. From what he'd told them, the *Border Rose* was battle torn, but still seaworthy, so Dillon wouldn't have abandoned ship because she was sinking. If there had only been twenty dead, as Maitland reported, where were the extra crew Dillon had carried along?

On the *Byron*, she told herself, settling against the cold pillow in her bedchamber a few hours later. The bed seemed twice as big without Dillon beside her, and a hundredfold as empty. She'd remained in the parlor until she could no longer bear Ellis Harrison's presence. Although she'd been careful not to reveal the plan Dillon had confided to her, the man hung on to her and her stepmother's every observation about the calamity like a dog with a choice bone and did his utmost to discourage any hope that may have resulted from their speculation.

If the bastard were the right size, no doubt he'd have donned Dillon's clothing by now, she thought grudgingly. Or worse, he'd follow through with the licentious looks he'd slipped her way from time to time and try to fill her bed. Although Rose doubted the man had the courage to dare such a thing, she'd put a silver letter opener under her pillow.

Rose shivered under the heavy layer of blankets. Her imagination was running wild at this point. She'd even seized on the parting "Your Lordship" Captain Maitland addressed Ellis Harrison as, although the mistake was an understandable one. The seaman had seen the mansion and assumed a titled heir was most likely privy to such elegance. Heaven knew, Harrison's haughty and demanding manner would rival that of the king of England!

Rose realized she was desperate for a clue, anything which might explain this catastrophe. The chances of Ellis Harrison being the same lordship referred to by

the shavers, however, was as remote as the real title
Amanda Mackay had told Rose he coveted. Her brother-
in-law was so eager to take over as Dillon's successor in
the family affairs that it was only natural to place the
blame on him.

A telltale creak on the opposite side of the room
struck Rose's contemplation still. She ran her hand up
under her pillow and grasped the letter opener as the
door continued to open in a gooseflesh-raising cre-
scendo. A sliver of light from the lamps kept burning
in the hall crept into the room and, although Rose
stared at the entrance for a sign of the nocturnal intruder, she saw neither shadow nor form.

After what seemed a thousand heartbeats, the door
closed as mysteriously as it had opened and Rose let
out a breath of relief. However, before it was fully spent,
she realized she was not alone. Someone was on the
floor, making their way toward the bed in a slow, muted
shuffle.

"Who's there?" Her nails bit into her the flesh of her
palm as she tightened her grip on the letter opener.

"It's me . . . Jerome!"

Rose nearly laughed upon seeing the child's round
head rising over the edge of her mattress. She tousled
his pale blond hair with a vengeance. "You scared the
life out of me, you rascal!"

"Nobody knows I'm here," he answered proudly. "I
snuck right out after Mavis left her room . . ."

Rose didn't have to guess where the nanny had
headed.

". . . an' hid under the hall table till she snuck into
Father's bedroom," the boy went on. "Then I came
right here."

Jerome crossed his arms across his nightshirt with a
little shiver. Uncertain as to whether it was born of excitement, the cold, or both, Rose threw back the covers.

"Well, climb in here until you take the chill off and tell me why you're wandering about in the middle of the night, young man."

In an instant, Jerome was beside her, snuggling as close under her arm as he could get. He was cold, Rose thought, carefully tucking the blankets over him. Such a little imp, but a sweet one. She planted an affectionate kiss on his forehead.

"How's that?"

"Better than sleeping with Alison. She wets the bed."

"Is that why you came here . . . to find a warm, dry bed?"

She felt the little boy shake his head in denial. "I needed to talk to you and I haven't been able to get away from that old Mavis!"

"About what?"

"About that man that was here earlier. He had a blue mark like some of the ones who turned over Mama's coach."

Rose had noticed a small tattoo of the fleur-de-lis on the back of Captain Maitland's hand, surrounded by a scarlet-ribboned heart.

"It was like a flower, but it wasn't like any I've seen in Mama's garden."

"It's a French symbol," she explained.

A tattoo proved nothing, she told herself, before her mind ran away with speculation. There were lots of Frenchmen about, now that the war with France had ended. Monsieur Benet might have such a tattoo somewhere on his person.

"Did his face look familiar?"

"No. Ally and I didn't see much of the men's faces because of all the hair and beards. That man's hair wasn't as long as the ones who scared us."

Neither the hair, nor calling Ellis Harrison Your Lordship, nor the fact that he had a French accent and a tattoo was sufficient to incriminate Captain Maitland, Rose reasoned. Besides, if he were responsible for the *Border Rose*'s misfortune, why would he come to the owner's house to report it?

Rose whistled silently in frustration. She'd check the captain out, although in Castine she'd have a better idea of how to go about it. Without Dillon, she'd never felt farther away from home.

As soon as she was up and dressed the next morning, Rose found Joeli in the kitchen and revealed her plan to visit the *Border Rose*. The maid, after a long night of assuring Audra Harrison that there were no monsters closing in on her, had been too weary to do more than caution her. When Rose slipped quietly through the front entrance, the rest of the household was still abed, including Jerome, who'd spent the remainder of the night in her room.

Dillon wasn't dead! She knew it, not because of Joeli's insistence that her mysterious bones had said so, but because she felt it in her heart. He was somewhere, needing her to piece together the puzzle he'd left behind.

Rose was able to pay one of the vendors on the way to market for a ride on his wagon. Although he was reluctant at first, the sight of a shining silver coin did away with his objections to a lady of her status riding on the seat beside him. By the time they reached Water Street, he'd become quite talkative about the little farm which had produced the milk and butter he carried in the back of the wagon in earthenware crocks and cisterns.

As he assisted Rose down off the wagon, she scanned the harbor and spied the *Border Rose* rocking gently at her moorings. Her sails were reefed, those on the one mast that remained in tact. Blasted pirates, the first thing they tried to do was cut the masts in two. Rose turned her attention to the docks.

That early, they were still, aside from a few salts who were stubbornly carrying on their celebration of the previous night. Most of the dockworkers were no doubt in the tavern on the corner where the smell of fresh bread and brewing coffee beckoned like a siren song to the damned. Feeling somewhat damned herself for failing to consider that no one would be about to hire out yet, Rose tightened her grip on her purse and stepped through the door beneath a sign of a banty cock squared off with feathers in full array.

She'd indeed found the warm haven of the men who put off going out to the water as long as possible with hot coffee and, in some cases, a stronger brew. Aware that talk had ceased and all eyes were upon her, she walked up to one of the sleepy-eyed serving wenches.

"A cup of coffee please, black," she added, slipping a coin into the woman's hand.

"That's handsome pay for a'that," the woman replied.

"There's also handsome pay for anyone who'll take me out to the *Border Rose* in the harbor," Rose said in a voice loud enough to reach the right ears. Surely there were some wherrymen about at this hour to transport her to her ship.

"Ye be the Mackay's Yankee bride, don't ye," a round-shouldered old salt observed from the rough-hewn table next to her.

Rose eyed the man curiously, uncertain whether or not to answer. Too many years of tobacco smoke and shouting above the roar of the wind and sea had coarsened his voice to a rasp, just as age had bent his body. His unwashed hair was dark with grease, his matted beard no better and bobbed of its own accord when he spoke.

"Aye, I am," she acknowledged slowly.

"I'd not go there wi'out me own men aboard, if'n I was in yer place, pretty boots."

"Whose men are aboard her?" Rose inquired, ignoring his presumptuous address. The old man motioned for her to join him and lowered his voice so that she had to lean toward him to hear.

"The same what brought her in."

Coffee and whiskey dominated what might otherwise have been unbearable breath. Rose backed away as he started to hack and cough. She'd not had breakfast and her stomach was already unsteady with want.

"So you think I should find some of the Mackay workers and board her with them?" she asked, taking the steaming mug of coffee from the obliging serving woman with a grateful smile.

"Makes no nevermind to me!" her companion answered in strangled voice. "Ye'll be hard put to find a wherry for such today, what with the hangin' on the admiralty ship this mornin'. I'll take ye out, but 'twill cost ye more." He peered at the purse wrapped about her arm. "Or I'll take ye to the Mackay office for a small fee. I know a shortcut through the alley . . ."

"No thank you. You've been helpful enough."

She hadn't been born yesterday. Shot with gray and bent as he was, her companion had not failed in strength, not if he rowed a wherry to accommodate harbor traffic. He could easily detour her through some abandoned alley. It was daylight, but not many were stirring to come to her aid, should she need it.

Her companion made no other offer, but concentrated on his own brew, while Rose sipped all of hers that she could stomach. The low ceiling and closeness of the room was bearing down upon her. Or was it the gaze peering out at her from under her companion's prominent eyebrows? Feeling like a small fish trapped in a shallow pond, Rose squirmed off the bench, leaving her mug of coffee half full.

"Thank you for your advice, sir. I think I shall wait."

Instead of answering, the old man shrugged and straightened his long legs under the table. Rose could see the holes in the soles of his boots, resting under the bench she'd just abandoned. The bits of rag he used to keep out cold poked through them, filthy as the rest of him.

Not the least at ease, she returned to the street and walked to the corner where the morning watch was stationed, huddled next to a burning cresset like a drunk to his bottle. After chiding her for being out and about in such a place at such an hour, the soldier obligingly gave Rose the directions to George Street and followed her with his gaze until she disappeared around the corner a few blocks up. Her booted feet were numb with cold by the time she arrived at the Mackay office building.

Once again she passed the time with a cup of coffee furnished by a disconcerted clerk before Dillon's business manager arrived. Already aware of the news concerning the *Border Rose* and her captain, Mr. Foster assured her that he had the matter well in hand and would keep her advised of any information they discovered. Again she was told that her business was at home with the senior Mrs. Mackay, but Rose would hear it no more. She cut loose with all the obscenities to which she could lay tongue, leaving the man speechless. "Now I'm going aboard that ship! You can tie to it, sir! And you'd best hope my husband does come back, because if not, it's your position that rests with my disposition!"

She folded her arms expectantly and waited for the stunned man to reclaim his wits. Rose had never been given to swinging about her authority, not aboard her father's ships, nor at the shipyard, but she'd wearied of being told what she could not do.

"W-well, I'll try summon what men I can, Mrs. Mackay."

Rose gave him a saccharine smile. "Please do, Mr. Foster."

She was shown to Dillon's office, where she sank into his upholstered chair, its oxblood leather worn and soft, suggesting that it had born his father's use as well as his own. It seemed to cradle her in the semicircle of its cushioned arms. As close as she could come to knowing her husband's assuring embrace, Rose leaned back in the sturdy confines of his chair and closed her eyes.

She'd find Dillon, she promised. She'd find him or at least find out what happened to him. She had to. She'd not rest until she did.

Twenty-three

"Mrs. Mackay, you are up and about early this morning."

Rose came upright in the oversize chair at Ellis Harrison's wry observation from the doorway of the office. She refrained from making any derisive remarks herself, although she wondered what had pried the man from his bed after spending the night with Mavis Adams. "So are you, sir."

"Mr. Foster says that you're insisting we replace Captain Maitland's men with our own," Harrison chuckled without humor. "Foolish lady, the captain's men consider the ship their prize and have every right to it until it is dispensed with at the prize court."

"But they know it's my ship!"

"It's a formality, madame, nothing more. However, if you insist on going aboard and are reluctant to do so with a strange crew in possession of it, then I shall be glad to accompany you."

Behind her unsolicited visitor, Mr. Foster cowered as though expecting another outburst. She supposed she hadn't given the man a chance to explain the details to her.

"My apologies, Mr. Foster," she said. "The news of Dillon's disappearance . . ." She refused to say demise. ". . . has reduced me to a state of near hysteria. I am collected now, however," she went on, addressing her brother-in-law. "And I accept your offer to accompany me to the *Border Rose*."

Sometimes meekness won more cooperation than bluster. "I told Joeli I'd be back for the noonday meal, however," Rose added, making certain Harrison knew that others were aware of her whereabouts. She didn't trust him.

As for Mr. Foster, she wasn't certain. He was certainly well dressed for an office manager, she thought, noticing the fine weave of his coat and costly brocade of his vest. But, according to Amanda, Mackays did pay well.

The fact was, she could trust no one, Rose decided as she accompanied Ellis Harrison into a hired coach to return to the waterfront. No, that wasn't true. She could trust Monsieur Benet! He was the one she'd have investigate Mr. Foster and Captain Maitland. Much as it aggravated her, as a man he would be able to find out more than she. In the meantime, she'd contact the admiralty about the whereabouts of the *Byron*.

After giving the coachman a stingy tip, Ellis Harrison helped Rose out of the squeaking vehicle and hailed one of the wherrymen who now gathered to the south of the King's Wharf.

"To the hanging?" a younger man asked, maneuvering the pointed prow of his boat alongside a floating ramp.

"To yon *Border Rose!*"

"I'm only taking folks to see the hanging!"

"Perhaps this will make it worth your while, sir." Rose produced a gold coin from her purse, enough to pay a boatload's passage for a flogging round the fleet, which would require moving from ship to ship as the poor victim was dealt his blows on each, and a hanging.

"You could have purchased him and the boat for

that!'' Ellis Harrison complained at her side as the young man shoved off from the dock.

"I mean to get to my ship, sir," Rose replied tersely, before smiling at the wherryman.

The tide was incoming, causing it to take longer to reach the moored ship. Rose's cloak, warm as it was, was no match for the chilling breeze that caused other harbor passengers to huddle close together in order to brave the weather long enough to witness the execution a distance away. A yellow flag fluttered at the flagship's mizzen top mast, signifying the seriousness of the punishment in store.

Rose shuddered at the recollection of the bodies hanging on the beach at the harbor entrance. Another would be added to them today, she supposed, although what brought the increasing crowds out to see a man hanged was beyond her. Doxies snuggled next to fur-decked ladies. Businessmen shared the flat plank seats with farmers seeking to fill their idle winter time with the grisly amusement.

The men on the *Border Rose* seemed surprised when the wherry veered toward them rather than the warship moored near George's Island. They scurried to prepare a sling for Rose, but she called out to them that it was unnecessary. She'd come prepared to climb up the side with a pair of wool flannel trousers from Dillon's chest tied under her skirts.

Without regard for the way the wind played scandalously with them, Rose climbed aboard, allowing the watch to assist her over the rail. While Ellis Harrison made the same trip, she surveyed the deck, oblivious to the embarrassed apologies made by the flustered man on duty.

"We wasn't expectin' a lady, yer lordship."

Again the phrase caught Rose's attention, but the sight of the sand-littered decks, splintered and darkened with blood, made her sway uncertainly. Ellis Harrison caught her arm as she steadied herself.

"The captain tried to warn you."

Rose forced herself to ignore the weakness as well as the comment and concentrated on the ominous scene before her. Some of the guns Dillon had had installed on the top deck were missing. Had they been thrown over the side to outrun the pirate attack? She'd heard of such maneuvers. Sometimes the heavy guns were abandoned in shallows so that they might be salvaged later.

"Where is Captain Maitland?" her brother-in-law demanded beside her.

" 'E's aboard the *Flora* over there!"

"And what is your name, sir?"

"Gimp, sor, what wid me leg as it is!" To demonstrate the seaman took a few hobbling steps away and back.

"Who is in charge here, Mr. Gimp?" Harrison demanded, unaffected.

"Tha'd be me, sor!"

"Where are you from, Mr. Gimp?"

Rose turned away from the deck, distracted by her companion's interrogation of the crew. "I'd like to go to the captain's cabin. Is there someone in there?"

"Naw, mum. We's scace enough to fill six hammocks, but who'd cause trouble 'ere amongst 'Is Majesty's whole bloody navy?"

Once again Rose assumed a mild demeanor. It wasn't hard, for the sight of her beleaguered ship was enough to make her feel as though her brain and limbs were stuffed with straw.

"I'd like to spend some time there alone, if I might, Mr. Harrison."

"I dunno," the watchman started.

"She owns this ship. Her late husband was Captain Mackay."

At that, the man's eyes widened. "By all means, mum, by all means!"

"You go on, Mrs. Mackay. I'd like to speak to the crew a bit more," Ellis Harrison told her. "Unless you'd have me escort you down the hatch?"

"No! I could maneuver the steps blindfolded, sir."

For all that she could see as she descended to the main, she might as well have been. Despite her resolve not to let her emotion run wild, her eyes were flayed with it and blurred. Dillon wasn't dead, she told herself sternly. This was all a nightmare and she'd wake up any moment!

The latch to the captain's cabin gave easily, as though it welcomed her. Once inside, Rose refused to gaze at the bed she and Dillon had christened as man and wife. Instead, she went straight to the carved rudder case and twisted one of the wood-petaled blossoms until it came free from the meticulous turnings the Wilson brothers had made.

She didn't know exactly what she expected to find as she reached inside the hidden cavity, but when her fingers closed around a folded sheet of paper, she caught her breath. She opened it up and began to read the note scrawled in Dillon's bold hand.

"Rosebud, go home before you ruin our plan! I told you I'd be safe and I am! Sorry about the ship, but it can be repaired." It was signed, "All my love, Dillon."

The sound of hurried footsteps coming down the hatch outside the cabin drove Rose to shove the missive into her purse and hurriedly screw the wooden rose blossom back in place. As the latch clicked, permitting Ellis Harrison entry, she started.

"Mr. Harrison, whatever is the matter?" She hoped her breathlessness did not betray her.

"You said you wanted to get home by noon. Those

bosun's whistles are signaling eleven . . . the hour of the hanging," he explained at her blank look.

Rose turned toward the window, trying to recoup her composure. Yes, above the excitement pounding in her ears, she could make out the Spit Head Nightingales, as the whistles were commonly referred to along the waterfront, playing all hands to witness punishment. Her spirit had no right to soar when a man was about to die, but she couldn't help it any more than she could help the color which flooded her cheeks.

"It's just as well," she managed, wringing the strings of the purse about her wrist in a show of dismay. "I'm in no humor to witness a show of death under the circumstances. It makes my blood boil!"

Hoping her act was convincing, Rose swung away from the stern counter and marched past her brother-in-law with pulses pounding. Anger was her only hope of hiding her excitement, for she could not manage a look of grief.

"It's just about to start, mum," the watch told her as she took to the rail to climb down into the waiting wherry.

"Then hurry," she said to the young man at the oars. "I've no stomach for this!"

As soon as Ellis Harrison was beside her, they shoved away from the ship. Traveling with the incoming tide instead of against it, the return trip was shorter. Rose kept scanning her surroundings, wondering where her husband was. Obviously they suspected Captain Maitland and were waiting for him to lead them to the mastermind, the insider Dillon suspected. She ventured a glance at Ellis Harrison, but he was too preoccupied with his own thoughts.

And Maitland had contacted her brother-in-law! Was she sitting next to the man who had engineered a plot involving the governor's people in three ports? She fingered her letter opener through the thick tapestry of her purse.

To her astonishment, Ellis Harrison paid the wherry-man again for their transport and hurriedly ushered her to a hired coach which had just put out a passenger at the wharf. Whether it was his urging or her own ecstatic tumult which caused her to trip on the metal rail was anyone's guess. Nonetheless, her purse hung on the doorlatch, jerking her arm back so fiercely that the corded string broke. Rose's chest seized as she scrambled for her balance as well as the handbag, which fell to the floor of the vehicle.

"Heavens, I don't think Joeli will have me with a broken neck!" she managed, snatching it up and tucking in the note which threatened to spill from it as she did so.

Her jest was lost on her companion. Still in a dither of his own, he took the seat across from her and motioned the driver to proceed. As the coach lurched forward, he took particular pains to peer through the flaps on the windows of each side.

"Something is wrong, very wrong," he muttered. Suddenly he looked at Rose with an accusing gaze that tightened her grasp on her sole means of defense. "So what did you see, madame?"

"More than I care to discuss," Rose answered with forced calm. Something had shaken Ellis Harrison. Had the crew on the *Border Rose* said something to alarm him? "I don't see how anyone could have survived a battle like that which rendered mast, deck, and rail in splinters."

She looked away at the waving window cover, hoping she'd sounded as dismayed as she intended. Perhaps if she were distraught, he'd leave her to the ride in peace.

"You looked as though I'd startled you when I entered the captain's cabin."

"You did, sir. It is customary to knock first."

"Did you recognize any of the men aboard the ship?"

Rose was so startled at the question, she stared at the man. "Of course not! That was why I wanted to put her in the hands of Mackay men."

Instead of looking at her, however, Ellis Harrison focused curiously on the handbag clutched in her lap.

"You were the one who said the notion was silly." With conjured pique, she focused on the window again, never dreaming of the coming explosion which struck the side of her face. It flashed white and then dragged her into a sickening swirl, where the window curtain flapped alternately—faded gold, then black . . . faded gold, then black . . . and black . . . and black.

Hunched over an oar fashioned into a crutch, Dillon Mackay watched the hired coach carrying Rose and Ellis Harrison disappear around the corner with an unsettling alarm. Had she read his warning? Was she going home? He motioned to one of Captain Stevenson's guards, a man disguised as a fishmonger. Rose's life wasn't worth the risk, he thought, climbing aboard the cart as the naval officer turned up the street.

"Something wrong?"

"Maybe," Dillon answered tersely. "Who'd believe Harrison was stupid enough to risk going aboard the *Border Rose*?"

He and Captain Stevenson hadn't. When Maitland went to Ellis Harrison with the news of the abandoned ship, they'd hoped his brother-in-law would lead them to the man who put together the macabre circle. Instead, he'd gone to gloat over his alleged victory! Or he'd suspiciously accompanied Rose.

He should have told her everything, Dillon bemoaned. He should have told her that they'd intended to offer the captain of the pirate ship parole if he revealed the identities of the men he worked for. He was to say he found the *Border Rose* abandoned in order to keep anyone from being suspicious until the entire ring was flushed out. The red paint on her decks and the broken rails and mainmast was all part of the scheme, though it had pained Dillon to do such damage to his own ship.

Now Stevenson's men were ready to arrest the culprits on signal, but all was halted until the ringleader was found out. The lower rungs of the ladder could always be replaced, like the shavers who'd been taken near the Grand Manan. Harrison's offer of freedom and profit on the high seas to those willing to work for him and his captains had been ingenious. After serving in the French navy, some of the captives had eagerly taken the opportunity to privateer.

One successful voyage provided enough bodies for burial to send to Melville Island in their place in order to account for the number of names Harrison was responsible for. The rest of those who fell victim to the marauders were killed only to silence any witnesses who might lead to their capture. As for the lost ships, it was as Dillon suspected from the start. They'd not been sunk, but taken to a nearby cove and repainted with new names. Just enough debris had been left to convince local fishermen and villagers.

Ellis Harrison and key men in Digby and Annapolis Royal had accumulated enough wealth in less than a year to retire!

"Hurry, man!"

"He'll know he's being followed if he sees us," his companion objected.

"Drive past the house . . . and don't forget your call!"

"Fish ready cook," the disguised guard called out. "Lobster, too! Buy 'em now, ladies, do so do!"

Dillon strained to see Rose climb out of the halted coach, but, so far, only Ellis Harrison had emerged. He was waving his hands in frenzy, motioning the coachman to the front door. The latter leapt from the high seat and landed hard enough to break his legs. Numbed from the jar, they carried him stumbling up the steps where he began to beat on the door. By the time Henry answered it, Dillon saw Ellis Harrison emerge from the cover of the coach again, this time carrying a limp figure in his arms.

Rose! Fear clutched his throat even as he snapped, "Drive to the corner and turn around. We're going to sell some fish at the back of the house."

"But he's not . . ."

"Damn it, man, something's wrong! Now do as I say and I'll take the responsibility."

As the cold darkness which claimed her consciousness thawed, Rose had the sense of being carried up a set of steps. She could hear Amanda Mackay's authoritative voice, but her head was starting to pound too loudly to make out what the woman said. All she knew was that there was some sort of argument going on. Then she felt a mattress beneath her and the chaos began to sort itself out in her mind.

"Madame, I am taking the young lady with me! As I told the others, should you call the authorities or in any way try to stop me, I promise she shall suffer more than a bruised skull."

"Ye're nae worth the dirt on my daughter's slippers!"

"There's considerable dirt there, believe me, madame," Ellis Harrison sneered.

Rose blinked her eyes, but was barely able to make the man out. He was pointing something at her mother-in-law. A pistol? Was that what he'd struck her with?

"Leave the lassie here, sir!" Amanda pleaded as Harrison turned toward the bed where Rose lay. "Dillon will ne'er let ye rest if one hair of her head is harmed."

Rose closed her eyes quickly. She had to pull her wits together. How did Amanda know Dillon was alive? Had he confided in his stepmother and not her? Or had Ellis Harrison read the note in her purse?

"Nor will he lift a finger to stop me as long as I have her in my custody. She's too precious to him to risk it." He traced a finger over the swelling on Rose's temple, causing her to wince. "Ah, I believe she's coming around!"

At that moment, the door opened, sparing her further examination. Mavis Adams entered the room in a panting rush carrying a traveling bag. "I've got my things, luv! The brats are locked tight in their rooms and the rest of the staff is sulking downstairs like dogs on a short leash. How I've waited for this moment!"

"The Frenchman?"

"Gone for his afternoon classes."

"And my wife?"

"Sleeping like a babe, what with the laudanum I slipped in her toddy awhile ago."

"God save ye, is that what ye've been doin' to me daughter?" Amanda Mackay's voice quivered with outrage.

"Just to keep her calm, madame . . . and to keep her from remembering," Harrison confirmed in a perfunctory manner. "As for you," he said, addressing Mavis, "wipe that gloating smile off your face and invite the coachman in for tea in the kitchen. Tell him I'll be awhile and . . ." Rose heard the clinking of change, "give him this for his trouble. 'Tis small enough price to pay for his vehicle."

Rose tried not to stiffen as Harrison turned her way

once again. The longer she pretended to be unconscious, the more time she had to figure out what to do.

"Bring me some salts, woman! She's heavier than she looks and I'll not be carrying her."

A rush of indignation swept more blood to Rose's face, increasing the pounding in her temples. Since he was determined she return to consciousness, there was no point in suffering a nose full of ammonia.

"I'll need no salts, nor the likes of you carrying me!"

"Well, well, the sleeping princess awakens."

"No thanks to you," Rose averred. She made no objection when Amanda Mackay rushed to her side to help her sit upright.

"Easy now, lassie. Ye've had quite a blow to the head."

"On your feet, madame, we've a coach to catch before your husband and his hounds converge upon us."

Rose stared at the folded paper her captor shook out before her eyes and her heart sank. She'd been nothing to Dillon but trouble since they'd crossed paths. Why hadn't she put it back where it was safe? she moaned silently.

Except that something had tipped the man off before he'd seen the note, she reasoned through the blur of pain that assaulted her when Ellis Harrison pulled her to her feet from the edge of the mattress.

"How . . . what put you wise?" she asked, swaying on her feet in confusion.

"Instinct, my dear. Your husband's little love note and the fact that I recognized none of the crew. Maitland might have taken on a few strangers on his own, but not that many."

"Where . . . where are we going?"

"Don't even think about using that poker, Mother dear! I've a pistol at this young lady's ribs and I should hate to panic and set it off by accident."

Rose felt the prod of the barrel through the folds of

her cloak and heard her stepmother mutter something under her breath in another language. No doubt it was a Gaelic curse of the basest nature.

A few French ones came to Rose's mind, but she was too dazed to utilize them. It required all her strength and concentration to maneuver the steps plummeting before her. Her hand clenched white about the polished wood rail, she carefully placed one foot in front of the other. She daren't trust her knees. They threatened to buckle with each step, as though somehow they'd become disconnected from the rest of her.

Upon reaching the landing where the two sets of stairs converged from either side of the second-floor gallery, she stopped a moment to steady herself. If only her head would stop throbbing. As she raised her free hand to the swelling at her temple, the front door opened unexpectedly and a rush of cold air invaded the hall.

"Bonjour, bonjour! Silly me, I forgot my papers . . ."

Rose meant to warn the unsuspecting Monsieur Benet, but at the same time her knees buckled and she dropped with a gasp on the carpeted landing.

Claude Benet started for her with an astonished "Madame!"

"Stay right where you are, Monsieur Benet!" Ellis Harrison's fingers bit viciously into Rose's arm.

Claude Benet did as he was told. "But what has happened?"

"My son-in-law's corruption has come to a head and he's takin' Rose as hostage," Amanda Mackay said from the gallery above. "He has a gun at her side, monsieur. Don't provoke him."

"That's right, Monsieur Benet," Harrison concurred. "You of all people should not provoke me."

"But I must help the lady! She is hurt!"

"No, I'm fine!" Rose insisted, struggling to her feet.

"Your face! *Mon Dieu,* did you do that?" he challenged Harrison.

"Miss Audra say de monster comin' all night, an' Joeli, she tink de little gal crazy. She no be crazy, *non!* Yes, she be smartest of all."

Joeli's chanting from the back of the house drove Ellis Harrison against the wall, dragging Rose with him, as if he expected the Maroon to impale him with a ceremonial knife. "Come out of there, you simple Maroon, where I can see you!"

Although he growled in demand, something about his manner continued to suggest panic. Claude Benet's arrival had sparked it and Joeli's chanting only added fuel.

"Dillon saw us leave the ship. I saw him."

"The devil you did!"

Rose winced, half expecting the pistol he jabbed at her to go off. Instinct told her she'd struck a raw chord. If she could keep him distracted, there was a chance she might pull away, provided she didn't fall down the remaining stairs in the process.

"He and Captain Stevenson know about you and your contacts in Digby and Annapolis Royal. He knows the whole bloody game you've been playing. The *Border Rose* was a decoy and your men snapped at it. I believe Captain Maitland has left you in still water, sir."

"Enough!"

She saw his pistol hand coming up toward her face and drew back as far as his hold on her would allow, but Rose could not avoid the blow. The noonday sunlight pouring in through the palladium window over the front door seemed to intensify to a blinding flash which knocked her legs out from under her. The pressure of the fingers on her arm gave way to a blast of agony which sent her sprawling against the table on the landing.

Glass crashed somewhere near her, tenor compared to the explosion of the pistol which burst in Rose's ears. Anticipating the bullet tearing into her flesh, Rose clung to the edge of the steps. Was she in shock and couldn't feel the shot? She forced her eyes open in time to see a shadow looming in front of her, a silhouette swaying and then teetering backward. It landed somewhere with a series of rolling thuds. Harrison?

Joeli screamed, a high-pitched wail that raked into Rose's consciousness. From upstairs there was a thunder of descending feet. Amanda's? she wondered, her fingers closing instinctively over a shard of the Canton vase which graced the mahogany table in the stairwell. Suddenly, she was jerked viciously to her feet again, but not before she hid the glass in the folds of her cloak.

"Everyone stop moving about or I'll slit her throat from ear to ear!"

Cold metal pressed against her throat, sharp as the glass Rose fingered until the keenest edge was away from her. Harrison had fired his pistol, which put them on more equal ground. She had to stay cool, like Amanda Mackay, who'd halted halfway down the steps at her son-in-law's newest threat like a ruffled hen behind a wire fence.

"Ye've killed a good man!"

Killed? Rose fought the wave of nausea that assaulted her as she realized who'd taken the shot in her place. Not daring to turn her head, she strained to look at the bottom of the formal staircase where the crumpled figure of Claude Benet lay.

"Shut up! All of you, into the pantry, quick!"

Where was Dillon? If he had everything under control, how could this be happening?

"What the devil do you think you're doing?" Mavis Adams hollered from the back of the house. "You've scared the bloody coachman off before I could get him inside!" Hurried footsteps brought the disgruntled woman into the hall. At the sight of Claude Benet lying on the floor she blanched. "Oh, lud, now what'll we do?"

"Fetch the pistols from Mackay's office! Quick, woman!"

Rose somehow maintained her footing and her hold on the piece of broken vase as she was tugged down the remaining flight of steps and past the dead man.

"You heard me!" Harrison shouted, his voice cracking with the anxiety that shortened his breath. "Into the pantry, now!"

Above the rush to comply, faint frantic cries echoed from the upper-story wing of the mansion, where the gunfire had frightened the children. Rose could hear them beating on the door Mavis had locked and was grateful that, at least for the moment, they were out of harm's way.

The shrill distraction lessened the pressure at her throat for a second, but Rose held back from using the shard of glass just yet. She had to get this madman away from the house before anyone else was injured.

"Send Mavis out to hail a coach. I'll go along peacefully. That driver's sure to bring soldiers back, so the sooner we're out of the city, the better!"

"Yes . . . yes!" her captor repeated, taking instantly to the idea. "As soon as I lock these good people in the pantry, madame, I shall do exactly that."

With the blade at Rose's throat, there was nothing any of them could do except obey the madman. One by one Joeli, Amanda, and Henry, who'd come from the back with Mavis, stepped into the shelf-lined enclosure where the fine linen and tableware were stored. Once they were crammed inside, Harrison kicked the door to and turned the brass key, locking it soundly.

Rose breathed a stilted sigh of relief. Three more safe. Now there was only her.

"Where the devil are you, woman?"

Taking his frustration out on Rose, Harrison dragged her through the dining room and into the hall without letting her establish her footing, nearly costing her her hold on her one paltry weapon. When he finally let her feet bear her weight, rather than his arm, she breathed in deeply, filling her crushed lungs. Her head hurt like the blazes, but at least it was clear, which was more than Ellis Harrison's was.

"Mavis!"

"I can't find the bloody pistols!" the woman shouted from the library.

Her captor ushered Rose unceremoniously into the room. "Damn it, woman, we haven't time to waste!"

Mavis Adams stood back against the bookcase behind Dillon's desk, staring at them as if she'd seen a ghost. The weapons case was exactly where it was usually kept, polished wood and shining brass on a table under the rear window.

"You simple-minded . . ."

The loud cock of a pistol hammer sliced through Ellis Harrison's curse, followed by an equally ominous warning.

"That's far enough, sir. Now take the knife away from my wife's throat . . . slowly."

Twenty-four

"Dillon!"

Rose could hardly say his name. Before the flood of relief she felt could affect the tension dominating her body, however, the pressure of the blade on her flesh increased.

"You must have as many lives as a cat, Mackay, but does your wife?" Harrison rallied without faltering. "Think now . . . one slip, say, caused by the involuntary reflex of my hand, should you have balls enough to shoot me and . . . well, you'd lose either way."

The ticking of the clock on the mantel grew loud amidst the time it took for Dillon to reassess the situation. Rose closed her eyes in dismay as she heard him ease the hammer down.

"He grabbed me soon as I came in," Mavis exclaimed. "I thought I'd choke on my own heart!"

"Stop babbling and take his bloody gun, you idiot!"

It seemed to Rose like a thousand heartbeats passed before the gun was handed over to Harrison and the blade, which had nicked her skin, moved away from her throat. She stumbled away and turned to run into her husband's arms, but instead was shocked into stillness at the sight of the old salt she'd had coffee with at the tavern that morning.

"Dillon?"

His shoulders were no longer bent, but his clothes were as ragged and his hair and face as scruffy as before. His eyes, she thought, looking into the river of emotion swirling in their whiskey depths, if only she'd been able to see his eyes, he'd never have fooled her.

"You stupid bluenose, why didn't you tell me who you were this morning!" she demanded, slinging his arms away as he reached for her. "Don't you touch me!"

"Rose, you're hurt!"

Rose wiped away the blood from the second blow her captor had inflicted. "You're damned right I'm hurt and you did it! You couldn't trust me with the whole truth!"

"Damn it, Rose, I had my orders! This wasn't my investigation alone."

Another wave of dizziness struck and Rose grabbed at the edge of the desk to keep from falling. Then Dillon's arms were about her, holding her, pulling her to him. She couldn't fight him, even if she wanted to. She'd feared him dead and now he was here, alive and embracing her as though he'd never let her go again. She didn't know whether to hit him or kiss him. Instead, she chose a more neutral course.

"You stink!" she said, turning her face away from the tattered coat of coarse serge. "Did you dip these in the back alley of a fish house before you put them on?"

Dillon ignored her remark and addressed Harrison. "She needs a bandage on her head. Let me get some linen."

"We can't take her out like that," Mavis agreed. "Not if we don't want undue attention."

"Who else knows we're here, Mackay?"

"No one," he lied. "I broke the surveillance when I saw you get in the coach with Rose."

Anticipating the worst, he'd sent his accomplice for additional help before speaking in the guise of a fishmonger to Henry at the servants' door in the back. The man hadn't recognized him, but said in no uncertain terms that they wanted no fish or lobster. Past Henry's shoulder, Dillon had seen Joeli rocking back and forth in front of the kitchen hearth as though in some sort of troubled trance while Mavis Adams stood next to the Maroon, clinging with uncommon interest to every word.

When the gunshot went off, he'd nearly blown his cover and charged in, but feared that would only set off more violence. Instead, he'd moved the fishcart to the blind side of the house and peered in through the dining-room window in time to hear the jist of what had happened. He'd liked Claude Benet, but there was nothing he could have done from the back to have spared the honorable Frenchman from his brother-in-law's madness.

Ellis Harrison was clearly at a loss as to whether to believe him or not. Keeping the pistol fixed on Dillon and Rose, he paced over to the window and peered out.

"Mavis, go around to all the windows upstairs and down and see if you spy anything suspicious."

"You don't have enough time to play games, Harrison," Dillon spoke up. "I'll be missed eventually. Leave Rose here and take me with you. I guarantee I will get you out of the city and on a ship."

"Do as I say, woman!" their captor barked at his accomplice. "As for taking you instead of your wife, I'd sooner travel with a lighted powder keg. You must think me a fool, sir." He waved the gun at them. "Now, you two lovebirds move over to the settle. Your wife looks as if she's about to collapse as it is and she'll need her strength."

"At least let me get a towel from the liquor cabinet for her head."

"By all means. Just remember, I have your beloved in

my sights and I am a better than fair shot. Monsieur Benet discovered that, I fear."

Above them, Rose heard Mavis's hurried footfall as she flitted from room to room. "All I see so far is a fishcart!" she called down from above them before going to the other wing.

Ellis Harrison's face lighted briefly with consideration as he watched Dillon fetch a towel and return to Rose's side on the settle bench. Rose wondered how desperate the pompous bastard would have to be before he stooped to escaping in a fishcart! The image of him in Dillon's disguise almost made her laugh, despite the sting of the liquor Dillon used to wash her head wound.

"It's just a small cut," her husband observed to no one in particular.

"It doesn't feel small!"

Dillon smiled at her and the room seemed to brighten.

"I'm a lot of trouble, aren't I?"

"Nothing worthwhile comes without a price," he told her. "Suffice it to say you're priceless."

Rose couldn't help but feel the rush of love his left-handed compliment spawned. She loved Dillon Mackay with all her being.

"No matter what happens," she began as Dillon carefully tucked in the edge of the bandage, forming a band about her forehead, "I love you. I have since I was a little girl on Father's ship."

"Ah, such devotion, Captain Mackay!" their captor derided caustically. "Your sister used to be that devoted to me until she developed a conscience."

"I'm surprised you recognized one, Harrison."

Dillon's insult only deepened the man's sarcasm.

"You think your sister is a misguided angel led astray by infatuation, but, sir, before her accident, I promise you, no more devious mind existed. At last I'd met a woman worthy of my own ambition, good for more than breeding heirs."

With a satisfied smirk that he'd gotten Dillon's full attention, the man went on. "We were destitute, dependent on the successful Dillon Mackay's charity to hold our heads up among our peers, when Audra struck on an ingenious plan."

Rose listened in utter amazement as Ellis Harrison recounted how his wife had sold her grandmother's jewels to purchase a ship, a ship which she had him outfit with French prisoners bound for Melville Island. Crewed with men who owed no allegiance except to its profitable enterprise, the privateer set out to prey on choice victims, whose papers were copied by a clerk on the payroll of the customs house.

"Imagine how good it felt to hear the same merchants and investors who'd shunned us when I lost my wife's dowry bemoan their losses time and again. Lud, it was glorious!"

Harrison went on, describing their foundling start. Prizes were taken to remote harbors and refitted with new paint and names. Until they'd captured enough, some of the lower-born volunteers set out in shaving mills which haunted the coasts. After the *Demand* debacle, the few who escaped disguised as local fishermen brought Harrison the news that the *Thorne* had gone down with captain and crew.

"That was the ultimate victory! Do you have any idea what it's like living in your shadow, Dillon Mackay?" Harrison challenged, marching up to Dillon and pointing the gun at his head. "You not only have money, but the respect of people from the meanest dockworker to the governor!"

"I can't believe Audra had any part in this," Dillon swore. "I gave her everything! If anything, I spoiled her."

"She planted the seed and nurtured it until it grew on its own!"

Rose could see the man was wounding Dillon with every word about his sister's involvement in the bizarre scheme.

"Don't fret so, she did get upset when she'd heard your ship was victimized by the shavers. Mavis, where the bloody hell are you?"

Rose started at the unexpected burst of anger amidst Harrison's glowing pride.

"Mavis!" he shouted again at the ceiling.

"She's in the other wing, I believe." Dillon was astonishingly calm considering their plight.

Did he know something they did not? Rose wondered, still fingering the shard of glass hidden in the folds of her cape? Were Captain Stevenson and his men on their way to the rescue? Considering that her husband was more in control than she at the moment, Rose worked her hand beneath her cape to her husband's thigh, pressing to gain his attention as Mavis answered from a distant corner of the mansion.

"I hear you!"

"Then get down here. We've wasted enough time!"

The clearly agitated man resumed a stiff perch on the edge of the desk where he could see both the door and the settle. "Now where was I? Ah, yes, dear Audra," he sneered. "It was well enough to prey on everyone, it seemed, except her perfect brother."

Rose pressed Dillon's thigh again and felt him jerk as the glass cut through his trousers. Mistaking his start as reaction to his blistering tale, Ellis Harrison continued.

"She became hysterical . . . totally unmanageable. Mavis and I had little choice—"

"So you were cavorting with your mistress while my

sister's brainchild made your fortune for you?" Dillon closed his hand over the shard of glass.

"Cold as a fish, that one," Harrison declared, pleased with Dillon's further irritation. "Her time and her use was over."

"So you sent your French picaroons to kill her?" Dillon snorted in contempt. "I'm astonished you didn't have them do away with the children as well!"

"But her little brats had an inheritance, to which, with you out of the way, I'd have access." Sliding off the desk, their adversary approached Dillon, again leveling the gun at his head. "How many more lives do you think you have, Mackay. I vow, I'd like to take the last one."

Rose held her breath, fearing the madman was readying for the kill. He was close enough for her husband to leap at him, but a sliver of glass was no match for a pistol. He needed a distraction. Just as she was about to slink down in the settle and onto the floor if need be, Mavis Adams returned.

"My brother has more lives than you do, Ellis!"

Rose looked at the sardonic woman again. It wasn't Mavis, but Audra wearing Mavis Adams's traveling jacket over her voluminous muslin nightdress. Poor, disoriented Audra, aiming a small pistol at her husband's back!

Harrison was so startled to see his wife that Dillon had the chance he needed. With a lunge, Dillon was on the man, wrestling with the pistol hand. Momentum carried the two of them down on the gaming table.

A shot went off, but it flew wild, striking somewhere in the wall of books beyond. Rose looked about frantically for anything that might be used as a cudgel and spied the bottle of whiskey Dillon had used to cleanse her wound rolling across the floor. Despite the room spinning about her when she rose from the cushioned settle, she threw herself at it.

The table legs splintered under the weight of the tousling men just as Rose's fingers closed around the bottle neck. With a terrible crash, they bore the top to the floor. Dillon recovered first, smashing his fist into his stunned opponent's face, but, to Rose's horror, the man on the bottom came back grasping a remnant of the table leg and knocked Dillon aside, dazed. Rose crawled forward with every intent of smashing the bottle against Harrison's head, when another shot shook the windowpanes.

Rose saw the man twist toward the doorway where Audra Harrison stood, one barrel of the cumbersome pistol smoking, the second cool and ready for its drawn hammer to send a second bullet sailing after the first. That, however, was not necessary. The man reached behind his back, as though frantically trying to undo the damage done by the tearing ball buried there, before his shock-stiffened limbs turned to water.

Dillon rolled aside as his brother-in-law sprawled where he'd been but a moment before. Her hand still clasped about the bottle, Rose returned her attention to Audra, who still held the pistol extended. Her seagreen gaze was wide and haunted.

"Give me the gun, Audra!" Dillon said.

"No!" The young woman took a backward step. "It wasn't all like he said!"

"I know you have a side," Dillon told her gently, not wanting to add to the wild panic in her eyes.

"Then sit down and listen! Don't try to take the gun or I'll shoot, I swear!"

"You don't want to hurt anyone. I know that."

A crocodile tear spilled down Audra's ashen cheek. "No," she said miserably. "I love my family. I didn't want any of them hurt by that monster, especially . . ."

A sob tore from her throat. "M-Monsieur Benet! How I hate that man!" Audra shook the gun at Ellis Harrison's still figure with fueled vehemence. "He was like poison to everything he touched!" Her Valkyrie-like expression suddenly faded and she looked frightened and wounded once again. "I didn't know they were killing all the prisoners on the prizes they took. I swear it!"

"I believe you, Audra," Dillon told her, trying to keep her calm. "He's gone now. He can't hurt you anymore!"

Audra glanced from Dillon to Rose and back again. "See to your wife, Dillon. She's bleeding."

In all the turmoil, Rose had hardly noticed the sticky wetness trickling down her face from where her bandage had slipped. Dillon helped her back to the settle and tenderly put the bandage right.

"Where's Mavis, Audra?"

Audra's pallid features took on a demonic glow of satisfaction. "She thought I'd been drinking that vile potion she kept slipping into my toddies. Everyone thought I'd lost my mind, but I knew Ellis had sent those men to kill me."

"Why didn't you tell me?"

"Oh, Dillon, I was so ashamed!" the woman cried brokenly. "Besides, he'd threatened to kill me and the children. That's why I ran in the first place. I've never been so frightened of anyone in my life. I didn't want to live, but then I couldn't die, not and leave Alison and Jerome in his hands. I watched his whore like a hawk with them, but I knew as long as they were here, they'd be safe."

"Where is she now?" Dillon asked again.

"She tried to smother me with a pillow!" Audra declared defensively. Cunning invaded her wild look as she added in a singsong manner, "But she didn't know that I kept a hatpin woven into the mattress." She smiled. "I ran it through her throat, right there!" The obviously deranged woman pointed the gun to where the pulse beat frantically in her neck. "She thrashed about like a chicken with a wrung neck! She's dead now."

"For God's sake, Audra, give me the gun before you kill yourself!" Dillon jumped up from the settle and started for her, but stopped as she held out her free hand in warning.

"No, don't move or I *will* shoot myself! Or maybe I will anyway." She glanced with something akin to envy at Ellis Harrison. "Look at him. He's free now." She sniffed and shook her head. "You're wrong, Dillon. He's still hurting me! I'm the one suffering. When he killed Monsieur Benet, he put that bullet right through my heart."

"*Non, ma petite,* he put it through our shoulder."

All attention flew to the door of the library where Claude Benet leaned against the jamb, his muslin shirt soaked as bright as he was pale.

"Claude!" Audra stared at the wounded man in joyful disbelief.

"*Ma pauvre petite,* give your brother the gun. Your nightmare is over! How can you even think to end your life when your children are crying for you upstairs!" Weak from blood loss Benet rested his head against the paneled jamb, clinging to the consciousness that threatened to abandon him again.

"He's right, Audra. Jerome and Alison need their mother," Rose injected, hopeful at the way the deranged woman furtively searched Benet's face for a reason to believe him.

"I'm no good for them. I'm too weak, you said so yourself."

Rose's heart was tugged by Audra's despair. Were she involved with Ellis Harrison, she wasn't so certain she'd not consider suicide herself. But he was gone now and she had someone who loved her.

"Give me the gun, my beautiful Audra," Claude Benet said, stretching out his hand without letting go his support. "Do not leave me half a man. Together we will raise Alison and Jerome and we will have many grandchildren, all of whom will speak fluent French," he went on with a hint of his jocular manner.

"You'd still have me, knowing what you know?" Audra asked uncertainly.

Dillon was close enough to her to snatch the gun now, but her finger rested on the trigger. The risk of setting it off was too great.

"I would, madame. Like you said, your husband was a poison. Now he is no more."

Dillon slowly retreated to Rose and sat down beside her. "The only witnesses to your involvement in this are dead, Audra," he said, drawing Rose against him.

"And you've suffered enough, living under your husband's irrational rule," Rose added. "It's small wonder you did not lose your mind."

"I lost my heart, Rose," Audra admitted with a sheepish look at Claude Benet. "Claude taught me more than French. He taught me the meaning of love. I'd never known it until I met him."

"Then live for that love, *ma petite!* Give me the gun!"

In his desperation to reach her, the Frenchman lost his tentative grip on the doorjamb and pitched forward.

"Claude!" Dropping the gun, Audra ran to him and lifted his head into her lap. "If I must live, then you must!" she sobbed, stroking his dark-brown hair off his forehead. "Dillon, please! Send for the doctor!"

"Go on!" Rose encouraged, when her husband hesitantly glanced at her. "I'm fine!"

She rushed past Audra and Benet on Dillon's heels to go to the pantry where the other household mem-

bers were imprisoned. No longer shaky, but filled with
relief, she turned the brass key and opened the door.
Suddenly she was engulfed in caring arms and besieged
by questions as to what had happened. They'd heard
the second shot and thought certain she'd been killed.

"No," she assured them. "I'm fine. Audra came to
our rescue. It's over!" Her voice faltered with emotion.
There was hope now—hope for her and Dillon, hope
for his tormented sister as well. "It's over!"

So it was. Later that night, when all the confusion
had passed, Dillon brought up a linen towel packed
with snow. Rose sat propped up in their bed against a
bolster of pillows. On the table beside it were the dishes
left over from the delicious supper Joeli had prepared.
Much of what had been on Rose's plate still remained,
but she had finished a cup of clam broth prescribed by
the cook to assuage her headache.

The doctor had told Dillon that she seemed well
enough, aside from the small cut at the hairline of her
temple. As for Claude Benet, the bullet in his shoulder
had been removed and the wound washed out with
Amanda Mackay's best whuskey. Like Rose, he was left
to the care of the Mackay household and, in particular,
Joeli, who'd made up a poultice once the physician left
and packed it against the Frenchman's freshly dressed
wound.

The clock had just struck the hour of one in the hall
and she was certain everyone was exhausted from the
excitement. There'd been red-and-blue coated officers
in and out of the house all afternoon, questioning everyone. Amanda had assumed the role of mistress of
the house and, with Joeli and Henry at her command,
seen to it that no one left either thirsty or with an empty
stomach. Dillon felt certain that all the names of those

involved had been revealed or would be when the Annapolis Royal authorities went through Harrison's office.

In the midst of it all were Alison and Jerome, silent and well behaved as little lambs after Rose spoke with them about being brave for Monsieur Benet and their mother. If they felt any remorse over their father's demise, they hid it well. Like everyone else, they were glad it was over.

"Is everyone asleep?" Rose asked as Dillon tenderly placed the cold pack against her swollen temple.

"Not Joeli," Dillon answered. "She's hustling from Benet's room to Audra's like a bee after wisteria. She says they're going to have two more babies."

"The bones?" Rose queried with a chuckle.

"That's not all!" Her husband gave her a lopsided grin as he stripped off his shirt. "She says we're going to have to build more rooms on the farmhouse."

"How many?" There were already four bedrooms, not counting the master bedroom on the first floor, which was intended for Dillon's office.

"Two more, lessen we wan' dem babies piled up on one anudder!" he mimicked the Maroon.

Rose pressed the cold bag to her temple to keep her brain from bursting out of her skull. "Five babies! We'll have our own crew!"

She closed her eyes and sighed as Dillon slid into the bed beside her. He was naked, but his flesh was warm as he snuggled against her.

"Ah, ah," he warned, kissing her eyelids open. "I can't let you sleep."

Sleep was the furthest thing from Rose's mind. Although he was covered sufficiently by the blankets, she could picture the ridged planes of her husband's manly body. Then there was the thickened manhood which rubbed in silent protest against the soft muslin of her nightshift.

"We could start on those babies."

"What about your headache?" Rose nearly laughed at the hoarse desire that inflicted Dillon's voice at her suggestion. She pulled his head to her breast and buried his face against the soft, yielding flesh. He was about to burst with want and yet he was willing to suffer, rather than cause her discomfort.

"If we're careful not to jar my head overmuch," she mumbled against Dillon's recently washed hair, "it might be just the distraction I need."

"You're certain?"

Rose felt her skin shrink with shivers of delight at the playful brush of her husband's tongue against the peak of her breast budding against the thin material of her garment.

"Umm," she moaned.

Sliding his hand with delicious intent up the inside of her thigh, Dillon lifted her gown until he cupped the down-soft mound awaiting it. With ever so talented fingers, he sought its erotic core and bedeviled it until her breath was ragged and Rose felt as though she were going to implode with the longing for more. She wriggled, forcing herself against his probing fingers, drawing them deeper with her yearning body.

"Whoa, Rosebud!" he teased when the cold pack fell away from her forehead with a gurgling sound. "Remember your headache!"

"I can't even feel it!" she whispered. "All I feel is you! All I want is you! All of you, Dillon! Hurry!"

As he covered Rose's body with his own, she embraced him, running worshipful hands over his back, tripping along the length of his legs with her toes.

"Now, Dillon, please!"

Rose braced herself for the initial thrust and was

stunned instead by the slow and easy slide which took possession of her, inch by inch, breath by breath, heartbeat by heartbeat. Ever so stirring, yet tender, agonizingly so, Dillon withdrew from the assault, only to submit her to it again . . . and again. Rose was rendered helpless to the sweet seduction until it became unbearable.

"Do something!"

Dillon laughed like the devil he was. "I thought I was, my love. As prospective parents, we must learn to exercise patience." He grunted as she kicked his buttocks soundly with her heels. "How is your headache?"

"You know bloody damned well where I'm aching, Dillon Mackay!" Rose swore at him. "If you're too tired, then roll over and let someone who can do it take over!"

"You always want to play captain."

"Well, you're not man enough for the job!"

"Then have at it, madame!"

Dillon rolled over pulling Rose with him, so that, amidst the tangle of the covers, she was now in command of the situation. The bandage around her raven hair gave her as savage a look as did the reflection of the flickering lamp he'd failed to put out upon climbing into bed to her flawless skin.

No sapphire ever blazed brighter. She possessed the fire of the gem, not just in her bewitching eyes, but in manner, in the delectable body which now writhed atop him.

Reaching for some semblance of control, Dillon grasped her gyrating hips, raising beneath them so that the fierce union afforded no slack. Like a graceful jungle cat, she'd pounced on him and was now devouring him in such a way as to riddle his body with the need to surrender.

Dillon moaned loudly with the climax she would not

be denied. Every nerve cried out in release to the thundering beat of his racing blood. He was grateful that he was lying down, for his head was light as a cloud. She'd wrested his bloody brains out!

He swore, not in anger, but in awe of the bewitching girl who leaned against his damp chest on folded elbows.

"I would have done better," she told him with wide guileless eyes, "but I had a headache."

Although he wanted to laugh, all Dillon could muster was a twitch at one corner of his mouth. She was unpredictable as the sea and twice as resilient. He'd weathered many a storm, but something told him it would take a lifetime of experience to learn all there was to know about his new mistress, his wife . . . his Border Rose.

Epilogue

The rich green fields and woodlands that rose and fell with the lay of the land about the estate of Chateau Beaujeu were as full of life as the newly renovated homestead. An orchard heavy with the fruit of the season swayed in the breeze which flowed through the big house. On the lawns, Beaujeus of all ages sought their pleasure in their own fashion. Some bowled. Others tossed horseshoes, while the older members of the family sat in the shade of the house and watched their juniors with pride.

At the center, Alain Beaujeu rocked back and forth on his chair, all the while holding his wife's hand. His Beaujeu blue eyes sparkled beneath eyebrows long ago whitened by time as he spoke to those he loved. Rose sat, like her brother Jack and their cousins, enrapt by the old man's gift of storytelling.

"It was here, *mon amis,* that it all began some . . ." He shrugged his shoulders, erect as they'd been in his youth, if not quite as mobile. "What is it, Tamson . . . *mon Dieu,* sixty years!"

"You must be old as the mountains, Grandpère!" one of James Beaujeu's brood exclaimed.

Of the thirteen grandchildren present, the eldest brother John had contributed two—Rose and Jack. Robert, the youngest of the Beaujeu boys, who'd followed his father's passion for adventure and gone west to establish a trading post, had brought the three beautiful children given him by his lovely Indian wife. Arissa, their half sister, had brought along not only her and Phillip Conway's two grown children, but the first great-granddaughter, who evened out the score to fourteen branches of the growing family tree! The rest of them belonged to middle brother James, who the family teased was as prolific at planting babies as he was keeping Annanbrae one of the grandest estates in the Hudson Valley.

"Sometimes I feel old as the mountains," Alain admitted with that special twinkle in his gaze which Rose's grandmother swore had stolen her heart some sixty years ago. "But life has been good to us, *non, ma petite?*"

"Aye, that it has," Tamson replied. Her face, while creased by time, always seemed to hold a smile, which was now directed at her husband. It was hard for Rose to imagine Grandmère Tamson with the fiery Scots temper her husband pretended to tremble before. "If only I could keep all their names straight!"

"So what happened, Grandpère?" a little girl sitting in grandmother Arissa Conway's lap prompted impatiently.

Alain rose to his feet and snapped his fingers in front of the child's nose, causing the auburn-haired waif to laugh in delight. "Well, *ma bonne grande petite-fille,* I will tell you!"

The other children ranging in ages four to Arissa's stepson Jonathan's forty plus had all heard the wonderful tale of Tamson's abduction by the fierce Acadian trapper she fell in love with, yet they never seemed to tire of it. Even the spouses who'd married into the clan, drew closer, as charmed by the old *voyageur's* storytelling as they'd been the first time they met him.

Robert put his arms about his petite raven-haired wife, placing his hands on her belly, which was swollen with the newest Beaujeu. "*He* might as well listen early," he teased, his dark cinnamon eyes twinkling with mischief.

"You're sure it's a boy?" Rose challenged, glancing at the three little girls pulling on the fringes of his buckskin trousers.

"It has to be!" the youngest Beaujeu brother claimed. "The tide doesn't always run the same way!"

"Tell that to James," Rose's father put in.

Seated on a bench with Aggie Prichart Beaujeu standing over him like a watchdog, he looked better than he had when Rose had left Castine the year before. At forty-nine, his new marriage had managed to erase a few of the haggard lines of his face and put a little more life in his step. It was Aggie who looked the worse for wear, not from her role as John's bride, but from the ocean voyage they'd made to get there. Not favoring sea travel at all, she and Grandmother Tamson had spent it consoling each other in their equal misery.

"That's not fair!" Tamson Beaujeu spoke up in her middle son's defense. The soft burr of an old accent still tinged the pleasing lilt of a voice not quite as steady as it had once been, but just as sweet. "Jamie isn't here to defend himself. Just because he had a run of five girls before Michael and Joshua were born!" she sniffed with a wry twist of her lips.

Rose had been there for that. Her uncle celebrated for three days. After five girls, not one, but two boys had come along.

"Well, if Mary hadn't come with the children, there'd be more than one more Beaujeu on the way."

To the embarrassment of the short, full-figured girl

James Beaujeu had married, the entire assembly of adults laughed at Robert's comment. The children joined in on general principle. "What can I say," Mary Beaujeu said, jostling one or the twins on her hip. "He's a man's man."

"You mean a woman's man," Arissa Conway teased good-naturedly.

Rose glanced over her shoulder as Dillon Mackay closed his arms about her waist. There was another Beaujeu on the way, maybe two according to the physician, but they chose to wait until the family saga was told in which destiny forced certain Beaujeus to love their enemies. After all, they had another chapter to add.

Alain walked about in the circle which had formed around him and Tamson, practically dancing from grandchild to mesmerized grandchild as he told of the viciousness of the savage war which had cost him his family and the farm on which he'd been raised.

"Where was it, Grandpère?" one of James's girls asked.

Alain exchanged a secret glance with Rose. "I will get to that in a moment, *ma cherie.*" He took up the little girl's hand and lifted it to his lips. "For now we will be patient, *non?*"

"I know where it is!"

Rose grabbed Alison Benet and pulled her niece against her skirts to shush her before the anxious child gave away the secret.

"Here, I'll take her," Audra Harrison Benet said apologetically. She grabbed Alison's hand and started to lead her to the orchard where Claude Benet and Jerome were climbing a tree to fetch a choice apple. "This story is for the other children."

"Because I already know it!" Alison informed her mother in a smug tone. "I showed them all around, you know. Can they be my cousins, too?"

Alison's voice trailed away, but Rose followed the mother and daughter with her gaze until they reached the crisp white orchard fence, which had just been added that year. Although Dillon's sister had never completely emerged from her emotional withdrawal after the hearings concerning Mavis Adams and Ellis Harrison's deaths, she had come a long way toward reentering the small family circle.

Claude Benet's unending patience and devotion was to thank for that. While the arm attached to his wounded shoulder had partly withered, he still had enough use of it to handle the young men who attended the school of education and etiquette for young boys, which Dillon had helped him start. He'd also adopted Alison and Jerome. The family lived in the huge Argyle Street mansion with Amanda Mackay, but were frequent visitors to Chateau Beaujeu, particularly in the summer months.

The end of the war between the United States and Great Britain had signified a new beginning for the Mackays. Audra had started over with a new husband and new life. Rose and Dillon began their married lives in a time of peace, where war no longer tugged them apart with impartial fingers. Their time was split between Chateau Beaujeu and the *Border Rose,* although now that Rose was expecting again, she was grounded.

What made it perfectly bearable was the fact that Dillon insisted on remaining with her. Sometimes he nearly drove her crazy with his concern for her. He always drove her insane with his desire.

"And so comes another war and a Beaujeu we did not even know about falls victim to the same fate!"

Rose leaned against Dillon as her aunt Arissa took over the tale. While she was not as demonstrative as her father in the telling, she was no less interesting. Occasionally, her husband of thirty-five years would put in a word or two, when he was not distracted by the grand-daughter his wife handed over to him. She'd been a doctor of sorts and administered aid to the enemy troops which occupied her family inn. Worse than that, she'd fallen in love with the man who had been their spy and cleared the way for their occupation.

Well able to relate to the pain Arissa suffered when she learned her Phillip had been killed in the attack on Quebec, Rose squeezed Dillon's hands and locked her fingers within his. Never again did she want to know that horrible void left by a heart that had been wrenched from her chest by grief. A tear slipped out the corner of her eye, but Dillon, ever watchful for her slightest need, kissed it away.

"I can see now, I never had a chance of getting away from you," he confided in her ear. "You knew what you were talking about that night on the island."

Rose grinned as he nibbled at the back of her earlobe. "Behave!" she whispered under her breath, backing even closer to him so that she knew the full length of his wonderfully masculine body.

"That's a pot calling a kettle black!"

"And now we have yet another war and another magnificent love to add!" Alain Beaujeu announced, glowing as he looked at Rose and Dillon. "That is, if you think you can keep your mind on it long enough for the telling."

Rose blushed deeply, aware that all eyes were on the two of them. "Well, it all started when he captured my ship!"

"No, now don't short them on the facts," Dillon objected. "It all started with a pink petticoat flying from the mast tops. Gentlemen," be went on, addressing the males of all ages gathered about, "if ever you spy such a banner and you're not of a mind to surrender to it for the rest of your life, take my advice and run the other way just as fast as you can make sail!"

"All right, you bluenose braggart, if you think you can tell this, be my guest!" Rose stepped away with arms crossed in a challenge which her handsome husband took up instantly.

Playing up the exciting parts for the sake of the younger listeners and down the more painful memories for Rose's sake, he made it sound like an adventure from the Arabian Nights with himself as Sinbad and Rose as the beautiful but troublesome princess.

"And now, I believe I'll let my wife and her grandfather finish the tale," he said, bowing out with a graceful sweep of his arm toward Rose.

"Actually," Rose said, "we'll let the house tell the tale. Everyone into the back kitchen! I believe Joeli has a delicious buffet prepared in the dining room, but there's something you all must see first.

Thoroughly intrigued, the clan straggled toward the kitchen attached to the main two-story house. Of all those who'd come, only Rose's grandparents knew of the secret there. They'd wanted to surprise the others.

It took a few minutes for everyone to crowd into the room. Phillip Conway's bad leg, injured in a fire during the Revolution, had become more troublesome and an invalid's chair was necessary to transport him long distances. The man who'd claimed a Montreal bride and resettled her in his native New York lived up to his reputation of making the best of a bad situation by giving his granddaughter and small nieces and nephews rides in it.

Once all the littlest Beaujeus were herded to the front where they could see, Grandpère Alain made a big show of putting his ear to the doorjamb of the small winding stairwell that rose to the kitchen loft. He listened, holding his finger over his lips to silence the restless group of youngsters.

"What is it, Grandpère?" the little girl on Phillip Conway's lap insisted in a hushed tone.

"Why, this wall, it is telling Grandpère about the children who lived here."

"Nuh-uh," one of James's girls said dubiously.

"Ah, but it is! Look right there. What is it you see?"

The kitchen had been repainted, all except for the doorjamb which had held the secret of the little cottage for sixty years. Rose didn't care that it stood out, faded and worn compared to the fresh look of the rest of the room. It was her heritage, her roots, the roots of the babe or babes she carried.

An older girl leaned over and read the name he pointed to. "It says Alain! That's your name, Grandpère!"

Alain Beaujeu's smile lit up the room. Emotion sparkled in his eyes as he told James's daughter to read on.

"Annette, Liselle, Laurette . . ."

A blade of similar emotion cut at Rose's throat and filled her eyes to brimming as he hugged his granddaughter and bussed her on the top of the head. "You see, *mes amis, mes coeur!* It is here in this humble cottage that it all began. This was my home, where I and my sisters were born. This was where the British came and took my family away, where the Beaujeus left their land."

He turned to where Dillon and Rose stood arm in arm nearby. "And this is where our story comes full circle," he said, his voice intense with feeling. "Such is life! It always comes full circle, maybe not in this world, but in the next. I, Alain Beaujeu, have been blessed to see such a circle complete itself in my lifetime. Someday, there will be more Beaujeus to put their names beneath mine and my sisters'."

"Sooner than you think, Grandpère Alain," Rose spoke up in a halting voice. She looked at Dillon, too filled with the joy of the moment to go on.

"Rose and I are expecting a baby . . ."

"Maybe two," she injected hopefully.

Dillon smiled down at her and she warmed as though basked in the full heat of the summer sun. "However many are coming will be here sometime during Christmas."

John Beaujeu broke the delighted silence by heartily shaking Dillon's hand. "Congratulations, son!" He went on to kiss Rose on the cheek and hold her until he trembled with the effort.

Soon they were surrounded by family, Beaujeus with dark hair, Beaujeus with light hair, some with dark eyes and others that blue which bore the family name. It was some time before Rose was able to make her way back to Dillon's side. As she did, he pulled her into his arms and whispered in her ear.

"I love your family and its motto!"

Rose radiated happiness as she drank in his whiskey gaze. She followed Dillon's meaningful glance to the cross-stitch which hung over the little stairwell. With tiny red hearts as quotation marks, it read *Love thine enemy.*

TALES OF LOVE FROM MEAGAN MCKINNEY

ROMANCE FROM FERN MICHAELS

DEAR EMILY   (0-8217-4952-8, $5.99)

WISH LIST   (0-8217-5228-6, $6.99)

AND IN HARDCOVER:

VEGAS RICH   (1-57566-057-1, $25.00)